WHEN DEATH FREES THE DEVIL

L.J. HAYWARD

When Death Frees the Devil
Copyright © L.J. Hayward

Cover Art: L.C. Chase, lcchase.com
Editor: May Peterson, maypetersonbooks.com/editorial
Sensitivity Reader: The Shrinkette, theshrinkette.com/2017/02/21/sensitivity-reading-services/
Layout: L.C. Chase, lcchase.com

ISBN: 978-0-6484460-8-8

First Edition
December 2019

Also available in ebook: ISBN 978-0-6484460-6-4
Also available in Kindle: ISBN 978-0-6484460-7-1

WHEN DEATH FREES THE DEVIL

L.J. HAYWARD

TABLE OF CONTENTS

PART ONE

ETHAN

THE TOWER

Blast.

Blast, bother and bollocks. This wasn't how the plan was supposed to go. If Ethan was honest, he hadn't expected it to work perfectly, but this was what he got for letting someone else do the planning. Maybe if he hadn't, he wouldn't be here right now.

Here, in the pitch black and the cold that permeated the air, the stones under the balls of his feet, and the chains that suspended him from the ceiling. He was stretched out to the point of discomfort, pulling at the rough stiches in the wound in his hip so they felt like claws slowly ripping through his flesh. His feet only just touched the floor, making him strain to take some pressure off his arms. The shackles around his bruised and tender wrists were warmed slightly from contact with his body, but the longer he dangled there, the more the chill seeped back into them. Into his skin and flesh and bones. He couldn't tell anymore if the burning ache in his arms was from the strain of taking most of his body weight, or the random shivers that wracked him.

Ethan couldn't hear much past his own laboured breathing and the faint thump of what might have been his heart struggling. The silence and the cold felt subterranean. Strung up and underground. This wasn't the plan. It was in no way any part of the plan. He shouldn't have trusted it. He hadn't worked it through himself, hadn't assessed and researched and accounted for all possibilities. This was his own fault for not taking charge, for letting his emotions overrule his training. He should never have done that, never have done that. He shouldn't have trusted anyone other than Jack.

The jittering discomfort started in his gut and his fingers itched for something he could straighten or untwist, something that needed fixing. Or a knife to flip, a familiar, repetitive motion to occupy his body so the chaos in his head didn't overspill and he could settle it down.

He concentrated on that thought. On imagining he had his tactical knife and it was turning in the air and landing perfectly in his hand. Tip to grip to tip to grip. It worked, and the rushing thoughts slowed and settled until he could focus on his body again. On keeping it ordered and still and concentrate on dragging in the few gasps of air he could. At least it was stale, tinged only with the sweat of his own body. No blood, thankfully, and no stench from the rotting corpse of whoever had last been cuffed up like this and forgotten about.

It felt like he'd been forgotten, even as he told himself this was just another one of their tactics. The dark, the suspension, the cold, the endless passing of precious time. All elements Ethan had used himself. Methods he'd been taught to resist through repetition as he grew up. He hadn't let them beat him then, and they *wouldn't* now. He was better than that, even though he had to bite back a bitter chuckle at the thought of all of his victims having the last laugh now because this wasn't training. It wasn't a test. They wanted him to crack, to be scared and vulnerable. It wouldn't work. The dark had always been Ethan's sanctuary and the waiting and cold could be ignored. The suspension was another matter.

He'd been here for at least four hours. Long enough that breathing was getting harder and harder. His lungs felt strained and flat, his ribs pressing too tight to them like a vice. A couple of times he'd relieved the pressure on his chest by flipping upside down and holding onto the chain with his feet.

Needing the flood of oxygen again, Ethan stretched up just that bit further and grasped the chain above the shackles. Lungs now burning, he curled his thighs up to his chest. Even though it pulled the stitches in his hip in new directions, it did offer some reprieve, so he held it, dropping his forehead onto his knees.

In the privacy it afforded him from the inevitable cameras watching him, Ethan allowed himself to think of Jack. His beautiful, stubborn, funny and endlessly contrary Jack. He could ignite so many different feelings in Ethan with a single look—love, laughter, frustration, fear, peace, lust—and yet they didn't overwhelm him anymore. His head and his heart could be still when it was just the two of them tucked away in a secure place.

How long had it been since he'd last seen him? Not much past the four hours he'd been awake in this cell? Or a day? Two? Longer? Was Jack a captive like him? Was he—

Ethan cut that thought out before it could form. Jack was all right. Safe the last time Ethan saw him, and he'd been reassured he would stay that way. So long as Jack didn't do anything stupid—not necessarily a given when Jack's heart was involved. Not that Ethan's decision-making paradigm had been much better of late, for the exact same reasons.

Would this never be over? All Ethan wanted now was to be with Jack. He'd thought he'd had that, and then . . . this.

Light flooded the cell.

Ethan startled and dropped from his precarious position, sensitive eyes burning. The sudden weight hanging off his shoulders jarred his whole body, setting him to swinging on the chain so he couldn't gain traction on the slick, cold stone floor. He scrambled for equilibrium, gasping for air while his eyes watered and his heart pounded in surprise and confusion.

He should have been expecting something like this. Should have been preparing for it instead of losing himself to memories of Jack. That he hadn't was humiliating. Frustration curled through him. Shame. Confusion. Surprise. He didn't like those feelings. They were weak. They meant he wasn't skilled enough or prepared enough. They meant someone else had the upper hand, and that was how one failed.

Ethan caught the edge of one of the floor stones with his toes. Muscles tensing, he froze his swinging and got his other foot on the ground as well. Eyes closed, he forced everything else aside and focused on his other senses, which he strained to their limits, needing to find the threat, work out what it was, and how to neutralise it.

Just in time to hear the lock on the door clunk open and someone enter. Just a few steps before they stopped.

Not yet ready to test his eyesight in the light, Ethan kept his eyes closed and listened. Muffled, distant voices, so soft he couldn't make out words, or even a language. Beyond them, nothing. No hint of traffic or birds or radio to give a clue as to where they were. The air wafting into his stale cell was sterile and warm, feathering his cool skin.

"Hello, One-three."

He had no chance of stopping the quiver that rolled down his spine, giving away his surprise.

The speaker gave a soft hum. A sound Ethan was incredibly familiar with. More than anything else in his childhood, that sound had shaped him. More than a mostly absent mother. More than Two's confusing blend of affection and abuse. It was a sound he had once cherished—and now feared.

"You know I'm disappointed, don't you?" the Doctor murmured.

Shame churned Ethan's stomach but he locked everything else down. Expression, limbs, breathing. Not that he had much control on the last, now he was suspended once more. But he wasn't going to struggle for air. Not in front of the Doctor.

Once, disappointing the Doctor had been the most terrible pain Ethan understood. It would curl him up in humiliation and agony until he'd redeemed himself, then he'd bask in the Doctor's pleasure. It hadn't just been him, either. All of them had, to varying degrees, lived and breathed by the Doctor's good word. It had taken Ethan a long time to get beyond that conditioning. A lot of time and distance and Jack.

"Of course you do. How could you not? You always were the smartest of the group, One-three."

Ethan struggled to not react.

"Oh, come now. Don't be like that." Another step and the Doctor's voice lowered, warming, so it wrapped around Ethan like a hug. "Look at me, One-three."

He tried, desperately, fiercely, not to obey. Froze everything this time. Even his laboured breathing.

The Doctor came closer, well within range of Ethan's capability to harm—and kill. "One-three, look at me."

When he refused, there came that little, dissatisfied hum again. It twisted like a knife in Ethan's chest. He could resist, though. He didn't believe the Doctor held all the answers anymore. Now, he *knew* otherwise.

"All right," the Doctor murmured, disappointment clear in the soft tone. "I see how this is going to progress. You've learned some bad habits since you left the group, One-three. Or should I call you Ethan?"

It was easy to not react this time, because "Ethan" had never been one of the Doctor's tools. The jobs given to the group and the names they had worked them under had nothing to do with the Doctor's goals. "Ethan Blade" hadn't been the Doctor's creation, then or now. It had taken a lot of time and some tough lessons, but One-three had finally made himself into a man he could live with, and Jack had named him in a moment of love and connection. He'd taken the word "Ethan" and made it into a name, something that defined him as a human and lover.

Letting the name and all it meant wrap around him, Ethan had no trouble resisting the Doctor's next words.

"Do you honestly think he loves you, One-three?" When the words didn't get a reaction, the Doctor continued in a soothing tone. "You know better than that, mon doux garçon."

The familiar words, in that voice, in French, nearly pierced Ethan's armour, but he steeled himself against it. He'd believed those words once, when he'd been desperate for something familiar, something soft and warm and comforting. Now, though, he knew it had just been a lie, so he kept still, didn't open his eyes, didn't let the Doctor know it still affected him.

His efforts were rewarded with a gentle chuckle. "Oh, I've missed you. Your stubbornness was always what defined you. Even when you stopped resisting, I knew it was just a ruse. The others might have believed you, but I knew the truth. You were simply biding your time, and when it came, you certainly surprised them all. But not me. Never me." A couple of steps brought the Doctor right up to Ethan, almost touching, minty breath wafting across Ethan's face in a whisper. "You may have shocked the others when you killed Two, but not me. I always knew you had it in you." A pause, then, "Paul St. Clair."

That broke his resolve. Never had the Doctor used that name, not even when Ethan had thought of himself as Paul. The shock of it wracked his shoulders, making the chains clank and his toes scrabble at the stones to regain their lost purchase.

The Doctor didn't push him. He never did when he found a chink he could exploit. He would wait to see just how he could manipulate the weakness he found in his subject, to judge the best way of using it to get what he wanted. So he left the cell, the sound of his even pacing marking his exit, leaving Ethan fighting an anticipatory shiver as the door opened, closed and locked.

Alone again, Ethan found comfort in the darkness. This had been his life for the first six years, unending black occasionally touched with the red of a light shone directly into his tissue-covered eyes. He had been able to see for the vast majority of his life, but those formative years hadn't left him entirely. He knew the dark and how to move in it. If he'd had to make the killing blow on Two with his eyes open, he knew he wouldn't have been able to do it.

Despite the Doctor's claim.

They left him alone for perhaps another quarter hour, then the door opened again. A single, silent man entered, the thump of his boots on the floor indicating he was large, though the fluidity of the steps meant it was probably all muscle making up his bulk. He moved around the outer edge of the cell, circling Ethan entirely, moving back and forth until he finally settled into position behind and to the left.

Ethan knew what was coming, even before the soft slither of leather over leather. Even before the man gave the short whip an experimental crack against the stone floor.

He was being punished. He'd disobeyed the Cabal. Run away. So they were punishing him and it wasn't entirely about causing pain. It was barely that, honestly. All of them had been made aware of what it meant to be wounded on their back—cowardice, weakness, betrayal.

As the first lash landed, a smarting snap across the taut skin of his back, followed by the sudden, sharp pain a second later, he wondered if this would end in scars again.

A second and third in quick succession, layering one on top of the other. No delay in feeling the pain now. It was instant, deep, and radiating. Ethan gritted his teeth against the urge to cry out. He wouldn't let them think they'd won. Not this time. He bore the bite of the leather silently and thought of Jack. Of the day they'd spent at the hidden waterfall in Vietnam, swimming, playing, rutting together under the sugary spray of water until they were gasping in shared pleasure. Of how Ethan had told Jack about Plutarch and his theory that scars were a sign of life. To have faced a danger and survived was a victory.

Ethan didn't want any more signs of survival. He was done with fighting. That life was supposed to be behind him now.

He should have known this plan wouldn't work.

The whip snapped across his spine, overlaying several other strokes. Fire lanced through his skin and muscle and a strangled cry erupted from his throat. Ethan bit back the whimpers that wanted to follow it. The one sound, though, was enough to encourage his torturer.

A series of rapid lashes, and it wasn't until they were over that Ethan heard his own gasps and grunts, realised the dampness on his face was sweat and tears. Even though it felt as if the skin on his back had been flayed off, every wet trail stung like a thousand needles, which meant it was salty sweat, not blood. Yet.

But the person didn't strike again. Between his heavy, pained breathing, Ethan heard the leather sliding against itself, then footsteps. The door opened, the torturer left and, after a moment, the lights went out.

There was no hope of relieving the strain on his arms and chest by flipping upside down again. Every little movement, including dragging air into his lungs, sent flashes of intense agony through his body. Simply hanging there was pure pain. He didn't even try to lose himself in thoughts of Jack. He couldn't associate the best thing in his life with this.

This wasn't the first time he'd been whipped. It wasn't even the second, when he'd learned just how soothing warm blood falling over raw skin could be. No, the first time had been like this. Full of pain but no blood.

He'd been nine years old, resigned to the strange new life within the group of Sugar Babies and being called One-three, and Bad Luck, and Freak. Resigned but still confused about why his mother had left him in this horrible place with hurtful adults and odd children who pushed and pulled him in all directions, who hated him for no reason, or who plied him with affection and harm equally. He'd still thought of himself as Paul then, still tested the limits of this new world, of the new rules of right and wrong they were teaching him. Tested the capacity of the carers to live up to their name until they'd had enough and strapped him to the bars and whipped him until he was promising to never question them again.

But no matter how hard the carers and instructors tried to bend Paul to their wills, he resisted. No matter what the Doctor said, Paul wouldn't give up on himself.

It wasn't until a year later, sitting in a shower stall, watching blood from the carved "TWO" on his foot swirl away down the drain, that Paul surrendered. Ribs aching, split lips stinging and whole leg throbbing, Paul St. Clair took his last, sobbing breath and One-three let it out.

So many years later, once again at the mercy of the Cabal, Ethan vowed he wouldn't give in this time.

TWO

They left him hanging for another hour. The pain of his lashed, stretched back outweighed that of his straining lungs and burning arms. Every drop of sweat from his head and shoulders ran in a stinging line down his back, giving him no reprieve.

The door opened before he passed out from the pain. Wreathed in agony so he couldn't concentrate enough to use his other senses, he slitted his eyes to see what was happening. Thankfully the lights had been dimmed enough he could watch as two men with guns trained on him come in first, followed by someone Ethan hadn't expected at all.

Zero rolled his wheelchair to a stop only a couple of feet back from Ethan's hanging body. The handler looked him over. "One-three." He shook his head slowly, then commanded the guards take Ethan down.

Once Ethan was on the cot, the guards left them alone and Zero manoeuvred around so he was next to the cot. "I can't say I'm pleased to see you here."

Ethan shifted to relieve his aching back. "This wasn't where I was hoping to end up, trust me."

"It never is the plan." Zero patted the armrest of his chair. "And yet it always seems to happen."

The handler hadn't always been "Zero." Ethan was certain of that. He was the last of the first experimental group. A sole survivor. Whatever number they'd given Zero originally had been changed when he became the handler for Ethan's group. Their contact with their masters once they'd been cast out into the world. His legs had been solid and muscular the first time Ethan met him, so he had only recently been paralysed. Zero had been bitter and mean at first, then he had seemed to become resigned to the chair and over the years, mellowed. While the buzzed grey-blond hair and diagonal scar across his face hadn't changed, he looked tired and defeated now. And his words and tone confirmed it.

"No one leaves the Cabal alive. Not even the bosses. People have tried but the Cabal usually finds a way to make it . . . beneficial not to. When they—" He cut himself off with a grimace, and when he continued, his tone was flat and dry. "When I was shot in the back, the damage was reparable."

They. Back. Was reparable.

With those few bland words, Ethan suddenly knew Zero better than he ever had, even after working with him for half his life.

Zero rocked his chair back and forth. "But I did think you'd be the one who managed it. I hoped you would at least."

"I had wondered if that was your goal when you told me I had to come in."

Zero gave a little shrug, then retrieved several white pills from a pocket. "For the pain."

Ethan wanted to snatch the pills out of his hand but resisted. While it seemed as if Zero was sympathetic with his desire to be free— for reasons Ethan was only starting to realise—he'd learned long ago that anything offered by the Cabal came with a commensurate price. He shook his head.

With an understanding nod, Zero backed up his wheelchair. "Then rest as much as you can. You're going to need your strength."

Once Zero had left, Ethan lay down. Zero was right and he needed to stay as strong as he could.

When he woke up, the Doctor was waiting for him.

"Good morning, Ethan." Standing next to the door, he pocketed a small screen he must have been looking at while waiting.

Stomach twisting from hunger to nausea and heart hammering in shock, Ethan struggled to sit up. His muscles had stiffened, a result of sleeping on the uncomfortable cot and unconscious efforts to keep from causing himself more pain in his sleep. Thighs, calves, and chest all ached, but it was the fire ripping across his back that pulled the gasp from him. Tears welled and he blinked them away. He didn't want the Doctor to see him hurting, even though a little voice in the very back of his heart cried for the comfort he remembered.

"I'm sorry that you're in pain," the Doctor murmured. The *but you only have yourself to blame* was clearly implied. "Would you like something to ease it?"

If he hadn't taken the pills from Zero, he certainly wouldn't take them from this man. "No, thank you."

The Doctor nodded. "As you wish. How about some breakfast?"

This one wasn't something Ethan could refuse, because the door opened immediately and three non-descript Caucasian men carried in a small folding table, a chair and a tray with hot food and a teapot. Another stood in the doorway, a rifle trained on Ethan while the others set down their gear. When they exited, the door was closed but not locked. Ethan didn't doubt the rifleman would be right outside it, waiting to take him down if he made a run for it. If they'd been told anything at all about him, they shouldn't have worried about a frontal assault.

The Doctor pulled out the single chair at the table and sat. He waved at the spread of food. "Come, Ethan. I know you must be hungry."

And just like that, he *was*, the nausea settling into hunger pangs. He didn't know how long it had been since he'd last eaten and it would help him regain his strength.

They'd set it up out of reach of the cot, so Ethan had to move, and by leaving only the one chair, he had to stand at the table like a supplicant. Both of which held him back, along with a healthy scepticism about the content of the plates and bowls. He wouldn't put it past them to drug the food.

The Doctor delicately spread butter on a slice of wheat toast. "Best hurry, mon doux garçon, lest I eat it all." He took a bite and chewed, his gaze locked on Ethan squarely as if knowing his thoughts and reassuring him.

Ethan was moving before he'd made the conscious decision to. He'd never suffered in the presence of the Doctor, always finding comfort and understanding with him. The pain always came at other times.

Mostly certain the skin on his back hadn't been broken by the whip, Ethan nevertheless felt as if he'd been flayed open, raw muscle burning as he stood, nearly crippling him. Yet he managed it, and one painstaking step at a time, reached the table. Despite the now gnawing hunger, he accepted the fine China cup of tea from the Doctor and sipped it. The heat felt good going down his throat and into his belly. It made him want to gulp it down, but if he did, the Doctor would make that disappointed hum of his and Ethan would fold up in shame.

Patiently, the Doctor put toast with butter and jam on a plate for him and handed it over. Ethan took it and, legs aching, retreated to the cot to sit and eat. Again he measured his bites, telling himself it was because he didn't want to risk upsetting his stomach, knowing, though, that he did it for the Doctor more than himself. After the first piece was down and settled, the Doctor offered him another. Ethan tried to refuse but a soft, "Come, don't be silly," had him staggering over to the table again.

When he'd returned his empty plate and cup to the table, the Doctor smiled at him, eyes sparkling warmly.

"You always were so polite and charming, One-three . . . sorry. Ethan. Such a lovely young man."

A lovely young man they'd turned into a cold-blooded killer. A child they'd abused and manipulated until he'd become what they wanted him to be. Ethan fought to remind himself that the Doctor had been a part of that, even if everything they had done together had felt so different, separated from the cruelty of the instructors and carers and experimental group by soft words, kind touches, and small gifts. Just a different way of creating a monster.

"Tell me about him," the Doctor said.

"About whom?"

The Doctor folded his hands together on the edge of the table, as he used to do on his desk in his rooms at the home. "You know very well who I wish to know about, Ethan. Tell me about Jack Reardon."

Nausea returned at the mere thought of talking about Jack to this man. Nausea because Jack was too good to be tainted by anything to do with Ethan's past, and because he wanted to tell the Doctor. Wanted to explain how Jack had given him everything this man and the Cabal had taken away from him. Wanted, blast it all, to let the Doctor know that he was happy, that he loved and was loved in return—that all of them had failed to break him completely.

"He's a very attractive man," the Doctor continued when Ethan didn't answer. "And intelligent, if a bit emotionally unstable. I believe it took him a deplorably long time to tell you he loved you."

"He didn't need to." Ethan hadn't meant to say it aloud and a blush heated his neck and cheeks as soon as it was out, which unsettled him further. He only ever blushed with Jack. No one else had ever made him feel that mix of arousal and coyness Jack could inspire in him with a dirty word or touch, or even just a look. Physical attraction and sex, or even the details of love, hadn't been part of his sessions with the Doctor. Admitting now that he felt wildly aroused not only by an attractive body, but the person himself, made Ethan want to squirm.

"Oh, Ethan." Pity lowered his voice and creased his brows into a frown. "Have you truly mistaken the pleasures of the flesh for love? Have you so thoroughly forgotten all you learned with us?"

"No, I haven't forgotten."

The Doctor made that little disappointed hum. "Tell me the truth, Ethan."

"That is the truth." Slowly, Ethan lifted his gaze and met the Doctor's. "I haven't forgotten anything I learned back then. But I have learned other things since, and one of them is that I'm not the monster you wanted me to be, that I am capable of being my own person and making my own decisions. The *right* decisions. I also learned that I am worthy of being loved, and capable of loving in return."

A fact he'd finally allowed himself to accept that night three months ago. After Jack had finally kissed him and they'd made love, Ethan had let himself believe they'd be together wholly and completely forever.

Then he'd heard that *ping*.

"I love him and he loves me. Why else would I have left him?"

THREE MONTHS EARLIER

P *ing.*

Something woke Ethan up, but before he could search out the disturbance, he was caught by the vision of the man lying beside him.

Jack lay on his belly, one leg bent part way, an arm tossed across Ethan's chest. Ethan trailed his fingers up and down his arm, loving the feel of his curled black hairs and the bulge of his biceps. Jack's long fingered hand, too, held his attention for a good while. The gunman calloused, the short nails a little ragged and chipped, the lighter shade of his palm compared to the back of his hand. How it felt to have it glide down Ethan's body. He shivered in recalled pleasure. Lord, those fingers on his skin, barely touching or gripping tight, and *oh*, when they were inside him. He bit his lips to keep from moaning.

Ethan pressed against his lover's side. "Jack," he whispered between kisses on his shoulder, leading up to his neck. "Are you awake?" Ethan had loved topping but now he needed Jack inside him. Needed Jack to drive him crazy and out of control.

Jack mumbled incoherently and rubbed his cheek over his pillow, then settled.

Disappointment mellowed by how gorgeous Jack looked with his face relaxed, lips parted and black curls falling across his forehead, Ethan snuggled closer. Head on Jack's pillow, he contented himself with gazing at this handsome man.

Never before had he believed this would ever be his. A real home, with someone he wanted to spend time with. Someone he could be himself with, who accepted that he wasn't "normal" and still wanted to be near him, be with him . . . love him.

Jack hadn't said it, but he'd told him all the same. Every time Jack came home to him, or let Ethan have space when he needed it and then welcomed him back with warm arms and smiles. Each time Jack pulled him close, just to be touching him without anything more. All the times Jack had laughed at him and with him. Whenever he forgave Ethan for making a mistake.

Every time Jack kissed him.

Which he seemed determined to make up for lost time with. They'd kissed over and over, soft and hard, dirty and chaste, each one as eloquent as the one before, all the way back to the first.

Ethan hadn't said it aloud, either. He wanted to, but it was so daunting. What if Jack couldn't say it back? What if what they had right now was all they needed and Ethan messed it up because he spoke aloud when it wasn't necessary? He loved Jack, had realised it several weeks back. The peace he felt with Jack, the warmth he found in his arms, the lightness in Ethan's mind and heart when Jack was near, could only be love. As was the way he didn't need to constantly analyse and survey his surroundings when Jack touched him, or the crazy swirling mess of emotions he felt when Jack took him apart in bed. He knew Jack loved him, the kisses told him that, so perhaps that was enough. They'd always been better at the physical side than the verbal side.

And perhaps Jack would say it, when he saw the present Ethan had got him in the morning. Maybe afterwards, Jack would take him to bed again and—

Ping.

No. Ethan refused to hear it. That part of his life was over. It had no part in this place or time.

Ping.

He would go to the Office and ask them to program a kill switch into his implant. He would prefer they turn it off permanently, but doubted Director Tan would allow it. After that, he and Jack would celebrate his birthday properly and maybe say *I lo—*

Ping.

Ethan buried his face in Jack's warm body. It was his choice to be here and they wouldn't make him change his mind.

Several minutes of blessed silence and Ethan let himself start to fall asleep.

Beep, beep, beep.

Blast it. A warning tone. Any second now, someone was going to remotely access his implant and sure enough an unknown voice spoke inside his head.

"One-three, confirm."

Ethan rolled away from Jack and stared up at the dark ceiling, counting the exposed beams. It helped focus his mind away from the repeated calls for acknowledgement. Still, his hands twitched for something to occupy them as well. Shoving down the sheet, he found the abandoned tube of lube and without thought, began flipping it.

"One-three, confirm receipt of transmission. If you do not confirm within twenty seconds, base will send an automatic location ping and a team will be dispatched to pick you up."

Twenty. Nineteen. Eighteen. Ethan searched for a way to stop them. Short of an electromagnetic pulse, there was nothing he could do. Fifteen. Fourteen. Thirteen. He and Jack could hold off whatever force the Cabal sent. Ethan had made sure it was possible when he'd bought the penthouse. Eight. Seven. Six. Of course, that meant in five seconds, the penthouse would no longer be their secret. The security Ethan needed would be destroyed. Three. Two . . .

"One-three, receiving transmission," he sent silently.

"Hold for command."

Ethan looked at Jack, and the peace he usually found in the thick brows, narrow nose, perfect mouth, and strong jaw wasn't there. All he saw now was everything he had to lose and just how much it would hurt when it was gone.

A new voice entered Ethan's head. *"One-three, the bosses are expecting a full report on the deaths of Two and Nine, in person. You'll have to come back."*

The first voice had been unknown. One of an ever-changing staff of people who had no real idea of who they were talking to, or who they worked for. This voice, though, Ethan knew very well.

"I don't work for you or them anymore, Zero. Remember that conversation we had after Vietnam? You let me go."

Zero sighed. *"I remember saying I would pass on your decision to the bosses, nothing more. You, of all of the group, should know that they don't do anything they don't agree to. They don't agree with you about leaving, so you haven't left the Cabal."*

Which was what Dejana had said when Ethan had told her the same thing, and then she'd promised to help him finish severing the ties that held him against his will.

"And don't think that accountant is going to do anything for you," Zero said, a touch of sympathy in his voice as he seemingly read Ethan's mind. *"They had her eliminated before she could, and not just because she said she'd help you."*

Of course they knew about Dejana. They found out everything. All the trouble he'd caused because of Dejana and her demands and promises, made pointless because of the Cabal.

Jack snuffled in his sleep and turned his face away, bent knee straightening, straight leg bending. He didn't know everything Ethan had done while Jack had been chasing a serial killer, but he would find out eventually, and when he did, would he still be able to forgive Ethan? History said he would, but there was always a breaking point.

"They're not just going to let you go this time," Zero said. *"They have contingencies."*

An alert told Ethan he'd received an image. Dreading the portent in Zero's words, he closed his eyes and slipped *sideways*. The image appeared on his overlay.

A daylight picture of a single storey house with a solitary dark-green bush in an otherwise empty yard. The walls were white stucco and the roof peaked, tiled in red, orange and yellow. An older model mid-sized SUV was in the short driveway and a woman stood beside it, green bags of shopping in both hands. She was perhaps in her late thirties, her long black hair pulled up in a neat ponytail, the skin between her brows wrinkled as she frowned. Even if the brown colour of her skin and the shape of her nose and cheekbones hadn't been sign enough, the expression told Ethan who she was.

Meera Reardon scowled exactly like her younger brother did. Jack's niece, a lighter skinned, younger image of her mother, laughed exactly like him. Matilda walked ahead of Meera, phone in one hand, the other swinging a brightly coloured shopping bag.

And the crosshairs of the rifle's site were centred right on the teenager's head.

Ethan's heart froze. The time stamp on the image said it had been taken at four fifty-one the previous afternoon.

Grimly, he asked, *"Are they still alive?"*

"Yes, but Seven is in place to rectify that if required."

Of course Seven was there. She was the Cabal's South East Asian operative and if it hadn't been for Samuel Valadian's well-known feelings about women, would have been the one sent to investigate and kill him. She was a brilliant hacker and could have undoubtedly found out everything the Cabal wanted to know, if Valadian would have ever let her do more than entertain him between the sheets. Instead, they'd sent Ethan. He, too, had had to let the target use him in bed, but being male, Valadian had also accepted that Ethan was capable of other tasks, as well.

Ethan often wondered how things would have turned out if Seven had gone to Valadian. She was, as they all were, an accomplished assassin, but her other skills far outstripped those she had for killing. Still, Ethan knew the moment she'd cleared Jack of being the Meta-State traitor, she would have eliminated him.

Just as she wouldn't hesitate to pull the trigger on a teenaged girl and her mother if Zero ordered her to.

"I have coordinates for your extraction," Zero said. *"I suggest you meet your brothers there and do what you have to in order to keep the women safe."*

Brothers? Both of them? That was overkill when Ethan's agreement to come in should have been enough. The fact that Zero even mentioned them felt significant, as well. It was a warning. Zero was right. The Cabal bosses had made sure they had contingencies. Ethan had to agree. It was the only way to ensure Jack didn't lose his family in one horrible, preventable, instant.

"All right. I'll do it."

FOUR

Ethan wrote a note for Jack—*Back soon, E*—and followed exfil plan number three. It got him out of the building without being detected by its, or his own, security systems and a couple of blocks away before he was caught on camera. If he wanted, he could have avoided them as well as he had those in the building, but he didn't because if Jack was going to have a life without him, then he needed his family more than ever.

He walked and let the mechanical eyes watch him. Around him, the storefronts were brilliant with Christmas decorations and announcements for holiday sales. Every now and then he reached out to touch a wall or a shop window. Quite apart from any practical reason, he wanted the texture and feel of this beautiful, vibrant city to soak into his skin.

Most of his work for the Cabal had been centred around Europe and South America, but he had done jobs in North America and the Middle East with Two and Ten, and all of them had worked together on big operations in China, Russia, and Africa. Ethan had seen some of the most beautiful cities in the world—Lisbon, Prague, Isfahan, Seville, Jaipur, Riga and many others—but the scenery had been peripheral to the reason he was there. Those places were always stained for him, if not before he arrived, then definitely after he left.

Sydney was different. Until a year before, he'd never worked there. He'd raced there and in Melbourne. The authorities—even the secret ones—had no idea the dreaded Ethan Blade had breached their borders. Sydney had always been clean for him. And even after he'd finished that job, it had only changed for the better. No blood, no stains. Just a successful job done—and Jack.

Casting thoughts of what he'd left behind aside before the ache in his chest became crippling, Ethan concentrated on the now.

On getting to the address supplied by Zero. On making sure nothing happened to Jack's sister and niece. On ensuring his brothers didn't get the chance to hurt anyone here at all.

The timing was close when he reached the designated pick up site. He could have moved faster but this wasn't something he wanted to rush. A final walk through the city Jack loved, the one Ethan was coming to love as well. The further he went, the more he wanted to go back. Wanted to curl up in bed beside Jack again and feel safe and content. It was so tempting. He believed the Office would do what it could to keep the Cabal at bay. Jack and his family wouldn't be hurt. The slow hollowing out of Ethan's chest would stop.

Tempting, but it would be futile. The Office had power, yes, but nowhere near enough to go against the Cabal. They had rules they had to follow. Laws to obey and politicians to appease.

Leaving Jack, giving him as much as he could to help his sister and niece, was the only option Ethan had.

There was no one on the footpath outside the entrance to Paddy's Market. The occasional car or truck passed on the mostly empty, early a.m. street. Ethan crossed the road and leaned against the orange brick wall of the building. It wasn't exactly blending in—a lone man on the street at this hour, wearing an overcoat in summer—but he didn't have to wait long.

A dark figure slithered down from the awning over the shopfronts across the road. Short and stocky, he nevertheless moved with a fluid grace and agile strength that saw him land on the footpath with no sound and barely a hitch in his momentum. Within seconds, he was approaching Ethan, hands swinging free by his sides, fingers splayed, showing no weapons. He was missing the ring and little fingers of his left hand.

"One-three," Four said in his low, gravelly voice. "Zero wasn't sure you'd show up. I knew you would, though." His white eyes gleamed in the ambient light of the night-time city.

When putting together their group of Sugar Babies, the Cabal had canvassed the entire globe for suitable candidates. None of them knew exactly where they'd been born—apart from Ethan who could narrow his birthplace down to southern France—but after they'd been released into the world to do jobs, they'd been able to guess. Two had probably been from a Nordic country, Nine from South Africa and Four central Africa.

"The bosses made it impossible to ignore the summons." Ethan had always liked Four. He'd been trained to be ruthless and merciless, as they all had been, but unlike some of the others, Four could confine it to the job. He wasn't overly compassionate but he wasn't cruel or manipulative, either. And his sweet tooth was worse than Ethan's, though Four had been thoughtful enough to share any pilfered chocolate or ice cream with him.

Four grunted. "They do that. This way. I have a car."

They fell into step side by side, familiar with each other's rhythms and actions. Ethan, Four and Two had all worked under the name "Ethan Blade" and as such had spent a lot of time in the field together before Ethan had broken away from the Cabal. The fact that they looked nothing alike had only added to the mystery around Ethan Blade.

With a silent gesture, Four indicated they take a narrow side street leading to a multi-storey carpark. As they went, Ethan surreptitiously scanned his brother for weapons.

They had been raised together, taught to work and fight together, taught to respect the other, and yet they'd also been taught to trust no one. They'd been encouraged to test each other's limits, to be merciless with their siblings in order to create stronger, deadlier tools for the Cabal. It didn't matter that Four had shared ice cream with young Paul. It certainly didn't matter that Ethan liked him. Four was what he was, what they all were, and that meant Ethan couldn't let his guard down.

Four had more than adequately proved that with the final test.

The dark street was a good place for an ambush, but they made it to Four's car without incident, and the stocky man threw a set of keys to Ethan as they approached a red Jeep Wrangler.

"Nothing fancy, One-three," Four said they got into the car. "We don't need anyone noticing us."

Ethan gave him a small smile as he inserted the key and turned it. "I am capable of keeping to a speed limit."

Gunning the engine, Ethan slammed the Jeep into reverse and they rocketed backwards. He palmed the steering wheel around, barely missing a cement barricade. Applying the brakes sharply, he brought the car to a sudden stop in the middle of the lane between parks, pointed towards the exit.

Four merely gave him a sidelong eyeroll.

Ethan didn't trust him, but he did like him. "Sorry."

With a grunt, Four waved him on and settled back into his seat, appearing to relax.

Much more sedately, Ethan drove them out of the carpark and onto the road. "Where are we going?"

"I'll let you know where to go. Head west for now."

Dutifully, Ethan turned them toward the A4 highway.

They had a number of standard exfil routes out of most places, and on top of those, they each had their own ways out, for the times when even the weight of the Cabal's gaze was too heavy. There were two Cabal options west of Sydney, and one of Ethan's own. He could discount his—only he knew about it—and he quickly ruled out the Cabal's. They wouldn't take the chance that Ethan had revealed them to the Office.

More so now than at any time in the past, Ethan was beyond the Cabal's trust. He'd severed all ties to them and his siblings—his *associates*—and put a signature to a contract with the Meta-State's Office of Counterterrorism and Intelligence. The signature wasn't real, but Ethan's plan to honour it was. At least, it had been when he'd thought it was the best way to stay with Jack and keep him safe.

Now, this was his only chance at making sure the greatest danger to Jack and his family was neutralised. He just had to be a bit more patient.

Dawn chased them westward into the Blue Mountains and beyond. In Mudgee, they stopped to switch cars.

Across the road from the carpark where Four was quietly breaking into a late model Holden Colorado—common enough on the country roads they wouldn't stand out—was a small corner store with faded posters in the windows for different ice creams. Glancing back at the man he'd grown up calling brother, Ethan's heart thumped heavily. If today went as Ethan believed it would, this would be the last time he and Four ever spent together. He'd been resigned to never seeing Four or Seven again when he agreed to live with Jack and made his commitment to the Office, but at least he'd known they were alive out there somewhere. There would have always been the slim possibility of seeing them, talking to them, once again. Ethan had left Seven's future in Jack's hands. Four's was now in his.

Maybe he could change that though. Maybe this didn't have to be a them-or-him situation after all.

Ethan was crossing the road even before he realised he was doing it. Four's hissed "What are you doing?" barely registered. It was too early for the store to be open but the lock on the door was simple and there was no sign of a security system. Ethan picked the lock and slipped inside swiftly. It didn't take him long to find what he wanted and he left money on the counter to cover them, then returned to where Four was already in the new car, waiting.

"What was that about?" Four asked as Ethan slid behind the wheel again.

"Breakfast." Ethan held out one of the ice cream sandwiches.

Once, Four used to take any sweet thing Ethan offered without reservation. Now, he eyed the gift warily, then slowly took it without looking at Ethan. He grunted something that may have been "Thank you," then tore open the packet and bit into the chocolate biscuit and vanilla ice cream. Four didn't have much of a conscience, but that he showed one now only made Ethan ache even more for what was inevitably coming.

Any interest he had in eating his own treat died in Ethan's chest. The hollow space that had opened up when he'd walked away from Jack widened. He ate for appearance's sake, started the car and followed Four's directions.

They passed Dubbo at eight-thirty a.m. and Ethan asked, "How much further?"

"Just be patient. We'll get there soon enough."

Ethan depressed the accelerator a touch more. Now that he was certain there was only one option, he was eager to get it done. It was still a delicate balance between dealing with his brothers and giving Jack enough time to ensure the safety of his family, though.

Jack was probably awake by now and realising Ethan was gone. The note he'd left wouldn't satisfy him for long, just enough to let Ethan get a head start on what he needed to do. After that, he didn't doubt that Jack would hit high gear and tear through any obstacles in his path. Ethan was counting on it.

He just had to give Jack enough time.

Two hours later, Four directed him off the road and onto a dirt track. The Colorado bounced over a clearly untended stretch of barely-there wheel ruts. The land around them was flat and open, empty pasture that hadn't seen a herd of grazing animals in some time. A few small clusters of trees broke the immediate surrounds, and the track angled towards a solitary shed in the distance.

Either alerted by the dust trail the ute was kicking up, or by Four via his neural implant, a large door began to open well before they reached the shed. As they got closer, Ethan saw it was a hanger and by the time he stopped the Colorado to the side of the door, a platform holding a helicopter had rolled out of the hanger on a set of tracks.

It was a Bell something or other with four blades. Ethan wasn't that interested in flying and only knew the basics of how to pilot most types of craft, enough that he could land one if required. He much preferred the visceral sensation of high speed on land and the immediacy of the surrounding dangers. It gave him something to focus all of his attention on, to quiet the constant buzz of assessing, planning, and strategizing that ran through his head. Over the years, he'd only found two things that banished it—racing and Jack.

Four got out of the car and went into the shed. There was no one else in sight, but Zero had said *brothers*, which meant Ten would be their pilot.

Ethan checked the Eagles in their holsters, the backup in the hidden holster on his back, under his shirt, the four-inch knives in their wrist sheaths, and the seven-inch tactical knife strapped to his calf. Only when he was satisfied they all there and ready to be used, did he exit the ute.

"Well, well," a cool, monotonal voice said from behind him. "The errant child returns to the nest."

Muscles tensing unconsciously, Ethan turned slowly. "Hello, Ten."

Ten stood by the back of the ute, scraping under a nail with the tip of a tactical knife. His aviators were directed at his hands, but Ethan could feel the weight of his gaze all the same. It was the same cold, penetrating sensation he'd always felt around this brother, similar to how Two made him feel when he'd been in the mood to torture. The difference was that Two had been able to hide it when required. Two could be warm and affectionate, luring people in close, only to turn on them in a split second. Ten had no such skill.

What really unsettled Ethan right then was how much Ten looked like Jack. The same light brown skin, the black hair that curled stubbornly, the tall, lean frame. He was of either Middle East or South Asia origin and as such had been centred in those areas for the Cabal, and thanks to his pure cold-bloodedness, tended to work alone, or on jobs where three or more of them were required. One on one, he couldn't be trusted to not kill his partner. Ten's confirmed kills on jobs rivalled that of Ethan Blade, and that been three of them.

If the Cabal had deemed any of the group a success, it had been Two. Intelligent, obedient—except when it came to Ethan—highly efficient and unaffected. They all shared those traits, to greater or lesser extent, but Ten had the added danger of being unpredictable. Generally, when they all worked together, any unsanctioned deaths were his.

The angle of the reflective sunglasses dropped down over Ethan's body and came back up slowly. Ethan resisted the urge to reach for a weapon, even as the gunshot scar on his left shoulder twinged.

"Did you finally tire of the target penetrating you? Is that why you're coming in?" The flat tone did nothing to make the questions any less disturbing, because although Ten had to know Seven was poised to kill Jack's sister and niece, that meant nothing to him. He had no empathy and couldn't understand it in anyone else, either.

"It's none of your business." Ethan matched Ten's even tone. He'd learned long ago to not react to his brother's nature. Ten couldn't help it.

Ten shrugged and slid his knife back into the sheath on his belt. He wore dark tactical clothing and boots, shoulder rig with his SIG on the right and his preferred hand cannon, a S&W 500, on the left. If Ten had one redeeming factor, it was that he didn't want his targets to linger.

Deliberately turning his back on Ten, Ethan started for the hanger door, wondering what Four was doing.

"You killed Two."

Locking down his reaction, Ethan ignored the words. Just as he was about to step into the interior, Ten spoke again.

"Congratulations, little brother. You passed the final test."

Four came out of the hanger as Ethan was forcing himself not to pull a gun on Ten. The stocky man stopped in front of him, a small bag slung over one shoulder, stance relaxed. Ten had moved up behind him, as well. To one side was the wall of the hanger, the ute to the other. Ethan was boxed in.

When he'd killed Two, he hadn't given a second thought to what it would mean to the Cabal, apart from the loss of their best weapon. All he'd thought about, all he'd *cared* about, was protecting Jack. And then Ten had mentioned the final test.

Was that why the bosses wanted him to come in? Had they decided Ethan had finally accepted his destiny?

If that were the case, though, they wouldn't have sent Four and Ten. Thanks to the loss of Nine and Two, there were only four of them left now. Seven was on her own job and Ethan doubted the Cabal could have spared the remaining two just to pick him up. Zero had been right to warn him.

By Ethan's estimation, Jack should be in furious motion by now. Hopefully he'd discovered the coded message Ethan had left him and his sister and niece were safe, but he couldn't risk it. He had to give Jack more time.

"Shall we get underway?" he asked coolly. "I'd hate to keep Zero waiting."

Four regarded him for a moment longer, then grunted and moved past him to toss the bag into the cabin of the chopper. Ten remained where he was, a silent menace at his back, and Ethan calmed his mind, ready for the instant his brother made a move. Which was to step aside, into Ethan's peripheral vision.

"Don't worry, little brother. You won't be late."

Leaving Ethan to parse his words, Ten went and began to warm up the engines on the chopper. Four came by, splashing petrol on everything, readying to burn it all. Clearly, this would be a one-use-only exit point.

Wondering if this was when it would happen, Ethan was both surprised and pleased when Four finished his job and motioned him into the helicopter. Perhaps they didn't want to risk it going haywire this close to their starting point. It worked in Ethan's favour, so he climbed into the cabin with Four.

The interior was relatively plush with leather seats for five passengers, cup holders and lots of bubble windows for site seeing—a potential charter craft used to allay suspicions. Ethan sat on the back bench and Four in one of the individual seats facing him. They all put on the headphones, for the noise cancelling properties only. All communication could be done through their implants.

In the pilot seat, Ten flicked switches, swift and sure, as the engine vibrated solidly. The only reason Ethan trusted him when they flew together was that crashing might kill Ten as well as anyone else, and Ten had a strong survival instinct.

Which meant that this might just work.

Overhead, the rotating blades swept shadows across the windows in increasing frequency, like they were slicing off the minutes and seconds of Ethan's remaining life. Each dark blur brought him closer and closer to the end.

Ten eased up the collective and pulled back on the stick, the chopper lifting smoothly, slowly taking them up and forwards. When they were high enough, Ten circled around the hanger and Four produced a remote trigger from a pocket. Flicking up the cover, Four put his thumb over the switch and pushed it.

The explosion was muffled and the pressure of it pushed against the chopper. Ten made another slow circuit so they could make sure everything had been caught up in the flames, which it had thanks to Four's liberal application of accelerant. Certain there would be little to no evidence left, Ten straightened out their trajectory and they shot into the sky.

When they levelled out, the chopper was headed in a northwest direction. Perhaps they were aiming for the Darwin exit point, though they'd have to stop and refuel a couple of times. Or they were just headed for the remotest, emptiest place they could find in order to kill Ethan and dump his body.

There was no doubt now in Ethan's heart and mind. Zero's warning had put the idea into his head and Four's reaction to the ice cream had confirmed it. This was most definitely a them-or-him situation.

Ethan didn't relax into his seat. There was no point in pretending. They all knew what was coming, even if Ethan didn't know when. All he could hope was that they would hold off long enough to give Jack as much time as possible. And that he would be able to do what was necessary when the moment came.

It was nearly midday when Ethan decided he couldn't wait any longer. It was likely they would wait until they landed to refuel, to make it two against one, but he'd given Jack as much time as possible. If he tried for more, the chances he wouldn't be the one to start things rapidly increased.

With a flex of his wrist, Ethan popped the clip on his hidden sheath. The knife slipped towards his palm. Locking down the memory of Four giving him the last scoop of ice cream, Ethan resolved himself. It was him or them, and if Jack was ever going to be safe, it had to be them.

FIVE

Ethan flipped the knife, caught it by the point and threw it at Four all in one swift move, but the man rolled forwards. His headphones pulled off his head as he went and the blackened blade of Ethan's knife thunked into the leather back of his seat. Expecting it, Ethan spun on the bench seat, back to the bubble window, and kicked at Four's face, ripping his own headphones off at the same time. One foot connected, the other Four managed to knock down even as his head snapped back. Ethan kicked again, finding ribs. Four oufed but lunged across the length of the seat. The chopper jerked sideways fractionally with the sudden movement and Ten glanced over his shoulder at them. Ethan's view of his face was fleeting, but Ten's expression was as bland as it had been on the ground.

Locked together with Four, Ethan had to twist away from his punches, deflecting them when he could. Four inched his way out of Ethan's hold, driving him harder against the window at Ethan's back. The chopper shivered with their frantic movements.

Seconds before Four threw himself back at Ethan, Ethan got a foot up and kicked him solidly in the solar plexus. Four tumbled backwards with a grunt, scrabbling at the back of the seat for purchase. Ethan levered himself up and followed him, grabbing the front of his shirt and aiming a short, sharp punch at his face. It landed on his hard jaw as Four pulled back. Four torqued his body, tossing Ethan off.

Ethan threw himself sideways, onto the backwards-facing seat. He slithered through the fourteen-inch space between headrest and cabin top. When he tumbled into the chair beside the pilot the tight confines meant he was almost upside down. Four, bulkier than Ethan, had no chance of making it.

Piloting a helicopter required concentration and coordination, so Ten couldn't immediately attack, giving Ethan a moment to roll into a slightly better position. Kicking the pilot in the face was not a good thing to do if you cared about not crashing—and Ethan didn't.

Ten tried to dodge Ethan's boot, but it caught him on the shoulder, knocking his hand off the collective. The chopper's nose dipped toward the brown ground far below.

Ethan kicked again, aiming for the stick. It jerked to the right and the chopper turned sharply. In the seat behind him, Four slammed into the window, thrown by the sudden change in trajectory.

Ten scrambled to regain control as Ethan kicked at him again. When he dodged to miss the blow, Ethan got his leg behind Ten's neck, then pressed his other calf to his throat. Ankles locked together, he twisted and Ten's grunt was strangled into silence.

The chopper careened wildly as Ten struggled to keep it steady and fight against Ethan's chokehold. Ethan braced himself and kept the hold as tight as he could. In the back compartment, Four was clambering across the seats, coming for Ethan, but the unpredictable flight of the chopper tossed him one way and then the other.

Then Ten went still. He hadn't passed out, just stopped struggling. His throat was working against Ethan's leg, trying to get air to his lungs, and his mouth gaped uncontrollably, but the rest of him was motionless. Then he let the collective go and pushed a button on the console.

The jolt as the chopper's course corrected rocked them all. Ethan was shaken free of his precarious position and crashed into the console. Ten landed half on him, half on his own seat and behind them, Four slammed into the backwards-facing seats. Within moments, though, everything was stable once more.

Then a large hand grabbed the front of Ethan's shirt and closed. Four dragged him up and over the backs of the seats. It was a tight fit but Ethan went without struggling, letting the broad man toss him onto the rear bench seat. Leaving the autopilot in charge of the chopper, Ten started over the back of his seat as well.

This couldn't go on much longer. It had to end before it became two on one.

Ethan leaped off the seat at Four. They clashed together, Ethan's trajectory taking them sideways. The chopper shuddered as they hit the side window behind the pilot seat. Ten, halfway over his seat, wrapped an arm around Ethan's neck and pulled him off Four. Ethan went with him, getting a hand between Ten's arm and his throat just before he was slammed into the backrest and pinned.

Four remained where he'd been, hands slowly coming up to wrap around the handle of Ethan's tac-knife. It jutted out at a downward angle under his sternum. The tip of the seven-inch blade was inside his heart. His chest jerked as his breathing faltered.

As Four slumped to the floor, Ethan fought against Ten but had no leverage, no room to get out of the hold on his neck. His remaining wrist blade was on the arm trapped under Ten's and his brother was staying low, using the chairback as cover from Ethan's other hand. Desperate, he let go of Ten's arm and freed his hand. The strong forearm crushed into his throat without hindrance and air became scarce very fast. Ethan couldn't tell what was the roar of the engine and what was blood rushing through his ears. But with a flick of his wrist, his last knife popped clear of the sheath and dropped into his hand.

Ethan slashed at Ten's arm, feeling the blade bite into material and flesh. Ten snarled and his hold loosened just enough to let Ethan pull in some air before tightening again. Desperate, Ethan thrust up and back wildly, meeting resistance for a moment and getting a cry of pain. He lost his grip on the knife as Ten thrashed. Weapon-less again, Ethan grabbed onto the arm across his neck and pulled. He got enough space to sip air but they were evenly matched in strength and they were locked in a stalemate. On the floor, Four was dying fast, his gasping breaths growing shallower and shallower as blood filled his chest cavity, compressing his lungs.

Needing some way of getting the upper hand, Ethan searched for a weapon. He had his Eagles, but if he took even one hand off Ten's arm, his brother would crush his throat. On the seat opposite him was the small pack Four had brought on board.

Bracing himself against the back of the seat he was trapped on, and using Ten's arm for leverage, Ethan got his feet hooked into the handles and wrenched them apart. The zipper broke and the contents spilled out.

The small EMP generator needed no further explanation. They'd stop to refuel and with the chopper off, Ten or Four would set it off and while Ethan was in pain from having the implant so cruelly disabled, they'd kill him. Its presence answered the question as to why his brothers had been speaking aloud to him. They had already had their implants disabled, so the sudden loss of it wouldn't affect them while taking Ethan down.

Right then, Ethan had only one option. One that guaranteed the Cabal lost the last of their weapons and make it just that bit harder for them to go after Jack. If they cared enough about him once Ethan was out of the picture.

Ethan held the EMP generator steady with one foot and pressed the trigger with the other.

The piercing screech of his implant dying ripped through Ethan's head. His violent, uncontrolled thrashing broke Ten's hold and he tumbled free, falling to the floor on top of Four's body. The pain dropped to a lingering ringing in his ears quickly and he became aware of an eerie calm.

The engine—and auto-pilot—were dead from the EMP. The only sound was the continuing *whomp whomp whomp* of the rotors still spinning. They were dropping fast but weren't plummeting uncontrolled out of the sky.

Just as Ethan wondered why, the chopper wobbled and started tipping.

Instead of coming after Ethan in those moments of disorientation, Ten coolly turned around and took up the controls once again. The chopper righted itself and their descent steadied but didn't slow. The ground was coming up very fast.

"How?" Ethan couldn't help but ask.

"It's called auto-rotation. Safety measure to help the pilot land the machine in case of engine failure." Ten's tone held no hint of alarm. Ethan had never heard him sound anything less than eternally unsurprised. "I'm going to kill you when we land."

Which was going to be very soon, the brown and green ground rapidly approaching. Ethan had maybe twenty seconds left to end this before things got more or less even between him and Ten.

He threw himself across the rear cabin, slamming into the back of Ten's seat just as Ten pulled the nose of the chopper up sharply. Scrambling for purchase, Ethan grabbed the headrest with one hand and wrapped his other arm around Ten's neck and, rather than choke, jerked his arm up. Ten's head snapped back and he lost his hold on the stick.

Everything was a chaotic blur after that. The chopper rolled and dropped, spinning blades hitting the ground first. Its body was flung over, rotors snapping off as it went, thrashing the rest of the craft about wildly. His hold on Ten shaken loose, Ethan tumbled, colliding with Four's body, the seats, and the central column. Then the chopper hit the ground, metal crunching, glass shattering, and rolled, once, twice, before coming to a rocking stop.

Ethan curled into a tight ball, hoping that was it, and for a breathless moment it was. Then it rocked a little too far one way, hit a critical point, and toppled over again. It rolled down a slope, crunching over rocks and hard dirt. Compared to the actual crash, this was steady and controlled. Ethan braced himself between seat and central column, only knocked loose when the craft hit water.

Waves splashed up around him and sprayed in through the cracked glass. The most violent motion stopped, replaced by an almost gentle rock and slow sinking. Water starting gushing in and the body of the chopper groaned under a new sort of pressure.

Ethan pulled himself out of the growing pool of water in the cabin. Ten was lodged between the front seats and the controls, a steady stream of dirty water pattering down on his chest. Blood smeared his face and neck, his head lolling back listlessly. Ethan clung to the back of the seat for a moment, watching his brother's chest for signs of life. As he waited, and the chopper sunk further and more cold water swirled around him, Ethan didn't know if he wanted to see Ten's chest move or not.

There was absolutely no love lost between them, but apart from Seven, Ten was the last of Ethan's siblings. Ethan grieved for Nine and wondered if he would ever stop. He worried that Seven would get to Jack's family before Jack did, because if that happened, nothing would stop Jack from killing her—nothing would stop Ethan from killing her in that case—but he hoped she would defy the Cabal this once.

He wished he hadn't had to kill Four. And some very small part of him wanted to see Ten draw breath and open his white eyes.

If he did, Ethan would kill him and not regret it, but there was that small, contrary part of him all the same.

Seeing no movement of Ten's chest, Ethan left his brother behind. After finding his plastic framed glasses floating on the rippling water he hauled himself through a shattered widow unblocked by mud. Sharp edges of glass caught his leg, pain tearing through his flesh as he pulled away from the wreck and swam upwards.

Ethan broke the surface of the murky water, gasping for air. Fumbling in his pocket, he found his glasses, put them on and opened his eyes. The chopper shifted in the muddy bottom, another burst of bubbles exploding from the cabin as the large machine settled into the bottom of the dam. His leg stung and he could feel it bleeding, warmth pooling briefly around his calf before the water diluted the blood away.

He paddled until his feet hit the mud, crawled onto the bank and caught his breath.

It was done. The last of his brothers were dead by his hand, and right then it didn't feel like a victory. It was a capitulation. A surrender to everything the Cabal had ever wanted him to be. He could kill without remorse and yet these deaths—and Two's—he felt in his own chest like someone had punched him in his solar plexus.

Ethan sat there and deep breathed until the anguish subsided, leaving the empty chasm inside him even wider. Which allowed the physical injury to be felt. He prodded at his leg tentatively. Yes, that sharp stab of pain was a decent wound. Tearing off his pant leg showed him several cuts, most of them shallow but one was large and bled freely. Ethan wrapped his torn pant leg around the cuts as best he could, then stood. It stung, but not too badly. Avoiding the freshly turned up dirt of the crash site and roll into the water, he headed up to the top of the raised perimeter of the dam. At the top, he studied the surrounding land.

Open, empty pastures as far as he could see. Just the occasional stand of trees to break the monotony.

A dam meant people, though. Ethan had no idea which direction they might be in, but he'd survived far more desolate treks with less.

Simply because it was where he eventually needed to get, he set out eastward.

It took him two days to find other humans. Or signs of them, at least. He'd passed scattered herds of cattle and a few sheep, but no people. At first sight of the house, he held back and studied it from a distance for several hours, seeing an old ute come and go several times, then it left and didn't return. He took half an hour to get closer, making sure that all residents had departed before breaking in.

Being a remote property, they had a very extensive first aid kit and Ethan cleaned the cuts on his leg, the deepest of which had started showing signs of infection the night before. He took the stock of painkillers and antiseptic cream, then moved to the kitchen.

He filled a cloth bag with canned foods and bottles of water, then set it by the door, ready to go if he needed a quick escape. Only then did he satisfy his empty belly with a simple sandwich, struggling to not eat too fast and upset his tender stomach. Then he left the house and on impulse, checked the large four bay shed out the back.

One bay was empty, another had a John Deer tractor and the next one was cluttered with farm equipment. In the last bay, however, was a low, sleek shape under a dusty cover. Not daring to hope, Ethan lifted up a corner of the tarpaulin. A hint of green, an angular fender and round, forward facing headlight. A further peak showed a flat black grill with a Holden badge.

Resistance was futile. Ethan tossed the cover off and revealed a late seventies Holden Monaro. Lime green, thick black stripes running up the bonnet. GTS350 coupe. Classic. His fingers itched to touch it, but if he went that far, he'd have to get in and feel the leather of the seats. Curl his hands around the steering wheel, and well . . . it was inevitable.

Despite the dust on the cover, which probably was barely a week's accumulation in this environment, the tank was full and the engine came alive smoothly when he hotwired it.

The whole idea was ridiculous. It would leave a path a mile wide for anyone to follow, but with the 5.7 litre V8 motor, they'd have to work to catch him.

He peeled the car out of the shed and onto the dirt driveway, back end fishtailing in the loose surface. Arcs of red dirt spraying up behind him, Ethan roared away. For the first time since his implant had *ping*ed while lying beside Jack, Ethan felt truly in control. This was something he could do without thinking. It was second nature to him now, to let the pulse of a powerful engine dictate the beat of his heart, to feel the speed in the weight on his chest, to let the world blur away and disappear. Like this, he could almost forget what he had done, or that in doing so, he might have destroyed the most perfect thing that had ever happened to him.

What if Jack hadn't got to his family in time? What if Ethan had left him to face Seven alone and he didn't prevail? What if Jack hated him for leaving without saying anything?

He ditched the classic Monaro in Tamworth and switched to an early model Toyota Celica guaranteed to have no GPS tracking devices onboard. Another car change in Newcastle and at nine p.m. that night he was cruising back into Sydney in a Hyundai Santa Fe. He couldn't imagine a more unlikely car for Ethan Blade to drive, given his reputation with the local authorities. This time, when he left the car behind, he didn't steal another one, instead making his way across the city via public transport and taxis, always careful to keep his face off any cameras. Just after midnight he was back in the building on Bathurst Street.

The penthouse was empty. No sign of Jack, no sign of recent habitation in fact. The *E* on the note he'd left had been crossed out and replaced with a *J*, but that and a few extra groceries in the fridge was the only change from when Ethan left. Hoping it simply meant Jack had gone back to his own apartment—which he could understand, given the circumstances—and hadn't succumbed to any dangers, Ethan went down to the garage.

He stopped dead in his tracks when he stepped out of the lift. The detachment he'd been relying on to get him through this vanished the moment he laid eyes on his Aston Martin Vanquish S Coupe. Victoria was in her usual place, but she was damaged. Dinted fenders, smashed lights, paint scraped back to undercoat in several places, bullet holes across her rear end. She was just a car, but one he'd invested a lot of his life into fixing, keeping pristine and getting to know so well he could drive her blind. He felt her damage in his own body.

Ethan ran his hand over the damaged areas, finding red paint in the scratches on the fenders. What had happened? It had to have been Jack who'd taken her out. He had access to the keys and, if he'd found and followed Ethan's clues, cause to need her. The damage wasn't so great the occupants wouldn't have survived, but were they uninjured? Was Jack okay? Were his passengers, if any, all right? Hopefully Victoria had taken all the hits for them and done her job well.

Turning from his car, Ethan's heart took another blow.

In the space next to Victoria, where Jack parked his Kawasaki Ninja, was instead a white-covered motorbike, red bow still in place.

Jack's gift. The bike Ethan had bought for him. The Ducati Panigale was second hand and had required some work before it was back to showroom quality. It had been Ethan's refuge in the week after Nine's death. Cathartic. Taking something he used to do for his sister—maintaining her Ducati SuperSport S—and now doing it for Jack had helped him deal with Nine's loss. When the bike was finished, Ethan had been able to look at it and not feel the gut-deep hurt of Nine's death. It had become solely Jack's. He'd organised for it to be delivered on Jack's birthday. Finding it here still, four days later and untouched, tore a hole in his heart.

Jack had been here between his birthday and now. He had seen the gift. And left it behind. Was it just a case of him not liking the model? Or did he not like whom it was from anymore? The possibility hurt like nothing else. Not even thinking Jack was sleeping with his old fling had sliced through Ethan's chest like this.

The hole in Ethan's heart simply joined up with the hollowness in his chest that had been growing deeper and darker since he'd walked out of this building four days ago.

It didn't matter why the gift was still there. It didn't even matter that his precious car had been through a trial and come out battered and broken. All that mattered was making sure Jack was all right, and that he would stay that way.

Or be avenged.

SIX

Ethan had to be certain before he left Sydney again. Certain that his plan had worked and that Meera and Matilda were safe. Certain that when he left again, it was to protect Jack and not avenge him.

And there was one fast way to do that.

In another stolen car, his first stop was to fetch a set of fake passports and IDs. Ones that even Jack didn't know about. The money he'd taken from the penthouse had been lost in the chopper crash so he visited a few other drop sites and collected another hundred grand in various currencies. From there, he took his time getting to Leichhardt, ensuring he hadn't picked up a tail. Parking some distance down the street from Jack's apartment building, Ethan scanned it with a high-powered rifle scope. It was after midnight yet there was a light on in Jack's corner apartment. No shadows moved inside but shortly after one a.m. a man appeared from the front entrance and walked towards a car parked on the side of the road.

Average height, lean, moving with an easy swagger, a satchel hanging by his left hip. He pulled a phone from the back pocket of his pants and as it lit up, his smiling face was revealed.

Ethan let out a breath he hadn't known he'd been holding. The growing pain in his chest eased away as he was watched Lewis Thomas flick through a couple of screens. He appeared fine and the light still shining from Jack's apartment was a good sign he was in there. Lewis had left Jack's place happy. He wouldn't have done that if his best friend weren't safe and healthy.

Ethan had met Lewis two weeks ago, when Jack had been recovering in the Office infirmary. Even though he'd helped Ethan negotiate his terms with the Office he'd also promised to bring the weight of the Office down on Ethan if he ever hurt Jack.

Was that what Lewis had been doing at Jack's? Comforting him because Ethan had left? Offering to hunt Ethan down and make good on his promise?

Lewis put his phone away, opened the car door, tossed his satchel into the back and got in. A moment later, he was gone.

Ethan kept a watch on Jack's place for the rest of the night. Earlier than he usually left for work, Jack appeared out of the underground garage on his Ninja. In his riding leathers and full-face helmet he was anonymous, but not to Ethan. He knew the body, the shape of the legs, the curve of the arms, the way he angled his head when checking for oncoming traffic. It was Jack and he was all right.

The pain in Ethan's chest sharpened as the bike turned towards him. His hand was on the door release without thought, ready to pull it and dash out in front of Jack. The need, the driving *ache*, to simply throw himself at Jack and hold on forever was almost too strong for Ethan to fight.

About to open the door, he shifted in the seat, twisting his injured leg and the flare of pain cut through the haze of want. It brought the memory of escaping the sinking helicopter, of the fight with Ten and Four. Of killing his brothers before they could kill him, because the bosses had ordered them too. Because no one defied the Cabal.

It was time they were stopped. Their shadowy global manipulations needed to end, yes, but it wouldn't be because they'd influenced presidential elections for their own political gain or started civil wars to earn themselves money. No, the reason they were going to die was because they'd raised a *family* of killers and then demanded that the brothers and sisters kill not only their targets, but each other as well.

Grimacing against the agony, both physical and spiritual, Ethan watched as Jack sped past his parked car, racing to catch the yellow light at the intersection, sweeping the bike around the corner just as the traffic light went red.

And he was gone from Ethan's sight. But not his heart. Never his heart.

Jack was all right. He was alive and well and working—possibly to find Ethan, or the Cabal, or to simply make sure his family was never threatened again. He didn't need avenging, but there were others—One through Twelve, from cold and calculating, to unfeeling psychopaths, to dead boys who'd never stood a chance of surviving their brutal childhood—who needed Ethan to make sure that the people who'd destroyed their lives didn't go unpunished.

Tap tap tap.

Ethan's reach for his Eagle stalled as he recognised the face peering in the passenger side window of the car.

The smart thing to do would be to ignore Rocco Cesare, start the car and drive away. Smart, but impossible.

It had been easy to avoid Lewis and harder to avoid Jack, but Rocco was right there, smiling at him through the tinted glass and motioning for him to wind the window down. Ethan leaned across the passenger seat and opened the door for him instead.

"Oh, thank you, son." The elderly man gingerly lowered himself into the leather bucket seat. "It's quite warm outside already. Shorty and I decided to cut our walk short today."

Hearing his name, the dachshund jumped up, front paws on the edge of the seat. His tongue lolled out of his panting muzzle, disappearing as he barked excitedly.

"Do you mind?" Rocco asked.

"Bring him in." Ethan wouldn't have cared even if this were Victoria. He wasn't about to leave the dog out in the sun while they sat in the cool interior.

Shorty helped Rocco pull him up by scrabbling frantically with his paws, and when he could, he clambered over his human and the centre console and straight into Ethan's lap. He nosed at Ethan's chin, then licked him.

All of his reserves spent on not chasing down Jack, Ethan lowered his face into Shorty's affection, letting the rough tongue leave tingling stripes across his cheeks and jaw.

"Shorty," Rocco murmured disapprovingly.

"It's all right." Ethan rubbed the dog's spine and Shorty stopped licking, his eyes rolling back in his head in canine ecstasy. "It makes him happy."

Rocco made a noise in the back of his throat that probably meant *not only Shorty*, and his smile was indulgent. "How have you been, son?"

Ethan had come to know Jack's elderly neighbour—*their* elderly neighbour—fairly well over the past month. It had been difficult to avoid him in the apartment building, not that Ethan had tried too hard, and not only because of Short Round. Yes, the dog had drawn him in initially, but the man had proved to be everything Jack said he was, sweet, kind, and welcoming. Rocco hadn't batted a single eye at two men living together, nor had he pried into Ethan's past when they chatted.

"I've been well." He hated lying to the man.

Rocco nodded. "Good. I'm pleased to hear that. I'm glad I saw you just now. I've wanted to thank you for what you did for Shorty."

Hands stalling on the dog's long body, Ethan blinked against the sudden sting in his eyes. "I don't know what you mean."

"I know you paid his vet bills, son."

As if sensing he was the topic of conversation, Shorty pushed and nudged at Ethan until he got his demands across. Succumbing, Ethan cradled the dog in one arm, so he could scratch the exposed and needy belly. Shorty sighed and rested his head on Ethan's shoulder, his hot breaths puffing contentedly on his neck.

"It wasn't hard to work out," Rocco continued softly. "They were paid when I went to pick him up and when I asked Nishant, he knew nothing about it." He only knew Jack by his Indian name.

"Then why think it was me?"

"Who else cares about Shorty so much?"

The tears surged forward. "It was the least I could do."

Rocco was quiet in the wake of the confession, only the happy snuffles of the dog filling the car.

When Rocco did talk, it was soft and hesitant. "Did you poison Shorty?"

Ethan's arm tightened around the dachshund reflexively. "Of course not."

"Then, son, it's not your fault and you shouldn't blame yourself for it."

But it is my fault. Ethan bit the words back. He couldn't admit that without telling Rocco everything. That it was Two who'd poisoned Shorty so he could get past him and into Jack's place without alerting anyone. That Two had only been there because Ethan had wanted something he should never have thought he could have.

Ethan nodded, setting aside that trap and moving on to what he needed to confirm before he could go. "Is Nishant's family all right? Has he said anything to you about them?"

Rocco frowned but shook his head. "Nothing to me, but when we chatted the other day, he seemed okay."

"That's good then."

"Except that he misses you, Ethan."

Shorty twisted around in Ethan's arm and licked his chin again.

"I know," Ethan whispered to the dog. "I miss him too. So much."

"Then why didn't you stop him from leaving just now?"

Ethan shook his head, mute from the impossible tangle of want and need and reality.

"I may not know everything that happened the other week," Rocco continued, the soft tone hardening a little, "but I do know you're mixed up in whatever mess Nishant got into when he was arrested. Whatever it was about, I knew he wasn't guilty of murder. He's a good man, a good soldier. But I saw the look in his eyes when he surrendered to the police. It wasn't anger or panic. It was despair."

Mouth open to ask him to stop, Ethan didn't get a chance as Rocco kept going.

"I've seen that expression before, son. On my daughter's face when she realised she had to divorce her husband. In the mirror when my Bettina passed." He paused, then added firmly, "On your face right now. So why didn't you stop him?"

"I couldn't. It's too …" Ethan closed his eyes behind his sunglasses, thankful that Rocco couldn't see the tears pushing forward. "Too complicated."

The older man snorted. "Everything's complicated, and if that were ever a real excuse, then it would be a pretty miserable world we live in."

"It isn't?"

"No. Not at all. Look at Shorty there. Two weeks ago, he nearly died but that doesn't matter. He's okay now, happy and excited to see his best friend. Whatever happened then, son, no matter how complicated it was, or how complicated it might be still, all that really matters is now. You want to be with Nishant?"

"Yes."

"And he wants you too. What else matters?"

It was tempting. So very tempting. Did Ethan owe any more loyalty to his dead siblings than he owed Jack? Was the Cabal his responsibility to take care of? Ethan desperately wanted the answer to be no, but he couldn't quite convince himself.

Rocco had seemed to instinctively know Ethan didn't like being touched and had never tried in the past, but now, he rested his hand on Ethan's arm. A simple, warm contact that lasted maybe five seconds before it ended, but one that Ethan knew he would be feeling for a long time yet.

"Think about it, son," Rocco said gently. "We all deserve to be happy, you included. Now, I had best get Shorty home and to his water bowl. It's rather warm out today and he's been carrying on like a pork chop." Opening the door, he patted his thigh and said, "Come on, Shorty. Let's go."

Short Round gave a little whine but squirmed out of Ethan's hold, hopped across to his human and let himself be scooped up and deposited back on the pavement. Rocco groaned and huffed his way up out of the low car. When he was standing, he turned and, one hand on the door ready to close it, stooped and smiled warmly at Ethan.

"Shorty and I miss you too, son. I don't think it will, but we'd like it if that helped you decide to come back."

Before he could respond, the door was closed and Ethan was alone again, watching his unexpected friends cross the road in front of him and go home. He sat there for a while longer, thinking about Rocco's words, eventually distilling them down into three that reverberated inside his head.

What else matters?

SEVEN

THE TOWER

"**H**mm," the Doctor said as he set his teacup down. Porcelain *clink*ed gently against porcelain as the cup settled into the saucer with a sound Ethan associated with warmth and safety. He knew now that they'd been false feelings. "Interesting. You attacked Four unprovoked."

Ethan sipped his own cooling tea. His throat was dry from talking and he needed a buffer before replying. "They were sent to kill me."

"Did you know that for certain?"

"There was no other reason for both of them to be there."

The Doctor sighed. "Is that how you were taught to operate? With nothing more than supposition?"

"It was more than a guess. The bosses had already gained my cooperation. They needn't have sent anyone to escort me in, yet both Four and Ten were there." Ethan left it unsaid that Ten was only sent out when death at any cost was required. He was simply too unpredictable.

"By your own admission, neither made a move against you. You made the first strike, Ethan."

"It's what we were taught to do." Taught. Conditioned. Abused. It all meant the same thing. "To be in control of every situation we find ourselves in, otherwise the probability of success is greatly reduced. Attacking mid-flight meant I had control of the situation. Neither of them would have planned to attack then. Ten's survival instinct was too strong and Four would never have expected me to make such a move."

The Doctor nodded slowly. "And you understood that such a move would most likely have ended in your own death?"

Ethan flinched, making his back sting. It had settled into a dull throb over the course of the session. "Yes."

"A sacrifice."

Ethan paused his drink halfway to his mouth. The word caught him by surprise. Ten wasn't the only one with a strong sense of self-preservation. They had all been drilled in the concept of survival. If they perished, who would finish the job for the Cabal? Ethan had been consciously working for years against most of the things they'd instilled in him, to greater or lesser success, and those things had stopped being a conscious choice with Jack. Ethan didn't need to plan when he was with Jack anymore. It was all natural now. New instincts, new reactions, new thoughts—new feelings. There had been no hesitation when he'd put himself between Two and Jack, but he had been certain Two wouldn't kill him. Hurt him, disable him, break him down, yes. Kill him? Never. And yet the Doctor was right.

"To save Jack and his family," Ethan said.

"But weren't they your brothers?"

Lips twisting into a grimace, Ethan shook his head. "You might have tried to make us think we were family, but we weren't."

The Doctor frowned. "Nine wasn't your sister?"

Ethan locked his body down before his reaction gave him away. "No."

"Truly? I was led to believe that you spent a significant amount of time with her in Johannesburg."

"I liked her," Ethan admitted tightly. "That doesn't mean I believed we had any sort of familial connection. Two certainly didn't display any when he killed her."

"I believe Two didn't fail his final test, unlike you. However, we're not discussing him, Ethan. Unless you want to tell me how you felt when you killed Two."

Like the knife had plunged into his own chest, instead of Two's. And relief. More relief than pain, he'd realised afterwards. Relief at his own freedom from a lifelong tormentor; relief that Two was no longer a threat to anyone.

Ethan shook his head.

"As you wish." The Doctor poured more tea into his cup and held up the pot, silently asking if Ethan wanted a refill.

The few mouthfuls left in his cup were stone cold but Ethan said, "No, thank you." He'd already given in too much.

The Doctor gave him a far too knowing look. "Still so stubborn, mon doux garçon."

"Why do you call me that? You didn't do that with any of the others."

"No, I didn't. You were different, though. You *are* different. It was a mistake, treating you as if you were the same as them, for which I apologise."

Was this what Jack felt when Ethan tried to say sorry for doing something wrong? Too much confusion to truly take the apology at face value.

"Why was I different?" Ethan knew why he thought it, but the Doctor had always offered an alternate view of subjects. "Was it because I joined the group when I was older? Because I remembered my mother and what kindness was like?"

"That's part of it. Since you bring it up, let's talk about your memories of kindness. What's something you remember from before you joined the group?"

Ethan pretended to drink to give him something to hide his hesitation behind. Of all the things the Doctor had talked to him about in the past, Ethan's time before the group was not one of them. They'd talked about life with the other children, what the instructors taught them and how Ethan felt about the things he was learning. Ethan had come to understand very quickly that any mention of his mother wasn't allowed, or anything about the world before the group. So he'd kept his memories to himself. They'd faded as time flew by and his head was filled with his new situation. He struggled now to recall something specific to give the Doctor, some proof that they hadn't completely eradicated Paul St. Clair.

"My mother," he whispered, then louder. "My mother. She was kind to me. She would sing to me. A lullaby." It felt like a lie as he said it. Jack had given him back a tiny part of his innocent childhood with the lullaby, but even when Ethan had been telling him about it, he hadn't been able to say if it had been his mother who sang it or not. He *wanted* it to have been her, but he didn't know for certain.

"Interesting. So how do you think that set you apart from the other members of the group?"

"Because it meant I had known something other than cruelty."

"And did that you make you better than the others?"

"No," Ethan bit out.

"So why did you refuse to partake in the final test?"

Ethan's teacup clattered against its saucer, a chaotic counterpoint to the Doctor's delicate *clink*.

Which was all the Doctor needed. "Was it cruel when you killed your brothers, Ethan?"

"It was self-defence."

"Or was it something else?"

Forcing himself not to visibly react, Ethan said, "They were going to kill me."

"How can you be sure of that?"

"It's what they do. They kill."

"And what do you do?"

Very carefully, Ethan set his cup and saucer on the floor. "I don't do that anymore."

"You killed your brothers."

"Not by choice."

"There is always a choice. Isn't that what you said when you refused to take part in the final test?"

Ethan closed his eyes. It was too much. Every word out of the Doctor's mouth sparked new questions, new doubts. Everything had felt so right when he'd been in the moment, but now he was confused.

"Did you give Four a choice, One-three? Or did you make it for him?"

Don't give them a choice. The repeated instruction echoed in his memories. *Make it for them. That way, you* control *them.* You *control the situation. When you control it, you* win.

Ethan hadn't given Jack a choice in the desert. He'd set the situation and laid the path for him to follow. Just as Ethan had done dozens of times in the past, from the very first job in Athens to the moment he'd walked out of the penthouse on Bathurst Street. Except that Jack hadn't kept entirely to the path. The contrary man had insisted on weaving all over the place, but it had been those detours that had caught Ethan's attention.

"Four made his choice." Ethan struggled to gain some control in this situation. "He chose to follow the bosses' orders. He chose to get me into the helicopter so he and Ten could finish the job and kill me."

"Yet you didn't give him a chance to change his decision," the Doctor said patiently. "You killed him before he could."

"I had to."

"So he wouldn't kill you? So you could survive?"

Ethan nodded numbly. He could feel the twist coming but it was like he was a dumb child again, blindly walking into walls the Doctor put up no matter which way he turned. It was one place Ethan hadn't been able to learn his way around because it kept changing.

"But weren't you willing to sacrifice yourself? For Jack and his family, you said. If you truly believed Four and Ten were sent to kill you, why not let them? It would have been the same outcome. Your sacrifice would have saved the Reardons either way, yes?"

"No." Ethan sought the confidence he'd had in the helicopter. It had felt so clear and straightforward then.

"Why not?"

"Because Four and Ten would still have been alive." Ethan jerked back at his own words. He hadn't meant to say that. Hadn't known he thought it.

The Doctor sipped his tea, set his cup back down with a *clink*, and waited patiently.

"They were dangerous," Ethan blurted out. "Too much of a threat to be left within the Cabal's control, or even left alive."

"But aren't you the same? Dangerous? Too much of a threat to be left alive, especially within the Office's control?"

"The Office doesn't control me."

"Don't they?"

"No. My relationship with the Office is different to what I had with the Cabal. Everything is different."

The Doctor studied him for a long while, until Ethan looked away, realising he hadn't convinced him of anything.

"How is it any different? Is it because the Office is *good* and the Cabal is *bad*?"

Ethan wanted to agree but his head shook before he could stop it. Neither entity could be so easily defined. The Office did use illegal and morally questionable means to perform their duty of protecting the Meta-State signatories. And the Cabal did work to promote stability and beneficial relations in some situations—they had, after all, sent Ethan in to discover a traitor to the Meta-State to prevent any upheavals he may have caused.

"Is it different because *you* are different?" the Doctor murmured. "Is it because you understand something other than cruelty?"

Hearing his own words turned back on him made Ethan cringe. It sounded so naively arrogant when the Doctor said it.

"You liked Four, didn't you," the Doctor continued relentlessly. "You used to share the sweets you stole from the kitchens with him. Why did you do that, One-three?"

Still. Ethan needed to be still and calm. That way he could order his thoughts and sort out this sudden tangle of conflict and confusion. He had to settle this uncertainty before he lost all control of the situation.

"Was it kindness?"

Ethan had been trained to resist interrogation, but this man wasn't the enemy. Or he shouldn't be. He never used to be.

"That's what you believe, isn't it? That you shared your pilfered goods with Four out of kindness. Or that you helped Nine with her lock picking skills because you liked her and didn't want to see her hurt by the instructors. None of the others ever did that, did they? Because they didn't know any better. They shared, but it always had an ulterior motive. Do you think your acts of kindness had ulterior motives, One-three?"

Except that the Doctor *was* an enemy. He always had been. Ethan had to remember that. He couldn't let the Doctor trick him into thinking he cared about him. Ethan wasn't a child anymore and he knew what the Doctor was trying to do. It was the same thing Two had done to him over and over when they were younger.

"Hmm."

That disappointed hum stung but Ethan absorbed the pain, dispersed it amongst the rest of it. All of it had the same cause, after all, so it belonged together.

"So stubborn. All right, One-three, don't talk to me. But you will listen." *Clink* went the porcelain. "Every act of kindness you performed back then was as mercenary and ruthless as anything any of the others ever did. You bought protection with your little gifts. When you helped Nine, or shared your sweets with Four, or stole pens and paper for Six, you effectively put them between yourself the others."

"I didn't do those things so they would protect me." Ethan sealed his lips against the next words. Admitting to a vulnerability was dangerous with the Doctor. With anyone in the Cabal. Saying he'd been trying to make friends because he was lonely and scared wouldn't prove anything to the Doctor.

The Doctor hummed. "Perhaps not at first, yes. But when you realised they would defend you if you gave them gifts, there was an ulterior motive to your actions. Is this kindness, One-three? Manoeuvring your brothers and sisters into taking punishments meant for you, or sending them into conflicts that were yours to fight?"

Ethan shook his head before he could stop himself. "That wasn't—" He clamped his mouth shut. He was walking straight into the Doctor's trap.

The *clink* of porcelain had a distinctly disapproving tone this time. "I think that's enough for now, Ethan. You're tired and clearly not willing to listen. I'm only trying to help you, but I can't do it all by myself. You have to acknowledge your own issues before you can hope to deal with them." He stood and fastidiously fixed his clothes before walking to the door. One hand up to knock, he cast a last, pitying look at Ethan. "Remember that Sugar Babies aren't like normal people. You can't be trusted to make your own decisions because you don't understand true kindness or compassion. That is why you killed your brothers. Not out of some skewed sense of kindness or sacrifice, but because it is what you are. A cold-blooded killer."

After the Doctor left, two men came into the cell and cleared away the table and chair, while a third covered Ethan from the doorway. When he was alone again, Ethan fought the urge to lie down and wallow. He wanted to forget the Doctor's parting words, but they swam through his mind unrelentingly. It had been hubris to think he'd cast aside the conditioning of his childhood. How easy it had been for the Doctor to reduce him back the scared creature he'd once been—still was, apparently.

He didn't want to be here again. Not in a cell, not with these people. He'd barely survived it the first time.

And perhaps he hadn't survived it. Paul St. Clair certainly hadn't. That blind boy was long dead, the first victim of the assassin One-three. For a brief time, he'd thought One-three had been buried under Ethan, the man Jack thought he was, but that was plainly wrong. Jack's Ethan wouldn't have been so easily reduced to this, surely.

He couldn't do this again. It was too hard, too painful. He needed to escape—any way he could.

Except that there was no way out of this cell. There was no one on the outside to help him and the enemy weren't the sort to underestimate him. They knew what he was capable of, what he could and would do to finish a job.

The plan hadn't worked like it was supposed to. Which only left him one way out.

Slowly, he stood and went to the middle of the room. The chain hung from the ceiling, solidly planted there so it could hold his weight. He reached up and touched the links. Thick, hard, cold metal.

He jumped and caught the chain, hauled himself up a bit higher, his back burning with each stretch and pull of his muscles. He lifted the shackles and locked them around the links, creating a loop big enough to fit his head through.

Creating a noose.

Soon, he'd be free.

EIGHT

The lack of air was starting to be an issue by the time the guards opened the cell door. As was the pressure of the chain against his windpipe. He hadn't let himself drop when he'd put the noose around his neck—that would have been contrary to his needs—but without any other tools or materials, Ethan hadn't been able to suspend his weight any other way than by his neck. The chain was positioned so his jaw took some of the strain but not nearly enough to spare his throat some damage.

But the guards weren't too tardy and they rushed in, swearing at each other, at him, at their superiors. Frantic to make sure the prisoner didn't die, two of them came right to him, guns slung over the shoulders as they reached for him with both hands. The third held back, gaping.

Ethan grabbed the chain, lifting himself so he could breathe. In the same instant, he kicked one guard in the face, a solid connection that broke the man's nose and hopefully his cheekbones as well. As he staggered, Ethan got both legs around the other man's neck. The guard had been going for his rifle, but the moment the strong calves closed over his throat, he dropped it and tried to pry Ethan's legs apart.

Slipping his head out of the noose, Ethan hooked an arm through the loop and hauled the guard closer with his legs. Grabbing a handful of the man's shaggy dark hair, Ethan swiftly shifted his feet so one was against the back of his neck and the other was on his throat. It was a matter of seconds to crush his windpipe. The guard's legs collapsed as he struggled for air. Ethan let him drop and, swinging back for some momentum, launched himself off the chain at the peak of its forward motion.

The guard still in the doorway had his rifle up and fired, but it went wide thanks to the wild swing of the chain. Ethan hit his chest feet first. The man wore armour under his dark khaki coat, but it didn't stop him from crashing over backwards. His head hit the solid brick on the far side of the hallway. The *crack* was loud and the smear of blood on the wall as he crumpled to the floor was very telling.

Ethan landed in an ungraceful heap on top of him. Stars danced before his eyes, his body still in need of more air. Gulping it down made his abused windpipe burn. It had been an incredibly risky plan but the only one he'd been able to think of so quickly. He'd needed to get out of the cell sooner rather than later, because much more time here, with the Doctor working hard to break him down—again—was intolerable.

Behind him, there was frantic scrabbling at the stone floor. The man with the crushed neck was taking his time to die. Under that was another sound, softer, steadier. Someone moving stealthily, trying to creep up on him.

Ethan moaned loudly and rolled over, making sure he made enough noise to cover the guard's approach. The man took the bait and rushed forward.

It was absurdly simple to catch him with a kick, sending him pinwheeling back into the cell. Flipping to his feet, Ethan followed. Barely upright, he dived into a roll under the trajectory of the man's raised rifle. He came up well inside the guard's range but even hurting for air, Ethan was faster and got the rifle pointed at the ceiling as the man's finger pulled spasmodically on the trigger in panic. A kick, a punch and a sweep of his leg had the guard tumbling over, his rifle now in Ethan's hold. One handed, Ethan spun the weapon, pointed, and shot the man in the head.

A moment later, he put the choking man out of his suffering.

Ethan stood in the middle of his cell, rifle at the ready, dead bodies around him, and closed his eyes. He stopped breathing so the sounds of any approaching backup wouldn't have to compete with that of his ragged gulps for air. So far, he couldn't hear anything, but he didn't doubt more of the enemy would be on the way. The gunfire would have alerted someone to what was going on.

Not taking any chances, Ethan dragged the body from the hallway into the cell and after finding the key, locked the door, with himself still inside. Swiftly, he pulled clothes off the body closest to his own size but had to cinch the belt tighter. Jack was right. He'd lost too much weight. It was a thin disguise and he had no real hope of it working, but it might give him a few precious seconds. One of them handily had a pair of sunglasses. The reflective aviators weren't exactly inconspicuous but they were better than running through an unknown place completely blind.

As he picked weapons off the bodies, Ethan massaged his throat gently.

He wasn't the cold-blooded killer the Doctor said he was. Well, not only that. He'd been out on his own in the world nearly as many years now as he'd been under the influence of the Cabal and Doctor. In that time, he had developed his own rules for taking jobs and how he carried them out. He had said no to the Cabal so many times now it barely required an effort anymore. He had thrown off the name they'd given him—One-three—and become his own man.

He wasn't Ethan Blade, or One-three. Not even Paul St. Claire anymore. He was Ethan, the man Jack had shown him he could be. Damaged and grey, but worthy of something better, of *being* someone better. Someone who didn't let the monsters from his past construct false walls for him anymore.

Now he just needed to get beyond these real walls.

Making sure the hallway outside was still empty, Ethan unlocked the door and slipped out. Blood smeared across his face to help obscure his features, he forced several deep breaths past his abused throat and then set out running.

The halls he ran through were the same brick as the cell, lined with similar doors. A detention level. There had to be more guards. And sure enough, he hurtled around a corner and ran right into a thick-bodied man dressed the same as the dead guards and carrying a rifle.

"What the fuck?" the man grumbled.

Ethan's gasps for air were real. "Thank god," he rasped out. "The prisoner's out. Killed the others. I barely got away."

The four guards came on instant alert. Weapons at the ready, one commanded Ethan to go to command and let them know what was happening while the rest went looking for the prisoner.

Which confirmed something. None of the guards were carrying a radio, and if someone had to convey information on foot, it meant he was at a Cabal black site. Highly secret and completely hidden, with no external power sources and all buildings heat shielded so no hotspots would show up on satellite images. It also meant absolutely no telecommunications that could be picked up. Relaying information was a pain, but not one black site had ever been compromised. This bid for freedom just became even more vital.

The second encounter didn't go as well as the first. Halfway through his grating explanation one of the five men recognised him. Two of them were dead before the first man finished saying "It's him."

Ethan rushed into the remaining guards. He spun and twisted in the middle of the enemy, punching and kicking. Within moments he'd worked out their strengths and weaknesses and from there, Ethan whirled into serious motion.

One man came at him with brute strength and a snarl. Ethan twisted at the last moment and planted his foot in the back of his knee. The big man went down with a startled grunt, his knee cracking into the hard stone. Ethan forced him the rest of the way down, smashing his face into the floor.

Another guard lunged at him, handgun first. Ethan smacked the weapon aside, grabbed his shirt and tumbled over backwards, feet in the man's gut. He went with a yelp, cut off sharply as Ethan dropped him on his head.

The third man didn't rush in but circled, waiting. With Ethan on the floor, tangled with the other two, he made his move. Two swift kicks to Ethan's back sent him sprawling. The whip damage flared supernova bright and Ethan jack-knifed at the intensity of the pain. He rolled, presenting his belly for the follow up blows, tensing his abdomen.

Ethan knew the moment his attacker decided he wasn't a true danger anymore. The kicks began to lack strength, with longer pauses between them. Which was when Ethan moved.

Grabbing the man's foot, Ethan pulled him off balance, then swept the man's other leg out from under him so he crashed down. Ethan snatched a knife from the side of his boot and rammed it to the hilt in the man's stomach.

Hands caught Ethan around the neck. His abused throat spasmed, but he threw himself backwards and into the chest of the man behind him. It became a scramble of elbows and fists and knees until Ethan got the other man into a strangle hold. Ethan held on as the man struggled, but he couldn't get free and went slack in Ethan's hold. Not trusting him, Ethan held on for as long as he could, but the others weren't entirely out of the fight yet.

The man Ethan had dropped on his head was crawling away and the other one, with the knife in his stomach, was groaning as he moved in short bursts. Either one of them could get to a gun in seconds.

Time was up. Ethan let the man go and he twitched as his body automatically pulled in air. Shoving him aside, Ethan scrambled towards the nearest gun. He closed his hand around the barrel of a rifle.

Bang!

Ethan was already moving. The bullet cracked into the floor where he'd just been. Flipping the rifle around, stock against his aching abdomen, he pulled the trigger and swept the weapon in shallow arcs. The man with the gun dropped and didn't move.

Movement behind him. Ethan rolled and repeated the move, taking out the stabbed man. One more bullet put the strangled one out of his quietly moaning misery.

Agony swept through Ethan. His back was ablaze, his stomach ached, and his neck felt even more crushed. He gave himself precisely five seconds to wallow, then Ethan slowly got to his feet, braced against the wall for a moment and spat blood out of his mouth. After a few deep breaths, he replenished his weapons and continued onwards.

Another fight like that wouldn't end as well, so he continued at a cautious stalk. The first group would have undoubtedly discovered the dead men in the cell and worked out that Ethan had been the one they'd sent to command. It was highly likely they were coming up behind him and just as likely he was going to encounter more resistance before he found the way out.

NINE

The next group didn't detect Ethan creeping up on them. Crouched behind a corner, he studied them as they milled before a set of double doors. They were the first of that sort he'd seen, so they had to lead somewhere significant. Hopefully out of the detention level. Whatever lay beyond them, though, it would be a new challenge and Ethan had no desire to endure another hand-to-hand fight before he discovered it. Sadly, while he was working out how to take them down as efficiently as possible, one pair from the original group he'd bluffed his way past came up behind him.

They must have had orders to keep him alive if possible, because the new arrivals shouted at him to put his weapons down. Which of course alerted the group by the door. They came on guard, weapons up and pointed down the hallway toward Ethan's hiding spot.

"All right," Ethan called. "I surrender."

"Put the weapons down," one of the pair to his left commanded. "Hands on your head and face the wall."

Ethan grabbed the two rifles he was carrying by their barrels and lifted, shaking the straps off his shoulders.

"Drop them," the other man shouted, his own weapon trained on Ethan.

"Give me a second," Ethan snapped back, irritably working the straps down his arms. "I'm a bit tied up here."

"Put them down!" More forceful, and perhaps a bit worried.

"Look," Ethan said patiently. "I'm doing the best I can."

One of the pair muttered to his fellow in German. Ethan pretended not to know his intelligence had just been insulted, and to have more issues with the rifle straps. The longer he took, the filthier the insults and, finally, the enemy rifles dropped to point at the floor.

Twisting, Ethan threw one of his rifles at the pair to his left and flipped the other one to his now free hand. A spray of bullets took them out as they ducked the flying weapon. As the bodies crashed down, Ethan sprinted for them. Behind him, the other group sprang into action, racing up the next corridor, yelling for information.

Just as they rounded the corner, Ethan hit the floor and rolled in behind the dead bodies. They were his only cover in the empty space. Bullets followed him, hitting the bodies he hastily pushed together and ducked behind. On his belly, he stuck the barrel of his rifle between the legs of the body on top and returned fire.

The position was untenable. Even as two of the enemy dropped to lucky shots, Ethan knew his time was severely limited. He could replace mags in the rifle with those pilfered from the bodies, but the enemy could most likely replenish ammo and bodies from beyond those doors. Plus, there were the last two men from the first group somewhere behind him. He doubted the surrendering ploy would work a second time, and he had no guarantee that they wouldn't just march him right back into a cell on this level.

He'd have to retreat. Take his chances with the other two guards and try to find another way out.

The enemy ceased fire.

Ethan let his own finger relax on the trigger and listened as the last echoes died away. Muffled voices, deliberately low so he couldn't hear. Then a familiar voice called out.

"Ethan, are you all right?"

No. Not this again, not so soon. The Doctor.

"You've done very well to get this far, but you won't make it any further alive. You know that, don't you."

It wasn't a question because it was plainly obvious to everyone there. Ethan was trapped. No way out. Surrender his only option.

Ethan brushed his hand over his hip, where Jack's rough and ready stitches still held his flesh together. Maybe here was good enough. There was a chance he wasn't underground, but the sterile air and coolness in the walls said otherwise. Below ground or not, the fact of the matter was he had no other choices right then if he wanted to survive this.

He pulled the rifle free and slowly held it up, then tossed it over the small barricade of corpses.

"That's good, mon doux garçon. I'm very happy you can see reason on this. Come, we'll have a session."

The word sent a shiver down his spine, but Ethan suppressed the urge to keep fighting. He didn't know if he could handle another "session" with the Doctor.

Swiftly and confidently, the guards advanced. Hands bound behind his back with cuffs around his wrists and a restraint tied between his upper arms, they hauled him up and prodded him forwards. Not back towards the cells, but through those doors. The Doctor walked ahead of them, hands clasped casually behind him, head bowed as if thinking.

The guards were rough, kicking and pushing him along even though he was going willingly. Another two joined them just beyond the doors, falling in between him and the Doctor. Occasionally a shove from behind sent Ethan reeling into those in front. They merely knocked him back, a pinball tossed between violent paddles. Ethan let them push him around. It would tire them out and if he didn't respond, they'd soon lose interest.

He studied the new hallway they came into. Still brick, but smooth and painted an off-white, or a white that had discoloured over time. It was short and led to a lift. Ethan was forced into a back corner, the Doctor at the front opposite. They weren't taking any chances with the man's life, apparently.

The journey upwards wasn't a long one. Ethan strained to see how many buttons were on the panel but when one of the guards worked out what he was doing, he stepped right in front of it and sneered at Ethan.

When the lift stopped and the doors opened, sunlight greeted them. The Doctor stepped out and murmured to someone Ethan couldn't see, then he was herded out into the warmth.

They appeared to be on an observation deck. A curving expanse of glass created the wall in front of them, slightly hazy with a coating that stopped it reflecting light—a must on any hidden installation. The lift was in a central hub, also round. Ethan didn't doubt that the glass extended all the way around, giving them unhindered views of the world outside. And so far, what Ethan could see of that world was water.

Endless, unmarred, deep blue water. Wave tips sparkled with sunlight, darkening only when a soft puffy cloud passed overhead. Around the clouds, the sky was azure and, like the water, unblemished.

"Let's walk, Ethan." The Doctor motioned him forwards.

Ethan went and the guards stayed behind. The Doctor kept them to a slow, patient pace but they were back where they started in under two minutes. The entire way, Ethan only saw water in the distance and, occasionally, rocky outcroppings of the island they were on. Even if he'd escaped the complex, he wouldn't have been able to avoid pursuit for long on the tiny land mass.

"Do you understand now?" the Doctor asked as they began another meandering circuit.

"There has to a boat, or a chopper."

"You'd think so, but the nearest transport is a two hour flight away, I'm afraid. And as I'm sure you're aware, we will only risk a transmission in the direst of emergencies. We're quite isolated."

Ethan shook his head. "All this for me?"

The Doctor hummed. "When did you become so arrogant, One-three?"

Shame flooded Ethan, more from the sound than the words. He hated the automatic response, especially here, after he'd failed at his escape attempt. And now, after he'd seen just how futile the attempt had been right from the start. The only good thing right then was that he was definitely above ground now. This was his chance, so he had to make the most of it.

"Then why show me this?" he asked in a small voice.

"Because I know you, One-three. You're tenacious. You don't leave things half done, even when commanded to."

There was a hint of reprimand, perhaps for Ethan's failed attempt now, or his disregard for orders during the Valadian job. After the desert, the Cabal hadn't wanted him to finish it. They'd been worried about his connection to Jack—rightly—but in the end, it was that connection which had allowed the job to be finished.

"This isn't a place you can escape from, my boy. I want to you understand that. You've proven you can get out of your cell and that eliminating the guards isn't a problem for you. But you can't try this again." The Doctor turned to him and lifted his chin, clucking disappointedly at the damage done to Ethan's throat. "For your own sake, as much as my peace of mind." Apparently he wasn't too concerned for the survival rate of the guards, though.

The Doctor encouraged him along and they returned to the starting point. A small table had been set up, this time with two chairs, a tea set and a tray of medical paraphernalia. Ethan sat and the Doctor checked his throat, inside and out, proclaiming it only bruised and made him a cup of hot water with honey. The guards were reluctant, but gave in and released Ethan's bonds after the Doctor assured them *he* would be safe now that Ethan knew there was no hope of escape.

Ethan gratefully sipped the hot drink, relishing the soothing warmth and honey as it washed over his abused tissues. He knew he would be made to pay for accepting this kindness at a later point, but right then, it calmed the fire in his throat and gave him a moment to order his thoughts.

The Doctor was manipulative. Ethan knew that now, but the learned responses from his childhood were still there, making him obedient. The Doctor was confident his conditioning was still strong, with good reason given Ethan's performance so far, but that didn't mean Ethan couldn't use it to his own advantage. It was just that it was hard to remember not to respond to the little cues when he was so sore and tired.

"Let's talk about Two's death," the Doctor murmured. "How did it make you feel?"

Ethan drank again and looked out at the vast view of water and sky. He ran his hand over his hip, found the slightly raised section with the stitches and pinched it hard. He felt the crack but didn't hear it, thankfully, and the physical pain diverted his attention from the other, difficult to understand feelings.

"I just find it hypocritical of you, One-three," the Doctor continued in a disappointed tone. "You refused the final test."

"Because it was cruel and pointless. We'd already been tested enough. It defeated so much of what we'd been conditioned to do." Ethan shook his head in disgust.

"It was a necessary test. Trust in your siblings was only one lesson taught to you. What was the last task testing, One-three?"

Swallowing against the urge to yell, Ethan winced at the pain it caused. After another drink, he murmured, "Obedience and survival."

"And you failed it."

Ethan had consciously decided not to partake in the final test. He'd been sixteen, the youngest of the group, and once the final test was done, they were going to be unleashed on the world under their own recognisance. Beholden to the Cabal but spread around the world, awaiting assignments in the territory they'd been assigned. Failure to complete the jobs would be punished. They'd all been punished enough over the years to know obeying was best.

There had been twelve children in the initial program, then Ethan had been abandoned by his mother and taken in as a late addition. He had never found out why they'd decided a six year old would fit into a system designed to take neonates and mould them from birth. Perhaps an experiment within an experiment?

Eleven of them had survived to reach the final test. After the final test, there had only been six.

Ethan forced the memory down and focused on the Doctor. "And yet you recommended they send me out regardless."

The Doctor nodded. "I did. A decision I have yet to regret. You've been much more difficult than the others ever were, including Ten, and yet your evolution has been fascinating. You are what we made you, One-three. An emotionless killer. You took down twelve trained men today and I know you're thinking about how to finish the job. If you got the chance, I'm sure you'd do it and walk away without a second thought for the lives ended by your weapons."

Ethan was careful to not react, but of course the Doctor would have surmised that. It wasn't that hard to predict the outcome when you'd created the program.

"But you've become so much more than that. Much of it, I believe, is due to your late inclusion in the group, but there's been another significant influence on the changes we've observed over the past couple of years."

It was harder this time, but Ethan managed to not let his thoughts show. His heart, however, gave a painful thump.

"Jack Reardon certainly is an interesting subject," the Doctor continued as if to himself. "He not only convinced you to leave the only life you knew and think you could be a *normal* person, but he repeated it with your sister. And he didn't even have to use sex that time."

TEN

"Jack Reardon, born to a Caucasian father and Indian mother. Australian citizen with an Overseas Citizenship of India, thanks to his mother," the Doctor recited. "Graduated with honours in applied science and acceptance into a graduate diploma in education, which he didn't complete due to joining the army after the death of his mother. Tested for and was accepted into the SAS, attained the rank of lieutenant and then burned out rather spectacularly. Only to be picked up by the Meta-State's Office of Counterterrorism and Intelligence, where he had a rather mediocre career as a domestic spy before encountering Ethan Blade in the Great Sandy Desert. Since then he's become the one person in the entire world to even come close to taking down the Cabal. Impressive."

Ethan kept his face impassive, though it was hard. Each mention of Jack was like the whip falling on his back. Sudden and sharp, the individual pains overlaying each other until all he wanted to do was scream.

"But he had help, didn't he?" The Doctor gave Ethan a small silence to fill and when he refused, nodded and continued. "I always knew you would excel with what we taught you, One-three. I am disappointed it took you so long to prove me right. All those years you fulfilled the bare minimum requirements of the jobs given to you, hiding your talent in mid-level assassinations. Number seven on the John Smith List for so long. Oh, mon doux garçon. Do you know how proud I was when you unleashed your true self as EB13? Five high-level assassinations within three months, while the Office, the CIA, MI6, the SVR and others, all tried to catch you and failed. It was . . . glorious. Everything I knew you could be. Relentless, ruthless, precise." He smiled warmly. "If only you hadn't targeted the Cabal."

Unable to stop himself, Ethan flinched.

"The Cabal took you in when your mother abandoned you. How did you describe her earlier? Kind. Loving. Affectionate. And yet she left you behind the first moment she could. I remember it. Do you, One-three? She'd heard rumours of a 'school' for Sugar Babies. One of the staff talking out of turn, I believe. So she sought us out and thrust her blind, malnourished, *bruised* child at the first person she saw and walked away. This is the woman you say taught you how to be kind. Think about it. She abandoned you, and we, the Cabal, took you in when we had absolutely no obligation to. We already had a full quota of Sugar Babies. The program had been working for eight years already, and yet we disrupted our work, our lives, our *home*, to take you in and care for you. Feed you. Educate you. Give you your sight. And yet it is us you come after."

"Well, it was easier than finding my mother."

Very slowly, the Doctor set his cup down with a *clink*. "Pardon? I didn't quite catch that."

Realising he's said it aloud, if in a whisper, Ethan tightened his jaw and refused to meet the Doctor's gaze.

That disappointed hum again, and then in a firm tone, the Doctor said, "I am curious as to why you felt you could come after the Cabal."

The view beyond the window hadn't changed, except that the clouds had moved on and new ones had taken their place. There were no ships, no planes. No sign of other life for as far as Ethan could see.

He'd done all he could and now just needed to hold on a bit longer.

"I did it because it's what you taught me to do. Find the target and eliminate it."

"Indeed. And who made you target the Cabal? Your Jack? His Office?" The Doctor poured more tea into his cup, added sugar and stirred it. He tapped the spoon on the lip of the porcelain. "You know we're quite secure on that front."

Ethan stilled. The Doctor was so confident, and he had every right to be. But it didn't mean he was completely safe.

"Do you really wish to know who made me come after the Cabal?" Ethan asked softly.

Setting his cup down, the Doctor folded his hands on the table. "I've said I do."

"You called him Eleven."

The Doctor's jaw twitched.

"Do you remember him?" Ethan kept his voice quiet so the guards wouldn't overhear. "He was maybe a year older than me, but smaller. At least he was after I outgrew him, once you began providing me with regular, healthy meals. You're right. I did like Four, and I had fun with Nine, and even Seven became someone I cared about, but I always felt closest to Eleven. He was always scared, as I was. He couldn't keep up with the others, as I couldn't. He was constantly targeted, just as I was. Like me, he kept failing the tests, kept getting punished or forced to redo the tasks until he got them right, even if it took all day and night. I felt like we could actually be brothers, not the pretend ones you tried to make us into. But he would never let me close. If I tried to be kind he shunned me, called me weak. If I tried to give him presents, as I gave to the others, he threw them back at me and told me I was wasting my time. There's only so long a child can resist that sort of rejection, so I stopped trying. Eventually I improved with my skills and lessons. Eleven did not. Do you remember him, Doctor? Do you remember what happened to Eleven?"

Ethan didn't stop the wash of memories that came forward with his words.

At fourteen years old, Paul St. Clair had long since ceased to be. One-three had taken his place, numbly falling into line, doing everything they asked of him. It had been so long since he'd been "bad luck" to the group, he was starting to feel proud of his efforts. The instructors weren't so quick to snap a cane or throw a punch his way and the carers hadn't picked on him as much.

"I do. I will never forget. It was the first day I ever won against all of the others. I was first to finish the obstacle course and I felt like I was the fastest, strongest and smartest. It was the first time I felt like I wasn't going to die in that place. And that's when I found Eleven."

One-three had heard the rush of water as he turned into the showers. Steam billowed out from the stalls at the far end of the white tiled room. He'd stilled. Everyone else had still been on the course. Who could be in there? Taking one of the towels from the shelf along the wall, One-three had moved silently towards the shower stalls. They were small cubicles, no doors, so One-three had come in from the side, so he wouldn't be seen. Carefully, he'd listened, hearing nothing more than the hiss of the water, the gurgle of the drain, and crying.

Curious, One-three slowly twisted the towel into a thick rope and, holding the ends in one hand, stepped out.

A body was slumped against the wall under the shower head, legs splayed out, head bowed under the spray. Eleven sat with his arms limp at his sides, palms upwards. The water around him was pink as it washed towards the drain.

One-three froze. For the longest moment he simply could not comprehend what he was seeing. Eleven was supposed to be on the obstacle course. The instructors had confirmed that One-three was the first to finish. How had his brother got here before him with enough time to . . . to . . .

He must have made a sound because Eleven looked up at him, his white eyes barely discernible in the pale expanse of his face. "Don't . . ."

One-three crouched by his brother and wrapped the towel he'd thought to use as a weapon around one slashed wrist. Eleven was too weak to fight him but he shook his head feebly and tried to pull away.

"No, One-three. Don't. I can't . . . not anymore."

"We survive," One-three said firmly. "We protect each other and we survive."

"Too late," Eleven whispered as his head dropped forward again, listless.

One-three ignored him and reached for his other arm, ready to wrap it in the towel as well. That was when he saw the knife.

It lay on the stained tiles between Eleven's thighs, where he'd dropped it after slicing his femoral artery. The water poured down and diluted the blood as it pumped out, washing it directly into the drain.

"Let me go. I want to go."

One-three's legs collapsed under him and dumped him onto the bloody floor. He sat there, getting wet and stained, and held Eleven's hand while he died. They found them there, still in the shower, One-three crying, his dead brother's head in his lap.

Two weeks later, they told One-three he would be sent on a job that required a young, innocent, beautiful boy to entice Moraitis, to be used and abused just so they could ruin his political agenda. Eleven's final moment still fresh in his mind and heart, One-three refused, knowing he would be punished. He refused and refused until they whipped him to the point of bleeding. Until the leather cut so deep it would leave scars that remained into his adulthood. Then they'd dumped him in the same shower stall where Eleven had died and made him watch his own blood swirl down the drain. After that, he'd agreed.

Two years later, when told the details of their final test, One-three had refused again. They hadn't punished him for refusing to take part in it, though. The Doctor had said he respected One-three's choice and sent him out into the world with those who passed.

But that had just been another lie. The Doctor hadn't respected—didn't respect—Ethan's choices. It had just been part of the experiment. The experiment within the experiment. Otherwise, Ethan wouldn't be here now, his back aching and throat sore, demanding the Doctor acknowledge the sheer inhumanity of what he had done to thirteen children, and take responsibility for it.

"Do you remember?" Ethan asked again, letting his pent up anger and pain show in his voice.

The Doctor didn't answer the question. His expression was as locked down as Ethan's, giving away nothing of his thoughts. Ethan could guess at them, however. The Doctor hadn't forgotten Eleven, just as Ethan hadn't. Each time he'd killed one of his "brothers," Ethan had seen Eleven in their place, so damaged, so broken, death was the only freedom he could find.

"All right, One-three," the Doctor finally murmured. "It's clear that you're not yet willing to listen. You're tired and in pain. We'll leave it at that for today." He nodded to the guards standing by the lift. "Restrain him and return him to his cell."

Ethan was hauled out of the chair and his arms and hands were tied behind his back again. They were at the lift when the Doctor spoke again.

"Once he's secure, break his leg."

He would have fought then, but the doors to the lift opened.

The cool blue eyes of the woman in front of him froze Ethan's plans before they'd even formed. She met his gaze for a long moment, then brushed past him, greeting the Doctor with an outreached hand and received a warm, familiar welcome in return.

The guards shoved Ethan into the lift and the doors closed.

ELEVEN

THE HEARING

"They're ready for you, Mr. Reardon."

Jack nodded to the blonde woman with the blue tinted glasses but didn't stand to follow her. Instead, he pulled in a deep breath of the perfectly temperature-controlled air, held it, the scent of floor polish and old leather pooling in his nose, then let it go slowly. Three more of them barely took the edge off the queasiness in his stomach. What he really needed was a cigarette or three, but they'd kept him waiting on a moment's notice. If he'd ducked out the back of Sydney's Parliament House for a smoke, he could probably guarantee that was when they'd call him in. So, he hadn't gone and now they wanted him in there. He felt like he was going into a war zone naked.

Standing, Jack did up his jacket button, picked up the leather case that held his files and, trying one more deep breath, followed the woman down the short corridor. Her heels clicked on the polished marble floor, a metronome keeping the time of Jack's march into battle. He let out the breath he'd taken, hoping that this would be the one that brought the serenity. This was not the time for him to lose control, or to even react. They would try their hardest to discredit him and his story. He couldn't do anything to help them.

"Through here," his guide announced and waved to a set of large, carved wooden doors.

"Thanks." Jack gave her another nod and, keeping the pace she'd set, pushed through the door. The queasiness disappeared as he entered the battlefield.

The room was set up like every other hearing he'd been in. A long bench at one end with five positions along it. A single desk and chair sat in the centre of the rest of the space, facing the table.

"Mr. Reardon, take a seat, please." Minister Simmons sat in the middle of the bench, flicking through a folder of papers even as he waved Jack to the solitary chair before him.

Karl Simmons was in his late sixties, with a full head of hair that was still more brown than grey and a face that tended to disappear in groups of similarly aged and dressed men. As Minister for National Security, he was nominally in control of the International Security Office, which acted to protect Australian dignitaries overseas. The ISO was also the cover for the secret Meta-State run Office of Counterterrorism and Intelligence, generally called the Office.

Simmons was the end of the line when it came to the operational integrity of the Office. The only person who could override a decision made by Simmons was the Prime Minister and Jack doubted the newly appointed leader of the country was too concerned with a preliminary hearing on the actions of one field asset. Jack's nuts were in Simmons's vice.

He sat, put his case on the desk to one side, and studied those who'd been called up to dissect his job performance this time. They looked like a firing squad and Jack wondered if he should just fuck with protocol and light one up then and there.

To Simmons's left sat Director in Charge Charles Lund, head of the Australian division of the Office. Next to him was Director Michelle Chan, the Singaporean External Threat Assessment director. On the minister's other side was Assistant Minister Roger Greene, who worked for the Minister of Defence. The last member of the review board was a man who's name Jack hadn't been told and hadn't been able to find. In a non-descript dark suit and blank expression, he was even more bland than Simmons. Sitting back in his chair, he was seemingly more interested in his pen than the proceedings. Jack guessed him to be from the Australian Security Intelligence Organisation or the Australian Secret Intelligence Service. Jack knew the type, knew his purpose in being here, and mentally tagged him as Quiet Man. He wouldn't take any part in the proceedings until absolutely required.

Finally, Simmons looked at Jack and gave him a perfunctory smile. "Sorry to have kept you waiting. I'm sure you can appreciate how much information there is to go through. But, we're ready now.

I have to say, Mr. Reardon, that I'm disappointed we're meeting again under such circumstances. This isn't as pleasant as our last encounter."

Jack carefully held his polite, open expression. "Our last encounter, sir, was when the previous Prime Minister presented a posthumous medal to the family of my dead co-worker. I wasn't particularly happy to be *there*, either."

Simmons's attempt at friendliness cracked for a moment, then smoothly he said, "Of course. It was a sad occasion though it was an honour to remember your co-worker's heroism."

The man couldn't even remember Harry's name. Jack dug his fingers into his thigh to keep from doing or saying something harmful to his chances of getting out of here sans handcuffs. The sooner this goddamned charade was over, the sooner he could hunt down Ethan.

"My intention was to simply convey my disappointment that once more, your actions are a matter of serious concern." Simmons's expression turned stern. "I needn't remind you that this is just a preliminary review, Mr. Reardon. The information we're gathering today will be used to determine if the matter of your conduct needs to be taken further. Are we ready to begin?" he asked his fellow reviewers.

After receiving nods and quiet affirmatives, Simmons looked at Jack with raised eyebrows.

This was it. All of his secrets were going to be revealed over the next several hours. He couldn't hold anything back this time. If they had any chance of this working, everyone had to know everything.

"Yes, sir," Jack said clearly.

"Good. Let's start with your relationship with Omega Subject. The man who called himself Ethan Blade."

Steeling himself, Jack said, "I first met Ethan Blade in the Great Sandy Desert two and—"

"No." Simmons cut him off with a shake of his head. "All that was part of the *last* conduct hearing, Mr. Reardon. Let's move on to the events at the end of last year. We have reviewed the files concerning the assassin called . . ." He consulted a bit of paper. "*Two*. Very confusing set of circumstances, but all in the past, I believe. Perhaps you could begin after you were released from the infirmary. I believe you left in the company of Omega Subject."

The repetition of "Omega Subject" grated on Jack's nerves just as bad now as it had the first time it's been bandied about in his presence. "I'm not going to call Ethan Omega Subject all day."

DIC Lund frowned. "Didn't he in fact confirm he wasn't Ethan Blade?"

"He did, but he also decided that he wished to be called Ethan." This was it. Time to be upfront. "Because that's the name I called him by."

Simmons's mouth downturned at the corners. "Hmm. Your relationship with Omega, sorry, Ethan. It was sexual, wasn't it."

"Yes, sir."

"At the request of Director Alex Tan, I believe."

Lund leaned forwards. "I don't believe Director Tan actually stated Mr. Reardon should enter into a physical relationship with the subject."

"No," Jack agreed. "He simply asked me to 'keep him happy.' He didn't specify how I was to do that."

"And Tan wished this because . . .?" Simmons prompted.

Jack blinked several times so he wouldn't roll his eyes. This was all normal. "Because he wished to have access to Ethan's particular skill set."

"Did he ever take advantage of them?" Greene asked.

"No, sir. He did not."

"Why not?"

It was far too early for Jack to be this irritated surely. "You'd have to ask him, sir."

Again, Simmons sorted through his papers. "We do have a couple of contracts pertaining to Omega, sorry, *Ethan*. The one we're primarily concerned with today says the assassin is to be on retainer for ETA, Sydney." Simmons held up the thin contract and raised his eyebrows at Jack. "This is what you used to justify spending hundreds of thousands of Meta-State tax payers' dollars to find your errant boyfriend, Mr. Reardon. *This* is why we're here today."

"Yes, sir." Jack dug his fingers into his thigh again. "That contract makes Ethan the responsibility of the Office of Counterterrorism and Intelligence. Like I am. Like DIC Lund and Director Chan. If either of them went missing under suspicious circumstances, no one would question spending the money required to get them back."

Lund and Chan both looked like they would say something but Simmons beat them to it.

"The DIC and director have been loyal assets to not just the Office for many years, but to the Meta-State their entire lives. Ethan Blade has been a violent, disruptive force across the globe for nearly seventeen years, Mr. Reardon. He may have signed this contract but we have no proof he was going to honour it. It may have been he was simply playing for time. Keep the lawful charges we should have brought against him at bay until he could escape cleanly."

"Then why did he wait nearly a week to 'escape,' sir?" Jack asked. "He could have walked the moment he signed, free and clear, but he didn't."

Simmons actually looked sympathetic as he spoke. "Do you think it was love keeping him here, Mr. Reardon? That he needed to make sure you were well on your way to healing before he left?"

Yes, Jack wanted to shout. *Yes, love kept Ethan here with me. And it would have kept him here forever but for what caused him to leave.* Instead, he said, "We have evidence he was coerced."

"Please, show us," Chan said.

They would have seen it before but Jack still withdrew the data stick and held it up. Greene fetched it and loaded it on his laptop. After a bit of clicking, a section of the wall to Jack's left split and moved apart, revealing a large screen. The video began to play a moment later, taking Jack right back to that horrible first day without Ethan.

THREE MONTHS EARLIER

When Jack awoke he was alone in the huge bed in the Bathurst penthouse. His bed at the Leichhardt apartment was a king, but this one had to be a super king or something. It was massive. Maybe Ethan had bought it so that if they argued, neither would have to sleep on the couch because there was enough room to have a clear demarcation zone down the middle. For some reason, that thought made Jack smile. He stretched luxuriously, feeling the healing wound in his back throb, but it was overridden by the pleasant ache in his arse as he clenched. Best early birthday present ever.

God. It had been perfect. Ethan on him, in him, all over him. They would definitely be doing that again. Jack would couch it as Ethan needing practice, even though he didn't. He *really* didn't. And why the hell had Jack pissed around for so long *not* kissing Ethan? Well, he knew why, but thank heavens Ethan had enough balls to get it done.

Speaking of . . . Jack got up and scrounged up a pair of track pants to wear while he went in search of more kisses. His implant informed him he'd slept well into the morning, which was okay. He was still recuperating and Ethan had thoroughly wiped him out the night before.

"Ethan?" he called lazily on his way to the bathroom. "Why didn't you wake me up?"

No answer, and Ethan wasn't in the shower when Jack passed the bathroom on the way to the separate toilet. Maybe he was out getting them something hugely calorific and birthday themed for brunch.

Relieved, Jack went to the kitchen to get a drink. There, pinned on the front of the fridge with a magnet shaped like a Desert Eagle, was a note in Ethan's neat hand.

Back soon, E.

Not the most eloquent of missives, but it was enough. Over the past ten days, Ethan had occasionally vanished for a couple of hours at a time, leaving similar notes if Jack wasn't awake or around when he needed to escape. The first couple of times it had happened, Jack had worried that Ethan had decided he couldn't do this anymore. Live with him, live within the law, live in one place, any or all of them. He'd worked out quickly that being alone was part of Ethan's grieving process, returning to Jack in either a pensive or lightened mood, but more settled than he had been before going. Jack was just grateful he was coming back without mysterious bruises.

After a quick breakfast and shower, and no reappearance of Ethan, Jack scratched out the *E* on the note, added a *J* and headed out to get a few ingredients he knew they didn't have for butter chicken. It was his birthday, yeah, but he wanted to do something nice for Ethan, too.

When he got back, bags in both hands, his shouted "Ethan" was quickly swallowed up by the emptiness of the penthouse. A quick check showed no further changes to the note on the fridge.

Okay, this was getting annoying. What could keep Ethan away for so long? Especially after last night? Especially on Jack's birthday?

Jack went to the control panel for the security system in the main bedroom. According to the electronic logs, Ethan had left at two twenty-six a.m. Playing the feeds from all the cameras, Jack watched as Ethan left the penthouse, got in the lift, and vanished. Nowhere could Jack find him leaving the building. Which wasn't unusual. For Ethan to feel safe here, he would have to have several ingress and egress points, most of them very well hidden.

Jack made the call to Ethan's implant automatically. Ethan didn't answer and the connection switched through several new lines until finally, an electronic voice asked him to leave a message.

The last time Ethan hadn't answered one of Jack's calls, he'd been hunting down his "brother," Two, a psychopathic assassin who'd decided Jack had to be punished for corrupting Ethan.

"Shit." Jack crouched in the back corner of the bedroom and triggered the hidden catch so a small section of floorboards slid to the side. Under it was a keypad and fingerprint scanner, which he cycled through as quickly as he could, opening the floor safe. Ethan had several around the penthouse, along with a dozen concealed weapons in various compartments. No matter where anyone was, they would be no more than a couple of feet from a gun or knife or stun grenade. This safe held their personal weapons, Ethan's fake passports and a large amount of money in different currencies. The passports were all there but the money was gone, along with Ethan's twin Desert Eagles.

That didn't bode well.

Grabbing his H&K USP, Jack headed for the front door once again. At the sideboard, about to snatch his keys out of the bowel, he stopped. If he found Ethan and he was hurt, piling his stupid arse onto the Ninja wouldn't be his best option. But even as he picked up Victoria's keys he hesitated. The last time he'd gone looking for Ethan, he'd had to admit he had no idea where to look for him and apparently that hadn't changed. The one thing Jack thought he might have been doing—racing to sooth his anxieties—was ruled out because his car was still here.

"Goddamn crazy bastard," Jack muttered and grabbed the car keys. There was one other place he could check, but after that, Jack would have to pull out the big guns.

Sending Ethan a message he hoped would generate a response— *I'm coming to drag you home, you crazy bastard. And I'm doing it in Victoria*—Jack backed the sleek car out of her spot, got her pointed for the door and roared out. Swinging into traffic, a dark, nasty thought slunk into Jack's head.

What if Ethan hadn't gone under his own volition? What if it had been the Cabal?

It was all too easy to remember Ethan shutting down when he talked about his childhood with Two inside the Cabal. Far too easy to remember the chills that had wracked him when Ethan showed him his scared foot, explaining that Two's mutilation had happened because he, Ethan, had been weak in the eyes of those he'd coldly referred to as "carers."

These days, Jack's first instinct was to protect Ethan, even from the traumas of his past, so it was hard knowing some of the things he'd suffered back then. Even harder knowing there was very little he could do now to help him.

So, Jack hadn't asked him about the Cabal. Hadn't wanted to make Ethan hurt more than he already was. The man was grieving, in his own silent way, for the woman Jack had known as Eve Garrotte, whom Ethan called Nine and sister, and had watched die right in front of him, killed by their brother. Jack had waited for Ethan to speak up, or for him to talk to the Office psychiatrist about it. His first appointment had been scheduled for tomorrow. Jack prayed he made it. Prayed that it was simply restlessness, or grief, that had driven Ethan out of the penthouse at a ridiculous time of the night.

Clutching at those hopes, Jack drove to the one place he thought Ethan might be if that were the case.

Middle Head had once been one of Jack's favourite places to visit. He'd loved the old military ruins as a kid. Had cherished the time he'd spent there with his father, talking about history, feeling it viscerally in the crumbling cement walls and rusted gun emplacements. Then Dad had fallen victim to early dementia and Jack had brought him to Middle Head, hoping to restore some of his memories. The visit hadn't gone well and now the place was a mix of recalled joy and pain. Perhaps that was how Ethan saw it, too.

From the carpark, Jack walked out to the main emplacement. There were a few groups of people enjoying the fresh air. This close to Christmas, summer was in full swing and the temperatures could easily soar. The shade of plentiful trees and the ocean breeze made the park pleasant for its visitors though. Would that still be the case if they knew what had happened here barely two weeks ago?

All signs of Two's presence had been cleared away. His body, Jack's blood, the mess left by Adam's imprisonment in the tiger cages, all gone. Yet it still lingered for Jack, a shiver down his spine and spike of remembered pain where Two had stabbed him. He didn't doubt that Ethan felt the same way.

Jack found the spot he'd been looking for. Right here was where it had happened. Where Ethan had spoken about maybe not surviving the night, about how he knew why Jack hadn't kissed him, and then kissed him anyway.

"Just so you know," he'd whispered afterward.

Such a big fucking declaration and two weeks later, he was gone again.

TWELVE

Frustration whirling around with his worry, Jack stalked back to the car, dictating another message to his absent lover. "Come on, Ethan. Where are you? I'm getting really worried."

Back in Victoria, with no reply to any of his messages or calls, there was only one place Jack could go.

He'd always tried to keep his work and personal lives as separate as they could be when his best friends were also work colleagues. Lines had seriously blurred once Ethan blasted his way into Jack's work life, and a year later, into his personal life as well. For a while, Jack had managed to keep them apart, then Two had arrived to stalk Jack professionally for what he'd done personally. On the same day Jack had confessed his relationship with Ethan to Lewis—and Lydia by proxy—he'd also had to come clean about it to his director—and the Office by proxy. Donna McIntosh, his immediate superior, wasn't happy with Jack's life choices, but since the Office had deemed it acceptable for their own reasons, she had to lump it. Jack's main concern, however, was how his friends had reacted.

After an initial outburst of anger and confusion, Lewis had settled down and seemed very accepting of the fact his mate was sleeping with an assassin who'd once thought of Jack as a target. Lydia hadn't said anything outright, but Jack could feel her simmering dislike of it whenever they chatted. Lewis assured him it was because Jack hadn't told her himself and that she would get over it soon. Jack hoped he was right because he needed Lydia as a friend.

To get any balls rolling as quickly as possible, Jack called Lewis.

"Hey, mate," Lewis answered on the first ring. *"Happy birthday! I was going to call you later, see if you and Eth wanted to come out for drinks at the No One's Inn. My shout."*

"Jesus," Jack muttered aloud so he didn't have to focus his thoughts while driving. "I hope you never call Ethan *Eth* to his face. He'll have you in a sleeper hold before you can even pretend like you were going to add the *an*."

Lewis laughed. *"Yeah, probably. So, is it a date? Do I get to give Lyds the 'be nice or I'm cutting you off from the splendour that is moi' speech?"*

Despite his grim suspicions, Jack laughed. "Hold off on pissing her off just yet, okay." Amusement falling away, he said seriously, "There might not be anything to celebrate. Ethan's missing."

There was a long pause on the other end of the connection, then just as grimly, Lewis asked, *"What happened?"*

"Nothing," Jack admitted. "Except that I woke up this morning and he was gone. Everything was good last night and now he's gone. Something happened while I was asleep to make him leave."

Jack waited for the obvious come back, the "Do you fart in your sleep?" or "Maybe it was your snoring." However, neither came down the line, nor did any other silly taunts.

"What do you need me to do?" Lewis asked.

Worried that some imposter had replaced his friend, Jack sped Victoria through a yellow light. "Are you at work?"

"Unlike some people on mandatory recuperation leave, *I sure am."* His faux cheer restored the world to rights. *"Just finished up the final reports on the Judge mess and submitted it all to the PTB so they can complain about how many paperclips I used. My arse already hurts from this one."*

"Console yourself with the Guinness World Record for longest paperclip chain. In the meantime, I need you to start pulling all CCTV footage from two to four this morning from every camera from Bathurst Street"—having the location of his new secret lair revealed to the Office should teach Ethan not to disappear without a word—"the park and everything for a five-block radius. For a start."

Lewis groaned but didn't outright complain. *"I'll see if I can snag that kid from Ex Mon who helped us with the Judge case. Surely he's got an algorithm or magic spell that'll cut through some of the chaff. Are you coming in or are you still bed bound? Oh wait, your boyfriend's gone, so you can get off your back and come* help."

"I'll be there in ten, don't worry. And Lewis, let's keep this on the eighth, okay?" Meaning the eighth floor of the Neville Crawley Building where they worked for the Internal Threat Assessment department. Also meaning, *don't let the directors on the tenth floor know*.

"*Yeah, sure, of course.*" Lewis sounded distracted, which hopefully meant he was starting to get shit organised. "*They're all out of the building at the moment, anyway. Something to do with that rumour about the deputy PM I think.*"

Despite working for a government agency that more often than not dealt with political entities—foreign and domestic—Jack wasn't very interested in the nitty gritty of government. He wasn't as intellectually opposed as Ethan was, just tired of being jaded and pissed off about things that would never change, so he didn't worry about it too much now. Lewis had a better understanding and appreciation of it all on a wide scale, but it was Lydia who minutely monitored every piece of information they had access to. She had probably given Lewis a detailed description of what was going on in the upper echelons of the government and he'd distilled it down to "that rumour about the deputy PM." Which was still more than Jack really cared about right then.

"Great. We should be able to get some real work done before they find out. See you soon."

Lewis signed off and Jack concentrated on weaving the car through the late morning traffic, annoyed that he hadn't started this process sooner. Ethan had already been gone for nine hours. He could be on the other side of the world by now and Jack had no idea why.

Or if he was even still alive.

Stuffing that thought into the filing cabinet, knowing it wouldn't stay there, Jack sent a silent message to Ethan, praying that this time he answered.

Just let me know you're okay.

When he reached the Office, Jack found Lewis and Fabian Haggenhauen in a spare operations room already immersed in the search.

"Pull up a pew." Lewis barely looked up from his screen as Jack entered. "Fabes is still sourcing footage, but we can start on the ones he's already got for us."

The External Monitoring asset sent Lewis a glare for shortening his name, his fingers never once faltering on the keys of one of the two laptops in front of him. Fabian was as skinny and harried seeming as he had been when Jack last saw him, after a marathon hacking session to discover where photos vital to the Judge investigation had been originally uploaded to the net. Knobbly wrists poked too far out of the ends of his sleeves and his eyes peered past their dark bags with over-caffeinated twitches. There were already three Redbull cans lined up beside him.

"Thanks for helping us, Fabian." Jack took the seat in front of the spare computer, knowing better than to offer a handshake with his gratitude. Fabian didn't touch and Jack respected that.

"I've already been here for thirty-seven hours," the Ex Mon wiz muttered sourly, but kept working.

"In my defence," Lewis interjected before Jack could protest, "I did ask him to recommend one of his highly talented co-workers, but he just gave me the *look*"—the *how do you even manage to dress yourself?* look they'd become very familiar with over the short course of the Judge case—"and insisted he help us out."

"Offered, not insisted." Fabian sent him another glare.

"You're here, either way." Lewis smiled sweetly at him. "Would you like another refreshing drink?"

"Don't enable his addiction," Jack said out of the side of his mouth as he pulled up a list of files Fabian had just sent him.

"It's not enabling, it's bribery. He *is* doing this out of the goodness of his heart and soul, you know."

Fabian muttered something under his breath and ducked behind his screens.

"I know." Jack opened the first video and hit play. "And I really appreciate the help, from both of you."

They worked in silence for the next quarter hour, going through the videos by order of location, starting with those along Bathurst Street and working out in concentric circles. On his second computer, Fabian had facial recognition software running, but the program wasn't fool proof, hence the manual checking as well. Jack had no hopes of the computer finding Ethan. The man knew how to avoid being picked up by such programs. The most Jack was really aiming for was to recognise the body, the walk, the gestures. Anything more would mean Ethan was being very sloppy.

"Got him." Lewis squinted at the screen. "At least I think it's him."

Jack got up and moved to Lewis's side, leaning over his friend to get a closer look. The video was paused on the image of a man who had the same build as Ethan. He was caught in mid-step, shoulders hunched, hands tucked into the front pockets of his pants. Despite the summer night, he was wearing a knee length black coat that looked like a suede one Jack had seen in the closet at Bathurst Street. If only he'd thought to check for missing clothes before leaving.

"Is it him?" Lewis asked.

The face was turned away from the camera, the body language not typical of Ethan and the lighting poor enough that even if he didn't have the other issues, it would still be a challenge.

"Maybe. Let's follow him. Where was this footage from?"

Fabian tapped madly for a moment, then answered. "ATM surveillance camera on Wilmot Street. Two blocks over from your starting address, heading south easterly."

"It's a high probability it's him." Jack was almost convinced. He had no doubts Ethan would have several ways out of the penthouse that avoided camera coverage. The only worry was that Ethan *had* been caught on camera at all.

Using the ATM and subject's apparent direction as a new starting point, they focused their search more intently and found more footage of him on George Street, then at the intersection with Goulburn. Afterward, they merely caught glimpses of him until he reached the Haymarket.

"Do you really think it's him?" Lewis asked Jack when searching beyond the Haymarket didn't net them any more footage of the subject.

"Has to be. If it was a random person, their face would have been captured at some point on camera. This guy's good at looking casual but is obviously avoiding easy recognition."

Fabian made a soft, disagreeing sound. "No one can know where every camera is over such a long distance."

This time, it was Jack and Lewis's turn to give the tech the *look*.

"This is Ethan Blade we're following," Lewis said, tone patient. "He infiltrated this building, *twice*, and got out unscathed both times. He led the local cops on merry car chases across most of this city, *twice*, and wasn't caught, either time. He singlehandedly killed a troop carrier full of special ops soldiers, and no one knows *how* he did it. Do you really think he wouldn't know where all the cameras are on a route he clearly planned as an escape path from his own home?"

Eyes wide, Fabian looked between them, like he wasn't certain Lewis was telling the truth and thought Jack might confirm his suspicions. When he didn't get the results he wanted, he frowned, looked back at his screen, at them again, then at his screen. "Fine. He knows where all the cameras are. So why did he let himself be seen at all?"

"Precisely." Jack sat back down at his own computer. "Can you compile all the footage into a single stream for me?"

Fabian grunted a positive and not long later, Jack had a single video that tracked their subject across several blocks. It was barely a minute of footage and he watched it over and over, looking for something meaningful, something that told him what Ethan was up to.

He was certain it was Ethan now. The way he walked and how he occasionally reached out and touched the walls of the buildings he was passing. Jack would know those hands anywhere, even in the often fuzzy images captured by cheap surveillance cameras.

It hurt, seeing Ethan walk away from the penthouse, away from what Jack had believed they were finally starting to build together. Hurt like the knife Two had rammed into his back and twisted. Ethan was unhurried but purposeful as he made his way as directly as possible to the Haymarket. He'd left a note but "soon" had variable meanings when Ethan used it. It had already been nearly ten hours since he left the penthouse. "Soon" could mean he was already back there, wondering where Jack was. Or it could mean he would be gone for months. If "soon" wasn't an outright lie.

Jack hoped Ethan had a fucking solid reason for leaving. Especially today.

Birthdays. Fuck 'em.

THIRTEEN

"**T**here's a pattern here." Jack watched the same footage of Ethan once more.

Lewis groaned and dropped his head back so he stared at the ceiling. "We've been over it I don't know how many times already. Fabes has run it through every analytical program he has and we've found nothing. Maybe we need to get a psycho-physical analyst."

"I'd rather we didn't involve too many others just yet," Jack said.

"He's been gone for how long now? Ten hours?" Sighing, Lewis looked back at his screen. "Face it, Jack, we've done all we can with what resources we have. Fabes is either going to slip into a coma or have a heart attack from too much caffeine. He shouldn't be here. *You're* not even supposed to be here. If you want to take this any further, you have to make it official."

His friend was right, but Jack couldn't quite make himself agree aloud just yet. Making the search official would mean involving Director Tan of ETA, Ethan's nominal superior. Tan had proved to be honourable in his dealings with Jack, yet the man had a ruthless reputation stretching out behind him a mile wide, and the fact he'd eagerly bent over backwards to get one of the top ranked assassins in the world on his team didn't make Jack feel any less wary of his motives.

Lewis groaned as he got to his feet. "While you stew in your own stomach acid, I'm going to get something to eat. Hopefully Lyds left something for me in the fridge." He left, twisting his torso so his spine popped as he went.

Jack looked across the table at Fabian. The younger man didn't appear as if he was going anywhere soon, but he did have a tendency to suddenly decide he needed to be somewhere else and just go without any preamble.

"Is there nothing else you can do?" Jack asked, half hopeful, half resigned.

"I can expand the parameters of the search. We lost him at Haymarket but that doesn't mean he didn't leave the area. Lewis mentioned that he was involved in a couple of car pursuits and didn't get caught. Chances are he got into a vehicle."

Jack mentally kicked himself. "Fuck. Of course." Even though Victoria had been left at home, Ethan probably had another car waiting somewhere, or could steal something no worries. "Let's go through stolen vehicle reports from this morning. List the more expensive sports cars first, then more standard models."

"I've already started it. There were only two cars reported missing in that general area, a Toyota Prius and a Nissan Skyline."

"Dig into those reports, find out what you can. I'll look for either of them in the Haymarket footage."

By the time Lewis returned with an armful of drinks and snacks, Fabian had ruled out both stolen cars—the Prius had been taken by the owner's daughter and the Skyline was found wrapped around a light pole in Paddington, driver currently in hospital with minor injuries. Undeterred, Jack told Lewis their new parameters and his mate sat back down before his screen.

They worked in silence, bar the sipping of drinks and the crackle of packets of biscuits and chips, for nearly fifteen minutes. Jack found himself going back to the video stream of Ethan's journey from Bathurst Street, the niggling feeling that there was a pattern to his hand movements not letting him concentrate on the car angle.

The answer came to him when he stopped fixating on Ethan and looked more at what he was touching.

"Fuck me. He left a message."

Lewis jerked, as if he'd been on the verge of sleep. "What?"

"Come here. Look at this." Jack waited until Lewis had scooted his chair around the corner of the table and leaned in beside him. "See how he touches the walls every now and then?"

"Yeah? I mean, it's a bit unhygienic, but nothing—"

"No. Look at what he's touching in particular."

Lewis had one of the best minds for deciphering hidden meanings, and as Jack played the video through at a slowed down speed, enlightenment dawned on his friend's face.

"Shit. Shit. How did I miss that?" Lewis all but clambered over Jack for a pen and notepad, then sat down again, at the ready. "Start it over. Slow it right down. We can't miss a thing."

For the first time since realising Ethan hadn't just stepped out for some air, Jack felt a spark of excitement. Perhaps Ethan was letting them know where he'd gone. Or why he was going. Either way, he was suddenly very grateful for the overwhelming amount of Christmas decorations in the storefront displays, because Ethan was spelling out words with his touches as he went.

"V," Lewis said as they watched for every touch. "I, E, T, P, A . . . Did he have a stroke? This isn't making much sense. N. Wait, go back a bit, I think we missed one."

"R," Jack said, reeling the video back second by second.

"R." Lewis wrote it down. "Are you sure about that one?"

"Fairly. The footage isn't great, it's right at the start of that clip and the next one doesn't start until he's almost at the corner." Jack looked at what Lewis had written so far. VIETPARN. It didn't make any sense. "Maybe this is in code, too."

"Maybe. Let's keep going, it might be more obvious with more letters."

Jack wasn't sure as they added T, M, I, and R, but as the next ones were revealed, A, M, A, T, I, he worked it out.

"Jesus Christ." All of the blood rushed out of his head, leaving him lightheaded and queasy. He stared at the screen where Ethan kept spelling out the name of his niece.

"What is it?" Lewis demanded.

"My sister and niece. Meera and Matilda. They're in danger."

Lewis looked from Jack to his notepad and back again. "I see the names now but how do you know—"

"We got the letter wrong. The one we weren't sure off. It's I, not R. Viet paint. Fuck!" Jack shot out of his chair and was halfway to the door when Lewis grabbed his arm.

"Jack, slow down. Explain."

Jack forced himself to not break free and sprint for the garage. The most important thing right then was getting to his family, but the best chance he had of saving them was with Lewis's help.

"After Harry's funeral, I went to Vietnam to be with Ethan. We stayed in a house owned by one of his associates. She paints, Lew. That's what he means. A fucking assassin is going after my family." A new thought hit him like a bullet. "Dad. Maybe they've targeted him as well."

Lewis was more than familiar with situations exploding into action on a moment's notice and he took it in stride now. "Get to your sister and niece as fast as you can." He shoved Jack towards the door. "I'll get some protection for your dad and mobilise a strike team to follow you and get it out on channels." Meaning he was going to alert the local police that something was going down and to stay the hell out of it. The Office kept tabs on the immediate family of their assets, as a matter of protection, so all the details Lewis would need to direct the strike force were on hand.

Trusting Lewis to do everything he could, Jack went after the most immediate threat—the one against Meera and Matilda. He flew through the middle of the eighth floor, dodging co-workers and cubicles as he went. Rather than waste time in the lift, he slammed through the door to the stairs and headed downwards. The Office had several choppers but they were kept at the airport unless required and it would take too long for one to come here or for Jack to go to them. Instead, he threw himself into Victoria and rocketed her out of the garage in a move worthy of Ethan.

And immediately ran into inner city Sydney traffic.

"Fuck." Jack slapped the steering wheel and searched for a quicker route through the mass of cars. This was where the bike was superior to Ethan's sleek supercar, but going back to Bathurst Street for the Ninja would waste too much time. Even signing a bike out from the Office garage would take too long.

Slower than he had patience for, Jack made his way out of the CBD and thankfully got onto the M1 before he started smashing into other cars in sheer frustration. Once on the motorway, he let the Vanquish fly.

Meera had moved out of Sydney when Matilda started school, wanting to raise her daughter in a smaller community. They'd ended up in Helensburgh, about forty-five kilometres south. Far enough away they didn't have to deal with large city problems but close enough they could easily visit. An hour's drive, on a good day, was still longer than Jack would have preferred right then.

With the road ahead clearer and what traffic there was moving at a decent rate, Jack took a moment to dredge up his sister's phone number and called her through the implant, only to go straight to voice mail. He tried again, and again, and on the third try connected. But the call was disconnected before it was answered. Jack kept trying for another five kilometres, then gave in and called Lewis.

"I can't get through to Meera." He slid Victoria from one lane to another and planted his foot to get past a semi. The car responded beautifully, gliding across the bitumen as if it had all the friction of smooth ice and easily outpacing the huge truck.

"Yeah," Lewis agreed. "Fabian's monitoring her phone and it's been in pretty much constant use for the last hour or so. Your niece is seventeen, right? Maybe she's on the phone to a friend."

"On Meera's phone? I doubt it. She'd have her own. And she should be in school at this time of day." If she wasn't being held hostage in her own home by a woman who would probably have few regrets about killing a teenaged girl.

"We're checking with her school now . . ." Lewis trailed off and then came back with, "And she didn't show up today. When they called Meera she said she wasn't aware of Matilda not going today. Either she's ditched or . . ."

Not even sparing a breath to swear, Jack just pressed down further on the accelerator. Victoria jumped forwards like a restless racehorse. Everything outside the tinted windows started to blur.

"You need to interrupt the call. Get through to Meera and find out what the fuck's going on down there."

"Fabes is already on it. Strike team is about fifteen minutes from getting airborne. We lucked out and caught Sturges's team as they came back from training in the hills. They were kitted out and pretty much hopping out of their chopper when I called for a team."

One thing going right for them, at least. If they got a bird in the air in the next fifteen minutes, they would beat Jack to Helensburgh, but depending on where they could land, he might still get there quicker. A chopper landing on a suburban street, disgorging six combat-ready, gun-toting personnel would alert Ethan's associate. If she was already in the house, they couldn't risk it and Jack told Lewis as much.

"Sturges is all over it, don't worry, Jack. We'll get them out safe."

Throat tightening, Jack could only nod, even though the gesture couldn't be seen. Trusting his friend and the entire Office to back him up, he just concentrated on the road ahead. Naturally, he picked up a police car near Hurstville, but after barely half a minute of sirens and lights in his rear vision, they disappeared as the cops were called off by Lewis. That, more than anything else, would draw the directors in like flies to a fermenting carcass.

Jack was just passing Heathcote, where Matilda should have been at school, when Lewis contacted him.

"The strike team is about to land near a fire trail on the outskirts of the town. In other good news, we got through to Meera. She won't talk to us though."

"Sounds about right," Jack muttered. "Did you tell her to answer my call?"

"Sure did! She's looking forward to hearing from her little brother."
The fake enthusiasm in Lewis tone wasn't lost on Jack. He could guess at much of the conversation that had taken place between him and Meera. Probably very much like the last one Jack had with her. Though he would have hoped a missing daughter would change her attitude somewhat.

"I'm about halfway there. As soon as I've spoken with Meera, I'll get back in touch," he told Lewis, disconnected and called Meera.

"Jack?" she answered, her tone tight but not particularly distressed.

"Hey, Meera. We've been trying—"

"I don't really appreciate having my conversation being interrupted by some government lacky. What's so important you couldn't wait?"

The chances that the assassin was in the house were pretty thin considering the bitterness coming down the connection. Surely if someone had a gun pointed at her or her daughter, Meera might have tried to be a bit more diplomatic. Not that Jack had ever seen much reason in his sister's opinion in the past.

"Your life and Tilly's life. Is that fucking important enough?" He was already on edge, but Meera's voice triggered his ire on top of it.

There were several moments of silence on the other end and Jack started to wonder if the assassin was there. Then Meera caught a breath sharp enough Jack heard it.

"What is it? Do you know where Mati is?" No more spite, just a restrained worry.

"No. Meera, listen to me. Are you secure right now?"

"I'm in the house, why?" Her tone got pointed again, ready to stab. *"What's going on? Where's my daughter?"*

"That's what we're trying to find out. Don't panic. Lock all the doors and windows, then stay away from them. Don't let yourself be seen and don't answer the door unless I tell you that you can trust the person knocking."

"Jack, what the fuck have you done?"

FOURTEEN

Jack's heart imploded with grief. Meera's words, spoken in anger and fear, and torn by tears, gutted him. His hands tightened on the steering wheel and his foot lifted off the accelerator.

This very moment was one Jack had dreaded, and one Meera had always accused him of potentially causing. She didn't know exactly what he did, but she was aware enough to understand it was dangerous, and her own prejudices and beliefs automatically took it to the worst possible scenario. She'd called him a government sanctioned murderer in the past and had accused him of being blind to the manipulation and brainwashing inherent in the military and higher administration.

Her worries, if not all of her accusations, had been right.

Jack's foot pressed down and the Vanquish leaped forwards.

"I'm on my way, Meera," he said grimly. "Nearly there. I won't let anyone hurt you."

"*Too late,*" his sister snapped. "*Mati's out there, Jack. She ditched school and I don't know where she is. Oh God.*" Her voice choked off in a strangled sob. "*If something's happened to her . . .*"

"I'll find her. I promise." Jack balled up all his fear and anger and shoved it in the filing cabinet in the back of his head. His compartmentalisation skills had been a trifle hit and miss lately, but for this, for something so fucking important, he would make it happen. "Remember what I said about locking the house and staying inside. Do it now. Then send Matilda's phone number to Lewis, the man who called you before me. He'll be able to track it and we'll follow it to wherever she is."

All he heard for several moments was Meera's ragged breathing, then, "*Don't let anything happen to her,*" and she hung up.

Hoping like hell she was calling Lewis back, Jack slammed shut the drawer on the filing cabinet. His stomach curdled for a moment only, then the calm settled over him, letting him know he was ready to do whatever was needed to successfully complete the mission.

Ten minutes later, just as Jack was going to crack and call Lewis himself, his friend contacted him.

"Sturges's team has landed and are sourcing transport right now. They should be at Meera's address within ten minutes. We have Matilda's phone number and Fabes is tracking it now."

"Good. Keep me updated."

"Right. We'll—"

"Got her!" The shout from the background was an excited Fabian. *"She's on Woronora Dam Road, heading west. Moving pretty fast."*

"Send me directions," Jack commanded.

"Coming through," Lewis said.

Jack grunted acknowledgement and a moment later, the file appeared. It was automatically opened by the implant and a dry inner voice gave him the way to go.

He'd just left the motorway and was curling around onto a highway that would take him back north and west when Lewis called.

"We have people on your dad. It was decided to leave him where he is for now, unless there's a clear threat against him."

Jack agreed. His dad didn't do well with new situations these days. "And the strike team?"

"Sturges is at Meera's. They're holding back, searching for the subject but haven't found any indication someone's watching the house. He's going to approach the house."

"Is Meera on the line with the Office?"

"Yeah. Lyds is trying to keep her calm. She's pretty worked up."

Yeah. That was Meera. "She's just worried. Go easy on her. And Matilda?"

"I think she's okay at the moment," Lewis said. *"Her signal's pretty much just going up and down Woronora Dam Road. If something bad was going down, I doubt it would be so steady."*

Jack let out a little sigh. He trusted Lewis's interpretation of clues above most others. "Let me know if anything changes."

The tiny respite didn't mean he stopped worrying or slowed down. The sooner his niece was as safe as he could make her, the better.

Minutes later, he came up to the turn for Woronora Dam Road. Victoria's rear swung out a little wide as he made it without slowing enough, but the sleek car corrected easily and sprinted on. There was no traffic on the narrow two-lane road and bushland bracketed either side as it wound into the hills.

"Where is she now?" Jack asked Lewis when his friend connected.

"About two kilometres ahead of you, heading away."

"Got it." Jack held the steering wheel in one hand and loosened his USP in its holster under his left arm. His little Tilly might not be in any direct danger right now, but that didn't mean he wasn't going in as if she were. "I'll call in when I have her."

"Right. Going silent here to direct Sturges." Lewis signed off.

As promised, Jack caught up to what he presumed was his niece several kilometres later. They were almost at the end of the road, just before a sharp turn right where it crossed the dam in question. Ahead of him, the dirt bike, which was the only other vehicle around, slowed and veered onto the side of the road. There were two people on the bike, both wearing open-faced helmets, but that was their only consideration for safety. Neither had on leather jackets or anything more protective than jeans on their legs. Still some distance back, Jack couldn't make out more details but he guessed the pillion rider was Matilda. The arms she threw up in exaltation were light brown, shown off by the rolled up sleeves of a flannel shirt, and the hair flying wild from under the back of her helmet was dark.

She'd ditched school to go joyriding on a dirt bike with some delinquent.

"Goddamn it." Jack eased off the accelerator.

The bike eased into a turn, getting ready to undoubtedly speed back the way they had come.

A small red blur shot past the Vanquish and right for his niece.

"Fuck!"

The red sports car braked sharply, smoke curling up from its tyres, as it passed the pair on the bike. Both riders' heads turned to follow the curvy little car, the bike slowing to a stop as they gawked.

The chances of someone bringing their sports car to this very road for hooning purposes at this very time were fucking ridiculous.

Beyond the riders, the red car drifted into a tight turn, the driver's side window rolling down as it came to a stop, sitting sideways on the road. Jack floored Victoria's accelerator and charged towards the other car. In the rapidly diminishing distance, an arm extended from the red car and pointed a gun at the kids, who were still staring at Jack.

"Move," he shouted uselessly and, trying anything available, flashed his headlights.

On the back of the bike, Matilda tilted her head, then turned to look behind them. A second later, she was bouncing and slapping the back of the other rider. He looked over his shoulder, too.

The crack of the gun was muffled by the Vanquish's sealed windows and the growl of the engine as Jack arrowed past the kids. He was going too fast to see if they were okay. Before Jack reached it, the red car lurched into abrupt motion, turning to chase after the bike again. The cars passed each other, barely a foot of space between their side mirrors. Jack's glimpse was fleeting, but the driver had a ponytail of white-blonde hair and sunglasses. Then they were past each other, her flooring it after the dirt bike, and Jack facing the entirely wrong way.

Victoria came to a shivering stop in the middle of the road. Turning around would take far too long, so Jack chucked the Vanquish into reverse and rocketed backwards.

Twisted in his seat, Jack saw the bike disappear around the next bend, both riders aboard and upright. The sports car followed them, closing the distance. Jack sped up, his heart hammering wildly in fear for his niece, and his own driving skills. If only Ethan were here. Around the bend was a bit more room and, praying hard, Jack whipped the Vanquish through a reverse one-eighty. It was not smooth or elegant, but it got him pointed in the right direction in a car all in one piece, and it let him catch up to the others around the next curve.

Jack cursed. There was a drop off to the left, hillside to the right. The sports car was right behind the dirt bike, which had no chance of outrunning the high-powered vehicle. You didn't need a gun to kill someone on a bike when you were in a car. Even as Jack tried to catch them, the red car nudged the back of the bike. Jack planted his foot as the bike took another hit.

The bike wobbled, then cut sharply right. It hit the dirt verge at top speed and launched off the slight ramp there and flew into the scrub. Two seconds later, Victoria's nose punched the rear fender of the red car. Both vehicles shuddered at the highspeed impact and Jack instinctively braked. Red car rocketing ahead, Jack let the black Vanquish slow right down. His hands were impossibly tight on the steering wheel and his stomach was trembling in a mix of adrenaline and anxiety.

"Well," he muttered, "that went better than last time."

Clear of the assassin for the time being, Jack put the car in reverse and shot back to where the bike had left the road. Leaving Victoria idling, he got out, USP in hand.

The air was warm and dry and smelt of exhaust, hot rubber, wattles and eucalyptus—nothing burning, thankfully. Moving cautiously on the rocky ground, Jack followed the short track of the bike's wheels up the slight rise. It disappeared very quickly, but the bike wasn't far away. It lay on its side just inside the scrub, the front wheel bent from impact. There was no sign of the kids, but it had barely been a minute since they crashed. They couldn't have gotten far.

"Matilda," Jack shout-whispered, side stepping past the bike, gun at the ready.

A rustle in the dry foliage came from his right, just over the edge of a rise.

"Tilly," Jack tried again. "It's me, uncle Jack."

It had been thirteen years since he'd last seen his niece. He felt confident he'd recognise her, but would she recognise him? She'd only been four the last time they were together and he doubted Meera kept a current photo of him around to remind her about the uncle Meera was keeping her from.

"Mati." Maybe using the name Meera had would inspire some trust.

Furious whispering started up. Jack let out a relieved breath. Both of them were still alive.

"Come on, guys," Jack hissed. "Let's go before she comes back. Hurry up now."

The leaves on a scrub parted and a soft brown face appeared, still encased in the helmet. "Uncle Jack?"

Transferring his gun to his left hand, Jack scrambled over to where the kids were hiding. He crouched and held his hand out for Matilda. "Yeah, it's me. Come on, we have to get out of here."

"Tate's hurt," she said, breathing hard. "He can't walk."

"Shit. Okay." Jack tucked the gun into the holster. "Let's get him out of there."

Matilda slithered out of the bush. She was slender but strong, reaching back into the bush and helping haul out her friend. The guy was probably the same age as her, thicker and browner of skin, probably South Pacific origins. He whimpered as Jack and Matilda got him free of the scrub. His left shoulder was dislocated and there was a freely bleeding gash on his left calf, his jeans torn from the knee down to the ankle.

"Let's wrap this up quickly, then we have to get going." Jack searched for something to wrap the kid's leg in. "Tilly, are you wearing anything under the flannel?"

In the midst of pulling off her helmet, Matilda scowled at him. "Yes, and it's Mati. Not Tilly."

Christ. She was exactly like Meera. Thankfully, Jack didn't need to prompt her any more. Once free of the helmet, she pulled the red and white plaid flannel off and handed it over, leaving herself in a white singlet top.

Jack wound the flannel around the kid's calf, making sure he bound the entire wound. Between pants, the kid asked, "Mati, you know this guy?"

"I think he's my uncle," she said.

"You *think*?" It came from both Jack and the kid, in exactly the same incredulous tone.

She glared at them both.

Jack couldn't help it. He chuckled and tied off the arms of the impromptu bandage. "Good enough for the moment. Let's get going."

Between him and Mati, they got the kid to his feet and back to the car. They'd just got him settled into the passenger seat and Mati was about to squeeze in beside him when the red car roared back around the corner and aimed right for the idling Vanquish.

FIFTEEN

From this angle, Jack clearly saw the distinctive V shape of the grill. Some sort of sporty little Alfa Romeo was about to smash into him and the kids—and Ethan's precious Aston Martin.

"Get in." Jack shoved Mati down into the car on top of the boy. Using the open door as a shield, he drew his gun and fired at the charging vehicle.

Mati and the kid squealed in shock and huddled as far down as they could. The red car kept heading for them, bullets pinging off the grill and bonnet. Jack counted down the seconds, pacing his shots, hoping to distract and divert before it became desperate. When the assassin failed to respond, he settled his arms against the top of the door and took very careful aim.

Jack put a bullet into the windscreen right in front of the driver. Only the craziest of crazies didn't flinch in that situation. The red car swerved and missed them, screaming past without slowing. Jack sent his last bullet after it, then slammed the passenger door, threw himself across the low bonnet of the Vanquish and got in behind the wheel.

Two pairs of big, dark eyes, completely rimmed in white, stared at him practically from under the dash.

"Sit up," Jack commanded. "And belt in as best you can. This could get scary."

He slammed Victoria into gear and, tyres smoking, got them going. In the passenger seat, the kids scrambled to do as he said, long arms tangling, bodies slipping sideways as they took a curve at speed. The kids were just clipping the seatbelt into place around both of them when the Alfa reappeared in the rear vision mirror. It roared right up behind them and smashed into the back of the black car.

Victoria lurched sharply forward. Mati screamed and the guy cried out in pain. Jack got the car back under control quickly and considered his one option—straight up running away. He had the kids with him now, all that mattered was getting them away from danger as quickly as possible. Surely he could do that in this car.

Decided, he relaxed into the seat, adjusted his hands on the steering wheel, and said, "Hold on."

"What are you going—" Mati cut off with a startled yelp when Jack stamped on the accelerator.

Victoria's big engine roared and they left the red car behind very quickly. They also left behind definable scenery and any guarantee of surviving every curve in the road. But they were coming down out of the hills and back onto mostly flat land so the road straightened out. Which was good, and bad. The Alfa might not have had the instant get up and go the Aston Martin did, but the driver was probably more skilled than Jack and the little red car started creeping up on their rear again.

"Shit." Jack coaxed even more ludicrous speed out of the Vanquish. At this rate, they were going to run out of road far too soon.

"What?" Mati asked, then looked in the side mirror. "Fuck."

"Language," Jack snapped at her. He lifted his left arm. "Grab my gun and switch mags."

"What?" Mati sounded horrified. "I can't do that. I don't know how."

"It's very easy. You won't shoot anyone. Please."

Muttering under her breath, Mati leaned across her friend, making him grunt in pain, and wrestled the USP out of the holster.

"Spare mag there." Jack pointed to the black plastic case sitting in the centre console cup holder.

He talked Mati through changing the mag while he focused on not killing them all in a fiery crash. When it was done, he lowered his window and then put the gun in the pocket on his door, grip up. Over the sudden rush of wind, he said, "Okay, everyone. *Really* hold onto something this time."

"What are you—" Mati didn't even bother trying to finish. She just clamped her jaw shut, put a bracing arm across her friend's chest, and the other against the dash.

Satisfied, Jack took a deep breath and before he could chicken out, whipped the car into a stupidly fast handbrake turn. The tyres smoked against the bitumen and the engine squealed when Jack slammed the handbrake back down and then shifted into reverse.

Nose pointed toward their pursuer and speeding backwards—again—Jack grabbed his gun and, hand resting on the side mirror, fired at the Alfa as it took advantage of Victoria's slower rate and caught up. The Alfa swerved to the side and the assassin's arm appeared, gun in hand. They exchanged shot after shot.

Then suddenly, the Alfa slowed dramatically. About to yell in victory, Jack choked to a stop as a large, dark shape swept in over the top of the Vanquish. His foot lifted automatically off the accelerator as he recognised the sleek, deadly Kamov Ka-52 Hokum B.

The Ka-52 had once belonged to a wannabe domestic terrorist, Samuel Valadian, who'd hidden out in the Great Sandy Desert. Jack had used the Russian built attack helicopter to escape Valadian's compound, giving Ethan some air support on his one-man, no-camel assault before hightailing it out of there due to damage done to the bird's engines. When Jack had returned to the Office, they'd picked up the damaged helicopter and, of course, fixed it up for their own use.

The Ka-52 arrowed over the top of the Vanquish, pointed right at the Alfa and unleashed two streams of tracer fire on it as it rapidly reversed.

While the kids cheered, Jack brought Victoria to a stop. The Alfa was on the run, weaving backwards as the Ka-52 swept around it. The pilot wasn't trying to hit the car, just to keep it off Jack and from running too far. Which meant backup had to be on the way.

Jack put the Vanquish back in gear and headed towards the Alfa.

"What are you doing?" Mati looked frantically between him and the Alfa. "We got away. Don't go back there."

As they got closer, the helicopter stopped firing and settled into a menacing hover behind the Alfa, bringing the car to a complete stop in the middle of the road. Jack angled Victoria across the road in front of the red car, pinning it in place.

"Stay here and get down," Jack instructed the kids as he quickly changed mags again.

"You aren't going out there are you?" the guy asked worriedly.

Mati was eyeing him with narrowed eyes, arms crossed over her narrow chest. "He is." The disgust and recrimination in her tone were exactly like those in Meera's.

Squashing his regret down, Jack got out of the car, gun at the ready.

The double thump of the Ka-52's coaxial rotors pounded on his chest and in his ears, but he could still hear the soft rumble of the Alfa's engine. She was ready to run, given the first chance.

Jack shot out the closest tyre, then put another bullet through the grill. After a second, steam started coiling up from under the bonnet. The engine spluttered out a moment later. With the car disabled, the Ka-52 lifted away, taking the noise and wind with it.

"Get out, hands up!" Jack trained his site on the driver's side door. He was about to repeat the command when the door opened.

The woman who stepped out was the same one who'd met Jack and Ethan in a shopping centre carpark a year ago. She'd exchanged a lot of damning information about one of the directors of the Office for Victoria. This was also the woman whose paintings Jack had admired in Vietnam. Such beautiful creations from a person who'd been about to kill a couple of innocent kids.

"Hands up," he said again to the blonde assassin. "Put them on the roof of the car. Legs spread."

Expression bland under her sunglasses, she complied without argument. She wore dark-coloured tactical clothing and her hair was pulled back into a ponytail, shorter than when Jack had last seen her. Wary of getting too close, Jack eased into position behind her, close enough to guarantee a kill shot if needed, far enough away she couldn't get him with a surprise attack.

"Is it just you?" he asked, aware of the Ka-52 moving in a slow circle high above them. If it went tits up on the ground, the bird was fast enough to still move in and assist. "Or is there another one of you crazy fuckers out there?"

Jack wasn't really expecting an answer and wasn't disappointed when he didn't get one. His implant *ping*ed and a message informed him backup was two minutes away. He could keep the assassin contained for that long and use that time to learn some things.

"Do you know where Ethan is?" He kept his tone even so she didn't know how desperate he was for the information.

She didn't respond, didn't move.

"Is it the Cabal? Are they the ones who sent you after my family? Why didn't you come after me instead?"

Nothing. Apparently Ethan wasn't the only one who clammed up in defence. Perhaps he needed a different tactic.

"I liked your paintings and I'm sorry we busted up your home."

Getting no reaction, Jack settled into his stance, prepared to stay there the entire time it took for ground support to show up. A minute in, the woman spoke.

"Thank you."

"You're welcome."

Then they waited in silence.

Ground support came in the form of a big silver 4WD that pulled up next to Victoria and disgorged four members of an Office strike team. One of them leaned into the car, talking to the kids, while the other three came towards Jack.

"Reardon," Sturges said when he was close enough.

"Sturges," Jack replied. "Nice to see you."

The big man gave him a curt nod and instructed his two assets to secure the subject.

"Watch her," Jack cautioned them. "She'll be as slippery as Ethan Blade."

The two assets nodded in acknowledgement and converged on the woman. Jack and Sturges kept her under cover all the while.

"My sister?" Jack asked as the woman was very thoroughly patted down and divested of several weapons.

"Very vocal, but safe. Two of the team are still with her. There was no disturbance at the house."

"That's good." At least the Cabal hadn't bothered to spare two of their assassins for the job. Under normal circumstances, one would have been more than enough, but anything Ethan was involved in wasn't normal.

The man Sturges had left with the kids came over and said they needed to take the boy to the nearest hospital. Sturges told him to take the 4WD and radioed his other team members for one of them to find another vehicle and meet them here, now that the assassin was in custody. Jack went with him to help transfer the injured boy to the bigger car. Mati hovered over them the entire time and when she tried to climb into the 4WD after her friend, Jack grabbed the back of her top and held her back.

"I'm going with Tate," she insisted.

"No, you're staying with me."

Now that they weren't racing for their lives, Jack really looked at his niece. He hadn't seen her in thirteen years, but he recognised her. Or rather, he recognised Meera as she had been at that age. The big, dark eyes; high, fine cheekbones; the shape of her jaw. She had been a bright, vibrant four-year-old when he last saw her, bouncing at Jack's feet, demanding to be swung around and told stories and assured she was the centre of her uncle's world.

Now, here she was. Tall and willowy with masses of dark brown hair lightening at the ends, and piercings all the way up one ear. Grown up, but still so young. Not bouncing, not laughing, but roughly pulling out of his hold and scowling at him. Oh yeah. She was Meera's daughter all right. He'd wondered if he would feel that spark of family with her. He shouldn't have been worried.

"I don't know you." She crossed her arms and clenched her jaw.

"I guess not," he said evenly. "But I am the person who just saved your life, and that of your delinquent little friend in there."

"Hey," the kid protested from inside the car. Jack slammed the door shut and told the asset to get going. He had to grab Mati's shoulder to stop her from trying to get in the car again.

"I want to go with him," she snapped.

"And I want to keep you safe. You stay with me."

As the asset pulled the 4WD away and left, Mati glared at Jack. "We were perfectly safe until you started Fury Road-ing us."

Jack snorted. "Perfectly safe? You were on a bike without a tear resistant jacket and pants, gloves, or proper shoes." He waved at the thongs on her feet. "You didn't have a visor on your helmet, or goggles. Your little friend got hurt badly when you came off the bike." He spoke over her protest. "And speaking of, is that delinquent even allowed to have a passenger?"

"Stop calling Tate a delinquent."

"What else do I call the kid who took you joyriding, without permission from your mother, when you're supposed to be in school?"

Mati crossed her arms and narrowed her eyes at him. "You don't know anything about Tate. You don't even know me."

"True, but I know more than you about what's going on here, so you will do exactly as I say. Get in the car."

"No."

"Get in. The car."

"Are you going to take me to the hospital to be with Tate?"

"Sure."

She eyed his sudden capitulation sceptically but turned with a flounce and threw herself back into the Vanquish.

"You're not going to the hospital, are you," Sturges murmured from behind Jack.

"No," Jack admitted. "*I* might need to go once her mother is through with me, though."

Sturges laughed and slapped him on the back. "Good luck, mate. We'll see your latest assassin friend back to HQ. Try not to break this one out, hey?"

SIXTEEN

"**Y**ou said we were going to the hospital." Mati crossed her arms and slouched in the seat of the car.

They were parked outside of Meera's home, a neat, single storey white stuccoed house with colourful roof tiles. The yard was bare of garden beds, just a single mock orange bush in the corner that had once been pruned into a ball shape but had since gone a trifle feral. It was covered in white blossoms, their citrusy scent floating across the yard and into the car.

"Maybe later." No matter what Jack thought of Mati's friend, she was clearly worried about him. Which said a lot about her. She had just survived an incredibly harrowing experience and she was more concerned for her friend than herself. "Your mum's worried. You need to let her know you're all right first."

The curtains on the window closest to the driveway kept twitching. Probably Meera ignoring the commands of the strike team member left with her. Jack had called ahead to let them know he would be approaching in the black Aston Martin, with Mati, so Meera knew her daughter was close. If he didn't get Mati out of the car soonish, Meera would probably take down her guard and march right outside, regardless of her safety.

"You called her," Mati grumbled. "She knows I'm okay. I want to see Tate."

"We'll hear about your friend soon enough. Trust me, we know what we're doing."

"Why should I trust you?" She'd asked it several times already, but this time, it was sulky instead of snappy. "I don't even know what's going on."

Jack heaved a sigh. "I'm sorry. This is my fault, but the worst of it's over now. We know the threat is there, so we'll do whatever it takes to keep you and your mum safe. Come on, let's go inside. Meera's going to want to yell at us both for a while. Best to get it over with."

Mati looked at him inquisitorially, then she smiled. "You must know mum, then."

He matched her smile. "Yeah. I guess she hasn't really changed, huh."

"Right. Like that'll ever happen."

Jack opened his door. "We can be each other's backup."

After an extended eyeroll, Mati got out of the car. Jack took a moment to tuck his gun into its holster, catching Mati watching him with a part wary, part fascinated expression, then he motioned her ahead of him.

"Thought I was your backup," she muttered, but went with her head high.

Liking her courage, Jack grinned and followed her up the three steps to the front door. Leaning over her, he banged on the edge of the security screen. "Bains? It's Reardon," he announced loud enough to be heard inside.

After a moment, a woman in tactical wear opened the inner door. She scanned around them quickly, then flashed Mati a bright smile as she unlocked the screen for them. "Welcome home, Mati. Your mother will be happy to see you."

Mati grumbled under her breath but slipped past the woman and disappeared inside.

"Reardon," Bains said in the same joyful tone. "Your sister is going to be *so* pleased to see you too."

Jack snorted. "I bet. Is everything here secure?"

"About as much as it can be. I've been organising with HQ for a safe house for them. We should be ready to transport in half an hour."

The assassin had been caught, but Ethan had never exactly said how many of his associates there were. Who knew what else this mysterious Cabal might throw at them? Jack wasn't going to take any chances with his family, no matter what objections Meera might have.

Meanwhile, Meera could be heard clearly chewing Mati out for ditching school. The diatribe was peppered with a few desperate

"Buts" and "Mums," yet Mati couldn't gain any traction against Meera and stopped trying after a while. Then Meera's words petered out and after a moment, she let out a loud sob.

Hoping the worst was over, Jack wandered into the house as Bains locked up again. There was a breezeway down the middle, with rooms off either side. He found his sister and niece in a bedroom between the front lounge room and rear kitchen. Mother and daughter were cinched tightly together in the middle of the room.

It was Meera's room, judging by the large bed, sombre stylings and the array of photos on the dressing table by the door. Their parents at Uncle Raja's wedding in Kerala, the same photo Jack had on his bookshelf at home. Another of their father, taken recently as Jack recognised the nursing home garden in the background. Dad was laughing and he looked like he had when Jack was younger, before Usha died and dementia had started stealing his dad away from them. Bright eyed and happy. Half out of shot was Mati, grinning back at him with an expression of wonder. A rare moment of clarity for Chris and a rarer moment for his granddaughter to see the man he once had been. Then there was a set of images showing Mati as she grew from baby to toddler to school girl and to now, pained resignation on her face as she posed with a boy in a badly fitted suit, clearly on their way to a school dance.

Jack was caught by an early picture of Mati, back when she had liked being called Tilly, in a pink tutu, face scrunched up in concentration as she balanced on her tip toes. Her arms were up, little hands clutching larger, browner fingers for support. Jack remembered that day. Those were his fingers and he'd scooted back out of the shot because Tilly had wanted to look like she was doing it on her own. She'd been four. One of the last, happy times they'd all been together. He wondered if Mati had kept up the dance lessons.

As if sensing him, Meera lifted her tear-streaked face from her daughter's shoulder and found him. They were of a height, mother and daughter. Meera hadn't inherited their father's long legs, or much else of his Caucasian genes. She was Usha's child more than Chris's, in more than appearance.

"What the hell did you do?" she demanded.

Mati pulled out of Meera's arms. "Mum, he—"

"No. Jack can explain."

"Meera, I didn't mean for this to happen," he began.

Shoving a mass of thick, dark brown hair over her shoulder, Meera scowled. "You never do and yet it happens. And someone else always pays for it."

Jack flinched. Meera's deadly accuracy with her verbal knives hadn't changed.

"Mum!"

"Go wash up, Mati. This is between Jack and me."

"But—"

"You have blood on you," Meera pointed out. "Go wash it off."

"He saved me."

"Mati," Jack tried but Meera glared him into silence.

"You've already lost your phone and Netflix," Meera said ominously to Mati.

With a parting grumble, Mati left. She mouthed "sorry" as she passed Jack.

When they were alone, Jack tried a little smile at his sister. "Can we skip the yelling and get to the hug?"

Meera just stared at him, her dark eyes narrowed, arms crossed. Christ. She looked like their mother. The familiar cheekbones, mouth, and eyes. A few patches of grey woven through her hair. That same steel spine and stubbornness.

"Meera, I'm sorry."

The eyes narrowed even further and Jack braced for impact.

Meera burst into tears.

Shit. Jack stood helpless while his strong and determined older sister cried. Her hands dropped to her sides, wringing worriedly at the hem of her top, and she gasped softly as tears streamed down her cheeks.

The Reardons weren't a family that cried easily. The only other time Jack had seen Meera cry was when Matilda had been born. She'd been in withdrawal from Sugar at the time and it had been possible Matilda would be a Sugar Baby, with the perceived stigma and all too real eye-related issues. She hadn't been, thankfully, but the fear of it had sent Jack into research mode, giving him the knowledge to know Ethan for one many years later.

Uncertain of what to do, Jack stepped closer and touched her arm tentatively. His own eyes were burning. Today had been close. Closer than Jack had ever wanted his family to get to being affected by his job.

"Jesus." He pulled her into his arms.

Meera cried harder and leaned on him, though she did start pummelling his back with her fists. This physical assault he could take. It was the emotional one that tore him into strips.

He'd done this. His actions, his job, his choices, had brought them here. His niece barely snatched out of the way of an assassin's gun, his sister in his arms crying in anger, relief, confusion. Dad would be so sad to see them like this. Would he forgive Jack for something this bad if he knew? Dad had never blamed Jack for Usha's death, unlike Meera, and had forgiven his son for his bad choices afterwards, and all the ones leading up to it. But this? This seemed even outside of Chris Reardon's capacity of understanding.

Mati came to the bedroom doorway at one point. She'd cleaned up and, in a fresh T-shirt and jeans, looked at them in wide-eyed surprise for a moment, before turning and exaggeratedly tiptoeing away. Jack smiled.

"She's wonderful," he whispered.

"I know."

As if speaking had broken the spell, Meera pulled back, then pushed him harder so he staggered back.

"You goddamn piece of shit." She grabbed a handful of tissues from the box on the bedside table and handed him a couple.

"Not arguing." Jack scrubbed his damp cheeks.

Meera patted her face dry, blew, and scrunched the tissues into tight ball. "I knew something like this would happen one day. What happened?"

And as much as Jack wished he could confess everything to his sister, he couldn't. Not just because there were national and international secrets to be kept, but because knowing too much would put Meera and Mati in even more danger.

"I pissed some people off through work and they decided to get back at me." True, as far as it went. And exactly what Meera had been waiting for.

"I knew it." Fire sparked in her eyes. "The moment you went to work for the ISO I should have changed our names. God knows I wanted to get further away from you, but—" Her eyes widened and she grabbed the front of his shirt in both fists. "Dad."

Jack caught her wrists gently. "Is okay. We have people with him. If there was any danger to him, they would have told me. He's fine."

Meera studied his eyes, looking for a lie or omission. Seemingly satisfied, she let him go. "At least you thought of him."

That fucking hurt. "Do you think I'm that horrible a person?"

"Of course not," she snapped, then softer, "It's just that you've missed too many visits. He'd remember you more if you saw him more often."

It didn't exactly mollify his feelings, but in an effort at not reducing this to a screaming match, Jack said, "Once you pair are safe, I'll go see him."

"Good. So who did you manage to piss off then? Our own government?"

"Jesus." It slipped out before Jack could swallow the sudden surge of irritation. "No. Not our own government. Not any government. I don't know who they are but they're nasty and big and they have my—" He managed to stop himself but Meera didn't miss it.

"They have your what? Nuts in a vice? Is that worth your niece's life, Jack?"

"No, it's not," Jack ground out.

"Then what is? What did you do that pissed them off? Why is my daughter in danger?"

"Meera, I can't talk about this. We have to get you and Mati ready to go. We'll put you in a safe house until this is all over. You should start packing."

"A safe house? Where?"

"I don't know. It's best I don't know. But not here."

"Why is it best you don't know?" Mati asked from the doorway.

They both spun. The young woman stood in the doorway, arms crossed, watching them intently.

"Are you not coming with us?" Mati asked.

"No," Jack admitted. "I have to keep looking for . . . for the ones who did this."

"Who's going to keep us safe?"

Mati's indignant question warmed Jack's heart. Half an hour ago he hadn't suspected she might end up on his side in this particular family argument.

"Another team like the one here today will be with you," he assured her. "They're the best bodyguards in the game. Go pack some essentials, Mati. If you forget anything, we'll be able to get it for you."

Meera huffed but pulled a medium sized suitcase out of the wardrobe.

Mati frowned. "What about Tate?"

Suitcase dropping, Meera whirled around and planted her fists on her hips. "That's who you were with today? I told you you weren't allowed to associate with that boy anymore."

"You don't know him. And he's in the hospital because we came off the—" She cut herself off as she realised the quicksand she'd walked into. "Because of the crazy lady who tried to kill us."

"You were on that bloody bike again."

"We were fine until he showed up and things got scary." Mati waved at Jack.

Great. Familial solidarity didn't last long, apparently.

"And we had helmets," she finished triumphantly.

Meera didn't buy it. "I don't care if you had full body armour. I told you not to get on that bike with him again. No phone, no Netflix, no Tate, no soccer, no music, no—"

"Life! Jesus, mum, I can't miss practice. They need me for the band and I'm the best striker on the team."

"Maybe you should have thought of that before you ditched school to go joyriding with that delinquent."

Jack snorted under his breath, but it caught Mati's attention and she screwed her nose up at him.

"Look," he said before either mother or daughter could launch another barrage. "Whether or not you're allowed to do all those things the fact is, you won't be able to do them. You'll be in a safe house for at least a couple of weeks, maybe longer. They'll probably have Netflix but not the rest of it."

Mati's jaw almost hit the floor.

"What about school?" Meera demanded. "She needs to go to school."

"That will be taken care of. We'll provide tutors and class work for her."

Mati glared from one of them to the other.

Meera pointed out the door. "Go pack, Mati. Now."

The girl huffed and stalked out.

"She's just like you," Jack and Meera muttered at the same time.

They gaped at each other for a moment, then Meera shook her head and started pulling clothes from the wardrobe.

"Anything I can help with?" Jack asked carefully.

"No. You've done enough." Meera dumped an armful of tops into the suitcase, took a deep breath and went to the drawers.

"Thank you for not fighting me on the safe house. It really is for the best."

"Well, I would fight you on it except that there's Mati. You put her in danger, you can keep her safe now. It's the least you could do."

And she twisted the knife.

"I know," he whispered. "Meera, I really am—"

"I know you're sorry, Jack. You're always sorry. But you go off and do these things without thinking them through and someone else always pays for it. Do you know how much I hated it when Dad excused all your shit when we were kids? You were his precious son and could never do any wrong. No wonder you grew up thinking you can do whatever the hell you want and screw everyone else."

He knew better than to interrupt, even to defend their dad. Looking back on it now, Jack knew he and Meera had never had to compete for attention from either parent. It had been shared equally, but that hadn't stopped their childish perceptions from skewing it in favour of the other over the littlest slight.

Meera packed in stilted silence, her stiff shoulders a more familiar sight than that of the woman needing comfort and release against his chest. The tension was building again, that palpable tightness between them that always preceded an epic explosion. Meera's thoughts were simmering and Jack was building walls to keep her barbs out. No wonder he instinctively shielded himself from even his best friends. Perhaps that was why Meera hadn't ever settled down with anyone after Mati's birth. Growing up with this sort of hostility hadn't done either him or Meera any favours.

"I met someone."

Jack hadn't meant to say it, but the growing pressure in the room had forced it out.

Meera paused in folding jeans. "What?"

"His name's Ethan. He's . . . different. Good but not the sort of person I would have ever thought I'd end up with."

"Congrats, I suppose, but what does that have to do with any of this?"

"He's missing."

Jeans dropping into the suitcase, Meera faced him. "What?"

"He disappeared early this morning. I don't know where he went but I know it was because of the same people who sent that woman after you and Mati. Ethan left me clues, to let me know to come to for you. He's gone and you're safe because of him."

Meera stared for a moment longer, then spun around and kept packing, but not before Jack saw her expression twist with compassion. "You came for Mati and me instead of going after him?" Her voice was tightly controlled.

"Yeah."

Neither of them spoke again while Meera finished up. When she was done, Jack helped her close the suitcase then hefted it off the bed for her. She watched as he headed for the bedroom door, then caught up and stopped him with a hand on his arm.

"Are you going after him now?" There was a tiny tremor in her words this time.

"If I can find him."

Meera squeezed his arm. "You found Mati. You'll find him." Then she brushed past him and left the room, yelling at Mati to hurry up or be left behind.

SEVENTEEN

While Meera and Mati were transported to their safe house, Jack returned to Sydney. This drive wasn't as wild as the previous one, only exceeding the speed limit when Jack's thoughts wandered too far from reining in the powerful car.

After checking in with Lewis and being assured his presence wasn't vital at the Office right then, Jack drove right through the centre of Sydney and into Forestville. It was a small Northern Beaches suburb, quiet, shady, and friendly. It was the sort of place his parents had always spoken about moving to when he was a kid. Family orientated but conveniently close enough to inner Sydney and the coast to not feel cut off from the lifestyle of the city. They'd never made the move as a family. After Usha's death, Chris had found an old soldier's cottage in need of renovation in Forestville and set to working through his grief. When his early onset dementia had forced his relocation to assisted living, then a nursing home, Jack had considered giving up his Leichhardt apartment to live in the cottage and finish what Dad had started. Before he could make a firm decision though, he'd been sent overseas on the mission that forever changed his career and life. Believing him dead, Meera had sold the cottage.

Jack drove down the street he'd once thought he'd live on and past the allotment where the cottage had stood. The new owners had knocked down the 1960s era house and built a huge modern home. Not even that much of his father's dreams remained.

A couple of corners later and he pulled into the nursing home carpark. Getting out of Victoria, Jack took a deep breath and headed inside. The usually sparsely decorated foyer was all but drowning in Christmas cheer. Green, red, gold and silver tinsel had been strung around the walls and across the ceiling. Brightly coloured baubles hung off every pamphlet rack and picture frame. In the corner was a plastic tree, nearly overwhelmed with a glittering plethora of homemade ornaments, and crowned with a large, slightly off-kilter angel. An elderly woman and a child of five or six stood before the tree, trying to find a free spot to hang a painted Styrofoam ball. In a chair in the waiting area, a man Jack recognised from the Office was reading a magazine. They met gazes briefly but that was the only acknowledgement needed. Jack's dad was being watched over, that was all that mattered. One concern settled, Jack let the others crowd in.

These visits on his birthday were important. Special but difficult. With it being so close to Christmas, it had been easy for people to overlook Jack's birthday. They'd combined presents and sung Happy Birthday while cutting a Christmas cake. Except for Dad. His father had always made sure Jack had something special just for him on his birthday. Something separate from the mad scramble to see friends, to make sure the Indian half of the family got their gifts, or preparations to travel to Kerala. The least Jack could do now was make sure his dad knew, in some way, how special that had been.

Jack went to reception and signed in.

Ngaire, a familiar face at the desk, noted him and scooted her chair closer, smiling. "Nishant, it's been a while."

"I know. Work's been extra busy." While Jack tried to visit as often as he could, time and circumstance didn't always allow it. And he didn't like showing up while he was visibly injured. Dad probably wouldn't notice, but Jack would do anything to keep his father from getting distressed. "How's he been?"

"Good," the Maori woman assured him. "A bit quiet but otherwise fine." She hesitated, then added gently, "Your sister was here a couple of days ago."

Jack nodded.

This was how Meera had known Jack hadn't been to see Dad lately. Ngaire had been working in the home since they'd admitted Chris and had witnessed firsthand the relationship between brother and sister. Since then, they only ever came in separately, keeping track of each other's visits through Ngaire.

"Your dad's in the garden today," she told him. "He wanted to see the sky."

Giving her his thanks, Jack went out to the garden. Another asset was here, walking casually around the garden beds. Jack nodded to the woman and she slipped away, giving him some privacy.

Chris Reardon sat on a bench in the aromatic section. His once square shoulders were curled in with weariness, head bobbing on a neck that looked thinner than Jack remembered. Hair still more blond than grey receded across his head and was scattered across his jaw. Either he hadn't bothered shaving that morning or he'd gotten distracted halfway through the process, which happened more and more often lately. A book rested on the seat beside him, open and face down, the spine cracked.

Jack's steps faltered. Once, Dad would never have treated a book that way. He'd always been shoving bookmarks in Jack and Meera's books when they were younger. Forcing himself onwards, Jack plucked a spring of lavender from a plant and then sat next to his dad.

"Hello, Dad." He kept his tone pleasant.

Dad frowned at him, lines deepening around his mouth as he watched Jack turn the book over and use the lavender as a bookmark. "That's my book."

"I know." Jack set it back where he found it and smoothed down the cover. *Casino Royale* by Ian Fleming. One of Dad's favourites. "Someone used to get up me for not using bookmarks when I was a kid, and now it's a habit."

His father picked up the book and firmly set it down on his other side. "It's my book." That done, he focused on the mint in the garden bed in front of them.

There had been no recognition in Dad's eyes when he looked at Jack. Not even a vague questioning, as if maybe he thought this Indian man was slightly familiar. Dad had a better chance of recognising Meera, but then he hadn't believed she was dead before he started losing his cognition.

"It's a good book." Jack's voice broke a little bit, but he kept his tone light. "I know someone who probably likes it as much as you do. I don't know for sure if he's read it, but anything that's got over the top action and situations appeals to him."

Dad crossed his arms and huffed a resigned breath. At least he wasn't telling Jack to leave him alone or giving him an order for lunch.

"He's a good man, Dad. Not exactly who either of us probably ever saw me ending up with, but he's it. The one for me. Like mum was your one. It took a bit of work, but we're living together at last." At least, he hoped they still were. "You wouldn't believe the place we're in. Inner city, penthouse, private lift. It's pretty swish."

Jack told his dad about Ethan, his humour and his cars and love of all animals. Talking about him helped Jack believe Ethan would reappear before the end of the day, with a story of fighting Cabal henchmen and winning decisively—just like James Bond. Dad occasionally looked at him, mostly with a frown, and once with his lips parted like he was going to speak but didn't. Instead, he picked up his book and took out the lavender sprig, twisting it between his fingers.

"Usha planted lavender," Dad suddenly said, talking over Jack's description of Ethan racing on the Gold Coast.

Stumbling to a halt, Jack stared at him. "She did." He spoke carefully, unwilling to disrupt his dad's thoughts.

"It didn't grow well. The soil wasn't right."

"She kept trying though."

Dad looked up at him. "Raja?"

Heart clenching in cautious anticipation, Jack shook his head. "Dad, I'm Jack. Your son. Raja is my uncle."

"You look like Raja." He touched Jack's face with the hand holding the lavender. Dry fingertips and soft flowers brushed across his cheek.

"I do, a bit."

"Are you Raja's boy?"

"No. Raja doesn't have any kids. I'm your son, Dad."

The hand fell away and Jack caught it in his own, holding on while even this small part of his father was present.

Dad looked at his pale hand between Jack's brown ones. "I don't have a son."

"You do. It's me, Dad. Jack."

With a frustrated grunt, his father pulled his hand free and shifted along the bench a bit. The lavender was left between Jack's palms. He concentrated on straightening out the sprig, instead of throwing himself at his father, pleading for recognition and love and comfort. Ethan was gone, Meera and Mati taken away for their safety, and Jack needed someone right then to tell him it would be okay. That he wasn't alone.

When he could look up again without crying, Dad had opened his book and was reading, moving a finger across the page. He kept tracing the same line over and over.

Jack settled back, letting silence fall. As long as his dad wasn't yelling at him to go away, then it was a good visit. Even if Jack had to keep swallowing his sadness so it wouldn't escape and ruin the peace.

Eventually, one of the staff came and told them it was time for afternoon tea. Dad got up and went inside without acknowledging Jack. Following, Jack watched his father for signs of weakness. Despite his bowed shoulders, Dad still moved easily enough and for a moment, Jack was a kid again, trotting to keep up with his dad's long strides, devotedly trailing after the most important person in his life.

Jack sat and had a couple of biscuits and a glass of juice with Dad. Chris told him how he didn't like pineapple juice and refused to drink it, even after Jack told him it was apple. Things began to deteriorate after that. Jack was stealing his bikkies. The woman across from them was watering down the juice. The cake was poisoned. Jack had taken his book and wouldn't give it back.

While a couple of the staff coaxed Dad into calming down and returning to his room, Jack fetched the forgotten book from the garden. He slipped a few new sprigs of lavender between the pages and set it on the bedside table in his father's room. Dad was sulking in a chair by the window and Jack knew that if he stayed, he would upset his father more.

In the doorway, he stopped and whispered, "I love you, Dad," then left.

He sat in Victoria in the carpark for small while, deep-breathing through the pain. It had been a good visit, but that only meant he wasn't too wrecked to drive at all.

By the time he reached the Neville Crawley Building, he'd locked away the visit and walked onto the eighth floor dry eyed, calm and more than ready to get back to work.

Lydia was waiting for him by the stairwell door and fell into step beside him. "How's your sister and niece?"

"On their way into protection at last. Thank you for keeping Meera centred through it all. I know she can be difficult."

She squeezed his arm gently. "Family trait. But it's understandable. She was panicked about her daughter, that's all. I'm glad it all worked out okay."

Jack liked the teasing. Things had been cool between them since he'd revealed his relationship with Ethan. Lydia's reaction had been what Jack had expected—confusion and antipathy towards both him and Ethan. He'd gone through it with his second, Harry McGill, only minutes before he was killed by terrorists in Canberra. They hadn't been given the time to work it out. Jack still had that chance with Lydia, and maybe this meant she was starting to accept.

"And your dad?" she asked, even gentler.

His friends knew about his birthday visits to his father and never failed to be supportive of however they left him.

"Good," he managed. "He thought I was my uncle, so family at least."

"I'm sure somewhere deep down he knows you were there with him." Stepping back, she waved him on. "Lewis and Fabian are still in the operations room. They've found information on where Omega—" She winced. "About where Ethan might be."

She was trying, that's all Jack could hope for. "Thanks. Where are you going?"

"Back to the official work." She didn't quite keep all the testiness out of her voice that time. "Lew and I aren't assigned to look for your boyfriend, remember."

"I'm sorry. Do you need him back?"

It took her a moment but Lydia managed a small smile, though it didn't reach her eyes. "No. At this stage of the job, he's more of a hindrance than a help. We're still gathering information. When that hits critical mass, I'll let him loose on it." Backing off, she added, "Just don't get him suspended over this."

"I'll make him back off if it gets that far," Jack promised. She was right. Looking for Ethan wasn't an official job. Neither had been going after Mati, but that was at least being upgraded now they'd secured the assassin.

Lydia headed towards a different operations room and Jack carried on to where he'd left the others. He found them working side by side, surrounded by a herd of coffee cups and their taller energy drink can cousins.

"Lyds found you?" Lewis asked.

"Yeah."

Lewis nodded and simply patted Jack's shoulder, knowing his partner had already done the sympathetic support bit. That done, he shoved Jack down in front of the computer. "It's pretty thin but it's a lead. Fabes found it following your car idea. Show him the footage," he said to the younger man.

A video appeared on Jack's screen seconds later. Taken from a security cam in a parking structure, the image was grainy but right on the edge of the vision, a Jeep roared backwards out of a park, turned sharply and came to a very abrupt stop. After a moment, it took off at a much sedater pace and left the structure.

"Do we have any images of who's in the car?" Jack replayed it.

"Nope, which sort of indicates Ethan. We did follow the car as best we could. It went west and we lost track of it just before the mountains. Then we found the Jeep abandoned in Mudgee about 9 a.m. this morning. Fabes put the description and licence plate out to the cops state wide. There's no CCTV cameras in the area it was found, but a silver Holden Colorado was reported stolen there this morning. We've already got a KLO4 out on the new car."

"Good," Jack said, unsure of how he felt about this. Was Ethan deliberately leaving them a path to follow? Was he expecting Jack to catch up and . . . what? Save him? Perhaps. Or was he simply working on the fly? Doing what he could in the moment and not quite reaching his usual standards.

Fabian's computer beeped. "Got a report on the KLO4. Police car saw a silver Holden Colorado heading northwest out of Mudgee on the B55 highway. I'll set the search parameters to follow it."

Moments later, they got another hit. Images from a volunteer firefighter crew after they'd put out a large fire at an isolated shed twenty kilometres away from where the police saw the Colorado. And if the burnt-out hulk of a dual cab ute wasn't the same car, the coincidence would be vastly improbable.

"Look at that." Jack pointed to a photo of the burnt ruins. "See those tracks? That would have held a moveable platform for a helicopter."

"Shit," Lewis muttered. "They're airborne. That makes it a lot trickier."

Jack shot to his feet. "I need a closer look at the shed. Is the Kamov still on the roof?"

"Yeah. Pilot should be around somewhere."

"Don't need a pilot." Jack headed for the door.

Lewis caught up to him. "Then you'll have a spare seat for a spotter."

Fresh from Lydia's warnings, Jack gave his mate a searching look. "Are you sure?"

No hesitation from Lewis. "No wukkas, mate."

Minutes later, they were strapping into the attack helicopter and Lewis was as excited as a kid at Christmas. Jack wondered if he'd witness Lewis's O face when they were up and the Ka-52's powerful engines were unleashed on the sky around them.

"Don't forget you're my spotter," Jack said over comms.

"I know, I know. Holy shit, this is amazing. Do some fancy flying. Do some fancy flying."

Jack smiled at his friend's not-really-fake-over-enthusiasm. The Kamov Ka-52 was very manoeuvrable and it would be fun to take the craft through its paces now it was working at top performance. Right then, though, he just needed the speed and the bird delivered.

However, they were still barely halfway to the site of the fire when Fabian's voice came over the comms, giving them a new destination. The sun was setting in the west when Lewis spotted it. A flare of reflected light off the tip of something metallic. Dipping the nose of the bird downward, Jack shot down towards the ground and sure enough, that was a chopper rotor, broken off and bent, lodged into disturbed dirt on the side of a rise of slope of land around a dam. The path of damage rolled down to the water, leaving debris scattered over torn up grass and sod. At its end, the tail assembly of a large chopper was just visible in the brown water.

Again, the coincidence would be astronomical.

EIGHTEEN

Jack and Lewis got back to Sydney just before midnight and were welcomed by a very sour Lydia, who directed them to McIntosh's office and stared daggers at Jack behind her partner's back.

Great. In trouble with Lydia and on his way to a probable dressing-down from his boss as well. The pit that had opened up in Jack's stomach at the sight of the crashed chopper gaped a little wider. He and Lewis had spent hours searching the crash site, looking for bodies—looking for Ethan—but found nothing. Once the salvage team had arrived, Lewis had convinced Jack they'd done all they could themselves and to return to the city.

Miller, sitting at his desk, looked sleep rumpled and harassed. The glare he laid on Jack and Lewis clearly said he blamed them for being dragged into work at this hour.

"She's expecting you." His cool tone held a hint of glee that their nuts were about to be freeze-dried and used as earrings.

"Sit," Donna McIntosh said as they entered.

The chill in the word sent a shiver down Jack's spine, and Lewis's judging by the little shake of his shoulders. They sat.

The director regarded them over the top of her tortoiseshell rimmed glasses, her blue eyes glacial, then she looked back at the screen beside her, angled so they couldn't see what was on it. "You've both had a rather surprisingly busy day. Especially since you, Jack, aren't even supposed to be at work, and you, Lewis, are supposedly working on an arms smuggling case."

"Ma'am—" they both attempted and cut off the moment she looked up from her screen.

"I don't need excuses, gentlemen." There was no warming of her gaze, but her tone did soften slightly. "I'm happy your family is safe,

Jack, and we're organising a more long-term residence for them right now. I've also authorised the use of the Kamov and Lewis's interactions with law enforcement. I'm sure I don't have to remind either of you that I am not fond of retroactively approving the actions of *my* assets."

"No, ma'am."

"The capture of a Cabal assassin is the only thing keeping both of you from being suspended. As it is, we will *all* be justifying today's events for a long time to come. Jack, since you seem well enough, I'm rescinding the remainder of your recovery leave. As of this morning, you were back on active duty. I expect you back here at 8 a.m. for a full debrief. Lewis, since Lydia assures me you're not vital to the arms smuggling case right now, you're reassigned to work with Jack on the assassin."

"Yes, ma'am." Lewis didn't look relieved because he still had to face Lydia in the privacy of their own home.

"Has anyone spoken to the assassin?" Jack asked as McIntosh waved for them to leave.

"Not yet. They only finished processing her a couple of hours ago. Designation Sigma."

So it would be another several hours before they tried to talk to her. Enough time to let her new situation fully sink in. Time to test the security if she wanted and to learn there was no escaping.

"Will I be given access?"

"If she proves as difficult as Omega Subject, I'm sure we'll have to try everything."

They left, dodged Miller's death stare and headed to the stairwell.

"Could have been worse," Jack said.

"Could have had a few more hugs and 'job well dones,' too."

Jack snorted in agreement, but they both knew how lucky they'd been.

Lydia was waiting in the garage at her car. She forced a smile when they explained how the meeting went, assured Lewis she could handle their current case, and even gave Jack a sympathetic hug.

"Do you want to come to ours tonight?" she asked.

Jack had been mostly numb since his visit with his father but Lydia's concern threatened to thaw out feelings he wasn't quite ready to deal with, so he shook his head, got into Victoria, and went home.

Which surprised him when he ended up at the penthouse. Ethan had always insisted it was *their* place but without him there, it felt a bit weird to show up in the wee small hours. That shock combined with seeing what had appeared next to his Ninja so that he almost drove the Vanquish into the wall. Stopping just in time, Jack sat for a moment and stared at the white covered shape with a huge red bow on the front.

Slowly, Jack got out and circled the new bike hesitantly. It had to be from Ethan. Jack's birthday present. The man had been hinting at it—badly—for the past week and Jack had pretended to be annoyed by it while desperately eager to see what could make Ethan smirk and tease. This was it. It had to be. A bike, but a special one, and not just because it bulked bigger than the Ninja next to it. But because it was from Ethan. His first gift to Jack, and possibly his last.

Jack's fingers itched to touch it, to lift the cover and see what Ethan had chosen for him. He couldn't do it, though. Not with Ethan somewhere out there doing something Jack couldn't fathom. Knowing would end it. Knowing would mean Ethan wouldn't be able to surprise him again. Knowing would mean Jack accepted that Ethan had walked away from him, for good.

He left the cover on the mystery bike and went up to the penthouse, but the moment he stepped foot inside, he knew he couldn't stay. Despite Ethan's assurances, without him here it didn't feel like Jack's place anymore. Most of his junk was still at the Leichhardt apartment, but the important things had been brought over. His medals, the photo of his parents, Mati's card from thirteen years ago . . . that was it. That didn't feel pathetic at all.

Recognising the direction his thoughts were going in, Jack dropped Ethan's keys in the bowl, picked up his own and, on the Ninja, went back to his old place.

He didn't sleep well, or much at all, and in the morning encountered Rocco Cesare in the hallway. At his elderly neighbour's feet was a subdued Short Round, looking up at Jack with huge black eyes.

"Morning, Mr. Cesare." Jack was genuinely pleased to see him. "How have you been?"

"Good, good." He smiled fondly down at his dog. "Better since Short Round came home."

Jack crouched and let Shorty nuzzle his hand before scratching his head. "And how have you been, Shorty?"

"Bit quiet since . . . well, since then," Mr. Cesare answered for his dog. "But the vet gave him a clean bill of health and his appetite has certainly recovered. Which reminds me, did you pay his vet bills?"

Looking up in surprise, Jack shook his head. "No."

Mr. Cesare frowned. "Well, I wonder who did then. When I picked him up they explained that someone had already settled the bill."

Shorty nudged Jack's hand and he patted the dog while he digested that information. "Ethan."

"Yes, of course." His neighbour's frown didn't shift. "I haven't seen either of you lately. Are things okay with you boys?"

"Well, they were." Jack couldn't meet his gaze, focusing instead on Shorty, who swooned under his hand. "We're . . . um . . . he's gone."

Mr. Cesare squeezed his shoulder. "Son, I'm very sorry to hear that. I really liked your young man. I hope you can work it out."

If Ethan wasn't trapped at the bottom of a dam under a chopper, Jack hoped so, too.

They walked together to the end of the hall where Jack took the stairs down and Mr. Cesare and Shorty got into the lift. Jack was glad he'd spoken with his neighbour, to know he was okay and that Shorty had recovered. And that Ethan had reverted to his usual sneaky tactics to make sure Mr. Cesare wasn't out of pocket for something Ethan likely blamed himself for.

When he reached the Office, it was to news that the chopper wreck had been hauled out overnight and Ethan's body hadn't been inside. They would dredge the dam but Jack was starting to believe Ethan had escaped and was alive. Which meant he was possibly wandering around somewhere in the vast open spaces, maybe hurt, probably alone. Trusting the organisation of search parties to Lewis, Jack went to find out whatever he could from the female assassin.

He met McIntosh in an observation room on the sublevel with the cells and as they stood before a screen showing an image of a cell interior, Jack flashed back to this almost exact same situation a year ago. Then, it had been Ethan in the cell and Jack had a mental filing cabinet full of secrets that were slowly haemorrhaging right in front of his director. This time, she knew as much as he did and yet he still felt nervous around her. Probably because the Arctic mood of the previous night hadn't totally defrosted.

"She's proving to be as uncommunicative as Blade was." McIntosh watched the woman in the cell.

The assassin sat at the table, hands resting on its top, neatly folded together. Her head was slightly bowed so she appeared to be looking at her hands. The blonde hair Jack remembered being long and bouncy had been cut to just below her shoulders and curled stubbornly about the sides of her face. The light in the cell was low enough she didn't need glasses and her eyes were large and framed in fine lashes. She had clear, smooth skin, a jaw squarer than it was narrow, and beautifully shaped lips.

"I'm hoping you can work your particular charm on her." McIntosh turned to Jack. "Her capture might not have been as sublime as Blade walking into this building and surrendering himself, but it was remarkably easy. You were factors in both of those incidents. Let's see if it continues."

In the moment, Jack wouldn't have called the assassin's capture too easy, but afterwards, he'd been able to see how and where it could have gone much worse. If the woman had really wanted to kill Mati and her friend, then she would have found a more effective means than a car chase.

"I'll do what I can, ma'am. What about the implant?" They hadn't known about Ethan's when it had been him in there and hadn't countered it.

"The techs disabled hers during processing. After our first encounter with a Cabal assassin, we're not taking any chances this time. Even if she had intel in the implant we could have used."

Jack nodded. Ethan had imported several malware programs on his first visit to the Office, which had fed information out of their supposedly secure network and right to the woman sitting in the cell. She'd been the one to actually parse it to find the evidence that sent the previous Intelligence director off to a highly secure secret prison.

"No bribes this time, Jack." A wry hint of caution warmed McIntosh's tone slightly.

"No, ma'am." He managed a weak smile, then went to talk to yet another assassin.

Once inside the cell, Jack hesitated. At least with Ethan, he'd had some sort of idea how things might progress. Sure, Jack had worried that all those secrets he'd been holding tight might be exposed, but he'd had history with Ethan. Knew Ethan wouldn't attack him. Or at least, was pretty sure he wouldn't. His only prior interaction with this woman had been a brief one a year before, where she hadn't been too complimentary about Jack being with Ethan.

And Ethan may have put a target on Jack but this woman had put them on two innocent kids, one of them his niece.

"Hi," he began, tone neutral.

The woman turned around. "Good morning."

At their first meeting, she'd used an Australian accent. Jack hadn't paid it much attention, too surprised to find a big sister attitude in the way she spoke to Ethan, and that she too was a Sugar Baby. Now, he both was and wasn't shocked to hear an accent very similar to Ethan's. British, classy and mildly condescending.

Wanting this to go as smoothly as possible, Jack asked, "What would you like me to call you?"

She regarded him for a long moment, expression not changing but the intensity increasing. He'd felt that from Ethan at the start of their relationship. That predatory weight, of being sized up, assessed, and then filed away under whichever target classification he fit into. He hoped it was "not easy, approach with extreme caution," but doubted it.

"Seven."

Jack blinked in surprise. He'd been expecting a fake name, a shield she could hide behind. "Like Ethan was Thirteen, or One-three."

"Yes, exactly like that." There were definite tones of contempt this time. Jack almost flashed back to Meera when they were teenagers.

"Let's sit." He took the chair she hadn't been using and waited for her to return to the table. "I'm sure you know who I am."

White eyes, so like Ethan's, but also nothing like his, narrowed. "Yes."

"Good. I just have to make this official before we can start chatting." Jack ran through the usual spiel for the recordings. Then he got to the potentially interesting things. "Please state your name, age, and occupation."

"Seven, thirty-six at best guess, and assassin."

"At best guess?"

Seven's gaze went over his shoulder. "Celebrating birthdays wasn't a thing where I grew up."

Ethan had already revealed that nugget to Jack. "No, I suppose not."

That got her attention focused on him again. "He's been telling you things he really shouldn't."

Presuming "he" to be Ethan, Jack shrugged. "Whether or not he shouldn't is a matter of perspective, I guess. For the record, I'm glad he told me. It's only going to help us"—he motioned between himself and her—"have a more cooperative experience. I know your history, sort of, and you know I have a sympathetic understanding of it."

No reaction from Seven, but he hadn't really expected one.

"First things first, tell me about the job involving my sister and niece."

"You and your family have been on our soft list since you showed up in the middle of the Valadian job. I did the initial research on you for it. Until it was decided Valadian would respond more favourably to a male than a female, it was my job."

Had this woman been sent in instead of Ethan, Director Harraway would still have been exposed as the traitor he was, but Jack doubted he would have been there to see it. Ethan had never said so, but Jack knew he wasn't supposed to have survived once Ethan had discovered if Jack was the traitor or not. If it had been Seven, Jack wouldn't have been able to change her mind with mind-blowing sex.

"None of us particularly liked how One-three changed after he met you, but neither did we care. Well, most of us, at least."

The wound in Jack's back twinged. Two had believed he was cutting into a kidney in the hopes it would make Jack bleed out quicker. Either Seven's research had missed the fact he'd lost the kidney years before, or Two hadn't read that far.

"The Cabal, however," she continued, "were less than pleased. Their targets are usually world leaders, presidents and warlords. It's not often they concern themselves with a mere spy. Congratulations, Jack Reardon, you're now of great interest to the Cabal."

NINETEEN

Fan-fucking-tastic. Jack's guts tightened at the prospect of the mysterious Cabal taking an unhealthy interest in him. Before he could fully comprehend the weight suddenly on his shoulders, Seven continued.

"Two was their pride and joy. In terms of obedience, effectiveness and ruthlessness, he was the most successful of us. And you took him away from them."

Was there bitterness in her tone when she spoke of how the Cabal thought of Two? He could understand if there was. Only yesterday Meera had said pretty much the same thing to him about their father favouring Jack over her, and he definitely knew there was bitterness *there*.

"So sending you after my family was retaliation for Two's death?"

About to shake her head, Seven stopped and seemingly considered it. "Perhaps. My instructions were to get into position and hold for the go, or if it looked as if there had been a tip off, to go anyway. They could have been relying on One-three getting a message to you somehow."

"And when I showed up, you went into action."

Seven nodded.

"But you weren't serious about it, where you." Jack decided to go out on a limb. "I've a got a pretty good idea on how you guys operate and chasing a pair of kids on a dirt bike isn't really your MO. It's not efficient or overly effective."

"I misjudged," she said dryly.

Which was as good as an admission as far as Jack was concerned. "Okay. Why do you think you misjudged?"

Seven met his gaze for several heartbeats, then she looked away and murmured, "I'm tired."

"Pardon?" Jack had to make sure he'd heard her right. "You're tired? Of what?"

A flicker of some emotion passed over Seven's face, pinching her pale brows and tightening her lips. Then, as if letting something go, she let out a long breath, her shoulders dropping a little and her hands, previously resting flat on the tabletop, curled together.

"I'm sure you know we weren't given a choice. We didn't even know life could be different, until One-three came among us. He was this weird, confusing, blind little *thing* with strange ideas and a penchant for touching. Not in anger or to hurt, but in curiosity. Because he wanted to *see* us. It was, I believe, the first kind touch any of us had ever known. We all reacted differently. Two became obsessed with him, Four used him to get sweets, Nine thought he was funny, but then she thought we were all funny. Eleven . . . Eleven was scared of him. Of being him, I think. One, though. She hated him as she'd hated nothing else before. She was used to controlling us, to being the alpha, I suppose. One-three wasn't a threat to her but she couldn't see it. One way or another, he changed us. Changed the dynamic. He was a catalyst."

Jack hadn't expected much, let alone so many personal revelations. He kept quiet, not wanting to interrupt this surprising source of unfettered information, but also because he felt any words he might have would be insufficient. Seven had gone after his niece, no matter her overall intentions, but he felt a sympathy for her his better judgement couldn't stop. It had made him follow Ethan through the desert, made Jack listen to him and want to get to know him, and it was happening again.

"Because that's what we were." Seven's words steadied up as she shifted the topic to something slightly less personal. "Ingredients in an experiment. They wanted to know if Sugar Babies really were born as psychopaths, and if not, were we more susceptible to being *made* psychopaths. They didn't hide it from us. They told us every day what we were. It wasn't just the numbers they gave us as names, but that they called us Experimental Girl Seven, or Experimental Boy Two."

Stomach dropping into his shoes, Jack fought the urge to swear and hit something. Experimental Boy Thirteen. EB13.

"They thought it was funny when we began running jobs in the outside world to give us operational names with the same initials. Eve Garrotte. Ethan Blade. Just another reminder about who we were, how they had created us, and still controlled us."

God. And Jack had been calling Ethan *that* for all this time. How had he let Jack do that? Jack believed Ethan had been honest when saying he wanted to be the "Ethan" Jack saw, but it must have been torture at first. How had Ethan really felt hearing Jack groan the name in ecstasy when it had been a cruel *joke*?

Jack forced the personal crisis into the filing cabinet. "Ethan said he broke from the Cabal at one point. How did they deal with that?"

Seven shook her head minutely. "One-three might have believed he *broke* away, but he didn't. Not really. He simply refused to take the jobs they gave him until they agreed to negotiate with him. Letting him pick and chose jobs meant little in the end to them. And when he began taking outside jobs and making money above what the Cabal gave us and he wasn't punished . . ." Her lips turned up in a smile that reminded Jack of Ethan's deadly smirk. "Well, then we all started making our own money."

The hidden house in northern Vietnam had certainly cost more than a few pretty pennies, and he had the feeling this woman wouldn't be spending her money on fast cars. From what Jack could guess, Ethan had lairs in several countries and they were probably like the one he'd had in Sydney, a converted warehouse where he could house his car of choice. Seven, though, had created a beautiful, secluded haven for herself with one of the most gorgeous—and isolating— views Jack had ever seen. She painted and played the piano and kept the world at a distance. Yet she was here by choice, talking without coercion or force.

He did wonder if perhaps it was all subterfuge. How could he not when Ethan had done it over and over? These assassins had proven to be particularly tricky, even the one he thought he knew better than anyone else.

"You didn't misjudge," Jack said softly. "You wanted to be caught. You wanted to be here. Why, Seven? Why all but give yourself to the enemy? I know why Ethan did it, both times, but I don't know about you."

The remains of her smirk fell away, leaving an expressionless mask Jack had to wonder about. Something made him think it wasn't a mask at all. The smile had been a mask, definitely, but he wasn't so sure this expression was. Unlike Ethan, Seven had no memories of a long-gone mother to judge humanity from. She was a pure result of whatever experiments the Cabal had put these unfortunate children through. Seven might remind him strongly of Ethan but he couldn't assess her the same way. Couldn't let himself fall into the same trap he had with Ethan. He had no clues that under the cold-hearted killer shell was a person he could relate to.

He pushed on with his theory. "I don't think you're here because the Cabal wants you here. The first time Ethan was here, it was for the Cabal. The second time, it was for him. I think you're here for you."

The blank expression didn't change and that predatory intensity increased. "I misjudged and you caught me."

"We can certainly put that in the official report, Seven, but if you let us know exactly why you're here, we'll be able to help each other much more efficiently."

The silence stretched out between them. Ethan could out-patience a saint, and Seven undoubtedly could as well, but Jack felt she wanted to tell him. Maybe he was transferring his experiences with Ethan onto her, but the absolute stillness of the woman was too similar to Ethan's to be coincidental, surely.

"He said you *saw* him."

Jack didn't react to the abrupt words. "What does that mean?"

"One-three said . . . *Ethan* said you saw him. Not the assassin or the Sugar Baby, but the man. The person. He said . . . you'd see me too, if I gave you the chance."

Swallowing a sudden lump in his throat, Jack nodded. "When did he tell you that?"

"Six months ago, in Vietnam, while we cleaned up the mess you left."

Some life had returned to her tone and Jack gave a little shrug acknowledging the sarcasm. "He's right, up to a point. If Mati had been hurt, I'd say your chances would have been a lot slimmer. Okay, that explains you being *here*, but I want to know *why*. Why you chose to be caught. Why you didn't come in six months ago if you knew I'd treat you fairly. Why come in and why now, Seven?"

"It was what they taught us. To finish the job first, to ensure our own survival second. I'm here to survive, Mr. Reardon. I want your protection."

He blinked. "You want us to protect you? From the Cabal? Frankly, you'd probably have a better chance on your own out there."

She shook her head. "I don't care about the Cabal. If they want me dead, they'll kill me no matter where I am."

"Then who's got you scared for your life?"

"Isn't it obvious?" She smiled sadly. "The moment the Cabal went after you or your family, directly, he decided enough was enough. I always knew it would happen one day, but I never thought it would be because of someone like you."

Jack's blood went cold. "What do you mean?"

"I want you to make sure that Ethan Blade doesn't kill me when he destroys the Cabal."

THE HEARING

Jack's throat was getting dry and he worked up some saliva to wet it as the review board whispered amongst themselves. They'd been mostly quiet during his detailed report apart from a few clarifying questions here and there. Assistant Minister Greene had been keen to pursue the dollar figure attached to putting Meera and Mati into protective custody for three months. His argument that, bar the original incident with Seven, there had been no further threats towards them was valid, up to a point. A point which DIC Lund defended, thankfully. He'd signed off on the protection, after all. Minister Simmons had ended the potential side-track by assuring Greene that the budget hearing was already underway in another part of the building. They were here to primarily decide if Jack needed disciplinary action.

"I understand that Sigma Subject was very forthcoming with information." There was more than a touch of scepticism in Simmons's tone. "After everything we learned about these assassins, excuse me if I find her sudden willingness to spill about the Cabal rather dubious."

"Yes, sir, and you're not the only one to question Seven's motives. We all did. Me especially. She was convinced Ethan was going to go after the Cabal, but the investigation into the helicopter crash turned up evidence of him coming back to Sydney, before disappearing."

Jack had to curl his hands into fists under the desk and dig his short nails into his palms to keep from letting his emotions show. In the days after discovering the crashed chopper and the first interview with Seven, Fabian had continued to turn up hints of Ethan—a classic Monaro stolen from a property 150 kilometres from the dam; hints of him on the CCTV cameras around the penthouse building; a stolen Nisan GT-R, later spotted on traffic cameras just down the block from Jack's Leichhardt apartment. Mr. Cesare had also confessed he'd spoken with Ethan during that time. He'd assured Jack he'd tried to convince Ethan to go back to him, but it clearly hadn't worked.

Ethan had been so close to Jack and yet he'd left—again. At least Jack had had Mr. Cesare's word that he seemed hale, if emotionally distraught.

"At which point directors Tan, McIntosh and Wells created an interdepartmental team to investigate the validity of Sigma Subject's intelligence," Simmons continued. "ITA unit leader Lewis Thomas, joint field leaders, yourself from ITA and Keira O'Reilly from ETA, and special investigator Jesse Feitt from Intelligence. A rather impressive group, all of whom were taken off other cases to initiate an investigation which failed rather spectacularly on all fronts."

Jack took several deep breaths to calm down. "We didn't fail, sir."

Simmons waved a thick file of papers. "I have here summaries of four weeks of data gathering that didn't find Ethan Blade in time to save lives. That, in my book, is a failure."

"With all due respect, sir"—of which Jack couldn't find much to begin with and even less now—"finding Ethan was tangential to our mandated goal. We were tasked with finding as much information on the Cabal as we could, using Seven's intelligence as a starting point. One month is barely enough time to scratch even the surface of what she knows, and she doesn't know everything about them. None of the assassins did. They had one contact point with the Cabal, their handler, Zero. He gave them jobs and was their conduit to the Cabal leaders. Everything else Seven knew, she'd worked out on her own. It's a lot of information, but nowhere near everything. One month isn't enough time to confirm the sky is blue when the source is suspect," Jack reiterated. "Someone once said to me that if the Office wasn't aware of it for at least two years, then it was a big fucking surprise."

The moment it was out of his mouth, Jack regretted it. Simmons had made him lose his cool already, and they still had a long way to go.

At least no one tried to chastise him like a naughty child for swearing, but Simmons did raise a warning brow in his direction. "And what, briefly, did Sigma Subject have to say about the Cabal leadership?"

Jack took a moment to modulate his attitude again. "She called them the 'bosses.' No one but Zero and a very small number of trusted allies know who they are. She worked out there were five of them. Sometimes fewer when one of them died, either naturally or unnaturally, but never more than that. Voluntary retirement isn't a thing for them, apparently. Once you're a boss, you're a boss for the rest of your life. Or at least, that's what Seven speculated. Nothing we discovered countered her intelligence."

"Hmm. She worked out all that, but not one hint as to whom the bosses were."

Ignoring the cynicism in Simmons's words, Jack nodded. "She is a very skilled hacker and incredibly intuitive. Given more time and our resources, I'm sure Seven could have pinpointed the bosses within a couple of years."

"Quite apart from the fact that we would never have allowed that woman near our resources, she didn't get that time, did she, Mr. Reardon." Not waiting for Jack to agree, Simmons barrelled on. "Four weeks after disappearing from Australia, Ethan Blade made the first of five high level assassinations over a period of two months. All of which your vaunted team failed to prevent. Or did I read the reports wrong?"

Jack gritted his teeth. "No, sir."

"Even when you predicted who his next victim was, you still didn't save their life. Isn't that what you're supposed to do, Mr. Reardon? Protect lives from threats exactly like Ethan Blade?"

Anger bubbled close to the surface, tightening Jack's whole body and making blood rush through his head. "That's my cover job with the ISO."

"At which I'm assured you're very good. Except when it comes to hunting down your boyfriend as he left a trail of bloody corpses across half of the world. Why was that?"

It still hurt Jack to think about what Ethan did in those three months after leaving Australia. According to Mr. Cesare, he'd been in a troubled state of mind, in pain, and not long later, he'd started killing again. And not with the usual subtle and flawless plans Ethan was known for, but straight assaults with signs of interrogation, even if the eventual deaths had his trademark swiftness.

"He was operating at a level we . . . *I* hadn't seen before. Ethan Blade sat at number seven on the John Smith List for years, a mid to high-level threat. What he showed us over those next two months was more than enough to put him in the number one position. No intelligence agency anywhere has ever knowingly caught or killed the JSL number one."

Simmons leaned back in his chair, fingers steepled under his chin. "And why do you think he suddenly showed that level of skill after years of pretending to be mediocre at his chosen profession?"

Chosen? Jack bit back the snarl that word inspired. It was a clear provocation from Simmons to incite Jack into something stupid. Something Simmons could use to discredit him, and that would make everything they'd worked for worthless.

"Number seven on the JSL isn't mediocre," Jack said instead. "But what changed for Ethan this time was that he wasn't working for the Cabal in any capacity. This time, it was personal."

TWENTY

"**P**ersonal? How so?" Simmons asked.

"Frankly, sir, because I and my family had been put in danger by the Cabal. But since I know that won't be enough proof for you, if you care to look at the images attached to each of the assassination files, you'll note something similar at each scene."

Simmons scowled. "I've seen what you're referring to. A bloody EB marked at each scene. Ethan Blade. I don't see how that will convince me of anything other than his guilt."

"His guilt isn't in question, sir." A little thrill went through Jack as he got to feed Simmons some of his own bitter medicine. "His motive is. And it wasn't EB, but EB13. Not Ethan Blade, but Experimental Boy Thirteen. That's what the Cabal designated him. EB13 is a message to the Cabal, letting them know he's coming for them. The only other time EB13 was found at an assassination, it was a Liechtenstein duchess who'd taken a ticket out on Ethan."

Apparently unable to find a suitably demeaning response to that, Simmons moved on. "Take us through the victims of Ethan's personal revenge campaign, Mr. Reardon."

For this, Jack had to refer to his notes, so he used the time it took to take them from his case to shove as much of his personal feelings into the filing cabinet. Not everything got in there by the time he was ready, but he'd just have to deal with the rest on the fly.

"To be absolutely clear, we don't believe these victims had hurt Ethan personally, only that they were steppingstones on the way to discovering who the bosses are," Jack explained. "The first victim was Franco Sosa. Argentinian. He was a CEO of an up and coming R&D tech company. Killed in his bedroom in his mansion in Córdoba. Single gunshot wound to the head. No witnesses at all.

It turns out he had under-the-table ties to the next victim, Paulo Oliveira, Brazilian foreign trade minister. Poisoned while attending a symposium in Halifax, Nova Scotia."

"I understand you believed you were close to catching Ethan in Canada," Simmons mused.

"I thought we had a good chance. Thanks to the symposium there was a lot of extra security on site and even as we flew up from South America, other agencies were closing in on him. However, he slipped through their net and left via a boat and, as best as can be determined, landed on the Maine coast."

"And while he disappeared into the US, you spent a further week in Nova Scotia."

Jack ignored the blatant patronising tone. "Yes, sir. The FBI were on Ethan's trail in the US, as were the CIA, I believe, though they claim otherwise." With no authority to work on domestic soil, the CIA had kept their part in the hunt very quiet. As had MI6 and the Russian SVR. "We remained in Nova Scotia to confirm the intelligence we had on Oliveira. The minister had connections to several suspect organisations across South America, which, very quickly after his death, began to fall apart thanks to internal upset. We're still tracing connections, but it is highly likely that these organisations were all, in part or fully, controlled by the Cabal through Oliveira. Once he was gone, the lines of communication broke down and things disintegrated."

The trail had gone cold after that. Jack had suspected Ethan was too busy avoiding all the letter agencies chasing him across North America. Unable to justify their presence overseas, Jack and the field team had returned home. Three weeks later, a Russian dignitary "fell" off a yacht in the Bahamas.

"I understand there wasn't enough evidence to link it to other deaths," Simmons said.

"There was some doubt about the validity of the 'EB13' found at the scene. The team and I believed it was real, but Director McIntosh wouldn't approve the travel." Jack had thought he could depend on McIntosh to listen impartially and trust his instincts, yet she'd not only stopped him from going to the Bahamas, but then stopped communicating with him altogether. It still stung, but there was little point worrying about it now.

"I can only assume that Ms. McIntosh's leave of absence was a relief for you."

That bland statement almost did what nothing else today had—get Jack to forget why they were here and launch himself at the minister. Yes, McIntosh's seeming disregard for Jack's instincts had hurt, but fuck Simmons if he thought he was going to use it against him.

"No, sir, it was not."

Simmons cocked a sceptical brow. "Not even with the appointment of your friend, Lewis Thomas, to the position of acting director? Wasn't one of his first actions to authorise your visit to the Bahamas?"

Jack took a moment to settle his stomach. Yes, it had felt like a boon when Lewis was promoted, even temporarily. They'd celebrated, Lewis had disappeared for a week of training and Lydia had taken over as unit leader of their team. Despite working together for years, and being a couple for nearly as long, Lewis and Lydia did not have the same leadership style. Lewis's philosophy was to live and let live. Lydia's was not. Between them, they ran one of the most successful teams in the entire Office. Separately, it wasn't quite the well-oiled machine it had been. Information hadn't flowed smoothly, causing their investigation to stumble in the Bahamas and after. A lot of the blame had been put on Lewis's shoulders as he trial-and-errored his way into his new role, but they knew now that intelligence-sharing had once again been stymied from inside the Office.

"Yes, sir. We did confirm the victim as one of Ethan's. The trail led back to several *bratva* groups in Russia, a couple with tenuous links to organised crime in Europe and China. The Office had already linked Cabal activities to Hong Kong triads and mainland black societies, but at the time we hadn't realised the mysterious group at the end of the trail was the Cabal. If you wish to insinuate I used my personal connection to Lewis to further my own agenda, sir, you should also remember that as *acting* director, Lewis had to filter most of his decisions through Directors Tan and Wells. And DIC Lund would have surely stopped anything that wasn't appropriate. In fact, sir, isn't that why DIC Lund is allowed to be part of this review board? Because there was no actual misconduct on Lewis Thomas's part in anything that happened."

Lund leaned forward to speak, but Simmons beat him to it.

"Need I remind you, Mr. Reardon, that this hearing is about *your* conduct, not Mr. Thomas's or anyone else's?"

"No, sir, you don't."

"As I shouldn't. Just as I shouldn't have to remind you of the severity of your actions. Or that two of the Office's most valuable assets are dead as a direct result of them."

Jack cringed and his chest tightened. "Of course not, sir." Jack forced his fists to relax. They had a long, long way to go before he could do anything other than let this man walk all over him.

Director Chan leaned over to Lund and whispered in his ear. The DIC nodded and in turn, spoke quietly to the minister.

"I'm fine to continue," Simmons said loud enough for Jack to hear clearly, "but if you feel it's necessary."

"Thank you, minister." Lund stood and nodded to Jack. "We'll break for fifteen minutes. Go stretch your legs."

The board left by a door at the back of the room and Jack by the one he'd entered through. He was getting a bottle of water from a vending machine when Lewis found him.

"I suppose it's too much to hope it's over?" his friend asked as the plastic bottle clunked down into the bottom of the machine.

Jack snorted and retrieved his drink. "Not by half. Fuck Simmons. Does he even know how to read? I'm pretty much just reciting the reports he's had for how long now?" He had a long drink to sooth his parched throat.

"Don't let it get to you. It's all a dog and pony show anyway. They've made their decisions already, before we were even called up for these hearings."

Agreeing with a wry nod, Jack looked his friend over carefully. "How are you doing?"

Lewis wore a dark suit, the strap of a satchel filled with his own reports slung across his chest. There were dark shadows under his eyes and his hair was messy, as if he'd been running his hands through it. Which he proved by doing again.

"My torture session hasn't even started yet. Apparently my inquisitor is 'held up in a meeting.'" His air quotes were about as sarcastic as they could be. "Because I've got nothing better to do than hang around this place all day waiting to justify myself to someone who can only get it up for a dollar sign."

Jack smiled, though it was as weak as his mate's attempt at humour. "I didn't mean this here. I meant . . . you know."

Lewis shoved his hands in his pockets and shrugged. "I'm getting there? It's just taking some getting used to, I guess."

"Yeah." Jack squeezed his shoulder compassionately. "It gets easier."

"So everyone keeps telling me." He shrugged again, then sighed. "I miss her so much."

"I know. Me too." Jack felt terrible. He hadn't been there for Lewis. His friend was hurting—they all were—and Jack knew he should be giving Lewis the support he needed. "Let's go get a drink afterwards. We haven't done that in, fuck, so long."

"Thanks, but it's okay. I know you've got your own things going on." Lewis threw on a ghost of his old grin. "I'll drag Fabes out. He needs to be socialised."

"Lewis Thomas on a bender is not the socialisation that kid needs. Look, let's—"

"Mr. Thomas?" The woman who'd shown Jack to his hearing appeared from a doorway further down. "They're ready for you now."

"I guess someone got a birdie on the ninth hole," Lewis muttered under his breath. "See you later, mate."

Jack sent him off with a nod and a "Good luck."

Ten minutes later, as Jack was pacing back and forth across the hallway, he was called back into his own hearing.

The board were settling back into their seats, murmuring amongst themselves as they set out folders, cups of coffee, and phones. Except for the Quiet Man. He slouched in his chair, working his tongue over his teeth, and watched Jack as he came in and sat down.

"Right." Simmons cast an enquiring look at his fellows at the big desk. "Are we ready to continue?"

The door they'd exited and entered through opened again and that same blonde woman came in. Simmons pushed his chair back slightly as she approached him. She leaned over to talk quietly to him, then handed him a small piece of folded paper. As she left, Simmons unfolded the note, read it, shrugged and handed it over to DIC Lund. The Office director in charge shook his head minutely, then passed it on to Chan.

"We should tell him," Chan said, not too loud but not so quiet Jack couldn't hear her.

"Why?" Simmons pulled his chair back into place. "It has absolutely no bearing on what we're discussing here today."

Dismissed, the note was put aside and the committee turned their full attention back on Jack.

Simmons shuffled through his papers. "Where were we?"

"The Bahamas, sir," Green supplied like the good little sycophant he was.

"Yes, of course. I believe you travelled directly to the Netherlands after the assassination of a Syrian diplomatic attaché in The Hague. Where you remained while Ethan also killed the President of the International Criminal Court. A serious failure on your part, since you predicted Lucas Van Dijk would be the next victim."

"I didn't predict anything." Jack's patience strained. "Van Dijk *was* on a list of potential targets and we were in the midst of assigning extra security to him. We were too slow. Ethan's always managed to stay two or three steps ahead of us. This time, he managed to get into Van Dijk's office, interrogate him, kill him, and get out, all without being seen."

Ethan had seen Jack, though. Couldn't have missed him. It was all there on the CCTV footage they combed through after finding Van Dijk's body. Jack had watched it over and over, replayed the moment in his head. Talking with the head of security of the ICC, less than five meters from the door to the President's office. A team of four security guards marched past on their routine sweep of the floor. The final man in line had been Ethan fucking Blade. An arms-length of space. That was all that had been between them. Ethan had been in disguise but Jack hadn't. He was there in his capacity as an ISO specialist, the best cover they had for getting into the ICC because it was real. There was absolutely no way Ethan would have missed Jack.

Not that Jack had expected Ethan to throw himself into his arms then and there, but he had, foolishly, expected some acknowledgement. A note slipped into a pocket. A gesture caught on camera that Jack could interpret as "I'm okay," or "I'm lost," or "fuck off forever."

But there had been nothing. Just an immense frustration and a growing sense that perhaps Ethan didn't want to be stopped. That he didn't even want Jack's help.

Before Simmons could make a snide comment about any of that disastrous affair, Jack continued. "Van Dijk's death was, however, a massive break for us. It allowed us to pinpoint Ethan's next target. Hermann Jäger, a German national and heir to his family's textile fortune. At first glance, he doesn't seem to fit the bill for a Cabal gold star flunky. He's not in control of his family money, he doesn't hold an influential position and he's not about to inherit a small European country. However, he does occupy his time flying to every corner of the world, supposedly to hobnob with the rich and famous and spark scandals with the daughters of dukes. He's the perfect courier for the Cabal. A messenger boy no one would suspect."

Simmons smirked. "What made you so certain he was Ethan's next target?"

"The fact that Jäger had been seen in the company of Duchess Alessia Banzer of Lichtenstein about ten years ago. He was apparently comforting her over the brutal murder of her riding instructor, and rumoured lover, at the hands of one of her security personnel. Motive enough to take out a ticket on someone even ten years later."

"Supposition on your part only," Simmons reminded him smugly.

"Yes, but it was enough for Lewis, and through him, Director Tan, to authorise us to go after Jäger before Ethan got to him."

"And where did you find him?"

Jack sighed. "In the worst place he could have been right then, considering everything that was happening here with the deputy prime minister." Between that mess and Jack's own feelings about his mother's homeland, it was a wonder he ever agreed to follow the trail. "Jäger was in India. Mumbai, to be precise."

PART THREE
ETHAN & JACK

INDIA

Mumbai in spring wasn't the most pleasant place to be. At least on the waterfront the smog wasn't so bad, given room to escape out across the ocean. However, it didn't lessen the humidity or the heat any, and sweat rolled down the back of Ethan's neck, soaking into the pale blue cotton of his kurta. Likewise, his lower face under the mask was rather warm. He didn't risk taking it off, however, and not just because it helped disguise him. The air pollution alone was enough of a reason for the mask.

He stood at the very tip of Nariman Point, camera hung around his neck and backpack dangling from one shoulder. The camera had photos of all the monuments of note in South Mumbai—the Chhatrapati Shivaji Terminus, Flora Fountain, the Gateway of India. From the majestic arch, he'd walked across the island to here, where he took pictures of the curve of the land around the water with a telephoto lens.

Around him, locals gave him weary side-eye, from the blond hair—a wig he could rapidly ditch if he needed to escape pursuit—to the camera and his scruffy sneakers. He was the very image of a tourist, right down to wearing the kurta over his cargo pants.

Leaving the point, Ethan walked northwards, along Marine Drive, stopping to snap photos every now and then. The sun was sinking over the water, casting a dark gold tinge into his pictures as he made his way to the Oberoi hotel. The white façade and crisp shape of the buildings were muted and softened by the haze of smog, but it was clear this was an exclusive establishment. The hedges were perfectly manicured and the tall windows on the foyer were pristine even in the blanketing pollution. Audis and Mercedes pulled up at the entrance while Ethan watched from across the road. Richly dressed people slid into and out of the expensive cars, returning after a day of sightseeing or business, or going out for the evening. The valet staff flowed around the patrons like award winning ballroom dancers, never in anyone's way and always exactly where they were needed.

Then a familiar sound caught Ethan's attention. A hoarse, gravelly engine that even in low gear conveyed a sense of imminent power and speed. The orange Lamborghini Huracán rolled into the driveway of the Oberoi and eased to an idle at the entrance. Heads turned to look at the low, sleek vehicle. Even at a high priced hotel like this, such a car stood out. The valet's expression was openly lustful when he got out of the supercar, yet the Oberoi had some of the best service in the world and the man's face was schooled into politeness when he handed the keys over to the waiting driver.

Hermann Jäger didn't look much older than the last time Ethan had seen him, although it had been nearly ten years. From a distance, it appeared as if his hair was still golden blond and thick, swept back from his strong brow and high cheekbones in perfect waves. Intense blue eyes that had lingered in Ethan's memory for years were hidden by black sunglasses and his lean frame was stylishly immaculate in a tailored Savile Row suit.

It had felt both surprising and inevitable when Van Dijk had spat out Jäger's name moments before he died. The connection made perfect sense. Ethan had never been able to work out why he and Two had been sent to Duchess Alessia Banzer in Lichtenstein. It had made even less sense when, after it all went haywire, the lady would turn to a German playboy billionaire heir for help. The then thirty-year-old Jäger had swept in and proceeded to clean up the body, calm the hysterical duchess, and generally swan about the place as if he owned it.

Now Ethan knew. Jäger hadn't owned the place, but the woman.

The Huracán glided out of the hotel driveway and into the thick traffic. In his afternoon of watching, Ethan had yet to see the dense traffic ease off at all. At the intersection, the car turned left and was quickly lost in a sea of vehicles.

Ethan hurried across the street and as he ducked between two bushes, discarded the kurta and mask. From his backpack he retrieved a leather jacket and put it on. He kept the camera, made sure the extra lenses for it weren't quite out of sight in the backpack's pockets and exchanged the cheap sunglasses for a pair of Versace wraparounds. Wig artfully tousled, jacket opened wide, showing off the silk shirt stretched tight across his chest, Ethan swaggered into the Oberoi.

Just inside the foyer he stopped and surveyed the open, airy space with a slight pout. In such a crowded city, so much square footage was pure luxury and the Oberoi didn't stint in showing it off. Tall, clear windows flooded the area with natural light, as did the skylights far above. The polished floor was sparsely used by a red grand piano, a statue of ballet dancers, and a few clusters of chairs and coffee tables. It was understated elegance done at its best.

With a dramatic spin, Ethan took in his surroundings, including egress points and potential obstructions—to his own escape and possible pursuit.

"Sir? May I help you?"

Ethan gasped and turned to the speaker, clutching his chest. An elegantly outfitted concierge in a dark blue kurta was standing a couple of feet away, expression politely enquiring.

"Oh my. Yes, darlin', yes, you can help me. Is *this*"—Ethan waved wildly at the foyer around them—"*the* Oberoi hotel? Please tell me it is, because I've been to two different places claiming to be the Oberoi so far today and I'm late. I know I'm late but it couldn't be avoided when there is, like, three different places called Oberoi in this one city."

The Indian man stood stoically in the frantic wash of southern USA-tinged words and didn't react other than to nod politely. "Yes, sir, this is the Oberoi."

"Thank heavens." With a massive sigh, Ethan grabbed the man's arm like it was a life preserver. "Now, if you could just be so good as to call Mr. Jäger and let him know I'm here, I'd love you forever."

Gently extracting his arm, the concierge tilted his head slightly, giving Ethan a very subtle once over. "Is Mr. Jäger expecting you?"

"I should hope so. I'm here to photograph him in your . . ." He sighed as if making a huge sacrifice. "*Stunning* hotel. But as I said, I'm late, so please don't keep him waiting any longer. I'll just be here when you're ready to take me to him." Ethan swept toward one of the chairs in the middle of the foyer and dropped into it as if he'd run a marathon and started fanning himself.

It didn't take long for the concierge to return and inform him that Mr. Jäger wasn't in at the moment. Ethan's declaration that he'd wait for Jäger in his suite was met with polite refusal, so in a show of gracious compromise, Ethan allowed them to book him into the suite next to Jäger's.

The suite was as spacious as the foyer, and as delicately appointed, and the view of Marine Drive as spectacular as promised. Sadly, there was no balcony conveniently adjacent to Jäger's, but after a quick search, Ethan found an access panel to the ceiling crawl space in the bathroom.

Over the next hour, Ethan kept a surreptitious watch on Jäger's suite, while making random demands of room service for drinks and food. He didn't think he'd need the guise of a flighty photographer in order to leave but keeping up the pretence gave him something to do while waiting to see if Jäger would return quickly. He didn't, and when the sun had been down for over an hour, Ethan decided it was time to stop waiting.

Zipping up his leather jacket, which doubled as light, flexible body armour, he hauled himself up into the ceiling and, moving extremely cautiously, crept across to Jäger's suite. Twenty minutes with his ear pressed to the access panel assured him there was no one in the rooms and he carefully opened it and dropped silently into the room.

Jäger's suite was a mirror of Ethan's and he canvased it efficiently, finding himself completely alone. Then he went through the man's luggage, looking for clues about why he was in Mumbai. Of course he found nothing. If Jäger was who Ethan believed him to be, then he would know better than to leave even the smallest hint about his motives.

Ethan found a spot by the windows at the front of the suite where he could see the road outside but not be easily seen in return, and settled in to wait. Two hours later, when the traffic had finally eased off, the orange Lambo returned, disappearing under the canopy at the entrance. Ethan moved to his next position, the ambient light from outside enough for him to see by without his sunglasses.

Pressed to the wall in the sitting room, next to the doorway from the small entryway, Ethan let all of his thoughts and worries go. His instincts were unparalleled, his training etched so deeply into his bones it was almost part of his DNA. The few small niggling injuries he'd accumulated over the past several months faded out of his conscious mind. He couldn't afford to let them slow him down in this fight. Jäger was so close to the end of the line Ethan had to succeed. If his target got away now he'd have to start all over again—and Ethan didn't think he had the reserves to do that.

Three intense months of hunting, stalking and killing had taken their toll. His already spare frame had lost mass, leaving his muscles ropy and even more starkly defined. Yet it wasn't his body Ethan feared for. The hollowing out of his chest that had started as he walked away from the penthouse in Sydney had continued until he felt completely empty inside. All the warmth and fulfillment he'd felt over the past year had vanished as if it had never been—except for that one place under his ribs that still burned hot, a sun sitting in the vacuum of space.

Jack.

Ethan had had to put his lover out of his head in order to get this job done, but he hadn't been able to cut himself off from the man entirely. No matter how far Ethan ran, or what he did, or who he did it to, Jack would always be with him now. The changes he had wrought in Ethan were as indelible as those the Cabal had made, as deeply embedded. At first, he'd allowed himself to long for Jack once a day. Then once every two days, every three days, then once a week. Distance between didn't lessen the pain, rather seemed to intensify it, until in The Hague Ethan had nearly forgotten why he was doing this.

Jack had been so close Ethan could have lifted a hand and brushed it across his back, like he'd done hundreds of times before. A light trail of his fingers over that broad, hard surface as he moved past Jack in the kitchen, or in the shower, or as they lay together in bed, Jack snoring and oblivious as Ethan explored him in wonderment. He knew that back so well it had been almost as if he could see Jack's St. Thomas Cross tattoo through the material of his ISO jacket and shirt.

All it had taken to stop him was the reminder of his knife sliding into Four's body. Of watching Ten's chest to ensure he didn't draw breath. Of the uncertainty of Seven's wellbeing. That's why he was doing this, not for Jack or himself, but to make sure his siblings' torturers were punished.

The click of the key card in the door's lock snapped Ethan back to the present and focused him on the immediate threat. The door opened, someone stepped in, and then closed the door. Three long strides brought the person down the entryway and into the living area.

It was the steps that told Ethan this wasn't Jäger. The man wasn't that tall. Then a hand appeared and he froze.

Brown skin. Long fingers. Blunt nails.

Ethan grabbed the wrist and pulled, then hooked a foot around the man's forward leg and swept it out from under him.

Even as Ten started to fall, he twisted and pulled Ethan over, both of them crashing to the floor. Rolling, Ethan hit the credenza against the wall. A vase of fresh flowers toppled over. Catching it, Ethan tossed it at Ten, who deflected it with a forearm so it smashed against the wall, then lunged after him. Ten piled on top of Ethan and they rolled, hitting the credenza again. A tray of cut crystal tumblers and a decanter of liqueur rattled but didn't fall. Trapped between Ten and the furniture, Ethan didn't have much room, but he slammed a fist into Ten's ribs twice with as much power as he could. Ten grunted and reared back, lips pulled away from his teeth in a vicious snarl. Ethan thrust the heel of his palm up and into Ten's face, hoping to break his nose and perhaps shove shards of bone and cartilage into his brain.

Ten dodged the blow and got an arm around Ethan's neck. He hauled Ethan up into a sitting position, swung around him and, forearm pressing on his throat, leaned backwards. Air cut off, Ethan scrambled at the floor, seeking the shards of the broken vase. The moment his fingers found wet ceramic, he grabbed it and slashed at Ten's arm. Ten let him go and shoved backwards.

Ethan threw himself forwards, tumbling over one shoulder and coming up to his feet. Ten was also up and came at him without a pause, forcing Ethan into the corner. Grabbed from behind, Ethan leaned back into the other man and ran his feet up the wall. Kicking off, he flipped over Ten, breaking his hold. He landed and skipped backwards as Ten spun and attacked again. Ethan threw up arms and knees to keep Ten from landing a blow on his core. They moved into the open area of the suite, between the grand piano and office desk with a view of the ocean through a wide window.

"They're not going to let you keep going, One-three," Ten said calmly, dodging a spinning kick. "They know you're coming."

"I made no secret of it." Ethan snatched a folded blanket off the back of a couch and snapped it out at Ten's face.

Dodging the material, Ten shifted right into Ethan's kick. He flew sideways, staggering into the desk. A lamp crashed to the floor. Ethan lunged for him, but Ten slid along the length of the desk, before sitting on the corner and spinning on the polished surface. Ethan threw himself out of range of the boots aimed at his chest, and Ten came after him.

"How did you escape the chopper?" Ethan followed the words with a fast series of punches to his ribs.

Ten grunted and broke off, dodging around a plush armchair, keeping it between them as Ethan circled.

"You're too quick to run, little brother," Ten said in his flat tone. "The water brought me round and I found an air-pocket which kept me alive until I found an exit." He traced a new scar running from under his hairline and down his right temple. "You left me with this souvenir." He jumped onto the chair, tipping it over backwards and riding it down. Using the momentum, he launched himself at Ethan.

Ethan met him, fist driving for his exposed side. Ten threw an arm up, shoving the strike high, delivered a solid blow to Ethan's guts, then spun. He wrapped his arm around Ethan's wrist, wrenching it around behind him.

Going with the turn, Ethan jumped and landed on his brother's back. Ten fell forwards and Ethan propelled himself into a tumble over his head. Flipping to his feet, he delivered double-barrelled kicks right into Ten's face.

Blood splattered the floor as Ten scrambled away. Ethan pursued him.

"Where's Jäger?" he demanded, keeping his brother on the defensive.

"You won't find him." Ten spat bloody phlegm. "The bosses wanted him brought in."

The bosses of the Cabal. Ethan's ultimate targets.

"Let it go." Ten angled around until he faced the view from the corner suite.

Back to the scenery, Ethan loosened his limbs, readying for the charge. "I can't. They have to end. What they did to us was wrong. It was cruel and they had no right." He may as well have been talking to a brick wall for all that Ten would understand.

Blood dripping from his nostrils, Ten was as blank as if Ethan had been talking about how pleasant the weather was.

Ethan hurt. Not just from Ten's blows or his strained muscles. He hurt in his chest. He'd spent the last three months believing he'd killed all of his remaining brothers, that he'd left his only living sister to the mercy of the Office. And yet, here was Ten. Alive. And it hurt to know he would have to kill this cold, distant man all over again.

Why couldn't this all just be over?

"They'll take you back, One-three." Ten took a few steps backwards. "You just have to go with me to meet Zero."

"I didn't fall for that last time, what—"

Ten was already moving though. He spun and raced for the door to the suite. Ethan sprang after him. Ten wrenched the door open, dashed out and slammed it shut behind him.

Barrelling outside, Ethan was a fraction too late narrowing his eyes against the glare of the outside lights and didn't see the trap in time to stop himself from springing it.

Ten hadn't kept running. He was, instead, crouched against the glass balustrade on the edge of the landing, which gave an unobstructed view of the hollow core of the building.

Ethan all but collided with Ten as he surged up to his feet. Shoulders rammed into Ethan's gut, lifting him. Hands grabbed the material of his pants around his thighs and hefted him up and over.

Ethan tumbled out over a lot of empty space, half blind from the light. He twisted, reaching for Ten, for the railing, for anything. Ten dodged his flailing hand and stepped back. His expressionless brown face was the last thing Ethan saw as he plummeted.

Something brushed his grasping hands and he closed his fingers around it. Soft leaves from the decorative vines draped over the edge of the balustrade were crushed in his fists. Momentum jerked the plants out of their shallow soil and he dropped again, his weight too much for the slender tendrils. But it slowed him enough to catch the lip of the balcony.

Thirty odd floors of space yawned wide below him and there was nothing but his fingertips to stop him from falling the entire way. Heart slamming, Ethan focused on getting his breathing under control. His fingers stung like they were being pierced with hot needles and his arms trembled with the effort of holding himself still. Slowly, slowly, he pulled himself up in the most daring chin-up ever. Ethan got one forearm onto the very narrow lip under the balustrade. Trusting to that, he let go with his other hand and reached for the thickest wad of plants he could find. The moment he tugged on them, they came loose and he jerked back. There was absolutely no purchase against the glass barrier, his hand sliding downwards even as his body swayed, pulling him away from the edge. His precarious hold on the landing slipped.

Then a hand appeared over the top of the railing.

Brown skin. Long fingers. Blunt nails.

Ethan didn't even have to think twice. He threw himself upwards, striving for that hand. Palms slapped against wrists, fingers closed tight, and Ethan was hauled upwards.

TWENTY-TWO

J ack pulled Ethan over the glass balustrade, taking his weight and staggering backwards until he was pressed against the wall, his errant lover clasped tight to his chest.

Ethan was shaking, dragging in shallow, gasping breaths. He tucked his face into Jack's chest and clutched at his shoulders, fingers digging into his muscles as hard as they'd clung to life seconds ago.

"Jesus," Jack murmured over and over, arms tightening around Ethan.

He'd rushed out of the elevator just in time to see Ethan be thrown over a balcony—on the far side of the hotel. His heart had stuttered to a stop, then slammed into frantic action as he raced around the landing. Across the way, a brown-skinned man had sprinted away in the other direction, not waiting to see if Ethan fell, or caught himself on the balcony below, which he had.

Thank fuck.

And now Jack wasn't about to let him go. Not now that he'd finally caught up and nearly lost him in the same moment. Nothing was going to—

Ethan twisted out of Jack's hold and put on a pair of wraparound sunglasses. "I have to go after him." He spun around, ready to run.

Jack caught his arm and dug his heels in. "No fucking way."

"He knows where Hermann Jäger is, and that's how I find *them*."

Ethan wasn't trembling anymore. He was still and expressionless, closed against the chaotic feelings that threatened to swamp him. As much as he'd brought turmoil into Jack and Ethan's life, the psychiatrist Adam Quinn had given Jack precious insight into this man. These deadly calms that had once scared Jack only left him concerned now, knowing that Ethan was battling against unwanted emotions.

"Okay." Jack didn't relax his hold. Ethan wasn't running away again. Ever. "But not alone."

For a moment longer, Ethan was statue still, then he nodded. Not so long ago, Jack would have accepted that nod at face value. Now, after three months of chasing Ethan as he assassinated his way around the world, after being so close they could have touched in The Hague and Ethan had simply walked on by, he wasn't convinced. Yet he had to show some trust or he'd never get Ethan out of here alive.

Jack let his hand drop. Ethan didn't run away.

"Do you have a plan?" Ethan asked.

Pointing to the stairwell the bastard who'd tried to kill Ethan had disappeared into, he said, "Follow him. He knows where Jäger is."

That rogue corner of Ethan's mouth twitched up for a second, then he was off and running. Jack was on his heels not a second later. They burst into the stairwell and both of them stopped on the landing, listening. In a hotel of this size and at this late hour, not many guests used the stairs, so it was easy to make out running footsteps . . . below them, heading downwards. Ethan in the lead, they raced down, taking stairs three at a time and leaping over railings. Thirty floors flew by and by the time they hit the wide, glossy floor of the ground level, it was just in time to see an orange Lamborghini peel out of the driveway.

Ethan sprinted through the largely deserted foyer for the front of the hotel. Jack veered off.

"This way." He didn't wait to see if Ethan followed him.

A valiant staff member dodged into his path. "Sir. Sirs! You can't—"

Jack flashed his ISO badge at the woman as he whipped past. "Official business. Ethan!" He opened the door beside the concierge desk, spinning through it so he could scan the foyer even as he left it.

Ethan was seconds behind him.

The office space behind the door only had a couple of occupied desks. Jack thrust his badge in their direction, claiming "official business" again.

"You're here with ISO?" Ethan asked as they turned down a short corridor.

"Sort of. This way." He hit the release bar on the door at the end of the hallway.

Dim light greeted them as they came out onto a loading dock. It was empty of vehicles, but they had to dodge around a couple of staff who were unpacking a palette of stock. Jack hurdled a box of bottled water and dodged around a man with a carton of booze while fishing in his jacket pocket for a key. Ahead, the deadly looking Kawasaki Ninja ZX-10R was where he'd left it, parked at the top of the ramp.

"A Ninja, Jack?" Ethan asked as he caught up.

Throwing his leg over it, Jack inserted the key. "Go steal your own bike, if you don't like it."

Another twitch of his lips, then Ethan was on the bike, arms around Jack's waist. The engine awoke with a healthy roar before settling into a satisfying rumble. Jack kicked up the stand and eased the bike around until it faced the ramp.

Somewhat smugly, he yelled, "Hold on," to Ethan, then shot them down the ramp and into the alley behind the hotel. Ethan's arms did tighten at the first burst of power, but then loosened when they turned out of the alleyway and onto the road so he could move with the motion of the bike. Then he let go completely and sat up, most likely looking for the Lambo.

"There." He tapped Jack's shoulder and pointed.

A flash of orange disappeared around a corner ahead of them.

Taking a gamble, Jack swerved the other way, leaning the bike over as he took the opposite corner. Behind him, Ethan tensed, then relaxed when it became clear where Jack was heading.

Another turn later, they exploded out onto the main road that followed the curve of the bay. Jack cut across the southbound lane and swung into the northbound one, several cars behind the racing Lambo. The road wasn't so crowded that either they or the supercar couldn't weave in and out of the traffic. Jack, however, could move through smaller gaps and they gained on the orange Lambo quickly. Seeing this, the driver planted his foot and the car leaped ahead, crossing over to the opposite lane to get around slower moving vehicles.

Instead of facing oncoming traffic, Jack went to the left and onto Marine Drive. It was thankfully empty of pedestrians at this time of night, so he throttled up to high speed and quickly drew even with the Lambo.

The passenger side window rolled down and the shadowed figure inside raised a gun. Jack barely touched the brake and the bullet missed wide in front of them. He felt Ethan reach down between them and retrieve Jack's USP from the back of his jeans. Throttling up, he caught back up to the Lambo and Ethan returned fire.

Neither had much of a chance of hitting the other, as the Lambo cut in and out of the traffic at a second's notice. Jack swung back onto the main road and came in tight behind the low profile car. Ethan leaned around him and aimed for the rear tyres. Bullets sparked off the rear fender.

Then one blew off the right wing mirror of the Ninja.

Jack threw the bike into a sharp sweep left. Ethan locked one arm around Jack's waist and twisted, firing at the new threat coming up behind. Glancing in his remaining mirror, Jack saw two bikes rapidly gaining on them. One of them had a handgun trained on Jack and Ethan, while the other concentrated on catching up to them.

Stopping the Lambo now a lower priority, Jack took them back onto the boulevard and opened up the bike again. As they roared past the supercar, it braked suddenly and turned onto a side road, heading into the city. For a few precious seconds he felt Ethan lean that way, yearning after it and whatever intelligence the driver had. Then he shifted back into alignment with Jack and the bike.

They were rapidly running out of Marine Drive. Ahead was the beach and a decision about how to deal with the pursuit still hot on their arses. Ethan kept sending bullets back at them but had no hope of hitting anything substantial as they all kept up evasive manoeuvres. When the dark water of the bay was replaced with yellow sand, Ethan stopped firing, tapped at Jack's shoulder and gestured.

"Move over," Ethan shouted over the engine noise.

"What's the plan?" Jack nevertheless followed the direction of Ethan's hand and swerved closer to the sand.

"Distraction. Please slow just a tad."

Trusting him, Jack did so.

Ethan threw himself off the back of the bike. Tucking into a ball, he hit the sand and rolled. Jack couldn't risk watching what he did next, having to focus on the way ahead. He did hear several gunshots in fast succession, followed by a smash and a protracted screech.

Goddamn Ethan and his reckless moves. He'd only just got Ethan back within grasping range and he was already throwing himself away from Jack. Anger warred with concern. What the fuck did Ethan think he was doing?

An intersection was coming up and Jack braked sharply going into the U-turn, planting his foot and skidding the rear tyre around. Cars honked and people yelled in surprise, then he was heading south again. Except that he was on the wrong side of a tall barrier between the two sets of lanes.

He caught a quick view of Ethan as he went past. One of the enemy bikes was down and Ethan was crouched behind it, firing on the other rider, who had stopped and was also using their bike as cover. There was no sign of the police yet but they couldn't be too far away. The 2008 terror attacks were still fresh in city's memory and Jack couldn't let them be caught up in the sort of response open gunfire would—rightly—instigate.

He didn't go too far in the wrong direction before he found a solution to his problem. Hitting the horn on the bike hard and repeatedly, Jack slowed and left the road, getting onto the footpath. The smallish number of pedestrians ran out of his way, and when he lifted the front wheel of the bike onto the stairs leading to an elevated walkway over the road, they flattened themselves against the railings. Jack revved the Ninja and powered it up the stairs. At the top, he slid it around and rode along the covered bridge, the engine roar echoing through the tight space. Out the other side, he bumped down the next set of stairs, swung around and got back onto the road.

He weaved through the traffic, using it for cover as he approached the scene of Ethan's stand against the enemy. Not much had changed, and at the last possible moment, Jack swerved sharply onto the boulevard and rode the bike into the back of the helmeted gunman firing on Ethan.

The man went down with a cut off yelp as the Ninja went over his legs, then launched off the angle of the downed bike's body. Air borne for a second, the Ninja landed heavily, wobbling. Jack braked hard, foot down for balance, boot tread skidding over the cement. In a curl of black smoke from the back tyre, Jack came to a shaky stop just in front of the second bike, heart racketing in his chest from excitement and sheer shit-scaredness.

"Very timely." Ethan popped up from his cover, ejected the mag from the USP and peered into it. "I just ran out of ammunition."

"Get on," Jack growled, on a hair trigger from the dump of adrenaline and Ethan's reckless actions. "We have to leave before the cops get here."

"I thought you were here officially." Ethan didn't waste time getting back on the Ninja however.

"As I said, sort of. Things are rough, politically speaking, right now."

Any questions Ethan had were lost as Jack took off so fast the front wheel lifted off the ground. It thumped back down as he got control of both his anger and the bike and moved them back onto the road. Thankfully, Ethan was a cooperative pillion rider this time, pressed to Jack's back and not throwing himself off at stupidly high speeds.

A police car swung in behind them as Jack took a corner too fast. Lights and siren going, it wasn't long before it was joined by another one.

Jack took them down a random selection of streets, alternating between wanting traffic they could slip through while hindering the police cars, and open stretches where he could race away. The call had gone out, however, and there was law enforcement closing in on the area in a great mass. Every corner they went around was a gamble as to how many flashing lights they would find. Finally, they seemed to lose their closest pursuers and Jack reduced his speed to the posted limits.

"Do you have a destination in mind?" Ethan asked after nearly twenty minutes free of lights and sirens. They were stopped at an intersection, playing the part of road rule abiding folks.

"Vaguely," Jack muttered. "It's just getting there."

There was a speculative pause, then, "Are you lost, Jack?"

Jack scowled. "It's been a very, *very*, long since I was last in Mumbai, all right? And we never came here much. How about you plot our course with your implant, if you want to be helpful instead of just the reason why we have cops crawling up our arse?" Now wasn't the time for an argument but he couldn't stop the growl in his words.

Ethan stiffened against his back. "That won't be possible. My implant is dead."

"What? Why? How?"

A blurt of a siren cut off any chance at an answer, even if Jack hadn't sensed Ethan closing down. Ignoring the red light, Jack shot them around a corner to a chorus of horns, and the chase was on again. It never quite gained the same urgency as the first pursuit had, and whether by pure luck or divine design they were free of tails when Jack saw his goal as they roared up an overpass across some railway tracks.

"Is that where we're going?" Ethan yelled over the engine.

"Yeah." Jack cut across a lane of traffic to make the turn. "We should be able to hide pretty well in there."

"Yes. I imagine so."

TWENTY-THREE

At Ethan's best guess, they were in central Mumbai and ahead of them was a large slum area. The mass of tightly packed ramshackle huts pressed up against rows of old, dilapidated buildings like lake waters lapping at the shore. The road they followed between the buildings was narrow and rough and they shared it with a few other bikes and cars as desperate looking as the scenery.

This was a good place to lay low. Ethan didn't think there would be much police presence here, and perhaps what there was wasn't altogether welcomed. The law was not often on the side of most impoverished and oppressed peoples.

Jack slowed the bike and Ethan kept an eye out for tails, but also noted their surroundings, needing to ensure he had a path out of this place, if required.

The buildings were old and bedraggled, weighed down by history and neglect due to poverty, covered in grime and patchwork repairs. It looked despondent and downtrodden but there were signs of a thriving community as well. Canvas awnings over now-empty market stalls, closed for the night, locked grills over windows to hole-in-the-wall eateries, an occasional old motorbike parked on the side of the road. It looked cleaner than Ethan would have expected but every now and then a waft of damp rot reminded him that sanitation wasn't a high priority of the city here.

There were a few people on the street, most of whom watched them pass on the sleek, expensive bike with narrowed eyes and thin lips. Even with a lack of an authoritative presence, he and Jack needed to be careful, and they were leaving clear memories of themselves with these people.

Jack seemed to have the same thought because he pulled over not long later. They got off and Jack lifted the seat. From the compartment underneath he removed another HK USP, spare mags, which he shared between them, and a roll of knives he tucked into the inside of his leather jacket. Lastly, he pulled out a peak cap and shoved it on Ethan's head, tugging it down low over his forehead.

"Keep that on. A white guy here is going to stand out."

Adjusting the cap so it didn't hurt his ears, Ethan eyed Jack carefully. His scowl was deep and the angry growl in his voice hadn't lessened since they lost the police. Which meant he was mad at Ethan as well. In moments of weakness, when he had let himself dream about reuniting with Jack, he'd imagined surviving his plan to kill the Cabal and then finding Jack to finally tell him exactly how he felt. In those dreams, there hadn't been near-death experiences or highspeed chases—or Jack's entirely justified anger with him.

Jack wheeled the bike into a narrow gap between buildings and started throwing trash on it. Ethan helped silently and when it was as hidden as it was ever going to be, Jack led the way to the far end of the gap and onto another street. There were a few more people moving around here and Ethan hunched his shoulders and ducked his head, hoping they didn't immediately notice his ethnicity. Even Jack stood out despite being half Indian. His skin wasn't as dark, his jeans and leather jacket too new and spotless.

They picked up a tail not long later. A skinny youth in ragged clothes who slinked along behind them, probably thinking they—non-locals—were easy marks for pickpocketing. Jack noticed him half a minute after Ethan did and with a few discreet gestures they agreed on a plan.

It took the kid another five minutes to get close enough, and the instant his nimble fingers dipped into Jack's pocket, Jack whipped around and caught his arm. The thief was young but he wasn't stupid. He twisted his arm out of Jack's hold and turned, ready to sprint, and ran straight into Ethan, who grabbed his wrist, spun him around and brought his captured arm up behind his back. The kid gave a startled cry, then another when Ethan's other arm wrapped around his chest and lifted him off the ground. He struggled and tried to kick out at Jack, who went for his legs, but didn't connect before Jack caught his calves. Ethan shifted his hand to over the boy's mouth and they got him off the street into the dark shadows between two buildings.

The youth went still, eyes widening in fear. Under Ethan's palm, he was still trying to speak, the muffled sounds desperate now, not alarmed.

"What's he saying?" Ethan asked softly.

"Not sure. He's speaking in Marathi and I don't know it." Jack let the kid's legs go but moved closer so he was pinned between them. He spoke quiet but fast in Hindi and after a moment, the kid shut up, eyes still wide and scared. "I let him know we're not going to hurt him," Jack explained. "That we just need some information." From a back pocket, he pulled a wad of purple notes. The kid stared at them, fear turning into desperate want.

Jack and the youth exchanged a rapid conversation in Hindi and after a minute, Jack motioned for Ethan to let him go. The kid shook out his wrist, then thrust out his hand to Jack. Peeling off two notes, Jack held them up, his tone firm, and when the kid nodded frantically in agreement, handed them over.

The money disappeared into the boy's clothes faster than Ethan could follow, and a moment later, the kid was gone as well.

"He'll be back," Jack whispered.

"Are you sure?" Over the general stink of their surroundings, Ethan could smell Jack. Sweat, leather, and soap that combined in Ethan's senses into an urge to touch and hold Jack. The sun in the emptiness of his chest burned brighter with the new fuel.

Watching the street with a frown, Jack shrugged. "I promised him twice again what I already gave him. That's more money than he'd see in a year here. I guess we hope that's incentive enough." His black brows pinched even further together and his lips got thin. "I hadn't exactly planned for this, you know. Hadn't planned on having to haul you back from a thirty storey drop, either."

The growling rumble in his words echoed in Ethan's guts, half memory of the deadly fall he'd almost taken, half an awakening of that part of him that only Jack had ever been able to touch.

All those months of training himself to *not* want to run to Jack, all of it ruined in one instant. The moment he'd seen the hand appear over the balcony he had known who it was. Just as he'd known the hand in the suite *hadn't* been Jack's. The moment Jack had caught him, every mote of that discipline had fled and all he'd wanted to do was stay in his arms forever.

This was why it would be better if he left now. He could get back to where they'd left the bike. Ten was still alive, and he knew where Jäger was, and where Jäger was, the Cabal bosses were.

The kid returned before Ethan could work out how to get away. He spoke to Jack, then gestured for them to follow him.

"He's got a place for us to stay," Jack told Ethan, then went after the boy.

Now. Ethan could leave now. Simply turn in the other direction and get away before Jack could stop him. But his feet automatically moved after Jack. He would make sure Jack was secure, then strike out on his own again.

The youth darted barefoot along the tight streets and ducked under low hanging laundry, occasionally pausing to make sure they hadn't gotten lost. Eventually, he came to a stop before a crumbling white-bricked building five storeys high. There was what had once been red trim but had faded to a pale pink, arched windows and a portico supported by chipped and slightly crooked columns. Material of all types and shades fluttered in the windows and there was a row of old, empty chairs out the front.

A knock on the door was answered promptly, the boy switching back to Marathi to talk to the woman who peered out him, then up at Jack and Ethan. When Jack produced the money she finally nodded and opened the door wider.

While Jack stopped to hand over the promised rupees to the kid, Ethan went inside—and caught his breath.

What had once been a foyer had been transformed into someone's home, but that wasn't the most astonishing thing.

The floor was covered in vibrant rugs in rich colours of red and gold. Hindu idols were placed in positions of pride on a carved oak sideboard. A plush sofa divided the room in two, facing a flat screen TV mounted on the wall. On the other side of the room was a formal dining table with eight chairs around it. Through a door next to the table, the aroma of cooking unchallenged by the smell of dirt and detritus made Ethan's mouth water. The whole place was lit by electric lights. A boy of about sixteen sat in front of the TV, turned away from the Bollywood action movie to stare at Ethan with wide eyes. Then, dismissing him, the boy focused on the show again.

The woman who'd answered the door was older, probably his mother or aunt. She wore a yellow sari over what might have been a Muse T-shirt, her hair a tumbling mass of dark brown lightening at the ends towards golden. A red bindi was set between her curiously arched brows. She spoke in Marathi and Ethan could only shake his head and look around for Jack. He was still outside, talking earnestly with their guide, probably extracting promises of silence from him with even more money.

"You speak English?" the woman asked.

Thrown, Ethan stopped the instinctual urge to find a weapon. "Yes. I'm sorry if we're intruding."

She pursed her lips, possibly at his British accent, then shrugged. "You are looking for room?"

"If that's all right."

Eyes rolling, she said, "We have white boys here before." Miming taking a picture, she added, "Documentaries." Her tone said she couldn't understand why anyone would care, though.

Resisting the urge to apologise, Ethan was saved by Jack coming in. He bowed his head to the woman, speaking in Hindi. The conversation was short and ended when Jack handed over money and the woman tapped the head of the boy watching TV, calling him Suresh and gesturing for him to move.

With the aggrieved groan of teenaged boys asked to do something by their parent the world over, Suresh got up and beckoned for them to follow.

Through another door, they came into a corridor with a winding staircase at the end. Doors lined the walls, those that were open showed various sized rooms from small to medium, all seeming to house at least two adults and some children.

"This is a chawl," Jack murmured as they followed Suresh up the stairs. "The woman we spoke to owns the building. She rents out the rooms to families. The boy who led us here said she often keeps a spare room for *emergencies*."

Ethan snorted. "Are we her usual definition of *emergency*?"

"Possibly. I got the feeling she's not very sympathetic towards the police and government."

They went up three more floors, the rooms getting smaller and corridors more crowded with overflowing furnishings and laundry. Part way along, Suresh gestured to what was either a set of very steep stairs or a permanent ladder leading up to a small opening in the ceiling. Ethan went up first, wondering what surprise awaited him as he reached the ceiling. Cautiously, he poked his head into the space above. It was dark so he took his sunglasses off and looked around. The room was perhaps half again as large as those he'd just walked past, open and ventilated by a window high on one wall. There was a table with a couple of chairs and a mattress with blankets.

Ethan pulled himself all the way in and stepped away from the opening in the floor. Jack came up quickly, squeezing his broad shoulders through the hole. Suresh slithered in lastly and flicked on a light switch.

Blinking in the sudden light, Ethan put his glasses back on and looked around again. A single bulb dangled from the ceiling, casting yellow light on the cracked plaster of the walls and showing off the surprisingly intricate pattern of faded black and discoloured white tiles on the floor. A few flies lifted off the walls and buzzed about but the place was clean and warm, if a trifle stuffy.

"Table," Suresh said in good English. "Bed. I bring you food soon. There is shower downstairs, but you have to get your own water for washing in the morning."

Jack thanked him and handed over a couple of bills. Suresh disappeared and Jack went to the window, stretching up to open it and let in some fresh air. "We'll lay low here tonight, then leave tomorrow. It'll be crowded enough to cover our movements then." His tone hadn't lost any of the tension it had held since the Oberoi.

"Jack."

Spinning around, Jack opened his mouth to speak, then closed it and ran his hands through his hair, grasping at the black curls fiercely. As if that was all that was keeping him from punching something. Or Ethan.

"Jack, I had—"

"No."

That was all he said aloud, but his eyes, oh, his eyes screamed.

Stomach churning with confusion, Ethan murmured, "Please tell me your sister and niece are all right."

Jack nodded sharply. "They're fine. I got to them in time."

"I'm glad."

Silence fell, awkward and tense. Weariness tugged at Ethan's body. The fight with Ten, the ride to escape the gunmen and then the police, the long journey over the past months to get this far, all dragged on his shoulders like a cape made of anchors. The one thing that had kept him going since The Hague—finally having the Cabal bosses in sight—felt like it was even further away tonight than it had been that morning.

His traitorous body sagged and ached and desperately wanted to fall onto the mattress and rest—preferably with Jack wound around it. But his thoughts raced between all the mistakes he'd made in order to lose Ten and all the decisions he should have made to avoid them. He shouldn't have closed with Ten. Should have hidden and followed him when he left. The trap Ten had laid outside the suite, that'd nearly cost Ethan his life, would have been obvious and easily avoidable if he'd just been thinking clearly. If he'd been thinking at all.

It was the situation with Two all over again. He was failing. He wasn't the assassin the Cabal had trained him to be. He'd failed the final test, even failed to kill Ten three months ago. He couldn't even keep Jack safe, because here he was, right in the middle of the whole mess, his life once again sitting in Ethan's hand.

He had to leave. Had to go back out there and find Ten, find Jäger—find the Cabal, and finish this.

TWENTY-FOUR

Jesus fucking Christ. Ethan was going to be the death of him. Either from a stray bullet or a bloody aneurism. Temples pounding with the effort to keep his anger in check, Jack shrugged out of his leather jacket, hoping it would cool his head. No real luck, sadly.

He knew part of his anger was an irrational response to witnessing Ethan's near death. But part of it, a large part of it, was entirely rational. Twice, Ethan had had the chance to reach out to him—literally— and he'd chosen to walk on by both times. He'd kept up his personal crusade on his own, nearly getting caught in Nova Scotia and fleeing across the USA with just about every letter agency in the world after him. All leading up to today, when Jack had had to rescue him from falling thirty floors to a hard marble floor.

God. He'd almost lost him. For good.

And apparently he was going to lose him again if he didn't stop the man from leaving.

Ethan was at the hole in the floor, one foot down on the ladder.

"Oh, no you don't." Jack marched over and grabbed Ethan's arm.

"Jack, I have to—"

"What? Throw yourself from a speeding vehicle again? Finish what that bastard tried to do to you today?" Jack hauled Ethan across the room and all but threw him into a chair at the table. "Not if I have anything to do with it."

"You don't understand—"

Jack held up a finger and Ethan clamped his mouth shut. "I understand more than you fucking think I do." He grabbed his jacket and pulled out the roll of knives. "Fucking hell. Haven't we had this conversation before? I work for an intelligence agency. I understand exactly what you're doing." Pulling free two plastic cuffs, he stood behind the chair and, one wrist at a time, fastened Ethan's arms to the back legs. "Christ. Did it ever fucking occur to you that I was trying to catch you not to stop you, but to help you?"

Ethan hadn't been struggling—probably because he had a way of getting out of even this usually effective means of securing a prisoner— but he went still then.

"Three fucking days I spent talking to Seven. She's fine, by the way. Couldn't do enough to help me *understand*." And suddenly Jack ran out of steam. He sank to his haunches behind the chair and leaned his forehead on the backrest, his hands still curled around Ethan's biceps. Not tight or restraining, but just to keep contact. "She told me so much. Nothing directly about you. That's for you to tell me. I asked her to leave you out of it because I know . . . I know you need to be the one to tell me. But everything else . . ." Tears gathered and he shook them away impatiently. He'd cried in the interviews with Seven—everyone who'd been listening had—and now wasn't the time to dwell on those horrors again. It was time to do something about them. "Jesus, I almost felt sorry for Two."

Jack grabbed two more restraints and tied Ethan's calves to the front legs of the chair. That was, of course, when Suresh returned with food.

Ready to explain, Jack found he didn't need to. The Indian youth just looked at the white man tied to a chair, shrugged, and left the tray on the floor by the hole.

Letting out a long breath, Jack retrieved the food and set it on the table. Then he looked at Ethan's face. It was stone, sunglasses pointed directly at the opposite wall, mouth a straight line, jaw clenched. Damp trails marked each cheek.

"Fuck." Jack grabbed one of the towels covering the food and dried the tear tracks. "I'm sorry. It's just that ever since Seven told me what you all went through, I've been crazy with worry. Ask anyone I work with, they'll tell you I've been real prick. Well, more so than usual."

The tension in Ethan's shoulders eased a fraction. "You would have truly helped me?"

Jack's heart thumped at the hollow hope in his man's voice. "Yeah. You know I would have. The Office would have as well. They are, in fact. That's the only reason I got here as quick as I did. I was coming after you no matter what, but they got me here as fast as possible." And just in time.

To give himself a moment, Jack stretched up and hooked the towel into the chain the light bulb hung from. The material draped over it and dimmed the room considerably, but left Jack enough light to see by. He set out the bowls and plates, discovering dal and naan and fresh fruit and yogurt. There were two bottles of water as well.

At a nod from Ethan, Jack took off his glasses. Ethan blinked, then looked up at him. Holy fuck, Jack had missed those eyes. White irises, too wide pupils, those stupidly long and thick lashes. He was still angry. Probably would be for a while yet, but his chest grenade went off, blazing through him for the first time in what felt like forever. It was lust for this beautiful, sexy man, yes, but it was so much more than that. Jack might have had his head up his arse for far too long, but he knew what that sensation meant now. It was a sign of so many things, but right now, it simply meant he had to take care of Ethan, even if he had to tie him to a chair to do it.

Jack opened a bottle of water and held it for Ethan to drink, which he did in slow sips until a third of the bottle was done. Jack took a couple of mouthfuls as well, then contemplated the food.

"I'm not really hungry, Jack." Ethan at least sounded like his usual self.

"You need to eat." Seeing a solution to his logistical problem, Jack swung a leg over Ethan's and sat on his lap, facing him. Twisting around, he picked up the bowl of dal and a piece of naan. He rested the bowl between their bellies and tore up the bread. He scooped up some of the legume dish on piece of naan and held out to Ethan.

"Isn't there a spoon?" Ethan asked mildly.

"Nope. Open up."

Lips sealed, Ethan cocked an eyebrow at him.

"Come on. Most Indian food is made to be eaten with the fingers. It makes it taste better. And you need to eat. And rest." When that got him nothing, Jack batted his eyelashes. "For me?"

The corner of Ethan's mouth turned up, but that was it.

"Eat it and I'll give you a reward."

"Will you untie me?"

"Maybe. Eat it and find out."

Ethan resisted for several more moments, then opened his mouth. Suppressing a triumphant smirk, Jack fed him. Chewing, Ethan watched Jack suspiciously the entire time, probably wary of this threatened reward. Jack ate as well, unable to stop the smile.

When he was finished, Ethan said, "And the reward?"

Jack swallowed his own mouthful. "Coming right up." And he leaned over and kissed him.

It was barely enough to be called a kiss. A brush of his lips over Ethan's, then he pulled back, heart in his throat as he waited to see what response he'd get.

Ethan licked his lips slowly. "You still want to kiss me?"

"Always want to kiss you. But that doesn't mean I'm not still angry. Open up."

Ethan did so and Jack popped another bit of naan and dal into his mouth. They both ate, then Jack kissed him again. Ethan's lips pressed back this time, capturing his for a moment longer, then released him.

Belly tingling with warming anticipation, Jack sat back and prepared the next morsel. Ethan didn't need to be told to open up this time and his tongue swept out to catch the food, brushing Jack's fingers.

Holy fuck was this the wrong path to take right now. The anger still simmered in his bones, but *Christ*, his blood yearned toward Ethan like the tide chasing the moon. They'd had plenty of angry sex in the past. It was unavoidable when Ethan was a little shit and Jack's anger had a hair-trigger. Generally, it worked for them because when the rage-sex was over, Ethan was a useless puddle and Jack had forgotten what pissed him off at the first sight of Ethan's blush. This time, though, Jack wasn't sure that was how it would play out, for various reasons. Yet he leaned in and kissed him again, his tongue delving into Ethan's mouth, welcomed enthusiastically.

He followed the same pattern until the bowl was nearly empty and the kisses lasted longer than the chewing. Ethan made plaintive little noises with each kiss, slowly growing into moans as he pushed harder at Jack, straining against the ties holding him to the chair.

Jack removed the bowl from between them and slid up Ethan's lap until they were touching from chest to groin. His dick was steel-rod hard, pressed against the inside of his jeans, aching for more than that inadequate friction. Ethan was just as hard, tenting up the front of his cargo pants. Jack ground against him, making them both gasp at the sudden pressure. Hips rising off the chair, Ethan panted into Jack's mouth, striving for more.

"Jack," he whined, then moaned, "Jack," when Jack met him hip thrust for hip thrust.

Jack touched him. Couldn't not touch him. Hands glided over his tensed biceps and across his torso, lamenting the too many layers of clothes that didn't let him trace muscles or ribs, or tease nipples until they were hard and making Ethan suck in a deep breath when he rolled them between his fingers. Fingers lingered along his stubbled jaw, stroking the pulse points in his neck, then up into his hair, getting a low groan and tipped-back head in response. Jack shifted his mouth to that exposed throat, licking and nipping until Ethan was a babbling mess.

Then suddenly, Ethan's hands were free and curling through his hair, pulling his head up so he could kiss Jack's mouth again, greedy and possessive.

Fuck. Take-charge Ethan was as mind-blowingly sexy as submissive Ethan. It was Jack's turn to melt and let Ethan have his way. He nudged his way under Jack's chin, tongue lathing its way across the soft skin, making Jack's shoulders shiver and his dick throb. Ethan's hands pushed under his shirt, hot and hard as they rubbed over his abdomen, around his waist and up his spine to grab at his shoulder blades and dig in. Teeth raked over Jack's throat, making him whimper.

God. The man was infuriating, but so fucking gorgeous like this. When Ethan decided what he wanted and went after it, no holds barred, Jack could only ever stare in awe.

Except when what he'd decided was to make a solo suicide run against one of the most powerful and secret groups in the world. Then Jack could only do his best to keep the man alive.

Ethan shifted under him, growling against Jack's skin. With a muttered, "Blast," Ethan's hands were gone from his back and before Jack could dazedly work out what was happening, Ethan had one of the knives from his kit. The silver blade flashed in the dim light as the assassin spun it around in his palm, grabbed the handle and slashed downwards.

Snick. Snick.

The knife clattered to the floor and Ethan slapped his hands to Jack's arse. "Hold on."

Jack barely complied before Ethan surged to his feet, chair falling backwards, and set Jack down on the edge of the table. Legs wrapped around Ethan's hips, Jack pulled in a startled gasp, then he was being kissed, thoroughly, deeply, demandingly. Ethan shoved the tray with its remaining food aside and pressed until Jack was leaning back on one elbow, his other hand clutching at Ethan's shirt, unsure of what it was doing.

This shouldn't happen. Not now. Not like this. But Ethan ground against Jack's dick and all he could do was hitch his legs higher and grind back. Then Ethan slid a hand over his straining bulge, rubbing and squeezing.

"Jack." The name was ragged and breathless.

"Present," he managed amidst the fogging lust. He pushed up into the touch, trying not to but helpless to resist. "Oh shit." Maybe this would be okay. Maybe Ethan could fuck him and this wouldn't end the way he dreaded it would.

Ethan popped the button on Jack's jeans and shoved his hand inside them. "I need you, Jack. Please." His fingers slid along the length of Jack's shaft.

Eyes rolling into the back of his head, Jack moaned. God. This was karma all over again, back to bite him in the arse.

A low rumble started in Ethan's throat, an almost feral leer turning up one side of his mouth. "Naked, Jack. Now."

"No."

It was the weakest protest ever but Ethan heard it and froze.

Jack groaned and pulled Ethan's hand out of his pants. "Jesus, I'm sorry, but no. Not now."

Slowly, Ethan closed his eyes and pushed off him, seeking distance. Jack locked his ankles together at the base of his spine and grabbed his wrist, holding him close.

"Jack, please let me go. You don't want me, so why—"

"Fuck you," Jack snapped, lust and anger about level. "You know that's not true." He put Ethan's hand over his still hard dick.

Eyes opening, Ethan looked at his hand cupping him, Jack's brown fingers around his wrist. The sight would normally send Jack over the edge but he reined the impulse back.

"It's not me who doesn't want this," Jack said softly.

Swift as a snake, Ethan reversed their hands so he was holding Jack's palm over his own bulge. "You were saying?"

Jack sucked in a deep breath. Oh yeah. That was definite need right there, but it wasn't enough. "Okay, you want me here." He pressed against the thick shaft for a moment, then lifted his hand and put it over Ethan's heart. "Probably even here, too." Tapping Ethan's forehead, he said, "But not here."

Ethan knocked aside his hand. "What does that mean?"

"It means I know you, you crazy bastard." Jack let Ethan go and got off the table. His dick ached as he rebuttoned his jeans and adjusted himself in search of any relief he could get. Which was scarce. "We're not secure here. Safe for now, yes, but not secure the way you need to be. If you fucked me right now, you'd regret it afterwards. Like the first time. And forgive me if I don't want to see that look on your face again."

One hand on the table edge, Ethan turned away and pressed the heel of his palm to his crotch. "Is that the only reason?"

Jack ground his molars together. "No. Because if I remember correctly, the last time you fucked me into a coma, I woke up alone."

than jerked like Jack had physically hit him. It felt like a gut punch, hearing Jack so angry, especially moments after they'd been so close to amazing pleasure.

"Just in case you were wondering if it still hurts," Jack muttered.

Cock deflating, Ethan sighed. "I didn't have a choice."

"Aren't you the one who said there's always a choice?"

"All right. There was a choice, between you facing down two Cabal assassins with no desire to play games like Two did, or me leaving on my own and doing everything I could to make sure you and your family weren't hurt."

Jack pulled his shirt back into alignment and sat at the table. He dipped a piece of melon into the yogurt, contemplated it for a moment, then popped it into his mouth. Around the food, he said, "Yeah, okay. But you came back afterwards, and then left, *again*."

"You spoke to Rocco."

"Of course I did. Do you know how upset he was when his little chat didn't work? The guy was so worried about you."

Ethan tried to deflect the words, not let them under his skin, but his armour was in ruins. Had been since he'd let Jack into his life, since he'd begun to believe he could have a real life with him. First Jack, then Short Round, rapidly followed by Rocco. Even Lewis, Jack's best friend, had started to creep in, during their short acquaintance. He couldn't bear to think about the hurt he'd caused Jack, because knowing he'd upset Rocco was bad enough.

What else matters?

That's what Rocco had said to him and it had lingered in his mind the entire time he'd been climbing his way up the bloody ladder towards the heart of the Cabal.

"I did it for them." The words were out before Ethan knew he was going to say them. Whispered, but the room wasn't so large Jack didn't hear him.

"Did what for who?"

"When I left Sydney the second time. It was for my brothers and sisters." Not wanting to talk across the room, Ethan righted his chair, sat and picked up a bit of fruit. The slippery slice oozed juice down his fingers and suddenly it was the red of blood. He put the fruit back and wiped his hand on a cloth. "You said you spoke to Seven. Did she tell you about the final test they put us through?"

Jack stopped with some pineapple halfway to his mouth. "She mentioned something about a test but didn't elaborate."

"Six out of eleven of us failed it. Five of those who failed died during the test. I survived even though I failed."

"Jesus." Jack's hand reached across the table towards him, then stopped before they touched.

Appreciating the consideration, Ethan shifted his own hand until there was only half an inch between their fingers. Close enough he felt the support without risking his instincts.

"Is that why they whipped you?"

Ethan shook his head. "That was for refusing to do a job, eighteen months before the test. I wasn't punished for this. Perhaps they felt watching five of the others die was enough."

Jack's nails scratched across the tabletop as he clenched his hand into a fist. "Seven said there were thirteen of you at the start of the . . . the, ah, experiment."

"Yes. Only eleven of us survived to the final test. My sister Three died . . ." Ethan swallowed. He'd never spoken any of this aloud before and the words were lodging in his throat.

Jack moved one of the water bottles closer and Ethan took it, drinking half of it in one go. It was cool going down but pooled like acid in his stomach.

"It's okay," Jack said. "You don't have to tell me if you don't want."

"I want to. At least I think I need to. I hurt you and you should know why."

"Then not now. Not tonight." He gestured to the bed. "You should rest. I'll keep watch."

Ethan shook his head. "You should know this. Three died when I was nine and she was thirteen. We had just learned how to snap a neck in a single move and Ten . . . he wanted to try it on a real person, not a dummy."

Jack flinched. "And I guess he wasn't punished for that?"

"He was. It didn't change him, though. All it did was make the instructors watch him much closer. Two was . . ." Ethan couldn't finish because it was still very raw. Not that he regretted killing Two— because he didn't—but the thought that Jack now knew all about him made him a little anxious.

"Was an abusive, deranged psychopath," Jack finished for him.

The firm tone made the corner of Ethan's mouth turn up. All of Jack's disgust was directed at Two, not him, and Ethan knew he could trust that would never change. Jack was stubborn like that. It made talking easier.

"Yes, he was all that, but he was also capable of hiding it. Very well." Well enough he fooled a trained profiler. "Ten's not like that. He could never fake it, probably thinks that there is absolutely no reason to. Two only saw targets when he looked at other people. Ten doesn't even see that. He sees animals. Ants. We're nothing but events to him." The old gunshot wound in his shoulder ached. Touching it, he confessed, "This scar is from him. We'd just finished a job, and we'd disagreed over a small matter. Afterwards, he shot me. Not because I'd argued, but simply because he could. Because he wanted to."

Jack's mouth opened, but it seemed he didn't have a curse powerful enough to express the rage in his eyes, because he closed it again, jaw clenched.

"Ten is the man from today."

"God damn that fucking piece of—"

Ethan grabbed his hand, holding him back from doing the stupid, angry thing that was growing in his eyes. "Jack, don't. He's gone. You can't do anything about him now."

"Yeah." Jack closed his eyes and breathed deep. "But when I do catch the fucking arsehole . . ."

The promise in the unsaid words both warmed Ethan and left him cold. Jack was one of the best soldiers he had ever encountered, but the thought of him going up against Ten made the food in Ethan's stomach curdle.

"I believed he was dead in the helicopter crash," Ethan continued. "Apparently, he escaped."

"We found an African man in the wreck. That was . . . Four?"

"Yes. I killed him. I had to do it, otherwise they would have killed me first." Ethan delayed the next words with another drink. Jack sat patiently while he finished the bottle. "Sixteen years ago, during that final test, I wanted to die. Three months ago, I couldn't let them do that, not this time. Back then, all I had was what the Cabal had given me and I didn't want it. Now, I have so much else. I've learned to live with what I do. I have ways of escaping it when I can. I have you. Don't I?"

Jack nodded emphatically and turned his hand over in Ethan's to squeeze it comfortingly.

"When I first agreed to live with you, I worried that I was becoming too dependent on you to give me the life I wanted. What I failed to consider was that I already knew how get it, I just needed the courage to take it. You gave me that courage, Jack. You showed me it was possible and now I want it so much more."

"Then why throw that away with this crazy scheme to kill the Cabal one by one? You got away from the others in the chopper crash. You came home. You were right there, and then you left again." Jack's anger was bubbling to the surface again, his hold on Ethan's hand tightening. "Jesus, Ethan. The worst of it was over. You know if you'd come to me, told me everything, we could have worked something else out. Together."

Ethan was shaking his head from halfway through Jack's speech. "No. You don't understand. If I'd gone back, and if the Office had agreed to go after the Cabal, they would have done it for their own reasons. *I* need to kill the Cabal, and they need to know why they're dying. They took thirteen lives, Jack, and destroyed them. Thirteen children who could have grown up to be anything they wanted, and they broke them into pieces and rebuilt them into monsters. I don't care how many important elections they've influenced, or how many peacemakers they've had killed. I don't care that they could overthrow half of Africa and South America on a whim. They're going to die because of what they did to my sisters and brothers."

In the silence that followed, their gazes locked and, perhaps for the first time, Jack seemed to fully see him.

Jack had always been able to look past the cold-hearted killer façade and see who Ethan really was underneath. He'd always been able to touch that hidden part of him, coax it out and nurture it. Now, he was seeing the whole of him. Understanding that the façade was an integral part of Ethan as well.

Quietly, Jack said, "Seven said she'd always known you would one day destroy the Cabal."

Ethan pulled in a sharp breath and stood, fight or scramble instincts surging. Seven had shown surprising insight into Jack's emotional state several months ago, but to find out she'd been more aware of Ethan's own feelings than he had been sent him reeling. Sent him right back to those sessions with the Doctor, where all of his thoughts and feelings would be discussed to the gentle *clink* of a teacup on a saucer. Reminded him how the Doctor had seemed to be able to read his mind and tell him what he thought without Paul or One-three having to say a word.

"Ethan? Hey, you okay?" Jack came around the table slowly, hand out as if gentling a skittish animal. "I didn't mean to upset you. I'm sorry."

Ethan shook his head. It wasn't Jack's fault. It wasn't Seven's, either.

"I think you need to rest. Why don't you lie down and I'll keep watch? I promise."

Not that he felt he could sleep at all, but Ethan agreed because it seemed the easiest way to stop talking about his past, and his present. He took off his leather jacket and lay down on the mattress. The USP he put next to his hand, ready to be picked up on a split-second's notice.

Jack watched it all with a concerned frown, then with a sigh, he sat down on the mattress. Back to the wall, long legs stretched out, he put his own gun on his lap, and picked up Ethan's hand and rested it on his thigh. "So you know I'm here."

Some of the tension melted out of Ethan's body and he nodded against the thin pillow. He ran through a meditation technique and dropped into a light sleep.

He woke when the firm thigh slid out from under his hand as Jack stood, tucking the gun into the back of his jeans before walking towards the hole in the floor. Sensing no alarm in the movement, Ethan simply rested his hand on his own gun and watched through half-lidded eyes. Jack crouched by the hole and whispered. After a moment, the landlady's head appeared and they talked softly for a minute, then she disappeared again.

Ethan sat up when Jack came back. "What's happening?"

"Balwinder just wanted to let us know the cops have been seen on the roads around this area but haven't gotten this far yet. We'll be safe here for the rest of the night at least. How do you feel?" He sat back down and left his hand on the mattress between them, an invitation and nothing more.

"A bit more refreshed." Ethan took Jack's hand in his. "Why do we need to hide from the police if you're here officially?"

Jack chuckled. "I said I was here *sort of* officially. In that this is an Office sanctioned job, but the Indian government isn't aware of it. Relations between Australia and India are not smooth right now."

"Why not?"

"Well, we were both otherwise occupied at the time, but an Aussie politician, Grant Owen, was arrested by the federal police for conspiring against the commonwealth. It seems he made a deal with parties as yet unknown for information our government would have preferred to keep secret. Namely the super secret SAS mission in Jharkhand eight years ago."

Oh dear. Ethan closed his eyes and hoped this wasn't what he thought it was.

"Anyway, *somehow* the deputy PM got hold of the information after Owen was arrested and started making threats about releasing it if the current PM didn't stand down. The PM, of course, refused, thinking Nelson wouldn't spill the information."

Sinking feeling in his stomach, Ethan said, "I guess he was wrong."

"So wrong. Now the Indian government is in damage control, because it was a Meta-State operation and not something they can admit to. So things are rather tense at the moment and we have to be very careful about crossing lines. I'm here because I have a legitimate Overseas Citizen of India card."

"Which won't count for much if they also find out you were there in Jharkhand."

"Exactly. Thus, no police." Jack tugged Ethan back to lying, going with him. "We've got a couple of hours until dawn. We'll make a new plan of attack then."

Ethan rolled over and kissed Jack's check. "Thank you, Jack." Then he settled down to sleep again.

TWENTY-SIX

When Jack awoke he was alone.

A note left by his head said, *Gone for water. Back soon.*

"Jesus." He rolled to his feet, stretching to work out some of the kinks of sleeping on an old, lumpy mattress. He tucked the USP into the back of his jeans, slung on his leather jacket and went to find Ethan.

The halls of the building were busier in the morning hours, filled with kids rushing from room to room and adults hustling out to get to work. Jack got a few curious looks but that was all. Outside, there was a line up of old men on the chairs.

He held his hands in a prayer pose and bowed his head. "Namaste."

There were several "namastes" in return and they happily directed him around the corner when he asked where the white man had gone.

There was an open field behind the building, mostly dirt and a few hardy weeds. Junk lined the edges—discarded sheets of tin, curls of wire, rotting wooden planks. In the middle of the field a bunch of kids had set up a pitch with a garbage can for a wicket. The fielding team had an average age of nine, some in school uniforms, and they were all yelling clashing advice in a mix of Marathi and English. The bowler rubbed a red ball on her pants and scuffed a bare foot in the dirt. She took a short run up and bowled.

At the wicket, Ethan swung his bat and the ball cracked against the wood. It flew out over the field and every member of the fielding team pelted after it, screaming and laughing as it hit the wall of the building.

Ethan dropped the bat and held up his hands in a victory sign. "That's a six."

He got a chorus of "no way" and "you cheated," which only made him laugh.

He was so beautiful Jack had to physically stop himself from rushing over and hugging him. Leaning against the wall he watched as the ball was retrieved and play started again. Ethan scored several more sixes until he was bowled out with a ringing hit against the garbage can. He was escorted off the field by several small brown hands pushing and pulling at him. Only when he was firmly set against the wall beside Jack did the team return to the game.

"Namaste, Jack," Ethan murmured.

Jack smirked. "Bowled out by a nine year old."

"I'm out of practice." He looked over. "What is that smile for?"

"Nothing. It's just a nice morning."

"It's not bad."

"Weren't you supposed to be getting water for showering?"

"I got called up."

Laughing, Jack dragged him away from the cricket field and they found water a couple of alleys over. Rather than cart buckets back to their room, they stripped to their underwear and poured water over themselves right alongside other men doing the same. Jack couldn't help but watch Ethan's lithe body as he sluiced water over his head, and it wasn't for the usual, lusty reasons.

Ethan had always been lean, taut skin over perfect musculature. Over the past months his muscles had gotten harder and his collarbones and hips were more defined, jutting out sharply. He'd been skipping meals or subsisting on protein alone. Jack should have fed him more of the dal and fruit the night before.

Dried and clothed, they went by a market stall and picked up a breakfast of grilled vegetable sandwiches, along with samosas, batata vadas and chutney. Back in their room, after breakfast, Ethan leaned over and kissed him, then started gathering their small amount of gear. It had been a small gesture, but natural and felt like they were getting over the anger and betrayal. Ready to go, Jack stopped when a familiar word started bouncing around the lower stories, loud enough for him to hear it.

Police.

"Not that way," Jack whispered, backing away from the hole in the floor.

Ethan moved to the window and opened it as slowly and quietly as he could. Jack made a stirrup of his hands and Ethan used it to reach up and pull himself out. Feet braced on the windowsill, he leaned down and grabbed Jack's hand, hauling him up. Jack scrambled through and looked around.

The wall of their building was plain and had no features they could use to climb, either up or down. Across the alleyway, however, was an open window. Ethan jumped first, tucking his legs up and rolling into the room, taking the thin cotton curtain with him. Jack made sure he was out of the way, then followed suit.

An old woman at a sewing machine, surrounded by piles of cut fabric, gaped at them.

Jack nodded. "Namaste. Can we get to the roof from here?"

She cocked a confused brow and he repeated it in Hindi. Then as if she had men fall through her window every day, she gave him precise directions up to the roof. Meanwhile, Ethan fixed the curtain and when it was done, said, "Thank you."

"Shukriya," Jack said and Ethan repeated it.

The woman stared after them as they left, then the sewing machine started up again.

This building was full of little businesses, one-room factories mostly churning out clothes that would be exported to first world countries and sold for a hundred times what these people were paid to make them. Nobody showed them much interest and they came out onto the roof within minutes.

Ethan crept up to the edge and scanned the ground. "The police are going in next door. We got out just in time."

From the opposite side of the roof, it was just a short climb down to the next one. Then across a small gap to the one beyond. Eventually, they left the multistorey buildings behind and came to the sea of tin shacks and huts that made up vast portions of the slum. They were, also, far from the only people making their way across the joined rooves. It wasn't a crowded thoroughfare, but they certainly didn't stand out as they trotted carefully from one home to the next. At one point, they passed a massive tree growing up through the middle of someone's roof. Five men sat under the shade of its branches, smoking and drinking. In the distance was a line of tall trees and not far beyond them, a row of white office buildings.

"It seems surreal," Ethan said as they headed that way. "Such poverty right here, and just past those trees, that. It feels like there should be something bigger between them. Something to explain why there's such a difference."

Jack could only agree.

An hour later, they were walking out of the slums, across a railway track, and back into a more familiar world. A couple of blocks along, Ethan swiftly broke into a small hatchback, hotwired it and they joined the overwhelming amount of traffic.

"Where are we going?"

"We have to get out of the city, so head east." Jack settled back in the seat and closed his eyes. "I'll check in and get any updates."

It took him a few minutes to get into the right headspace to slip *sideways* and call up the overlay of his implant. The past twenty-four hours hadn't been exactly stress free and he was still worried that Ethan would try to ditch him again, so it took a bit to calm himself down. When he managed it though, the overlay showed several new files from the Office and several waiting messages.

Leaving the larger files for later, he read the messages first. Most were from Lydia, with brief updates on the political situation and further warnings to stay off the radar. Jack quickly sent through a few replies, confirmed another check in within a couple of hours and slid *sideways* back to full awareness.

"Did you have a destination in mind?" Ethan asked.

"Not exactly. We'll get out of town and find somewhere to hole up for the day."

It was nearly midday by the time they got out of Mumbai itself. They saw several police cars in that time but picked up no interest from them. Once finally away from the city, Jack turned them southward. Not long later, Ethan insisted they change cars, and Jack settled into the old SUV with a grimace as the seat sagged under him.

"Problem, Jack?"

"No. Just wondering at your choice of cars. This"—he gestured at the ripped upholstery and dirty floors—"isn't your usual standard."

"Stealing cars is too disruptive. However, when required, I prefer to take cars that won't be deemed as worthy of police follow up. I also avoid newer models that have inbuilt GPS tracking that require disabling, which only slows down a quick getaway."

Jack smirked. "So that's your excuse for having the harem."

"It is part of the reason, yes." Ethan's tone was mildly miffed.

"And you don't have a car in India?"

"This is my first visit to India, actually."

"What?" Jack gaped for a moment, then shook his head. "I thought you would have been everywhere. Ethan Blade, global terror."

Ethan smacked his chest with the back of his hand. "Don't forget, there were three of us under that name. I worked mostly Europe and North and South America. As did Two. Four and Nine were Africa. Seven was in South East Asia and the Antipodes. Ten is the Middle East and South Asia."

Jack's stomach swirled uneasily. "So he's . . . ?"

"Middle Eastern, we believe. None of the others knew where their birth countries were."

The scenery passed in silence for several minutes, then Jack sighed and asked a potently dangerous question.

"Do you want to try to find your mother?"

Another long stretch of nothing but the car's rattly engine. Ethan focused on the road ahead, hands tight around the steering wheel.

"We could start a search," Jack said gently. "We have a general area to look in. And a name that has to be in some hospital records somewhere. I mean, it would take a while, but we could do it. If you wanted."

After a moment, Ethan simply shook his head.

"Okay." Jack squeezed his thigh. "Offer's always there, though."

They stopped in a small village at lunch time for food and fuel. Ethan hid under his hat and stayed in the car. Jack got them lunch and filled up the tank. They travelled a little further until they found a side road leading to a small patch of trees.

In the mild seclusion it gave them, Ethan got out and stretched, wincing as his shoulders popped.

"Sore from yesterday?" Jack asked.

"Hmm. A little."

Jack made him sit on a grassy patch and got behind him to massage his shoulders and neck. Ethan moaned and melted into the touches, head tipping forward, giving Jack the endless temptation of his neck and hair.

Maybe Jack could convince Ethan to give up this dangerous quest. To go home with him and let the Office deal with the Cabal. He did understand Ethan's driving need to punish those who'd caused him so much pain and trauma. For years after his mother's death—in this very country—he'd been dedicated to doing what he could to make sure her killers were found and punished. It had hurt his relationship with his dad and turned the sibling rivalry between him and Meera into a cold war. Then when he'd finally had the chance to catch those responsible—or at least part of the organisation responsible—it had ended in one of the worst military losses in recent history. Still not having learned the lesson, Jack had moved onto his next target. The all-consuming need to hurt the CO who'd sent him and his squad into Jharkhand had been initially satisfied by smashing his face in, but it had taken Jack years to recover from that nightmare mission—and he knew now he would never be fully healed. The only lasting result from hitting his superior officer had been his discharge from the army.

None of that felt equal to a childhood of abuse, though, so Jack kept his opinions to himself. He knew he would be speaking from a selfish position. He just wanted Ethan safe. He wanted him happy and content. He wanted Ethan with him. He also knew he would get none of that until Ethan had satisfied himself with his vengeance. So he would keep Ethan as safe as he could while he did it. He would do it to make him happy. He would follow him anywhere, just to be with him.

TWENTY-SEVEN

than sighed as Jack's hands worked magic on his sore shoulders. He had missed this type of contact. It was surprising how used to a kind, tender touch he'd become over such a short time. Possibly missed it more than the passion and sex. Missed the quiet moments like this, when it was just the two of them and nothing to worry about.

Except that there was something to worry about. They still had to be careful of the authorities, and there was still the Cabal. He'd worked too hard to get here, almost to the core of evil itself, to let it go now. It was a wonder that Jack hadn't tried to talk him out of it. The help of the Office had been completely unexpected and only warily accepted. Good intentions or not, the Office was still part of a governing bureaucracy.

A soft kiss landed on the back of his neck and Ethan couldn't help but smile. This softness was a facet of Jack that continually surprised him, in very good ways. That trek through the desert hadn't shown Ethan this side of him. He hadn't seen it until they'd been together in Singapore, where Jack had tended his injury, then lay down with him, not for sex, but for comfort and rest. They'd had four days together, and it wasn't until the evening of day three that Jack had given in to Ethan's seductions and taken him to bed for more than sleep or an incredibly thorough blowjob.

Just as the night before he'd stopped Ethan's lust before it went too far. Jack had been angry, yes, still hurt from being left behind without a word, but there had also been concern for Ethan as well. He'd been correct. Ethan would have regretted sex, hating how he'd been so weak as to give in to his selfish desires, rather than be prepared for the enemy. He'd made so many stupid mistakes while Two had been in Sydney, he couldn't afford any more.

"Jack?"

"Yeah?" He rapid-fired kisses up and down Ethan's neck, his hands now more caressing than therapeutic.

"I assume there is a larger plan in the works. You said the Office was working to help me, after all."

Jack stopped kissing him and, with a sigh, rested his chin on Ethan's shoulder. "We have things in play. Our analysts and technicians took the information we gathered from each of your kills and extrapolated with regards to current political and economic models and, at last count, pinpointed a hundred and thirty odd candidates for the Cabal leadership."

Ethan's jaw dropped. Then he pulled away from Jack and turned around to face him. "Truly?"

"Truly." Jack mimicked. "See, we're good for something."

Leaning in and lowering his voice suggestively, Ethan said, "Good for many things." He kissed him, slow and lingering.

Jack was smiling when Ethan pulled back but lost it when he continued. "With each new body, we narrowed it down even more. When we worked out you were going after Jäger, that gave us seven likely suspects." He took a deep breath. "Three of whom happen to be here, in India, right now."

This was . . . it was . . . Ethan didn't know what he felt as those words sank in. Didn't know if he felt anything at all. Should it be relief at knowing he was closer than he'd believed? Rage at the people ultimately responsible for tearing him apart as a child? Gratitude that he wasn't on his own anymore?

"Do you know where they are?" He tried not to sound too eager.

"No. We just know they all came into the country within the last week. One through Mumbai, one through Chennai, and another through New Delhi. After that, they haven't been on anyone's radar."

"Who are they?"

Jack closed his eyes and, clearly reading from his implant, said, "Yanis Mylonas, Poseidon Shipping Company. Osamu Sakamoto, Sakamoto Industries. Karyna Seaver, Seaver-Randal Incorporated. They're all up there in the top one hundred richest in the world, but they're not the big names. It could just mean that they're not reporting their true wealth to keep a low profile, but between them, they have connections to over a quarter of the world's economic and political spheres." Opening his eyes, he added, "They seemed like they fit the requirements for megalomaniacal super-dick."

The corner of Ethan's mouth turned up. Trust Jack to sum the Cabal up so eloquently.

"I have heard of Seaver and Sakamoto in conjunction with Cabal interests, but not Mylonas. I've never heard of him before."

Jack looked away for a moment, then down at his lap, and said very quietly, "He was a business partner of Stefanos Moraitis. He, ah, profited a great deal off Moraitis's death."

He knew. Jack knew about Moraitis. Ethan locked down the surge of conflicting emotions—fear, anger, shame, relief. He'd known the Office, and by natural extension Jack, would learn of it when they began truly digging into his history. That's what it was. History. It meant nothing now.

"Then yes." Ethan heard the distance in his own voice. "He is a likely candidate for a member of the Cabal's leadership."

"Ethan." The word was filled with concern.

"I assume the Office is working to track all three of them down?"

Jack eyed him worriedly, then sighed and nodded. "Yeah, of course. In fact, I should probably check to see if they've sent any good news."

Ethan stood, brushed off his arse, and said, "I'll keep watch while you do." Without waiting for Jack to agree, he turned and walked a tight perimeter around him and the car. When he came back to Jack, his man was lying on his back, eyes closed, and a certain *absence* to his body that meant he was deep in his implant.

Unable to resist, Ethan crouched and brushed black curls off Jack's forehead. It was something so simple, something few people probably thought much of at all. But for him, it was a privilege to touch Jack like this, to be able to make such a small yet intimate motion. Such a small thing, but so profound.

Perhaps he shouldn't insist on following through with his ultimate goal. Jack was here now and reminding Ethan of what he had. Not just

Jack himself, but a life he'd been slowly but surely learning how to live on his own. A life not ruled by the Cabal.

A life none of his siblings had ever had a chance at.

That's what he was fighting for. Why the Cabal had to end, one way or another.

Jack opened his eyes and, instead of startling at how close Ethan was, smiled. "Is this keeping watch?"

"It is," Ethan whispered. "On the most important thing to me."

Smile fading, Jack seemed to wrestle with several different reactions, finally settling on, "I'd fuck you right now, right here, if I thought you'd say yes."

Ethan was straddling him so fast he felt lightheaded. Or maybe that was because he was then leaning down and kissing Jack like he was the only source of oxygen in the world. When he stopped, he said, "I'd let you, if I thought I'd say yes, as well."

Jack laughed and pulled him down into a tight embrace that swiftly turned into a definite cuddle.

Before he could decide this was worth more than revenge, Ethan broke Jack's hold and sat up. That was as far as he got though, sitting back on Jack's thighs, only their hands still locked together.

"Do you have good news from home?"

Instantly serious, Jack nodded. "There's been a little breakthrough. I sent the details of the Lambo we chased to the Office. It's only a lease, so we can't trace an owner, but we did manage to hack its GPS tracker and find it."

Ethan squeezed Jack's hands. "Where?"

"It's in Goa, further south down the coast. It's about a ten-hour drive. We could get there before midnight."

"We'll have to change cars again soon." Still holding his hands, Ethan stood and hauled Jack up as well. "You can tell me everything else while we look for something suitable."

With a grumble that sounded less real than usual, Jack said, "And a map. If we can't file share via implant, then we'll need another way to plan. Why did you kill your implant anyway? To stop them from tracking you?"

"No." Ethan let Jack's hands go and dug in his pocket for the car keys. "The Cabal didn't give us that option, for obvious reasons. Mine died in the EMP blast I set off to crash the chopper with Four and Ten in it."

Jack blinked slowly, then again. "You what?"

"I had to do something to end the fight with Ten before he got the upper hand on me. Here, you drive and I'll look out for a new car for us." He dropped the keys into Jack's hand and turned to get into the passenger side.

"You what?" Jack said again, staring after him. "You *crashed* a chopper to win a *fight*? With yourself in it?"

"It seemed to be the most expedient way of winning."

"Jesus." Jack got behind the wheel and started the SUV.

Instead of heading south toward Goa, they went east until Ethan found a suitable car. Jack dropped him off a small distance away and then ditched the SUV in the next town along. An hour after they'd parted, Ethan picked Jack up off the side of the road in an old, boxy Maruti 800 from the eighties.

Ethan drove so Jack could check his messages again, reporting the updates to Ethan.

The Lamborghini Huracán was located in a house isolated on top of a hill near the coast. There was only one road leading up to the large house, winding around the hill in an almost continual spiral.

"It belongs to Mahavir Balakrishnan," Jack recited. "He's the tenth richest person in India, though that may be a conservative number if he's associated with the Cabal and hiding his true worth. Inherited the family business when he was forty-seven and managed to increase their profit margins when he introduced full automation into their pharmaceutical production. The automation systems were designed and built by Sakamoto Industries."

Ethan nodded. "He's part of the Cabal then. Was he one of your candidates for the leadership?"

"We noted him but he didn't have the wealth or global connections the others do. He's right down the bottom of the long list."

"It makes sense they'd use him as a connection then."

"Yeah. But remember, this is pretty much conjecture at this point. We're only going on the word that Ten said he was taking Jäger to the Cabal leaders. He could have been lying. This could be a trap."

"It could be." At Jack's raised eyebrow, Ethan added, "All right, it probably is. But knowing that we can plan accordingly. Do you have schematics of the house?"

"Not yet, but they got satellite images of the property."

For the first time since the chopper crash, Ethan regretted the loss of his implant. It would have been much more efficient for Jack to send him the images than describe them. He did, however, enjoy listening to his lover's voice as he described thirty square hectares of lush trees and vegetation surrounded by a twelve-foot wall with towers at each corner and a guard station at the front gate.

"The drive goes around the house to what's probably a garage at the back," Jack continued. "There's a pool in front of the house. Christ, people with money have a really warped sense of perspective. Wait until you see this bloody place."

Ethan chuckled. "I asked you to tell me everything, Jack."

"I don't know that I can do this thing justice."

"Try, please. The more I know, the better prepared I'll be."

"Ugh, okay. I'll tell you now though, you aren't going to like it."

When Jack had finished, Ethan had to agree. He didn't like it. "This isn't going to be simple."

"No. No it is not."

They tossed ideas back and forth as they continued south to Goa. Nothing either of them came up with had a chance of working, sadly, considering the nature of the house they were going to attempt to infiltrate. Ethan was starting to despair that they would have to wait another day and lose any element of surprise they might still have.

As the sun set, Ethan dropped Jack off on a corner in a largish town and drove away. It was Jack's turn to boost a car. Preparing to ditch the Maruti 800, Ethan wiped down the interior and as he did so, accidentally popped open the glove compartment. A brown faux-leather case fell out. Reflexively, Ethan caught it, feeling small shapes shift around inside it. He unzipped it and found a basic set of make-up. About to put it back, an idea occurred.

Half an hour later, Jack rolled to a stop at their agreed meeting point in a Nissan Bluebird.

"You said old and unlikely to be missed," Jack said as Ethan got in, unable to stop the grimace. "If I'd asked, they probably would have paid me to steal it."

Ethan snorted. "It sounds like the engine is going to fall out at any moment."

Jack patted his thigh. "I'm sure it'll be something you can fix."

"Your faith is comforting. Before we leave, there is something else we need to pick up."

"What?"

Smiling, Ethan said, "I have a plan."

TWENTY-EIGHT

"I'm not sure this plan will work," Jack muttered.

Ethan gripped his chin tighter. "I said, don't move."

"I didn't move."

"You're moving your face and that's the part I specifically need to not move."

"You never said so *specifically*."

With a short, sharp sigh, Ethan let his face go and sat back on his heels. "Jack."

Jack couldn't help but smile. He'd missed the whole-sentence-in-his-name thing Ethan did so well. Even when that whole unspoken sentence was full of frustration and command.

"Okay. I'll behave. I just want it on record that this plan has a very thin chance of—" He was cut off by a kiss.

This plan, he was very much on board with. Especially with Ethan straddling his lap, but before he could take things further, Ethan pulled his mouth away and frowned critically as he looked Jack's face over closely.

"Did you mess it up?" Jack asked warily.

"No, thankfully."

"Then why kiss me?"

"It was the most efficient way of shutting you up. Now, hold still. And I mean everything, Jack."

Jack gave one last pained groan then did as told.

Shaking his head, Ethan dipped the tip of the fine brush into the palette of colours in his left hand. "It's almost done."

Holding still, Jack closed his eyes as Ethan brushed the make-up over his forehead.

They sat in the front passenger seat of the car, the overhead light on so Ethan could see what he was doing. The car was hidden behind a cluster of trees off the side of the road so the glow wouldn't be seen by passing traffic. Ethan had been working on him for nearly an hour, trying a few different approaches until he got the desired effects he wanted. For all his doubts about the plan working, Jack was willing to go along with it because it was the best either of them had managed to come up with, given their limited resources.

After another ten minutes, Ethan sat back again. "I'm done."

Jack opened his eyes. Ethan was studying him, frown pinching his dark brows together.

"It doesn't look good enough?" Jack asked.

"No. I mean, yes, it does." Ethan sucked in a quick breath. "It does."

Understanding Ethan's reaction, Jack just nodded.

"I always knew you and Ten shared some similarities of appearance," Ethan said softly. "But seeing you like this . . . it's . . ."

"I get it. It's okay." It wasn't okay. Jack hated being the cause of any discomfort for Ethan, but this was his plan. The only one they had.

Ethan gave a single nod, then scrambled off him, over the centre console and back behind the wheel. Jack angled the rear vision mirror so he could see the final product of an hour's work and a dozen pieces of pharmacy bought make-up.

He barely recognised himself. His cheekbones were sharper, eyes darker, eyebrows thicker, and lips thinner. A scar ran from his hairline down towards his right eye. His black curls had been loaded with product and slicked back. He looked leaner and starker.

"Ten moves differently to you." Ethan's tone was neutral as he put away the brushes and pens. "You have this sort of lose swagger when you walk. Ten is more precise. There is intent in every move he makes. He doesn't gesture needlessly. He's very . . ."

Psychopathic was the word Jack wanted to use, but he went with, "Robotic?" so as to not push Ethan further away.

Ethan's emotional relationships with his siblings were complicated. Jack had watched helplessly as Ethan mourned Two, one of the main people who'd made his childhood a horror story. He'd chased Ethan across the globe as he hunted vengeance for those other brothers who'd tried their hardest to kill him. While Jack and Meera weren't exactly poster-worthy when it came to familial harmony, neither had actually ever tried to kill the other. He had no real understanding of the turmoil it had created in Ethan's head and heart. All he could do was be supportive, and if that meant boldly walking into the enemy's stronghold pretending to be a deranged, cold-blooded assassin named Ten, then that's what he'd do.

After all, he'd already walked back into India for him.

"Hm, yes. Robotic." Ethan started the car and headed to the road. "He also speaks with an accent like mine."

"No worries. I can do British."

"Jack, I've heard your English accent. It is atrocious."

"Come on, old chap. It's not that bad." Jack started out in his exaggerated mimic of Ethan's accent, then slid into a more natural sounded one. "Never fear, I can pull it out when required. It's just that teasing you is so much fun."

Ethan cast him a sceptical, sidelong glance, sighed, and proceeded to tutor him until he was talking in a monotonal flat voice that bled any warmth out of the accent.

It had been several years since Jack had done any true undercover work. The stint with the Sydney police hadn't really counted because he'd gone in as himself, mostly. His soul had been too close to the surface on that job. It had been like having a filling done without anaesthetic. This time, though, it was like it had been in the desert with Valadian's organisation. A different name and look, new speech patterns and physical attitude. A protective layer of armour over himself was very welcomed.

Even if the closer he got to meeting Ethan's expectations, the more Ethan drew away from him. Perhaps it was his own defence mechanism, a coating of ice to shield him from the coming combat. Or perhaps it was that Jack was doing too well in bringing Ten to life in the tight confines of the car.

Once Ethan was satisfied with Jack's Ten impersonation, the interior of the car got very quiet. Just the hum of the noisy old tyres over the road and the clattering of the out-of-tune engine. Jack kept pouring over the satellite images of the house where Ten had supposedly taken Jäger to meet with the Cabal bosses. A wall, some guards and piles of vegetation. Jack had been required to get into more fortified places before, and undoubtedly so had Ethan, but he didn't believe people of the calibre they were dealing with would trust to so few security measures. Whatever else was in place was something he and Ethan would have to discover on their own, taking days or weeks they couldn't afford. Which was why they'd gone with this desperate subterfuge.

It was after midnight before they reached Canacona in southern Goa, where their target was situated. They had found a paper map at the same time as the make-up and Jack directed Ethan towards the southern end of the region and into a forested area, the road slowly rising towards the peak in the distance. Even though they knew the house was there, they could see no sign of lights to pinpoint it, probably camouflaged by the surrounding trees. Ethan switched off the headlights and navigated by his heightened night vision alone.

The road up to the house wound around the hill, a continuous curve that held potential threats every couple of hundred meters. Jack found himself tensing unconsciously, his USP in hand, ready to spring up with a second's notice. The further they went, the slower Ethan got. At oh dark hundred, the road was deserted.

As they reached the final side road—more an extended driveway to a property nestled on the slope below them—Ethan pulled onto it and then off into the trees and parked their stolen car.

"They'll most likely have passive surveillance from here on," he said. "Any car on the road ahead should be one they're expecting."

"And any car they're not expecting is one they can prepare for." Jack kept up his Ten voice, committing to it so he didn't slip up.

"Exactly. Wait here. I'll see what options we have."

Ethan was out of the car and melting into the night shadows before Jack could wish him luck. His man didn't need luck, but that didn't mean Jack couldn't hope it upon him.

Jack got out and stretched. He'd been sitting for hours on end and while their plan should circumvent the need to fight his way into the house there was no guarantee of that. From his small kit, he slid knives into his boots, into the back of his pants, and hung one around his neck under his clothes. The shoulder harness for the USP went on under his leather jacket.

A soft night breeze eddied through the trees, bringing a faint hint of salt from the Arabian Sea. He breathed it in deep, using it to convince himself this wasn't Jharkhand. This wasn't a secret SAS mission doomed from the start by a lack of intelligence and the willingness of one man to sacrifice the soldiers under his command. No. It was a secret Office mission potentially doomed from the start by a lack of intelligence and one man willing to sacrifice himself for what he thought was the right reasons.

But Jack trusted Ethan more than he had trusted his COs. Didn't he?

The hurt of Ethan's disappearance from their life was still there. One of those knives they were all made of, poised to thrust or slice at the least little provocation. It hovered close now that Ethan was out of his sight. What was to stop the crazy bastard from simply hiking up the hill on his own, leaving Jack behind again, to confront his personal demons alone? He'd already proven his penchant for self-sacrifice with Two, and then with this reckless hunt.

"Christ." Jack spun around, ready to go after Ethan, stealth be damned.

A low rumble caught his attention and Jack slid back into the deeper darkness amongst the trees. Seconds later a slow-moving car came up the side road, headlights off. It was an Audi of some species. Sports wagon, silver, and rather generic, but probably more in line with whatever Ten might drive than the beat up old Nissen.

Ethan pulled up, left the car in idle and got out. Feeling a little bad for doubting Ethan's word, Jack met him between the two vehicles.

"No one was home," Ethan reported. "I believe it's a holiday house and this is probably the car left here for the staff to use."

Jack wasn't hard up by any means. He had a well-paying job, often received bonuses and danger money, and didn't have family other than his father in a nursing home to support. He did, however, live in Sydney. The idea of leaving an Audi for staff to use was foreign to him.

"Leave me about fifteen minutes to get into position." Ethan adjusted his weapons and stretched his arms and legs. "Once inside, I'll do my best to meet you around the back of the house, but don't wait for me if you can't. Our priority is getting in and—"

Jack cut him off with a kiss. It was brief and chaste because the last thing he wanted was Ethan to get pissy with him for mussing the make-up. But it was enough that Ethan was silent when he pulled back, staring at him with wide, white eyes and slightly parted lips.

"Seemed like the easiest way to shut you up." Jack smiled and patted Ethan's chest. Finding what he needed, he pulled out the sunglasses and slipped them on. The night became so much darker Ethan was just a blob amongst the inky black shadows. Without contacts to make his dark eyes white, however, it was the only option. "I know the plan. I won't forget it in fifteen minutes."

That rogue corner of Ethan's mouth turned up and he reached out to push the glasses up onto Jack's head. "Perhaps only put them on just before you reach the gate. I would hate for you to crash the car before we even get inside the wall."

"I don't crash every car I drive you know."

"I know. Just a large percentage of them."

God. Jack had missed this. So fucking much. The urge to plead with Ethan to forget this risky plan, to forget his need for revenge, rose so fast and sharp it took Jack's breath away. He wanted to drag Ethan out of this country that had hurt him so much, before it had a chance to hurt Ethan as much, if not more, and go home with him. Jack didn't care if they lived in his Leichhardt apartment or the Bathurst penthouse, or a ramshackle stable in an abandoned homestead in the middle of the desert—so long as they were together and not facing an unknown enemy in an unknown stronghold.

But that would be the quickest way to lose him. No one, not even his beloved dad, had been able to stop Jack from doing what he could to get payback for what had happened to his mum. It had been something Jack had to do. Couldn't imagine his life going forward without making the terrorists who'd killed his mother understand just what they'd taken from him. Nothing dad or Meera had said had broken through his grief and guilt. So how could he expect any different from Ethan?

"Be safe," he whispered.

The smile Ethan gave him was sad and serious. "I will. Don't do anything stupid."

Jack managed a wounded "who-me?" expression, then got into the Audi as Ethan melted into the trees. It was hard waiting the fifteen minutes, and just because Jack apparently liked torturing himself, he waited a couple extra to give Ethan a bit more time to get up the hillside. Then he started the car and eased out onto the main road. Headlights on, he wound around the hill, all the tension from before intensified by his imminent arrival at the gates to Balakrishnan's property. He needed a smoke or three. The pre-combat nausea was right on cue, curdling in his belly.

Then he came around a final curve and the road straightened out into a direct line to the solid steel gates.

"Holy fuck." It would take more than a grenade launcher to get through that barrier. A few rounds from an M1A1's smoothbore gun to reduce structural integrity, then the tank itself ramming the gates might just do the job. Sans heavy artillery and a tank, all Jack had was the plan.

Dropping the sunglasses over his eyes, Jack cruised up to the gates, coming to a stop next to the guardhouse. Two Indian men with the bearing of soldiers emerged and approached the car. Jack hit the button to wind down his window and, remembering Ethan's lessons on how his brother moved, slowly and deliberately turned to face the guards.

One visibly stiffened and held back when he saw Jack, hand hovering close to the butt of his holstered gun. The other didn't notice and rested his hand on the car roof over the open window.

"Sorry, sir, but this is private property. You're going to have to leave," he said in Hindi.

"No. I'm not." Jack spoke in Hindi, which Ethan assured him Ten knew. The flat tone got him a double-take from the guard. "You will open the gate before I call Balakrishnan and inform him that I cured you of your stupidity." He made sure to put no threat on the words. It was simple fact, according to Ten.

"Mahesh." The second guard came forwards. "That's *him*. You know, the one who . . ." He trailed off as Jack turned his gaze on him.

Mahesh's eyes widened and he snatched his hand back from the car. "Oh. Sorry, I didn't recognise the car." Recovering quickly, he added in a firmer voice, "We will have to check the vehicle before you go in."

This was something Jack and Ethan had planned for, so he nodded curtly and faced forward again, patiently waiting for them to do their job. The two guards hurriedly gave the Audi a thorough check, including opening the boot and poking around in it, feeling under the seats, looking under the bonnet and, with a camera on an extension pole, ensured there were no "extras" hitching a ride on the undercarriage. With the car cleared, one of them stepped into the guardhouse and opened the gate while the other covered the area around them with his rifle. Anyone trying to make a dash from the trees through the gate wouldn't get far.

Slowly, Jack eased the car through the opening and into the lion's den.

TWENTY-NINE

It had been tight, but Ethan had made it up the hillside to the wall in time to be in place when Jack arrived in the car. The run had left him a little winded—three months constantly hunting and killing had taken its toll—but he had a chance to catch his breath while the guards confirmed Jack's identity and checked the car over. They even obligingly gave him half a minute to dash from the tree cover to the car and roll under it. He'd just hauled himself off the ground when it rolled into the combat zone.

From his precarious position, Ethan couldn't see anything more than the paved driveway and the precisely trimmed edges of the lawn on either side. He was trusting Jack's judgement on where it would be the best place for Ethan to drop down and let the car move on without him. They'd talked about somewhere between the gate and main house, but the car didn't slow down, the signal for Ethan to detach, for several minutes. Unless Jack had misjudged the distances on the satellite photos and the house was further away than they'd thought—which Ethan doubted—then there possibly wasn't a good place for Ethan to leave the car without being seen.

The dark under the car got lighter as they angled up a steep part of the drive, growing to a point where Ethan wished his backup sunglasses weren't in a pocket he couldn't reach right then. By the time the road levelled out again, he had his eyes narrowed so far all he could see was a very narrow slit of light most people would probably find barely adequate to see by. And this was where Jack decided to come to an almost complete stop.

Hoping that this was the signal, Ethan let himself drop from the undercarriage and the moment the car had cleared him, he rolled blindly to the right, hit grass and a second later, dropped. Stomach lurching, Ethan tumbled down a sharp decline, his passage somewhat soothed by the fact it was lush, manicured grass under him and not rocks. Then he crashed to a stop against thicker foliage. Scrambling onto his belly, he wormed his way into the plants, rough woodchips under his hands. Under cover, he put on the spare glasses and looked around.

He was in a garden bed of ferns, broadleaved plants and palms of various heights. The groundcover was thick enough for him to hide in, but not so bad he couldn't move easily. In a crouch, Ethan surveyed the area. Jack had continued around the house and down the far side of the hill to the garage. In front of the house was the pool, sunk into the slope of the hill, its exposed side made of rock covered in vines and flowers. The water within glowed crystal blue thanks to submerged lights. The house itself was something else altogether.

Jack's description of "It's just glass. All glass," hadn't been entirely correct. The rear wall was brick and the rest of the framework of the house was thick, mahogany-coloured wood, as were the floorboards, which could be clearly seen through the glass walls. Front, sides, and interior walls in the two-storey structure were glass, as was the roof. The ground floor was lit up, letting Ethan see all the way through to the garden on the far side. There was a kitchen in the rear of the house, dining and lounge rooms, what was probably an office, and in the centre of it all, what might have been a Zen garden with sand, rocks and a small tree that extended up to the second storey. The rooms on the second floor were shrouded with thick curtains, presumably bedrooms afforded some privacy.

Sneaking up on anyone on the first floor would be hard. And there were people inside. A half dozen men in dark body armour were spread throughout the ground floor and a dark-skinned man—possibly Balakrishnan—stood in the central garden with a phone to his ear. There was no sign of the three Cabal leaders on the ground floor.

Ethan slowly made his way around the building until he found the garage. It was as wide as the house with four bays undercover and room for several more cars on a flat expanse where trees had been cleared to make way for a helicopter pad, a white chopper sitting in its centre.

The Audi was parked next to a pair of dark-coloured 4WD on the driveway. Inside the garage was the Lamborghini Huracán that had led them here, a silver Porsche Cayenne and a sleek black 1969 Chevrolet Corvette Stingray.

Jack was standing in the middle of the empty bay, legs spread and arms raised as a guard patted him down, removing the array of weapons he'd been carrying. A second guard stood watch, SIG Sauer MCX Rattler covering Jack. The situation looked routine rather than alarmed, so chances were good they hadn't seen through his disguise.

Using the 4WDs for cover, Ethan moved around to the far side of the garage, slid to the ground and rolled under the Porsche. Next to it, the Stingray didn't have enough clearance for him to move under, so he crawled around its rear end and paused between it and the Huracán.

The pat down ended and the guards warily watched Jack unbutton his shirt, having already removed his leather jacket. They were checking him for wires, which they wouldn't find, but the moment Jack took off his shirt, they would know he wasn't Ten.

Ethan tensed, readying himself. On the far side of the supercar, Jack shrugged the shirt off his shoulders and, letting it dangle from one hand, turned to show off his wireless torso.

The first guard to see the St. Thomas Cross tattoo frowned and asked something in Hindi, alerting the other man, who didn't bother with asking questions. The barrel of the Rattler came up, aimed directly at Jack.

Ethan sprang up and slid across the bonnet of the Huracán. Jack was already moving, swinging about and flinging his dangling shirt into the gunman's face. The man flinched, then flew backwards as Ethan's feet ploughed into his stomach. Hitting the cement floor of the garage, Ethan rolled and flipped to his feet, USP in hand.

Jack had closed with the other guard, that man's rifle trapped between one of Jack's arms and his side, while he pounded his other fist into the guard's face. Leaving that guard in Jack's more than capable hands, Ethan pounced on the other one, who was dazedly trying to aim his rifle at Ethan. Ethan kicked the Rattler away and then dropped, knees first, onto the man's chest. The man cried out in pain as his body armour compressed his ribs, the sound choked off when Ethan slammed the butt of the USP into his nose. It was fast and easy to then break his neck.

One enemy down, Ethan stood and turned. The other guard was on the ground, the hilt of a knife protruding from under his jaw, the blade sitting inside his head. Sightless eyes stared at the bland ceiling of the garage.

"Nice timing." Jack removed the knife from the body, contemplated the bloody blade and used his own shirt to clean it off. "I was starting to wonder if you were stuck under the car."

Ethan crouched and began undoing the fastenings on the body armour of the man he'd killed. "I took a moment to do a quick recon. You're right about the house. It won't be easy to move around unnoticed." Surmising that his own pants were similar enough to those of the guard, Ethan only swapped out his shirt for the dead man's and his armour.

Likewise stripping his target, Jack stretched the guard's shirt across his chest, frowned, and looked at Ethan, swimming in his stolen clothes. Wordlessly, they swapped.

Once fully dressed and carrying the Rattlers, they approached a door, which probably led into the house. Jack crouched and studied the keypad for the electronic lock. After a moment, he said he could hack it and went *sideways* into his implant. Ethan kept watch over him and their surrounds, thankful that Jack still had his implant active and that he was very well versed in most security systems. It took longer than Ethan was comfortable with, but Jack finally shook his head and stood.

"I couldn't crack their codes, but I did manage to put a new one in. It should get us through any lock in the place." He made sure Ethan was watching, then typed in the code. The red light on the keypad went green and the lock clicked open. "Can you remember that? Seven sevens?" Jack smirked at him.

"Very funny, Jack." Ethan slipped past him.

"If it's good enough for you, it's good enough for me."

"I hope you realise I chose that code for the entire purposes of making it *easy* for *you*."

Jack snorted and followed Ethan into the house, but all levity was forgotten the moment the door closed behind them. The area they came into lit up with motion sensor lights, illuminating a narrow, brick-walled staircase leading upwards. Rattler at the ready, Ethan went first, Jack ascending backwards to keep a watch on their six.

At the first landing, there was a door, unlocked, and with Jack covering him, Ethan slowly eased it open. Beyond was a dim, narrow space opening into the kitchen. Gleaming stainless-steel appliances nestled into cabinets made of the same rich mahogany as the house's frame. Between that and the glass walls giving an unimpeded view of the surrounding greenery, it gave the appearance of the house having grown around these metal intrusions. It was an incredibly surreal sensation.

"There is a study opposite the kitchen," Ethan whispered to Jack, motioning behind them. "Directly in front of us is an internal garden. Sand, rocks, single tree. It extends up to the roof, I believe. On either side are lounge and dining rooms. There were six guards twenty minutes ago, and a man who could be Balakrishnan."

"Did you see Ten?"

Ethan shook his head. He would know his brother from a distance.

"Right. I'll take this floor then." Jack settled his sunglasses back in place and slung the Rattler from its strap under his arm. "Keep them down here while you go up to the next floor."

A small measure of the tension in Ethan's shoulders let go. At least he wouldn't have to fight with Jack about what was about to happen. If the Cabal leaders were here, they were most likely on the second storey. And they would not be leaving it alive.

Ethan gave Jack a firm nod, then started up the next set of stairs. The door closed quietly between him and Jack. Locking away his worries—Jack was smart and incredibly well trained, he would be perfectly fine on his own against six others—Ethan focused on the task ahead.

This was it. What he'd fought so hard for over the past months. His goal, finally within reach. Three out of five leaders of the Cabal, those who had been the ultimate conductors of the ruin of his childhood and that of twelve other innocent lives. People who believed their wealth—and the power that went with it—gave them rights over the lives of everyone else, to manipulate and exploit on such a wide scale it encompassed whole countries. All to gain more money—more power.

The door on the second storey landing had a keypad. Ethan pressed seven seven times and the light switched from red to green, a soft clack signalling the unlocking of the door. As with the floor below, this door opened into a small, secluded space so as to not interrupt the aesthetic flow of brick and glass. All he could see this time, however, was a curtained glass wall. Which of his tormentors was behind that thick emerald velvet? Mylonas? Seaver? Sakamoto? It didn't matter. They would all be facing the monster of their own creation tonight.

Rattler held diagonally across his chest, Ethan stepped out into the open. There were guards outside of three of the four doors along the central hallway. The space was interrupted by the trimmed upper branches of the tree in the garden below, extending almost to the glass ceiling. The closest guard was Caucasian, his bare, massive arms crossed over a wide, muscular chest. A tattooed winged skull and Force Recon banner was prominent on his left biceps. The next one was Japanese, medium height, lean, dark haired, scar puckering his left cheek, and had a pair of long bladed knives sheathed at his sides. Across from him was a tall Nordic woman Ethan found familiar but couldn't quite place.

The male guards both eyed Ethan warily, but it was the woman who recognised him, either personally or as a threat. She drew a Glock 17 with a silencer and pointed it at Ethan, turning side on to present a slimmer target. Instantly, the men came on guard.

Rushing forwards, Ethan used the tree for cover from the woman, bringing himself into range of the Marine. The big man was uncoiling himself for combat and Ethan sprang up and kicked out sideways. His boot caught the man in the solar plexus. Gasping in surprise and pain, the Marine staggered backwards, hitting the glass wall. The scarred guard came forwards, knives in his hands. Ethan threw himself in the other direction, keeping the tree between them. Putting himself directly in line with the woman's gun. Diving to the floor, Ethan rolled under a suppressed gunshot, the sound still echoingly loud inside the glass walls. Shoving with his hands, Ethan slid into her legs. Or into the space they would have been if she hadn't dodged away.

The corridor between the rooms ended in a balcony. Ethan's boots hit the glass balustrade, the glowing water of the pool all he could see. He immediately pushed off again. Glock's boots landed where he had been, but her gun tracked him nevertheless. Ethan flipped over backwards, coming up onto his knees, just in time to fall flat on his back under the scything pass of a knife. Continuing the tumble, Ethan scissored his legs up and over, knocking the blade from Scar's hand, and kicking him in the face.

This time, when Ethan sprang to his feet, it was right into the waiting arms of Marine. As those meaty weapons locked around him, Ethan smiled.

Time to get serious.

THIRTY

The door closed softly behind him and Jack hoped Ethan found the peace he was so desperately looking for up there. Unfinished vengeance was a weight that dragged everything down with it, compressed the heart and mind until there was little room for anything else. Jack had had his need for revenge very soundly beaten out of him. Hopefully Ethan wouldn't experience that same gutting disappointment.

If he had any chance of helping that not happen, Jack needed to keep these guards from rushing upstairs the moment a ruckus started.

Two of the six guards turned as he entered, Rattlers coming up to ready. Jack, face schooled into his approximation of Ten, merely looked from one to the other, supremely unconcerned with them and their weapons. They hesitated, then checked in with the suited man sitting in a chair in the lounge room that opened onto the garden, his view of Jack clear through the pristinely clean glass walls.

He appeared to be Mahavir Balakrishnan, in his late fifties, designer suit, tie missing and top buttons of his shirt undone. He held a small tablet in one hand and a tumbler of amber fluid in the other. His dark eyes behind wire-rimmed glasses skated up and down Jack, and then he gave a slight nod.

Guessing it meant he'd been accepted as Ten, Jack returned the nod and checked back with the guards. The pair that had come alert relaxed, but then moved further away from him. Like those on the gate, they seemed to have developed an understanding of what Ten was. Using that, Jack moved towards the garden in the centre of the house. Like water parting before a boat, the guards peeled away into the rooms on either side.

"Any sign of your counterpart?" Balakrishnan asked in Hindi, sounding bored.

"Negative," Jack answered.

"Maybe he's not as determined as you claim."

Jack gave him Ten's bland expression and a corner of Balakrishnan's mouth turned up in a sardonic smile before he went back to reading.

Close to the tree, Jack could hear only faint noises from the second storey. Footsteps, then a patter of more rapid ones, a few muffled thumps, then a silenced gunshot.

Everyone on the ground floor heard that. The guards turned, weapons raised, eyes going to the ceiling, then to Balakrishnan, who in turn looked at Jack.

Jack held up a hand in a "wait" gesture. Above, there were thumps and crashes, grunts and an exclamation in what might have been Japanese.

"Ten?" Balakrishnan stood, tablet forgotten as he peered upwards.

The sounds of the fight clattered from the back of the house to the front.

Around Jack, the guards started moving restlessly towards the stairs.

"Ruko," Jack said in Hindi, wondering how far he could push the quasi-authority Ten seemed to have here.

The guards obeyed and stopped but there was definite doubt in their expressions.

"What is this about?" Balakrishnan strode toward him, apparently very confident as he questioned a known psychopathic killer.

Again, Jack used the "wait" hand. Balakrishnan paused, frowning.

Shit. Time was running out and the sounds from above were only amping up. Jack had to do something decisive, and soon.

With a startled grunt, a body dropped down through the tree's hole. A big white man with tattoos thumped into the sand, head narrowly missing a large rock. After a moment, the man lifted his head and looked up at Jack with a shocked expression.

In two strides, Jack stepped down into the garden and went to one knee beside the huge man, Rattler aimed at his head. Down but not out, the man knocked the rifle aside. However, he missed the long-bladed knife Jack rammed into his neck from the other side. The man convulsed once, life bleeding out of him swiftly. Jack jerked his knife out of the body and stood, red droplets plunking into the sand.

"That was Seaver's bodyguard," Balakrishnan said. "Why did you—" His eyes went wide and recognition—or lack thereof—crossed his face. "You're not—"

Jack threw himself at the man, catching him around the thighs and taking him to the floor. He was spry for his age, but Jack was faster.

With Balakrishnan face down, Jack planted a knee in his back, the point of his bloody knife against the base of his neck, and the business end of the Rattler directed at the suddenly converging circle of guards.

"Guns down and back up," Jack said to them. "Or Money Bags gets it."

"Do it," Balakrishnan said, tone curt if a little shaky.

It worked and the guards stopped advancing. Jack gestured with the rifle and they retreated into the dining room.

Uncaring of the knife at his neck, Balakrishnan turned his head so he could see Jack from the corner of his eye. "I should have recognised you quicker. I've been waiting for you and One-three to show up all night."

Jack snorted and, keeping a watch on the corralled guards, let his Rattler hang from its strap while he fished some plastic restraints from a pocket. "Sorry, we got delayed looking for just the right shade to highlight my eyes."

"It's a masterful job."

"You, of all people, shouldn't be surprised at his talents." Jack bound the industrialist's hands behind his back, then turned to his ankles.

"Actually, I wasn't part of the Cabal when the experiment was underway."

Prisoner secured, Jack stood and pushed Balakrishnan onto his back with his foot. "Look at you, moving up in the world. Guess you're going to be there when the experiment ends, though."

Balakrishnan smiled. "I guess so."

That wasn't right. The man was too smug for someone tied hand and foot while one of the world's most successful assassins was in the house with death on his mind.

Rattler directed towards the milling guards, Jack closed the sliding glass door on the dining room, locking it by the simple means of smashing the keypad. Several of them would have handguns but Jack doubted that when building this frivolous house, Balakrishnan had skinted on the bullet-proof glass. After kicking the dropped Rattlers into the garden and covering them in sand, he hauled Balakrishnan into the lounge room where he'd been earlier and into a chair.

"Tell me about the Cabal," Jack said.

"Don't you already know it all? With your Office of Counterterrorism and Intelligence, and the Meta-State. You got the Messiah's data. Surely you know everything."

"Yeah, it was very helpful in tracking down you and the other elite members of the Cabal. Helped us narrow down the list of scumbags running the whole thing, as well. But what it didn't tell us is why. Is it just the money?"

Balakrishnan laughed. "Are you truly that naïve?"

"When it comes to your level of sociopathy, yeah. Spell it out for me, Scrooge."

Settling back into the chair as well as he could, Balakrishnan smirked. "Tell me about your Meta-State first. Why was it formed?"

Jack could see where this was going and he played along, hoping that the lack of noise from the second floor meant Ethan had won through whatever guards had been stationed up there.

"To protect its signatories from internal and external terrorist threats. We're working for the people, not using them for our own gains."

The smirk turned condescending. "I know that you know very well that it has been manipulated for monetary gain."

"If you're talking about Glen Harraway then you're as naïve as I am, because he was a traitor and we dealt with him. Very fucking harshly."

"And you're doubly naïve if you believe he was the only one." Balakrishnan continued over the top of anything Jack might have said. "But that is not what I'm talking about. This current trouble between our two countries—*your* two countries, I believe—is a perfect example. Or is that something else you need explained fully?"

Jack moved away from Balakrishnan and towards the tree, listening for a clue as to what might be happening upstairs. He needed a moment as well. Balakrishnan probably knew exactly what he was doing bringing up that topic right now. He was on a rung just below the leaders of the Cabal. He had three of them in his house right now. There was no way he didn't know exactly what had happened in Jharkhand all those years ago, and that Jack had been there, in the thick of it.

He heard nothing from upstairs. No movement, no voices. Hoping it meant Ethan had finished his bloody business and would be appearing on the ground floor any second now, Jack checked on the guards—still in their see-through prison, still glaring at him—and went back to Balakrishnan.

"I think it is something you need to hear, Jack Nishant Reardon." His tone dropped into a conspiratorial hush. "Let me tell you exactly what your Meta-State got out of the deal."

A loud crash came from above. Several booming gunshots. Feet running, bodies colliding at speed, voices snarling. Jack spun on the spot, trying to track the ruckus through the wooden barrier between him and Ethan. Across the way, the guards took it as their cue to move. Bunched together, handguns up, they all fired at the wall between them and the central garden at once. The glass crazed with impacts but held—for now.

Jack whirled and took cover behind Balakrishnan's chair, knife back at his throat.

"Kill me and you will never learn the truth about Jharkhand."

"I know the truth already."

"Do you?"

Fuck. Fuck, fuck, fuck. Things were quickly going tits up and right now was when this dickhead decided to dangle that bit of bait?

The guards ran out of bullets but the glass wall was still standing. So they started throwing furniture at it and three heavy wooden chairs from the dining suite was all it took to shatter it.

Jack threw the chair with Balakrishnan over sideways and crouched behind it, opening up with the Rattler. Men dived for cover but two of them fell to bullets before they could. Taking the rifle off automatic, Jack kept the rest of them pinned with strategic shots, but his ammunition wasn't going to last forever. He just had to hope—

A body clad in the same armour as the guards—as Jack and Ethan had stolen—sailed through the air from the second storey, arms flailing, and landed in the pool, water splashing up a great fountain.

Ethan?

One of the guards took advantage of his momentary distraction and dived from the dining room and into the sunken garden. Jack fired and grazed him, getting a cry of pain, but the man got one of the buried rifles and aimed it at Jack.

Ducking back behind Balakrishnan, Jack had the joy of hearing the industrialist scream "Don't shoot" just as the guard opened fire.

A spray of bullets arced over the chair, uselessly high but keeping Jack pinned. Then the Rattler jammed thanks to the sand in its mechanisms. While the man scrambled for another weapon, Jack leaped up, aimed, and put a bullet through his head.

Three down. The rest of them remained obediently behind the dining table they'd overturned.

Flicking a glance to the side, Jack saw no movement in the pool, but the blue water lapping gently at the edge was now stained pink.

Had it been Ethan?

"Bait."

Jack refused to look at Balakrishnan. "What?"

"You were bait. That's the truth of your deployment to Jharkhand. The Indian government needed something to draw the Maoist terrorists out of hiding without committing their own troops to a no-win situation. Foreign soldiers in a place they really shouldn't be was the perfect lure."

"Shut up." Jack really didn't want to hear this. He'd finally found something meaningful enough to drag him back here. Made enough peace with what happened back then to return now. God, he wanted to know, but finally learning exactly why he'd almost died, why he'd had to watch half his squad be picked off one by one by the enemy might just send him over the edge once and for all.

"Of course, your precious, altruistic Meta-State got paid for it. Preferential trade and economic resource agreements. Does that make the blood you and your men spilled there easier to accept, Mr. Reardon?"

The moment Balakrishnan had brought up this line of discussion, Jack had wondered if this was where it would end. Speculation never equalled certainty, however, and Jack was convinced the man was being honest. Lies could be disproven and never cut as deep as the truth.

He shoved it in a drawer in the filing cabinet in the back of his head. He would deal with it when he and Ethan were home and safe, not while he had at least three enemies and a prisoner, and he wasn't sure of Ethan's exact whereabouts or welfare.

Jack was turning when a gunshot rang out. The glass of the internal wall spider-webbed at the exact height of Jack's head. Instinct sent him to the floor, rolling behind the nearest couch for cover. Coming up to his knees, he aimed the Rattler at the new threat.

He stood at the back of the house, as if he'd just come down the stairs. Middle Eastern, scar across his forehead, sunglasses, a massive S&W 500 pointed at Jack.

Ten.

Calmly, the assassin walked towards him, his aim never wavering.

"I succeeded this time," Ten said and Jack realised just how bad his imitation had been. There had been too much life in the droning tone he'd used. Too much warmth. Too much soul.

Jack suppressed a shiver. Christ. Ethan had never made him feel this unquestionable *wrongness*. Neither had Two, for all his creepiness and homicidal hobbies. This was more than a psychopathy. It was an absence of something Jack couldn't define right then, but he suddenly empathised more with Ethan's need to punish the Cabal. They had not only created this man, but then unleashed him on the world.

Behind Jack, Balakrishnan started to chuckle.

Fighting the urge to shoot the industrialist, Jack said, "Succeeded at what?" He really didn't want to fucking engage with Ten but he needed time to find a way out of this mess.

"In getting my brother over a balcony."

Heart skipping beats, Jack's finger tightened on the trigger. Shooting now would do him no good. He didn't have enough ammo left to shatter the wall and Ten had too many options to take cover.

"Was he dead? 'Cause that's the only way I can see you actually managing it."

Ten's expression didn't change. "He wasn't dead, but he probably wished to be." When he reached the shattered wall, Ten backed into the dining room, never taking his site off Jack.

"What the fuck does that mean?"

Balakrishnan laughed harder.

"Shut the goddamn fuck up," Jack snapped at him, then at Ten, "Tell me what you mean."

Unslinging a backpack, Ten dropped it behind the table. "I mean, my brother was always too caring. Too . . . soft. He learned to kill as well as any of us, but it cost him dearly. We always knew he would want that price back. It is a pity he will never get it now."

Oh fuck. Oh God. What the hell had happened upstairs? Jack's stomach tightened so hard he nearly doubled over. He had to get to the pool, find Ethan. Get them both the fuck out of there.

It was Jharkhand all over again.

The three remaining guards stood up, now sporting new weapons provided by Ten. They advanced in two waves of two, covering him and each other. Jack was trapped, even though he could bloody well see freedom through the goddamned walls of this stupid fucking house. He could lose himself in the trees, like he had all those years ago, running with Nigel and dragging Lionel, desperately trying to evade and escape the insurgents who'd killed their mates. He'd all but carried Lionel out of the hot zone, he would do the same for Ethan.

Except that he couldn't. The enemy, once again, knew so much more than he did, understood the terrain better.

Jack dropped the Rattler over the front of the couch and stood, hands on his head. Two of the guards moved in rapidly and searched him for the rest of his weapons. As they were divesting him of his knives, the third man cut Balakrishnan free and helped him to his feet.

Mouth open to undoubtedly say something ultra smug, Balakrishnan was drowned out by a roaring engine. Everyone turned in time to see the orange Lamborghini race by the side of the house and down the steep driveway so fast sparks flew as the undercarriage scrapped over the sharp angle in the road. It curved around the pool, fleeing like all of hell's devils were on its tail.

"It appears he did not drown after all," Ten said as the red taillights grew further and further away.

"At least he's getting away." Jack's gratitude was real. Even if Ten put one of those absurdly large bullets through his head right then, it would be worth it because Ethan was free.

"Perhaps One-three wasn't a total loss after . . ." Balakrishnan trailed off, frown creasing his brow. "What is he doing?"

In the distance, the Lambo's brake lights flared brighter in the pre-dawn darkness as Ethan hit the brakes so hard the car slewed across the driveway. Then, before anyone could venture a guess, the white reverse lights came on and even in the house, the sudden burst of power from the engine was clearly heard.

As if released from a cannon, the supercar shot backwards up the driveway, moving faster and faster while everyone watched in surprise and confusion.

Jack and Ten worked it out before the others did.

"Holy fuck!" Jack broke out of the abruptly slack hold of his captors and dived to the right.

Ten went left, dragging Balakrishnan with him.

The Lambo hit the top of the incline, wheels turning at the last second so that when it launched off the improvised ramp, its rear end was pointed directly at the front wall of the house.

THIRTY-ONE

Marine dropped through the hole to the first floor, leaving just Glock on her feet. Scar was crumpled against the brick wall, his own weapon rammed forcefully through his chest. The other knife was in Ethan's hand and he tossed it at the woman as she raised her gun again. She dodged the flying weapon, dropping and rolling behind the tree.

Not bothering to run around the gaping hole in the floor, Ethan threw himself across the gap, caught a branch and swung over to the other side. He landed in a slide, boot colliding solidly with his final opponent's chest as she tried to rise out of her roll. She flailed backwards, gun flying from her hand. Ethan kicked up, catching her chin, and with a snap, her neck broke.

He lay for a moment, breathing hard. Three very skilled opponents in tight quarters had been a challenge, especially considering the gaping hole in the floor right in the middle of the combat zone. Ethan rolled over and peered through the hole, finding Marine lying in the sand, blood soaked into the yellow granules around his head. Someone—Jack most likely—had finished him off very quickly, judging by the lack of disturbance to the sand. Which meant Jack was most likely still active.

One stress eased, Ethan flipped to his feet, picked up Glock's gun and his abandoned Rattler and went to the door where Marine had been standing guard. After a few deep breaths, he punched in Jack's code and the lock opened.

The room was large and dark, shrouded by heavy velvet curtains in forest green. It was also suspiciously quiet. No one could have slept through the noise of the fight, or the one that appeared to be starting up below. All the gunfire was a good sign. If the enemy were shooting at something, then Jack was up to his usual tricks and making people very upset with him.

That didn't explain why the only reaction to the sudden ruckus below from the person in the bed was a faint mumble and twitch of a hand.

Cautiously, Ethan scouted the room, keeping one eye on the bed. As with the first floor, furniture was scarce and what there was, was made of the same wood as the house frame. Bed, bedside tables, dresser, two chairs and a low coffee table between them. A bathroom took up one corner, frosted glass walls around a free-standing shower, vanity, and toilet. The amenities were incredibly basic, but then this didn't seem to be a place one lived, but rather a showpiece for Balakrishnan's wealth.

A soft moan drew him to the bed, borrowed Glock in hand. The woman was perhaps in her sixties, a bob of artificially auburn hair messed up on the white pillow, wide, worried eyes looking up at Ethan as he came to stand over her.

Karyna Seaver. Scion of the New York Seavers, CEO of the multinational conglomerate holding company Seaver-Randal Inc and one of the richest women in the world. Ethan had worked for her, indirectly, several times over the years. He had suspected she was very close to the Cabal leadership, if not actually one of them, but had not been able to prove it.

Seaver's throat worked but no sound emerged apart from a few quiet gasps. The one hand resting on top of the covers twitched towards him, fingers stretching uselessly. Something had been done to her. A strong sedative perhaps. Or poison.

"What did they give you?" Ethan asked.

Mouth opening and closing in silent desperation, Seaver's eyes grew even wider and panicked.

"One blink for yes, two for no."

She blinked once.

"Do you know who I am?"

A slight tremble overtook her, whether from the paralytic agent running through her body or fear of him, Ethan didn't know. Didn't care. She blinked once, slowly, almost reluctantly.

"So you know what I do for the Cabal?"

A fast blink. She strained with her hand again, pleading. Ethan ignored it.

"Are you one of the five leaders?"

Two blinks.

Ethan pressed the barrel of the Glock to her forehead, right between her eyes so she could see it. "Are you one of the five leaders?"

The trembling grew and her eyelids fluttered, but made a single, jerking blink. Something like "please" stuttered out of her mouth.

"Then you know exactly why I am here."

Though pulling the trigger felt more like a mercy than a punishment as the tremble turned into convulsions and her struggle for air became a losing battle.

Ethan had rarely felt anything more than a passing bother for any death he caused. There had been worry when he hadn't been certain of a target's guilt, or relief when an enemy was no longer a threat, or sorrowful determination when he was killing his brothers. But those instances were few and easily lost amongst the vastness of nothing.

He had wanted to feel something now, though. Satisfaction? Release? Happiness? Something to mark this as the moment he felt free.

There was nothing.

The poison had robbed him of any agency in her punishment. The poisoner had stolen his freedom from him.

In the next bedroom, Osamu Sakamoto was already dead, sheets torn and rucked up thanks to the convulsions that had marked his final moments. Not even imaging the agony or fear that must have overtaken Sakamoto in those last minutes was a balm.

Yanis Mylonas was on the floor, one arm outstretched towards the door, as if he'd been trying to alert his guard. His body was still warm. He'd probably died during Ethan's fight with his bodyguard.

So close, but still nothing.

The chasm that had opened up in his chest when he'd walked away from Jack, that had only just started closing since reuniting with him, pulled wider again. He felt cold and empty. This was where he'd wanted to be, where he'd worked so hard, sacrificed so much, to get to, and now . . . it had all been for nothing. There was no fulfilment here. Just hollowness.

He'd risked Jack's life—their life together—for nothing.

Purely out of form, Ethan checked the final bedroom.

"Hello, brother."

The Glock's site was trained on Ten even before Ethan saw Hermann Jäger. He was bound hand and foot, Ten's arm around his neck holding him up as a shield, a blade pressed against Jäger's throat. The S&W 500 in Ten's other hand was pointed right at Ethan.

"Why did you kill them?" Ethan asked.

"Because I was told to."

And that was all it had ever taken for Ten to do a job.

"Who told you? Was it Zero?"

It happened very fast but Ethan saw the smile flit across Jäger's face.

Was this a coup? Was Jäger making a play for a leadership position? Why kill three of them if it was just Jäger? Unless it was a joint plan between him and Balakrishnan. And if it had been Zero who'd given Ten the job, then he was part of it as well. Either way, both Jäger and Ten had misjudged this moment, no matter what else their plan was. Jäger might not—yet—be part of the leadership, but his hands certainly weren't clean, either.

"Not Zero," Ten answered in his usual monotone. "He has not been trusted since you escaped in Sydney. He's favoured you one too many times. Orders are coming from higher up now."

Which meant the bosses were directly interacting with Ten, the last of their loyal assassins. Things must have become desperate.

"Then you made a mistake in your choice of shield." Ethan shifted his aim to Jäger.

Jäger jerked in Ten's hold, who only tightened his arm, keeping the man in place. Frowning at Ten, Jäger tried to get free again.

"And your mistake was thinking Jäger was a shield." Ten slit the man's throat.

Jäger slid out of Ten's now loose hold, hands pressing against the gushing wound in his neck. "You said . . . you . . . promised . . ."

All Ten did was step over Jäger's flailing body and advance.

"Why?" Ethan backed out of the room, keeping as much space between him and his brother as possible.

"To deny you the satisfaction."

It had all been part of the plan. A coup, and a punishment for Ethan. Take away the targets he had been aiming at for so long. Deny him *taking* his freedom from his captors. Leave him with an unfinished job—a defeat for Ethan in particular.

Ten followed him out of the room. "You had to be taught that no one ever defies the Cabal, One-three, and this is the only way you ever learned." He kept up his steady pace, never taking his aim off Ethan. "It's time for you to accept that and return home."

That was why Ten hadn't fired yet. Another brother trying to take him home, but not for personal reasons this time. Ten wouldn't have cared unless he'd been instructed to. But then Ten wouldn't care about taking him back wounded, either. Or dead.

Ethan spun and sprinted for the front of the house. Ten's rapid footsteps followed him. The huge Smith and Wesson boomed and fire blazed across Ethan's left hip. His leg gave out under him and he dropped to the floor. Rolling he came up against the glass balustrade on the balcony. Another bullet smashed into the glass just above his shoulder, making him hunch down instinctively.

"This did not end well for you last time, brother."

Ethan reached up and grabbed the top of the balustrade. "Last time wasn't my choice." He hauled himself up and over as another bullet—meant to kill—scorched across his ribs.

A single storey drop wasn't enough time to control his fall and Ethan hit the water badly. He impacted on his injured side, agony spearing through him even as the water engulfed him. He sank, pink tinging the swirling current. Ten peered over the edge of the balcony, his face wavering through the watery screen. Ethan let out bursts of air bubbles, smaller and smaller, until there was no more air. Ten watched him, much as Ethan had watched Ten in the crashed chopper. Ethan's lungs ached and his throat burned to breathe in, but he controlled his body's needs. Even after Ten disappeared back inside the house, Ethan held to his subterfuge for as long as he could. When it was no longer possible, he propelled himself across the bottom of the pool towards the far side. Breaking the surface, Ethan dragged in massive gulps of air, grabbing onto the edge for support as his oxygen-starved body quivered.

A familiar gunshot sounded in the house. Spinning, he saw Ten aiming at Jack through a wall of fractured glass.

This plan was lost. There was no salvaging it now. Ten had the upper hand. He'd always had the upper hand. Ethan's only option was to get Jack and get out. The problem was no one could sneak up on anyone in this place. Ambush was out of the question. Which gave him only one option.

Frontal attack.

THIRTY-TWO

The front wall of the house shattered, jagged hunks of glass flying wildly as the orange Lamborghini crashed to a stop in the middle of the lounge room. Jack curled up on the floor, arms over his head, knees to his chest, back to the worst of the destruction. There were a couple of screams behind him as the car or flying glass took out the guards too slow to move. Someone was far enough out of range of the danger zone to open fire on the car.

"Jack, get in."

Rolling over, Jack took a lightning fast sitrep. One guard was pinned between the back of the car and the inner wall. Another was on the floor, head bleeding from impact from a large chunk of glass. And there was the third, back in the dining room behind the overturned table, firing wildly at the rumbling Lambo. The driver's side door—closest to Jack—was open and inside, Ethan was scrambling across the console to the passenger seat.

Jack crawled to the car, keeping it between him and the idiot wasting his ammo in the next room. He tossed his Rattler into the car and clambered in behind the wheel.

"Show off." Jack slammed the door and put the car in drive.

"I do like to make an entrance."

Snorting, Jack stamped on the accelerator and the car burst out of the glass house. He spun the wheel to get them around the pool, rather than in it. One of the back tyres may have gotten a bit wet, but he got them onto the driveway and headed in the right direction.

"Jack, the gate is that way." Ethan helpfully pointed behind them.

"And did you see the gate? We won't be getting through it in anything less than a tank." Jack drove the Lambo around the side of the house and down to the garage. "Our real getaway vehicle is— Shit!"

Two people dashed out of the garage and across the open space towards the helipad. Instinct took over and Jack jerked the wheel and slammed on the brakes. Ten grabbed Balakrishnan and hauled him out of the way of the car, diving after the tumbling industrialist as the Lambo careened through a juddering turn. It went through a full one-eighty before it came to a stop.

Already moving, Ethan had the window down and the Rattler up. He unleashed the rifle at Ten and Balakrishnan, who scrambled into cover behind the black convertible.

"Keep them pinned." Jack got out and raced for the helicopter.

It was a Sikorsky S-76. Jack had flown one they'd confiscated off arms smugglers in Afghanistan so he was familiar with it and powered through the start up in record time. As the blades began rotating overhead, Jack yelled, "Ethan! We're leaving."

Ethan sent out another burst of bullets, then rolled through the interior of the Lambo and out the side closest to the chopper. He was almost to the aircraft when Ten popped up from behind the black car and aimed his hand cannon at Ethan.

"Ethan, down."

Ten fired just as Ethan dropped and rolled. The bullet smashed into the side of the chopper. The assassin kept up the barrage so Ethan was trapped on the ground and unable to get into the cabin of chopper.

Well. Fuck that shit.

Jack pulled up the collective and the chopper lifted into the air. Ethan peered up at him, frowning, then smiled when he saw what Jack was doing. Once high enough, Jack tilted the chopper so the lethally whirring blades formed a spinning shield from the bullets. Within their protective barrier, Ethan jumped up and caught the bottom of the open door. Certain he had a good hold, Jack lifted the chopper, keeping it angled so Ten didn't have a clear shot. Only when he was on the far side of the house did he right the chopper's angle and hover so Ethan could finish boarding.

The black car shot out around the house and down the driveway, Ten and Balakrishnan hunched down inside it. Pity the chopper didn't have any guns.

Ethan dropped into the seat beside Jack, panting, hand pressed to his left hip. Jack tossed a headset at him. When it was in place, Ethan asked, "Do we follow them?"

Jack considered it, then studied Ethan. He was pale and wet, sans sunglasses and sagging in his seat. Weariness was etched in the slowness of his movements, in the cast of his eyes, and the dull tone of his voice.

"No. We've put them on the run. That's good enough for now."

Ethan looked like he would protest, but after a moment, he just nodded and let his head fall back. His eyes closed. "As you wish, Jack."

Fishing the glasses Ethan had given him out of a pocket, Jack reached over and slipped them on him, which got him a smile.

"Okay, let's get out of here." Jack got the chopper heading in a southeast direction, aiming for the Arabian Sea. There would be fewer witnesses to their flight on the water.

"Where shall we go?"

"Somewhere safe."

Ethan sighed and shifted uncomfortably. "Is there any place here that's safe for us now?"

"Just one." Jack hoped, at least.

"Mm. Good." Ethan undid the body armour and wrestled it off in the confined space. It clattered to the floor of the cabin behind them. "Do you have a knife, Jack?"

"Bad guys took them all, sorry." Jack eyed Ethan's stiff movements warily. "You okay?"

"Mostly." Ethan ripped a strip of material off the bottom of his wet shirt. He wadded it up and stuffed it down the side of his pants until it sat over his hip. When he pulled his hand out, Jack saw the blood.

"You got hit?"

"It's not bad. Just a surface wound."

"Right. *Just* a surface wound." Jack coaxed some more speed out of the chopper.

Ethan squeezed Jack's forearm gently. "I promise, Jack. It's not that bad."

Jack grumbled but decided he would put the craft on autopilot when they were on the right heading and insist he check the wound. However, by the time they were over the water and soaring south, Ethan was asleep. Head listing to one side, chest rising and falling evenly, the blush of the dawn colouring his cheeks and putting a touch of red in his stubble, he looked so peaceful Jack couldn't bring himself to wake him. Ethan needed the sleep and if he felt safe enough with Jack in control of the situation, then that was all Jack needed.

He did have to wake him nearly two hours later when he was preparing for the next step of the plan. Since the Cabal was probably tracking the chopper, they had to ditch it sooner rather than later, and hopefully divert any parties sent after them. While Jack put new settings into the autopilot, Ethan scrambled around the back of the cabin. His cry of success made Jack smile. The utter weariness so soon after the action at the house had worried him, along with the blood. This sign of life was heartening.

When everything was ready, Jack joined Ethan in the back and then opened one of the side doors. Air rushed in in violent swirls. Without the headsets and the words stolen from their lips before they could be said aloud, they fell back on hand signals to coordinate.

The yellow parcel Ethan found went first, then Ethan, and finally Jack. They speared feet first into the water, going deep before popping back up to the surface close to the uninflated raft. Overhead, the chopper was flying onwards, on a trajectory that would take it further out to sea. Eventually it would run out of fuel and drop into the water and hopefully mislead anyone looking for them.

With a pull of the tab, the raft inflated and Jack hauled himself, and a wincing Ethan, into it. Paddling ashore, Jack watched Ethan favour his left side. There was more than the "surface wound" on his hip.

Even though it was an empty beach they washed up on, there was an old man with a truck at least as old as he was who offered them a ride into Mangaluru. He dropped them right at the train station, where they only had to wait a couple of hours for the next train south. There were enough tourists around Ethan wouldn't have been remarkable, but he spent the time staying out of sight so he wouldn't be closely associated with Jack. After scouting the station and finding it free of suspicious characters, Jack went back to the secluded corner Ethan haunted with drinks and food. Ethan perked up a bit with the nourishment, but he was quiet and withdrawn even when no one else was around.

Something significant had happened on the second floor of the glass house. Something that had sapped a lot of Ethan's natural energy and vitality. Jack was familiar with the stooped shoulders, the lax awareness, the dull lilt to the voice. He'd seen it in the mirror, heard it from his own mouth, in the months after Jharkhand. Ethan might have lost another fight to his brother, but he'd lost something else as well. Something more vital than some blood.

Jack boarded the train just after lunchtime. Ethan, assuring Jack he would make it, snuck on at the very last moment. He appeared at the door to the A1 sleeper Jack had booked fifteen minutes after the train pulled away from the station. Jack let him in and Ethan bee-lined for the long seat, which doubled as the lower bunk, sitting with a sigh. His hair had dried and hung lank over his forehead, his skin looking paler than usual against the dark of his stubble and sunglasses.

"All right." Jack locked the door and drew the curtain across its window. "Let's look at that *surface wound.*"

"It's fine, Jack. I'd really rather just rest."

A few extra hundred rupees in the right hand had furnished their sleeper with a first aid kit and Jack set it on the bed beside Ethan. "And I'd rather not drag another sick person out of this country. Drop your pants, Ethan."

There was a hint of Ethan's usual spirit in the look he gave Jack, who didn't relent and went after the fastenings on his lover's pants instead.

"Jack." Ethan made a weary swat at Jack's hands.

"You can do it yourself, but it will happen." Jack waited until Ethan was complying before opening the first aid kit to look through its contents. It was very basic but had enough for him to deal with "surface wounds." If it was anything more than that, it would give him a good reason to tie Ethan down so he couldn't do anything stupid for a while.

Ethan undid his pants and pushed them down far enough to expose his hip. Rolling to his side, he let Jack peel back the still slightly damp material of his boxer-briefs to expose the wound. It was a shallow slice running horizontally over his hip, gaping when Ethan moved and still bleeding. Jack prodded it gently, assessing the extent of the damage.

"What happened?" he asked.

"Close call with a bullet."

"Jesus." Jack resisted the urge to chew Ethan out. He didn't need Jack telling him to be more careful. The fact this was the only damage the bullet did meant he *had* been incredibly careful already. "At least you were right. It's a surface wound."

"Of course I'm right."

"But only because there's not enough flesh here for anything other than surface, you crazy bastard. Let's just hope it didn't hit the bone."

Ethan scowled, sitting up to twist and look at the wound. "I'm certain it didn't. It would have hurt a lot more if it had."

"Yeah, well, it still needs to be stitched." Jack put his hand over Ethan's face and gently pushed him back down. "Lie still or you're going to have wonky stitches."

Ethan's indignant "Jack" was muffled under his palm, but he went down and pillowed his head on his arm. "Wonky stitches won't bother me."

Any smart response Jack might have had dried up at the return of the lifeless tone. He worked silently while the train rattled and clunked along the track. Occasionally people passed by their sleeper, talking loudly in a couple of different dialects and sometimes English. Jack kept an ear out for anything that sounded like someone looking for them, but it was all innocent and no one lingered. Ethan was quiet, except for a soft grunt when Jack used a disinfectant spray on the open wound but didn't move or make a sound when he started stitching. There were two medium sized dressings in the kit and Jack pressed one over the wound when he was done.

"One down." He reached for Ethan's shirt. "Show me the other one, crazy bastard."

At least Ethan didn't protest this time, lifting his torn shirt up to show a dark, blooming bruise on his ribs. "One of Ten's .50 calibre bullets to the body armour."

"Sit up, I'll bind your ribs in case they're cracked." Testing something, he added, "You crazy bastard."

Again, no protest from Ethan and he sat still while Jack wrapped a bandage around his torso. Once done, Jack let Ethan right his clothes, then leaned over and kissed him. Soft and chaste, just enough to make a connection. Ethan sighed against his lips and touched his cheek, tipping his face forwards to rest his forehead against Jack's.

"You okay?" Jack asked gently.

"Better now. Thank you."

"Good." Jack pulled back, still worried. "Then you can give me my 'half right, Jack' now, thanks."

Ethan stilled. "I don't think it's true anymore."

The dull words tore at Jack's heart. "Hey, you never were, and you're still not, a bastard."

The sound Ethan made may have been amused, or heartbroken. "If my mother even knew who my father was, they were definitely never married."

"I'm talking about the other definition. Because you've always been crazy."

"Perhaps I have been."

Jack gave him another quick kiss, then sat back. "Get some proper sleep. I'll keep the watch."

He thought Ethan would protest, but after a moment, he just nodded and lay down on his uninjured side—which put his back to the rest of the sleeper.

More worried than ever, Jack sat on the bunk beside him, back to the wall, gun resting next to his thigh, out of sight but close at hand.

than didn't fall into a deep sleep. The rattling of the train was just a touch too arrhythmic, lulling him one moment, clashing with his senses the next. He was tired enough to want the sleep, not just need it. Tired and sore and weary. All this way, all that effort—all those deaths. Only to have it all ripped away from him. But they were dead. Three fifths of the Cabal leadership were gone, which was what he'd wanted. So why didn't he feel released?

Jack woke him when they were an hour out from their final stop. It was dark, almost midnight, and Ethan barely felt refreshed. Guilt speared him, too, when he saw the drawn cast to Jack's face. His lover had obviously stayed awake, doing as he'd promised—keeping watch. Had he slept since Dharavi? Perhaps a few short naps while Ethan had been driving, but nothing substantial. He hadn't woken Ethan to swap places once during the twelve-hour travel time.

"Do we have much further to go?" he asked as they prepared to leave the train. Rather than waiting until they reached the terminal, they were going to jump off on the outskirts of the city.

"Couple of hours." Jack shrugged ruefully. "It's been a while, remember. I might get us lost."

Ethan squeezed his arm reassuringly. "I trust you."

Jack nodded, and then they left the sleeper. The companionways of the sleeper class carriages were mostly empty, just a few night owls wandering the confined spaces. The general carriages were more chaotic but it added confusion as they made their way to the rear of the train. They jumped off while still outside of Trivandrum, capital of Kerala. This was where Jack's mother had lived before moving to Australia to be with his father. Ethan suspected Jack's safe place might not be an Office one.

The pace Jack set wasn't taxing, whether because he was accommodating Ethan's injuries, or simply tired himself, Ethan couldn't work out. It took them just over three hours of walking, through a city that was very British colonial in appearance, until they reached the beach.

"Oops." Jack looked out at the dark water. "We overshot."

"By much?" Ethan could have kept going but the urge to be somewhat secure was pushing on the edges of his hollowness.

"Nah. Unless we're still too far north." Jack turned around slowly. "It's been so long." The words were quiet, pained.

About to reach for him, to say something comforting, Ethan didn't get a chance when Jack moved into a darker shadow between two buildings. "I need to check a map. Can you keep an eye out?"

"Of course." Ethan leaned against the wall of the building next to Jack's hidey-hole, scanning the street.

Jack was barely a couple of feet away, but the space between them felt greater. He'd been quiet during the walk from the outskirts. Perhaps it was weariness, or perhaps it was Ethan's fault. It had been his crazy need to hunt down the Cabal leaders, dragging Jack into danger over and over while doing it. Forcing Jack into a flimsy plan that had failed to do anything other than hurt them both.

Jack swore softly as he joined Ethan. "We're only a block off target. Shit. I should remember this."

"Jack, it's all right. You got us here, that's all that matters."

Jack mumbled something under his breath, then gestured down the street. "It's not far. Come on."

Ethan followed obediently, not wanting to annoy Jack any more than he already had.

One block down, they turned into a narrow, pitch-black alleyway. Part way along, Jack stopped and looked around.

"How much can you see?" he asked Ethan softly.

"Some. What are you looking for?"

"A marking on the wall. It should look something like two interlocking circles."

Ethan studied the brick walls of the buildings on both sides, finally finding the faint remains of spray paint several meters further down. "Jack, over here."

Jack joined him and crouched, gingerly shifting some of the detritus away from the wall under the mark. "Here it is." With a grunt, he hauled open a small hatch in the base of the wall. "There should be a ladder there. Can you see it?"

Crouching beside him, Ethan peered in. His eyesight was better in the dark than most, but even he couldn't penetrate the gloom within the opening. "I can't see anything down there." Wanting to prove he wasn't just a burden, he turned and lowered a leg into it, feeling around until he hit what he hoped was a ladder rung. "There's something here. I'll go first." He continued down before Jack could protest.

"Fine," Jack sighed. "It should only be about ten or twelve feet. I was much younger the last time I used this passageway."

Definitely not an Office initiative, then. If it was family associated, then what could Jack's Indian family be into to require a secret entrance?

Curiosity starting to grow, Ethan slowly made his way downward, finding the floor moments later. The darkness was almost complete, just a faint lightening around the opening above, but the soft echoing of trickling fluid and the stagnant water smell suggested they were in a storm drain.

Jack landed beside him, one hand out and groping until he found Ethan in the dark. "Can you see much? I'm totally fucking blind."

"I'm not much better, I'm afraid."

"There used to be fluorescent marks on the walls. Hopefully they're still there. Let me just close the hatch."

Once the hatch closed, Ethan's slight eyesight advantage was gone. Then he made out a faintly glowing arrow on the wall and pointed it out to Jack. With a triumphant grunt, Jack grabbed Ethan's hand so they wouldn't lose each other in the dark and went in the direction of the arrow. Although the marks were regular, their progress was still almost painfully slow. Jack moved his feet in a shuffle, looking for ground obstacles. Ethan actively paid attention to the corners they took and the number of steps between, just in case he needed to get them out of this place. The familiarity of the exercise kept him focused and alert, less like he needed to just stop and curl up into a ball. Jack, however, seemed to be flagging the longer they moved through the dark. Ethan was about to suggest he take the lead when Jack stopped.

"Jack?"

"I think we're here." He dropped Ethan's hand and felt over the wall. With a relieved sigh, Jack grabbed something and pulled on it.

"Where are we?" Ethan traced the same area Jack had been touching and found a metal handle on the end of a nylon rope that dangled from the ceiling.

"Under a hotel on the shore of Veli Lake. Before they changed the laws about homosexuality, this was one of the few places people could come and be themselves. Though I suspect it's still in use. Minds and hearts don't change as fast as laws."

Right then, a creak of old hinges echoed from above and then a sliver of faint light cast a pale illumination over Jack.

"Namaste?" Jack asked softly.

A male voice said something in a language that didn't sound much like the Hindi Jack had been speaking. Jack replied in the same tongue, but when he was done, the other person didn't respond for so long Jack tensed up and Ethan readied to either fight or run.

"Jack?"

Jack jerked, then, in a soft voice, "Raja?"

The hatch above was opened fully. Ethan and Jack both flinched from the wash of light.

"Sorry, sorry," the man above said hastily.

"It's okay." Jack held a hand up to shield his eyes. "I didn't think you'd be here."

Ethan hurriedly put his sunglasses on and peered up at the man. It was Jack in twenty years. Skin slightly darker, wrinkles around his eyes and grey at his temples. Still a striking man, especially when he smiled. It was a confused smile, but happy as well.

"Let me get a ladder." Raja disappeared from the opening.

"Your uncle?" Ethan asked softly.

"Yeah. I haven't seen him in fifteen years."

Looking upwards, Ethan tried to see what lay beyond. "He runs the hotel?"

"Owns it. We used to stay here when we came to visit. Had a whole floor for the family. Meera loved it because she could go days without seeing me. I loved it because there seemed to be a large amount of very good-looking men walking around the place at all hours." His smile was sad. "I was sixteen when I worked out why they were here. Mostly because I followed this gorgeous young man down to the basement and watched him kiss his male lover goodbye, then leave through that hatch." He pointed to the opening. "So of course I had to go through it and explore. I got lost. Took me nearly a whole day to find my way to the entrance we used. There are a couple of others, as well."

"Your family must have been worried about you."

Jack laughed. "They barely even realised I was gone. Raja worked out where I'd disappeared to and fetched me back. I adored my uncle so I promised to keep his secret for him."

Ethan didn't miss the past tense. "It must have been nice knowing you would have a sympathetic uncle when you came out."

The humour vanished in an instant. "He wasn't sympathetic."

"But . . . this place. Surely that meant he—"

"Here you go," Raja said just then, and a rope ladder rolled down into the storm drain.

Jack went first, then Ethan went and emerged to find nephew and uncle sharing an awkward hug. Raja was speaking softly, patting Jack's back. Jack nodded but didn't relax.

The basement was dim and filled with old furniture, boxes, and cobwebs. A single shaded bulb hung from the ceiling and a door in the far wall was slightly ajar. The room smelt musty and stale.

When he could, Jack pulled away and reached for Ethan. The urge to back away flared. Jack knew he didn't like being touched in public. But this wasn't really public, it was Jack's uncle, and the tremor in Jack's hand spoke of a need other than the usual distracting affection. Jack had been very patient with him the past several days, willing to do whatever Ethan wanted, and had ended up in danger for his loyalty. And what had Ethan done for him?

He moved before he knew he would do it, leaning into Jack and clasping the hand of the arm Jack wrapped around his waist.

In English, Jack said, "This is Ethan. Ethan, my uncle, Raja Munjanattu."

"Pleased to meet you, sir." Ethan held out his hand.

Raja looked between them, at the hands resting low on Ethan's hip, then at his nephew's face. He took Ethan's hand in a firm shake. "Pleasure to meet you, Ethan." His accent was thick but clear. "Though I wish it had been under better circumstances." To Jack he added, wryly, "I assume this isn't a happy visit, considering your choice of entrance."

"Yeah. We need to stay out of sight for a while. Will you help us?"

Another assessing look between them, then Raja nodded. "Of course. You're family. No need to ask." Then he smiled. "I won't even ask why. I'm just glad you felt you could trust me."

Jack ducked his head and the arm around Ethan tightened.

"Thank you," Ethan said to Raja.

Raja gave him a vague smile. "You both look very tired. I'll take you to a room now."

"One of the *private* ones," Jack said.

His uncle frowned, then nodded. "You're in luck. The private rooms are all empty at the moment. I'll have to make up the bed for you."

"Just bring us sheets and we'll do it."

Jack's perfunctory tone and words got Raja moving, but there was a slump to his shoulders. This reunion probably hadn't gone the way he'd imagined it would. Perhaps because Ethan, a stranger, was there, or perhaps because Jack had shown his uncle just *why* Ethan was with him. Though if Raja facilitated clandestine assignations between gay people, while knowing Jack was gay, Ethan's presence shouldn't be that surprising. Maybe he disapproved of how they'd arrived, secretly and hoping to hide, meaning Jack's whole motivation was about protection, not getting in touch with family.

Ethan brought up the rear of their little convoy, following the other men through the door, up a narrow staircase, across what appeared to be another storage room and into another dark staircase. They went up four flights and came out into a lushly decorated salon. Thick carpets covered a polished wooden floor, intricate patterns in red, gold, and brown. Large, wingback chairs where paired up around small, circular, marble topped tables. A couch ran along one wall, a divan along another. The other two walls had two doors each.

Raja pulled out a key and unlocked one of the doors. "This room was cleaned this morning. I'll get you some sheets and toiletries. Look around and let me know if there's anything else you need."

Jack didn't move, so Ethan went in and switched on the light by the door. The room was a full suite, with small kitchenette, lounge area, and through another door, a large bedroom with a full bathroom.

Returning to the lounge to see if Jack had made it in, Ethan heard him and Raja talking softly in the salon. They spoke in the same language as earlier so Ethan had no chance of understanding, but the conversation didn't sound relaxed.

Raja caught sight of Ethan in the suite's doorway and broke off what he'd been saying to Jack, and asked in English, "Is everything okay with the room?"

"Yes. I was hoping we could also impose on you for something to eat?"

"Of course. The chef has gone home, but I can bring you a few things until the morning shift arrives and prepares breakfast." He glanced at his watch. "Which won't be long, actually. In fact, you're lucky I heard the bell ring for the hatch. I'd been out and was just returning when you rang it."

"Lucky us," Jack muttered as he turned and came towards the room. "Let me guess, you were out with your wife?" Not waiting for an answer, he brushed past Ethan and went into the suite.

Raja watched him disappear, expression blank. He dragged in a couple of deep breaths and, voice slightly harsh, said, "I'll be back soon with your stuff."

No. Not a happy reunion at all.

THIRTY-FOUR

God. What had ever possessed Jack to think this was a good idea? He should have just hauled Ethan into the middle of nowhere and called for an Office extraction, damn the fucking political situation to hell. But the lassitude that plagued Ethan had scared him and he'd wanted to get him somewhere warm and as safe as possible as fast as he could. This place had lasted thirty odd years as a secret from everyone but its clients; it would be a good enough space for Ethan to recover for a couple of days.

If only it hadn't come with boat loads of bad memories for Jack.

Standing in the lounge room of the suite, Jack rubbed his hands over his face, trying to scrub away the anger and resentment. He hadn't thought Raja would be here. His uncle had pretty much left the hotel in the hands of his managers—who were aware of the secret rooms—for years, spending most of his time in his new resort at Ponmudi. His wife, Lavanya, had her own apartment complex she managed at Valiathura Beach. As far as Jack was aware, Raja and Lavanya hadn't lived together in near a decade.

It was all just so much shit, and Jack had willingly walked back into it. Fuck it, coming here felt worse than coming back into India itself.

"Jack?"

Right on cue, there was Ethan with his wary but curious whole-sentence-in-his-name. Answering any of the questions he might have right now would only make Jack angrier.

"I'm going for a shower." Jack spun on his heel and headed for the bathroom.

Ethan trailed at a safe distance. "There aren't any towels."

"Raja will have brought some up by the time I'm done."

"As you wish, Jack. I'll bring one in for you when he does."

"Thanks." Jack's current mood wasn't Ethan's fault, but he couldn't look at him right then either.

In the bathroom he stripped fast and threw the sweat and salt encrusted clothes into the bottom of the shower. It wouldn't be as good as a proper wash, but it was better than nothing. He forgot to care about having nothing to wear afterwards the moment the hot water hit his skin, though. Christ. How long had it been since he'd gotten properly clean? Not since he'd been back in India, that's for sure. From the moment he'd touched down in Mumbai he'd been racing after Ethan, or with him. It felt good to be out of those clothes and washing away some of the grit and debris under the hot, hard spray.

A knock on the frosted glass of the shower broke through his momentary bliss.

"Jack? I have soap and other things for you."

Sliding back the door, Jack accepted the handful of products from Ethan. "Thanks."

"Towels and sheets have also been delivered. And there are snacks and drinks as well."

Before Ethan could back away, Jack leaned out and gave him a swift kiss. "Thanks." He meant it more this time. "I just . . . I didn't think he'd be here."

Ethan nodded and, instead of leaving, turned off the light. The open door allowed some light from the bedroom in, but it was low enough Ethan could remove his glasses. Then he removed his clothes and the bandage around his ribs. The clothes joined Jack's in the bottom of the shower, and he stepped in as well.

"Shit," Jack hissed as Ethan pressed up against him. Arms going around him automatically, Jack buried his face in Ethan's neck.

Ethan held him tightly as the water cascaded over them. "I'm sorry, Jack. This is all my fault. If I hadn't pursued this doomed affair, you wouldn't be here."

Jack laughed. "Can't argue with that, but it's okay. I know why you did it. And I chose to follow you."

"We're one as bad as the other."

"Seems like it." Pulling back, Jack ran his hand through Ethan's wet, greasy hair. "We're as disgusting as each other at least." He grabbed the shampoo and squirted a generous amount into his hand. "Stand still." And he rubbed the product into Ethan's hair.

Ethan tried, but after only half a minute, he was biting back moans, tilting his head into Jack's massaging fingers, and backing into him. Shower sex would be amazing, but more than a general contemplation of the subject left Jack feeling even wearier. What he really wanted was to fall into a bed between clean sheets, wrap himself around Ethan, and sleep for a day. Possibly two.

At least Ethan seemed to have revived. He moved with his usual grace as he washed the suds from his hair, then returned the favour. Neither of them got more than half hard and didn't try to take it any further, even as they shared the soap and worked it over each other's bodies. It was just the closeness, the simplicity of being able to take some time with each other, that soaked through Jack, leaving him warm and settled.

As much as he then wanted to crawl into the bed Ethan had made before joining him in the shower, Jack let Ethan direct him in wringing out their wet clothes and hanging them up as best they could to dry. Then it was into the bed with the tray of minibar snacks between them. Jack ate a couple of packets of biscuits and an apple and drank a bottle of water before sliding down under the sheets. Ethan put the tray aside and rolled into his arms.

"We're safe here?" Ethan pushed his back into Jack's chest.

"Yeah. Raja and I have our differences, but he's family. He won't betray us."

"Good."

Jack made sure he wasn't putting pressure on any of Ethan's injuries. "Are you feeling better?"

"Much." After a hesitant moment, he added, "Raja brought some ibuprofen with everything else. He said he thought it might be needed, considering your penchant for getting into trouble."

It was probably the exhaustion and pending coma, but Jack laughed. "That's pretty fair, actually."

"I gather you were a rather rambunctious child."

"Rambunctious? If you mean I didn't back down from a fight, then yeah. You'd think Meera and I would have fitted in here better than we did at home, but kids can be very exacting. We didn't sound right or act right. They had strong opinions about that. It was fight or run. Meera would run, so I fought."

Ethan chuckled. "I bet you did it just to be contrary."

"It is every brother's sworn duty to make their sister's life hell."

"Hmm. Maybe that's where I went wrong." His tone was pensive.

Fuck. "Sorry. I didn't mean to bring up a touchy subject."

"It's all right. I know what my relationship with them was like. It doesn't change how I feel about them or what I did for them."

"You did everything you could." Jack kissed the back of his neck.

Ethan shook his head. "I didn't. I was wrong to leave you and go after the Cabal by myself. You're right. I should have told you, told the Office. If I had . . ."

Jack waited for Ethan to finish, but all he did was push his face into the pillow. The silence felt like those hours after the events at the glass house. If only Jack had thought before opening his mouth. Or perhaps now was the right time to ask.

"Do you want to talk about what happened?"

Ethan was quiet for a couple of minutes, then sighed. "Not particularly."

"It might help."

"When does talking ever help? All it does is point out your shortcomings, your failures, every bad decision you ever made. It warps your perspective."

His tone was so dejected Jack felt an actual pain in his guts to hear it.

"It can give you another perspective. Something to help you work through whatever problem you have." Jack gave Ethan a gentle squeeze. "And you know I would never hurt you. Talking helps. I'll listen, let you get it out."

Ethan wriggled out of Jack's arms and rolled onto his belly, head turned away from Jack. "I'm tired, Jack. Can we just sleep?"

"Yeah." Jack ran his hand down Ethan's bare back. "I only want you to be okay."

Silence fell and Jack relaxed into the mattress. Maybe Ethan would feel more positive after a good sleep. And maybe Jack would know how to get over himself where Raja was concerned. He was just dropping off to sleep when Ethan spoke again.

"They were already dead."

Jack blinked in the darkness. As surprised as he was at the words, he kept his mouth shut. He had promised to listen.

"That was the target I was aiming for. My entire reason for pushing myself that far, for that long. And they took it away from me. Just as they took everything away from me."

The pain in his voice tore through Jack. He wanted to touch him, hold him, but this was one of those times when Ethan wouldn't accept it. When he spoke of his past—when he was at his most vulnerable—he needed to be in complete control.

"I wanted them to know, *needed* them to know why they were dying. They destroyed our lives, Jack. They gave me brothers and sisters, and then told me to kill them. Told them to kill me. My sister, One, hated me. I don't know why. She didn't seem to hate any of the others. But she was obedient and she never touched me outside of training. Then they told us the final test. To prove our loyalty and our training, we had to kill one of our siblings. I refused. I'd already watched one of them die, saw another one lying lifeless at my brother's feet. I couldn't do that again. One had no such compunction. She came for me with every measure of hatred she had."

Ethan rolled to face Jack. It was too dark to make out his features but Jack could guess his expression well enough—nothing. He was locked down, emotions sealed away so he could say these things.

"I was prepared to let her kill me. They'd already forced me to kill for them and I wasn't sure I could do it again. Not because it was hard, but because it was easy. Their training had worked, in that regard at least. If I died, I wouldn't have to make that decision again. Clearly, it didn't happen that way. Two killed One before she could finish me."

Jack never would have thought he'd ever be grateful for that psychopathic arsehole's existence, but here he was.

"They did that to us, and they needed to die for it. But that won't happen now. Ten poisoned them to take that away from me. The remaining bosses made sure I would have nothing. That I would be nothing but what they created. I killed my brothers for nothing, Jack."

"Jesus," Jack hissed and reached for him.

Ethan fought to get free, but Jack wrestled the other man underneath himself. Clamped his knees around Ethan's thighs and locked his arms around his chest. Silently, Ethan struggled, but he wasn't at his full strength. Neither was Jack, but his absolute need to keep Ethan safe was greater than Ethan's desire to get away. His twisting and turning weakened quickly, his breathing became ragged, and then he was crying. Quiet sobs that shuddered through his whole body. Jack changed his hold from restraint to embrace, shifting so he could hold Ethan to his chest and stroke his hair. He murmured soothing nonsense and kissed his temple while his lover suffered through this pain.

When Ethan went slack against him, Jack decided he would apologise to Raja for his shitty behaviour. Compared to what Ethan had gone through in his life, a few disagreements from nearly two decades ago meant nothing. Yeah, they couldn't see eye to eye on some things, but that didn't mean they weren't family, or didn't care for each other. His uncle was more than that. Jack was more than that.

Ethan was more than that.

"You're not only what they made you," Jack murmured.

Against his chest, Ethan's head shook a slow negative.

"Trust me on this, okay? You're not just an assassin."

"Aren't I, Jack?" Ethan pulled back but only enough to see him. "I went in there last night with the intent to *kill*. That was all I wanted. To let them know why they had to die, and then kill them. And when I couldn't do it, I fell apart. There is nothing else in me if three missed targets leaves me empty."

"That's just the shock. It'll wear off." Jack cupped his cheek, thumb brushing over his damp skin. "They taught you to hunt and kill. The army taught me that too, and is that all I am? A soldier?"

Ethan shook his head once.

"So neither are you just an assassin. Did they teach you to be a mechanic?"

"Yes. They taught us all basic engine maintenance."

"No. They taught you mechanics. You *became* a mechanic on your own. When you got your first fancy car and fixed it up, gave it a name, and then went out and got *another* car."

The huff from Ethan might have been amused.

"Those silly books you read."

"They're not silly. They're—"

"They're silly, Ethan, deal with it. Did they give them to you as a textbook or a what-not-to-do guide?"

"No." It sounded a bit sullen.

"No. You found them on your own and, for whatever crazy reason, decided you liked them."

"They're entertaining."

"If you say so, but you decided that, not them. I bet they also didn't have a petting zoo so you could play with the baby animals, either, and yet here you are, befriending half-feral camels."

"There were guard dogs."

"You snuck them treats, didn't you."

Ethan snorted. "I tried but they were too well trained to take food from me. I felt very sorry for them though. They never got to play."

Just like Ethan never got to play? Jack squashed that question into the filing cabinet. It never needed to be asked. If Ethan wanted to tell him, he would. Eventually.

"Do you see what I'm saying?" he asked instead. "There is so much more to you than you think there is. They may have turned you into a killer, but you made yourself into a car nut, an animal lover, and a reader with questionable tastes." Before Ethan could protest that one again, Jack added, "And you're someone I want in my life so fucking much it hurts me when you're not around."

"Jack," Ethan whispered, then kissed him.

Pulling him closer, Jack returned the kiss. It heated quickly, so they were writhing against each other, touching and teasing, and then it slowed down into tenderness, before slipping gently into just holding each other until they fell asleep.

THIRTY-FIVE

It was bright enough even with the thick curtains drawn for Ethan to scramble for his glasses when he woke up. Behind the dark shades, he surveyed the room, ensuring nothing was disturbed or missing. He'd slept deeply, and waking in a strange place always sparked his wariness. Nothing was amiss, thankfully.

Beside him, Jack was sprawled on his belly, still asleep and giving no sign of changing that state of affairs any time soon. When Ethan slept that deeply, it was rare for him to wake before Jack, so he took the chance to do something he loved and traced his fingers over the shape of his tattoo. He'd missed it over the past months. Or rather, missed this simple little action that nevertheless made him feel connected to Jack.

A knock at the outer door made Ethan roll out of the bed and to his feet, ready to pounce.

"Boys? Are you awake?"

Raja.

Ethan called, "A moment please," then hurriedly found his pants. They were still a little damp but he pulled them on. His shirt was torn so he grabbed Jack's and was buttoning it up when he answered the door.

Raja was waiting patiently with a trolley carrying cloche covered plates and a stoneware pot of something that smelt incredibly good.

"Is that butter chicken?" Ethan stepped back and let Jack's uncle wheel the food in.

"It is." Raja smiled widely, the corners of his eyes wrinkling. "Jack told me it was your favourite and it's one of the staples of our kitchen. Usha's recipe."

Mouth already watering, Ethan followed Raja into the lounge room and helped him set out the food on the coffee table. As well as the curry, there was rice, naan, lamb kofta with yogurt, palak paneer and gulab jamun and halwa for dessert. Ethan's stomach was growling by the time they were done.

"Is Jack still sleeping?" Raja looked to the bedroom door with an expression of cautious hope.

"Yes. We've been constantly on the move for several days. He needs the rest."

Raja nodded. "I'm glad you found somewhere you could stop."

"Thank you for this. We truly appreciate it. I know you and Jack have your differences and that this must be awkward for you."

Raja smiled sadly. "More like we are too similar, but for one point of view where we disagree." He shook his head and backed up. "I should leave you to your meal. If you need anything else, just dial three on the phone. It's a special line, it only goes to me."

Ethan walked with him to the door, where Raja stopped and sighed.

"Jack and I might disagree, but he is my family and I have missed him. I never thought I'd ever see him in India again." He gripped Ethan's shoulder warmly. "I'm very grateful to you that he's here."

"To me?" If only Raja knew how much danger Jack had been in because of Ethan.

"Yes, to you. Jack swore he would never return and yet here he is. I'm sure you've worked out by now that once Jack makes up his mind, he sticks to his guns."

"He is very stubborn," Ethan agreed.

"Stubborn, and passionate. Did he tell you what he did at my wedding?"

Ethan shook his head.

"It was an arranged marriage, but both Lavanya and I wanted it. We were friends, *are* friends still. Jack didn't like it." In response to Ethan's raised eyebrow, Raja said dryly, "He had his reasons. We might have disagreed, but I can understand it. We were going to have fireworks at the reception, but Jack stole them and placed them around the outside of the church. He set them off in the middle of the ceremony."

"Oh dear."

Raja laughed. "I was angry at the time, but I was impressed as well. It took a lot of planning and ingenuity for a seventeen year old, but he felt that strongly about it he didn't give up. And that's why I'm grateful to you. There's only one thing that could make Jack break his promise to never return here. Love. The loss of it kept him away. The love he has for you brought him back. Thank you for that."

Before Ethan could do more than gape, Raja turned and walked across the salon to the hidden staircase.

Ethan closed the door and went back to the lounge room. Jack was sitting on the couch, piling food on a plate. His hair was disarrayed, eyes still sleepy, and all he wore was his wrinkled pants.

How much had he heard? Was he cranky that his uncle revealed so much?

"Come and eat before I finish it all," Jack said.

Ethan hurried over and sat beside him. Jack gave him the plate he'd already prepared, then began assembling another for himself.

"Did we wake you?" Ethan shovelled in a load of butter chicken and rice.

"Nah. Had to piss." He started with dessert, popping a gulab jamun into his mouth. Chewed, swallowed, and added, "Heard you two talking though."

"Oh."

Jack smiled. "It's okay. I need to apologise to Raja."

"For the fireworks at the wedding?"

"That too. But I meant for that thing we disagree on." Jack loaded some naan with paneer. "Remember when I said I discovered the secret entrance to the hotel by following this hot guy?"

Ethan nodded, mouth full of kofta.

"The lover he said goodbye to was Raja."

He'd suspected it since Jack had explained the purpose of these secret rooms.

"I'm telling you because I trust you won't spread his secret. The old law was against acts of homosexuality, not identifying as homosexual, or queer. There were, and still are, a lot of people who object to even that, though. It was risky to come out, even if you didn't act on it."

"And Raja chose the safe path."

"Yeah. And I didn't like it. I mean, I wasn't even out to my parents. Meera knew because she has this sixth sense about finding anything I wanted to keep hidden. But I had a boyfriend and thought I was in love and couldn't understand why Raja would deny himself that. Then he announced his engagement." Jack's lips twisted up into a wry grimace. "I was a complete dickhead about it."

Ethan nodded emphatically as he spooned the last of his butter chicken into his mouth.

"Yeah, okay, no need to be so agreeable," Jack muttered. "Anyway, I need to say sorry for all that shit."

"What language were you and Raja speaking? It wasn't Hindi and it didn't sound like Marathi."

"It's Malayalam, the language of this region. My mother's language, though most people also speak English, or some Hindi. I don't speak Malayalam unless I absolutely have to. Hindi is less ... painful to hear." Jack set down his plate and cleared his throat. "I should go talk to Raja."

"I suppose, but later." Ethan set his plate aside as well and swung a leg over Jack's thighs and settled onto his lap. "First, this." He leaned in and kissed him.

Jack tasted sweet and spicy from the food, and Ethan teased the seam of his lips with his tongue until Jack parted them for him. A moan welled up in Ethan's throat as he delved into his lover's mouth. It was answered with a growl from Jack as his arms went around him, hands fisting up the material of his shirt. They kissed hard and forcefully, all the banked desire from that night in the slums unleashed. Ethan pushed into Jack, needing the contact, wanting the solidity of Jack's body to assure him that they were finally together and had no reason not to give in to the passion.

"Christ." Jack's mouth was barely far enough away for him to form the word. "Yeah. This. Now."

They both started undoing the buttons on Ethan's shirt at the same time, Ethan from the top, Jack from the bottom.

"You've eaten enough?" Ethan asked breathlessly.

"Yup. Probably need a snack after this though. Jesus, what is with these buttons?" With a grunt, Jack yanked the shirt open. The last couple of buttons pinged off in different directions, quickly followed the shirt itself.

Ethan laughed, then gasped as Jack flicked his tongue over a nipple. His head dropped back, spine arching towards Jack. The bruise on his side sent a wave of pain though him, just to remind him it was there, but he lost it in the exquisite sensation of Jack's teeth scraping across his gunshot scar.

"Jack!"

His man smiled against his skin, then pushed him back further as he trailed his warm, talented tongue down his sternum. It was only when Ethan felt something wet on his shoulder that he realised how far over backwards he was.

"Jack." Ethan scrabbled at Jack's shoulders. "Let me up."

Jack sat back after swiping his tongue back up and over a peaked nipple. "Sorry, did I hurt you?"

Laughing, Ethan shook his head. "You dipped me in something."

"Oh fuck. That's hot." Jack flipped Ethan around and his mouth landed on the damp patch. "God, the yogurt tastes better this way."

Torn between laughing and groaning, Ethan said, "Didn't you say the food always tastes better when eaten with your hands?"

"Hands, back, same difference." Jack lapped up the tart yogurt.

When he was done, Ethan turned back around, the bowl of yogurt in his hand. "Hmm, let's see if your theory holds up."

They spent a delicious while testing it, getting creamy smears on each other and the couch until the bowl was empty and they were too busy sharing the last of the yogurt in a long, deep kiss to worry as it tumbled to the floor. Then their hard cocks were free of their pants and Jack's hand was wrapped around them, stroking slowly.

Ethan melted onto Jack as trails of fiery pleasure curled up from his cock and balls. "Jack." His fingers wound through Jack's curls, tipping his head back so he had access to the tender skin under his jaw. He nipped and licked in time with Jack's hand, whimpering as a rough thumb rubbed across the head of his cock, collecting moisture from them both to slick harder and faster strokes.

It had been so long since he'd had a hand other than his own to offer release that this was working too well. Jack, too, was getting close, his breathing getting faster and shallower. Ethan had desperately missed watching Jack fall apart for him and he needed it more than he needed his own orgasm. Needed to know Jack still wanted him after

Ethan had walked out on him, after Jack had said no in Dharavi. Ethan replaced Jack's hand with his own and took control.

"Oh fuck," Jack gasped, head thrown back. "Jesus, Ethan. Too good. Too close."

"Do it, Jack. For me."

Jack growled, his free hand grasping the back of Ethan's neck and pulling him in so their mouths clashed. Ethan bit his lower lip, then invaded him with his tongue, sliding it across Jack's even as he sped up his hand. Barely half a minute later, Jack tore his mouth away and came with a strangled groan. His hips bucked up, thrusting his cock through their hands, rubbing against Ethan's shaft, slicking it with his semen.

That was all it took for Ethan and his orgasm lashed through him.

When he caught his senses and breath, he was slumped on Jack's chest, face pressed into his sweaty neck. His hand was still closed around both of their cocks and he gave them a lazy jerk.

"Christ." Jack's hands snapped around Ethan's biceps.

Ethan's laugh was muffled against his skin.

"Sadist."

"Hmm. Just making sure you'll be ready for round two." He softened his grip and gently rubbed them together.

Jack's groan was a long suffering one, but his hold turned into caresses up and down Ethan's arms, then down his back to grip his arse and squeeze. "Round two?"

"When you come inside me."

The air caught in Jack's throat with an audible hitch. "Yeah? What are you going to use for lube? We ate all the yogurt."

Sitting back, Ethan smiled at the dishevelled glory that was post-coital Jack. "Your uncle didn't only provide soap and shampoo with the toiletries."

Between Jack's grumbles that he most definitely did *not* want to talk about Raja during sex, they made it back to bed, lube fetched from the bathroom on the way. They spent a long while slowly working each other back to full arousal, getting there when Jack went down on Ethan for a slow, thorough blowjob. Ethan was lost to the pleasure right from the start, incoherently begging for each slicked finger that Jack worked into him, until all he could do was clutch at Jack's shoulders and haul his mouth off his cock and back to his.

"Now, Jack."

"As you wish," Jack returned with a fierce kiss.

Then he was easing inside and all the air left Ethan's body. His spine curled up, legs wound around Jack's waist. The pressure was exquisite, the sensation of being filled up one of completion. Jack let out a low moan when his balls touched Ethan's arse. The sound rippled through Ethan like a warm current—and it pulled towards Jack with gravitational force. He found Jack's mouth with his own and sealed them together as Jack started to move. Leisurely thrusts that slid his whole length in and out, taking his time to pleasure them both.

It was sweet and tender and by the time physical needs drove them both into frantic motion, chasing down their climax, Ethan felt the chasm inside his chest close.

THIRTY-SIX

The post-fuck snack turned out to be the rest of the food shared between them while they sat in bed catching up on the past three months apart. Once finished, Jack took the empty plates and bowls back to the lounge room and returned to find Ethan sprawled out on his back across the mattress. All of his naked glory was on display and Jack thought there might be a third set of orgasms in their very near future.

"Ugh," Ethan moaned as Jack joined him again. "I ate too much." He patted his taut and defined abdomen.

"No. *I* ate too much. You're just catching up." Jack poked one of Ethan's sharply jutting hip bones.

Ethan swatted his hand away. "I haven't lost that much weight."

"You didn't have any to lose," Jack pointed out.

"Fine. The only recourse is to live here forever so you can feed me Indian food."

The very thought of it made his stomach's contents shift uncomfortably. It also successfully deflated the hopes his dick had for more fun any time soon.

"There's some very good Indian restaurants in Sydney." Jack tried to sound casual.

Ethan rolled onto his side, head propped up on a hand. His expression was carefully neutral. Jack knew that look and his already unsettled guts churned even more. He was about to get sliced open.

"It wasn't just Jharkhand," Ethan said gently.

Great. This again. "What wasn't just Jharkhand?" It was easier to give in. Ethan would get whatever it was out of him eventually.

"That made you swear to never return to India."

Jack threw an arm across his eyes. "I don't want to talk about it."

"Didn't you tell me talking helps?"

"Didn't you tell me it just points out all your failures and twists your perceptions?"

It was Ethan's turn to poke Jack in the ribs. "And yet I talked."

Uncovering his eyes, Jack considered his man for a moment. Ethan sounded casual but his lips were pressed together and he was very studiously watching Jack's chest rise and fall.

"I'm sorry if I forced you to talk about what happened," Jack said.

After a moment, Ethan shook his head and when he met Jack's gaze, smiled sadly. "You didn't. And I think I feel, if not better for it, then at least lighter. A burden shared, perhaps? And had it been anyone other than you asking, I wouldn't have talked."

Ethan held Jack's gaze for long while, breaking it only when Jack levered himself up to kiss him. A chaste touch of lips that nevertheless made Ethan sigh and lean into him. That simple confession had a keen edge and it cut into Jack so neatly he didn't even feel it. All he knew was that he started talking.

"It's my fault my mum died. She was taking part in an educational program for remote teachers in the rural areas in the northeast. Showing them new techniques and courses to help reach the children, and I was going with her as an aide. It was supposed to give me extra credit for my post-grad degree in higher education. I was going to be a teacher, like both my parents. I'd finished my bachelors and was taking six months off before starting the post-grad, and . . ." Jack hesitated, then went with, "And Meera was pregnant with Matilda. She was also going through withdrawal. Did I ever tell you that? Meera was a Sugar addict when she was pregnant. That's how I picked up on you being a Sugar Baby. I researched it all back then. Thankfully, Meera got treatment in time and Mati wasn't affected."

"That's good," Ethan agreed, a touch of sadness in his words.

"Anyway, the fuckface who'd gotten her hooked decided he didn't want a kid, but when Meera said she wouldn't end the pregnancy, he threatened her. She got her shit together and came home. He followed her, making a lot of noise and trouble for her and our parents." Jack smiled apologetically. "He was inordinately proud of his car, a Nissan Skyline, so I set fire to it."

Ethan's eyes went wide. "You did?"

"Yeah. Rambunctious, remember?"

"Not quite the term I would use."

"Which would be?"

"Protective. Fierce. Loyal. Loving." Ethan kissed Jack's mouth.

"You could also add 'almost arrested' to that list. The only reason I wasn't charged was because the arsehole ran at the first hint of cops and there were no other witnesses. Anyway, mum delayed leaving until we knew Meera was going to be okay, and by that time I'd changed my mind about going. I thought it would be better if I stayed home so I was there when Meera had the baby."

Ethan's eyebrow quirked up. "Your sister was all right with that?"

"No. She yelled at me a lot about it, and not all of it was due to the withdrawal." Jack closed his eyes. It was the only way he could say the next bit. "She was actually yelling at me because she knew the real reason why I didn't want to go with mum. I was single and I was having too much fun fucking around. The last thing I wanted to do was come here, where I couldn't have sex or be myself. Being a monk for six months when I was twenty years old really didn't appeal to me, so I made the excuse of wanting to look after Meera and stayed home. And mum was all alone in a remote schoolhouse, doing prep work I would have been doing if I'd been there, when the Maoists decided to make a statement and blow up what they thought was an empty building."

The room was silent for a long while, then Ethan's finger drew a gentle line up Jack's cheek, collecting the tear that had escaped from under his lashes.

"I'm very sorry you lost your mother, but you shouldn't blame yourself, Jack."

Jack's laugh was bitter and ugly. "Which is what everyone says. Everyone except for Meera, of course. She always tells the truth, no matter who it hurts or what it costs."

"Hmm. I'm not exactly sure about that."

"You've never met her. Just wait. You'll be a believer when you do."

"Perhaps. But have you ever considered that Meera blames herself, not you?"

Jack sighed. "She's always been very adamant about where she thinks the blame lies."

"All right, let's look at this logically, shall we?" Ethan sat up and leaned back against the headboard. "Had you been with your mother on that trip, it is highly likely you would have been in that building when the Maoists attacked, not Usha. Either way, Meera was going to lose a family member."

"Yeah, and it's no national secret that mum was her favourite out of the two of us. That's what Meera yelled at me several times afterwards. That it should have been me, not mum."

Ethan nudged him with a foot. "Put that aside for the moment. Consider this, if Meera hadn't been pregnant, if she hadn't had to flee an abusive partner, if she hadn't gotten hooked on Sugar, your mother wouldn't have delayed her trip. Chances are she wouldn't have been in that district at that time if she hadn't."

"I guess, but the fact is, it *should* have been me, either way."

"Forget about yourself for a moment. Put yourself in Meera's position. If you had been the cause of the delay, how would you feel?"

Jesus. That was a low blow. Jack scrubbed his hands over his face. "She's hidden it incredibly well for a long time."

This time, Ethan's foot was a soothing rub along Jack's hip. "Family trait, I believe."

Catching the errant foot, Jack gave it an absent massage. "Probably."

"Now that you've talked and been given a different perspective, do you feel any better?"

Jack poked his tongue out at Ethan, who pulled his foot back and gave Jack another gentle shove with it.

"Wasn't there something you wanted to talk to Raja about, as well?"

"Christ. Okay." Jack huffed his way off the bed and grumbled his way into the bathroom. "Now he's all about the deep and meaningfuls. I should have kept my trap shut."

If he was going to talk to his uncle, he didn't need to smell like sweat and sex. In the shower, he turned the taps on and stood under the hard spray, face turned into the water.

The truth was he did feel, as Ethan had said, if not any better than at least lightened. He had a point about Meera. Jack had been too tied up in his own guilt, compounded by Meera's seeming conviction it was his fault, to ever contemplate what his sister wasn't saying while she laid all the blame on him. Meera had gone through so much in such a short span of time it was a surprise she'd come through it as well as she had—and Jack had barely even noticed. She had every right to hate him, especially to hate the choices he'd made that took him away from a fragile family that had been struggling to cope without a wife, mother and grandmother, and then nearly cost them a son, brother and uncle.

Goddamn Ethan and his cutting insight.

After his shower, Jack pulled on the same pants he'd been wearing for five days now and went looking for the shirt Ethan had been wearing that morning. Ethan himself was still on the bed, curled up and dozing. Jack hoped it wasn't a return of the despair that had followed him out of the glass house. He plopped a light kiss on his shoulder and whispered that he was going to find Raja. Ethan mumbled something like "all right," then snuggled deeper into his pillow. Resuming the search, Jack found the shirt on the floor in the living room, smeared in places with dried yogurt and, of course, missing buttons. Sighing, he pulled it on and went to find his uncle.

Raja, he discovered, had to make an urgent run up to his other hotel in the hills with some supplies they were drastically short on. Putting off a potentially uncomfortable conversation with a surge of guilty relief, Jack settled for rummaging through the pile of clothes left behind by forgetful visitors. He found jeans and shirts for himself and Ethan, drew the line at borrowed underwear and, in newish clothes, sunglasses and cap, made a trip out to buy undies and a few other essentials.

His uncle still wasn't around when he got back, so he made his way up the hidden staircase, thinking that lazing away the evening in bed with Ethan would be lovely before Jack contacted the Office to get a location for an extraction.

Those thoughts vanished the moment he opened the door to the salon.

"Hello, Jack," Donna McIntosh said.

His Internal Threat Assessment director sat in one of the leather chairs, legs crossed, hands draped over the armrests. Her dark blue skirt suit was immaculate, blond hair curling in thick waves over her shoulders. When Jack's brain failed to cough up a comprehensible sentence, she continued.

"I thought it best to wait out here for you to return. It's been some time since I was in the field and I don't believe I'm quite up to holding my own against Ethan Blade."

She sounded pleasant enough, but her blue eyes didn't exactly hold the warmth they usually did when she was being personable. They weren't quite Artic either, but an intermediate degree Jack had become familiar with the year before, when she'd been doubting his loyalty to the Office and his country. Coupled with the fact that the last time McIntosh had gone into the field, it had been to extract Jack from the Sydney police when he had been arrested for suspicion of being a raving psychopathic serial killer, it couldn't be anything good that brought her here.

"Ma'am," he finally managed. "This is a surprise."

"Well, it was rather last minute all around." She gestured to the chair opposite her. "Why don't you sit down. We need to talk."

Jack glanced towards the suite, wondering if Ethan was still asleep, or if his finely honed senses had let him know someone else was here. Was he listening at the door? Or was he so tired he had dropped into a deeper sleep?

"If you wish Mr. Blade to be a part of this, I can wait."

Snorting, Jack dropped his shopping by the door to the suite and himself into the chair. "I don't even know what this is yet."

She gave him a tight smile that did nothing to illuminate her reason for being in India, or in this supposedly secret salon. "I suppose. First things first, the Cabal is in turmoil. The loss of two of its leaders has thrown the rest of them into crisis management. Territory is quickly being—"

"Wait," Jack snapped. "*Two* of its leaders? Three died in that house, not two."

"New information came into light in the aftermath of the deaths. Sakamoto was not a Cabal leader. He was in position to step up into the role, should one become vacant, but he wasn't one of the five."

"Shit." Jack sank further into the chair. How would Ethan take that news? He'd torn himself up about this enough already. Jack couldn't imagine how he'd feel when he found out there were still three of the bastards out there, not just two.

"It gets worse," McIntosh said gently. "Mahavir Balakrishnan isn't just a high-ranking member of the Cabal. He is one of the leaders."

And he had been right in Jack's hands. Right at the end of his gun. He could have solved a third of their remaining problems then and there. If only he'd known.

"Don't blame yourself, Jack. None of us knew then. This isn't the first time a subject has slipped by us. There *will* be another chance."

"Good. When do we make that chance happen?"

"As soon as you and Mr. Blade are ready to—" Frowning, McIntosh reached into her jacket and pulled out a phone. One glance at the screen and she stood. "Excuse me. I have to take this." She strode on her three-inch heels to the far side of the room, phone to her ear.

Jack got up and, gathering his bags, went into the suite. "Ethan? You awake?"

A tousled head poked out of the bathroom. "Just drying off." He saw the shopping bags and smiled. "Please tell me there is underwear in there."

"Bingo." Jack fished out a pair of the boxer-briefs and threw them at him. "And as an added treat, McIntosh is here."

Ethan froze, half in, half out of the undies. "Why?"

"Get dressed and I'll fill you in."

Jack returned to the sitting room, closing the door to the bedroom to give Ethan privacy in case his director was in there. She wasn't.

McIntosh leaned in the main doorway of the suite, shoulders slumped, one hand pressed to her downturned face. Jack had never seen her look so defeated.

"Ma'am? Something wrong?"

She looked up, almost startled. This time, her eyes were warm, but not because she was pleased with something. Quite the opposite, apparently.

Ethan emerged from the bedroom, pulling on a new T-shirt. "Jack, is Ms. McIntosh . . ." He trailed off as he saw her. "What's wrong?"

McIntosh didn't even glance towards Ethan. Her sad gaze was fixed on Jack.

Oh God. Oh fuck.

Jack swallowed hard. "Is it Meera? Mati?" What the fuck had the Cabal done to them? He would burn down the world if one hair on either of their heads was even so much as snipped a bit short.

"No. They're fine, Jack. I'm sorry, but it's your father."

THIRTY-SEVEN

Thanks to the continuing contention between India and Australia, extraction took a day to organise, and it was another day to travel to the exfil site. Then thirty-six more hours via chopper to Sri Lanka, a rackety old twin-prop across the island and finally, a private jet to Sydney by way of Singapore.

Jack was quiet for most of the journey, sitting by himself when there was room to put distance between him and Ethan and Ms. McIntosh, barely communicative when there wasn't. Ethan watched him worriedly.

"How?" Jack had asked when his director had given him the news in the hotel suite.

Ethan had inched towards him, ready to hold him back if Ms. McIntosh said the wrong thing.

"A fatal stroke. There was nothing anyone could do. Jack, I'm so sorry."

As far as Ethan could tell, she had told them the truth. If the Cabal had somehow engineered the death, there were easier ways to make a murder look like natural death than imitating a stroke, especially in someone as already compromised as Christopher Reardon.

Ethan's efforts to comfort Jack hadn't exactly been rebuffed, but they hadn't been encouraged while they waited for extraction. Jack had remained stiff in Ethan's embrace, had barely acknowledged his kisses, and spoke only in single words, single syllables if he could manage it.

Raja had taken the news hard, as well. He'd crumpled into a chair, shoulders wracked with silent sobs. McIntosh had sat with him as his nephew shut himself away in the bedroom. Raja's wife had rushed to his side, his best friend if not his lover, and they had travelled together to Sydney openly, both of them cautioned against mentioning Jack's presence in India.

There had been phone calls with Meera as well. Ethan had been able to hear her angry cries at Jack through the handset McIntosh had given him. Jack had taken the abuse quietly, only speaking to agree with the details for the funeral. It would have been easier to witness if Jack had bitten back, or at least defended himself. So soon after Ethan had encouraged him to talk about his mother's death, he worried that he'd damaged Jack's relationship with his sister even further.

The layover in Singapore gave them time to shower and pick up the black suits McIntosh had organised. They did manage to sleep on the final, seven-hour leg to Sydney, landing mid-afternoon. Already dressed, they stepped out of the jet and straight into the car waiting to take them to the funeral home.

Mourners were already seated in the large chapel, the service moments away from starting, when they dashed in. A seat waited at the front, between Matilda and Raja. Ethan recognised Jack's niece and sister from the image Zero had shown him. Gone were the smiles and scowls, replaced with a sadness that made Ethan's chest ache. He'd said goodbye to Nine three months ago and the ache it had left inside him was still fresh.

A couple of rows back from the front sat Lewis Thomas. He'd saved several seats and McIntosh headed towards him. Ethan went to follow her, but a hand caught his arm, holding him back.

"Jack?" he asked softly, aware that everyone was waiting for them, watching them. "Are you all right?"

Jack's face was blank, but his eyes . . . his beautiful eyes were screaming in pain. "Sit with me."

"Of course." Ethan couldn't even contemplate abandoning Jack right then.

The shuffling of chairs caused a minor disturbance, but helpful funeral home staff accomplished it quickly. Meera's scowl made an appearance during the rearrangement, but as she stood to allow them to add an extra seat, Jack wrapped her in his arms and held on tight. His sister resisted, pushing against his arms and chest, but then

Matilda wormed her way into the hug and Meera's hostility melted into grief. She buried her face in Jack's shoulder and wept.

It was Raja who gently coaxed them into the chairs. Meera and Matilda resumed their places, Jack next to niece, Ethan between him and Raja. Jack and Meera each put an arm around Matilda, and Jack's other hand griped Ethan's tight enough to bruise. Ethan didn't care.

The service was short and basic. A celebrant conducted it gravely but with a touch of humour as she recounted Chris's accomplishments. Details were saved for his teaching trips to India, especially the one where he met and fell in love with a fellow teacher, Usha Munjanattu, and the joy he found with his children. When the celebrant invited speakers up, Matilda looked from her mother to her uncle. Meera nodded and gave her a gentle nudge. The young woman stood and, taking a deep breath, walked to the podium. She unfolded a piece of paper and smoothed it out several times. When she looked up, eyes so similar to Jack's met Ethan's for the briefest moment, then moved on. Ethan squeezed Jack's hand, getting a sad smile in return.

"I didn't really know my grandad that well," Matilda began, her voice trembling. "He got sick when I was still really little, but I remember what he was like before. I remember him laughing a lot. In my memories, he's always smiling. Mum would always say he told the worst ever dad jokes, too."

Jack and Meera both let out soft laughs, then glanced at each other and fell silent.

"One she said was one of his favourite is this . . . Two goldfish are in a tank and one looks to the other one and says, 'Do you know how to drive this thing?'"

It took a moment, but wry chuckles rippled through the crowd. Matilda smiled and told a few more of the terrible jokes. When people were laughing more freely, Matilda relaxed and told a couple of stories Meera had relayed about when she was a baby and Chris's attempts to stop her crying.

"A couple of years back, when mum and I were visiting him in the home," she said, turning serious again, "grandad had a really lucid moment. Mum, you'd gone off to talk to one of the nurses so you weren't there. Grandad and I were sitting in the garden and he turned to me and said, you're smart like your mother, and you're loyal like your uncle. You got your grandmother's strength and my humour. You are the best of all of us." She paused and wiped at her eyes. "I don't know about being the best, but I really hope the rest of it is true, and I hope he knows that I'll try my hardest to make him proud."

Meera was half out of her chair, tears falling freely, when Matilda held up a hand to stop her.

"No, mum, stay."

The gathering chuckled as Meera slowly sat back down.

"Wow. She listens to someone else," Jack whispered.

"I'm not finished," Matilda continued. "I have a poem as well. Do you mind?"

There were no objections so she read a short, beautiful poem about not lingering on the passing of a loved one, but rejoicing in their life and the legacy they left behind. Jack was crying by the end, but smiling as well, and when Matilda stepped down from the podium, he and Meera both stood to embrace her.

The celebrant concluded the service and the casket slowly rolled through a set of dark blue curtains at the rear of the stage. A reception had been set up in the next room, and as the people rose from their seats, they filed past the family, murmuring words of support and shared sorrow. Most people gave Ethan a polite little smile, some ignored him, one woman embraced him while sobbing. He managed not to throw her to the floor and pin her arms across her back, but it was a near thing. Moments later, Lewis Thomas appeared before him.

"Hell of an introduction to the family," Lewis said softly.

"It could have been better."

"Could have been worse. Thank you for giving Jack what he needed to save them. I'm glad he caught up to you and got you back."

The words were soft, but Jack heard them, looking over and nodding to his friend.

Matilda also heard and she leaned around her uncle to stare at Ethan. "You're the assassin?"

"Mati," Jack hissed and put a hand over her mouth.

The woman waiting to talk to Meera, who'd introduced herself as Mrs. Peterson, turned to look at them, eyebrows raised.

"Yes, he's an assistant," Lewis said pointedly to Mati. "To the governor. Of New South Wales."

Mrs. Peterson eyed Ethan up and down and said, "Well done then, I suppose," and moved on to talk to Meera.

Lewis stepped up and gave Jack a hug. "So sorry, mate. He was an amazing dad. You need anything at all, let me know, okay?"

Jack hugged him back. "Thanks. Glad you could make it." Releasing his friend, he looked around. "Is Lydia here? Did McIntosh leave?"

"No and yes, respectively." Lewis's expression soured. "McIntosh got a call and had to take it. She never came back so I guess she's gone for the day." He looked away, sighed, and added, "Lyds couldn't get away from work. She told me to give you a big kiss and a hug from her. A hug is as far as I'm willing to go though. In public."

Jack's smile was tinged with worry. "Tell her thanks and I'll probably see her tomorrow."

Ethan opened his mouth to protest but Lewis beat him to it.

"Dude. Take a week. Everything will still be there when you come back. You've been going for three months straight." He leaned in close. "And your dad just died. Take two weeks. Back me up, Eth."

"Eth?" Ethan repeated drily.

"Told you," Jack muttered. "I'll be in tomorrow for an update. We left . . . the other place in a rush. I need to know what's going on."

Matilda was looking between her uncle and his friend curiously. Even in his little experience of the young woman, Ethan could see the wheels turning in her head as she absorbed everything they were saying. He doubted anyone had outright told her he was an assassin, and yet she'd deduced it.

"Perhaps we should table this discussion for later," Ethan said. "You're holding up the line."

Both Jack and Lewis grumbled and Ethan saw why they were friends in that moment. Lewis moved on and allowed the rest of the people to come forwards. There weren't too many left and they all moved into the next room quickly. Jack gave Ethan's hand a final squeeze then went to talk to family and close friends. Ethan happily slunk into a quiet corner and observed.

Jack was hurting and vulnerable. He needed someone watching his six. Only a few people approached Ethan, asking how he knew Chris. Ethan gave them a polite "I didn't know him, I'm here with Jack," and most went on their way. Some gave his sunglasses odd looks, and one man muttered a homophobic slur as he left. One person, however, he couldn't dissuade with a few curt words.

"You're my uncle's boyfriend, aren't you?" Matilda leaned against the wall beside him.

"I believe so. Shouldn't you be with your mother?"

"She's fine. Probably off telling the staff how to do their job. It's her grieving process." She tilted her head, dark hair falling over her shoulder. "It's her process for everything, really. You should just be happy she's not here telling you what to do, too."

Unable to help it, Ethan smiled.

"Don't worry about it. She'll find you soon enough," Matilda said ominously. "Once she's finished yelling at Jack for disappearing for so long."

"If that happens, you can direct her to me. I'm the reason he was gone for so long."

Matilda eyed him warily. "You're not going to take a hit out on her, are you?"

"Ignoring for the moment your atrocious terminology, what makes you think I'm an assassin?"

"Are you saying you are one?"

"I'm merely asking why you think I am one."

"You still haven't denied it."

"I don't need to deny it in order to ask a simple question."

"People who aren't assassins who get accused of being assassins usually claim they aren't assassins."

Ethan's gaze left Jack's dark-suited body and arrowed in on Matilda. "You are your uncle's niece."

She frowned. "I'm not sure if that's a compliment or not."

"It's an observation."

She grinned at him. "Assassin or not, I think I like you."

Matilda stayed where she was, telling him about this and that person as they came into view. Her comments were usually amusing and more often than not very insightful. For all that they were at a funeral, Ethan found he was enjoying himself. Even when Matilda told him about Jack's daring rescue of her and her friend Tate from Seven.

"Then this helicopter came sweeping in overhead," she said breathlessly, showing him with her hands how the aircraft had moved. "And it started firing at the Alfa . . ."

Her words faded into the background as Ethan noticed Jack stiffen. He was not far away, talking with the bigot who'd insult Ethan earlier. It appeared he wasn't any more restrained with Jack, who looked about a hair's breadth away from punching the man, arms crossed, feet spread to balance his weight, and a very familiar, belligerent gleam in his eyes. Even Meera, across the room, noticed and began to make her way over. Ethan was closer so he murmured an apology to Matilda and headed for Jack.

Not even bothering to acknowledge the other man, Ethan stepped between him and Jack, unfolded his lover's tensed arms, took one hand and led him out of the room. Jack came reluctantly, grumbling the entire way.

Finding an empty office, Ethan pulled Jack in, locked the door, put a chair under the handle, and then opened his arms. Jack was inside them instantly. He embraced Ethan with a desperate strength, his face buried in his neck. Shivers ran down his back, almost like he had a fever. Ethan soothed him with firm rubs along his spine and soft words assuring Jack he was there.

"Don't leave me again," Jack said hoarsely. "I can't lose anyone else. Promise me, Ethan. Promise you won't go away again."

It was easy. So incredibly easy to say, "I promise, Jack. I'll never leave you again," because this right here was worth more than the Cabal, more than any vengeance Ethan could exact on them for himself or his siblings.

Jack was right. The Cabal had forced him to become a killer, but Jack had shown him how he was so much more than that, and that was what mattered the most—that Jack believed in him.

After a couple of minutes, Jack stopped shaking. He lifted his head and looked at Ethan for a long while, then said, "I love you."

THIRTY-EIGHT

t felt good saying it. Right and true. Jack had felt it for a long time, but it had only been while he was expending so much energy and emotion on chasing Ethan down on his trail of self-destruction that he'd admitted it to himself. And now he'd said it to Ethan.

"I love you."

Ethan went still and Jack let him have all the time he needed to work through it. He knew Ethan wasn't contemplating his best route for escape, not anymore. This stillness was just Ethan trying to deal with emotions he had trouble processing. Hopefully it would be a good outcome, which came when Ethan swayed forwards and kissed him.

It felt like that first kiss, at Middle Head, when Ethan had said without words what he'd been feeling. What Jack had been feeling as well, but had been too scared, too damaged, to say aloud. So Ethan had kissed him, just as he kissed him now.

Kissing was intimate. More so than fucking. For Jack, kissing was an expression of his heart and mind and soul. He showed himself, his thoughts, emotions, and beliefs, in his words, from his lips and tongue. They were the conduit through which he gave himself to others, and to the person he loved, he gave them everything through kisses.

Ethan drew back and studied him carefully. "I'm taking you home."

"But Meera—"

"Will understand. You're exhausted, Jack. I'm taking you home and we're both going to sleep."

Ethan was right. Jack had nearly punched one of his dad's colleagues and the old fart hadn't even said anything truly inflammatory. The suit felt like it weighed a tonne and if another person told him how much they'd miss his dad—not that any of them had missed him enough to go visit him in the home—he'd probably scream. So he nodded and let Ethan guide him out of the office, down the hallway and left him leaning on the wall by the front doors while Ethan went to tell Meera they were going. Mati found him there, wordlessly falling into him, head tucked under his chin, arms around his waist. They were still like that when Ethan returned. Mati let Jack go, gave Ethan a small smile, then waved them goodbye.

McIntosh had left the car for them, and Ethan gave the driver the Bathurst Street address. Jack was too wiped to question it, barely able to drag himself out of the car, into the elevator and then into the penthouse. Ethan hastily changed the sheets on the bed while Jack undressed. Once they were ensconced, wound in each other's arms—secure—Ethan spoke.

"I love you, Jack."

It was the perfect way to fall asleep and forget.

They both woke at some point through the night, reaching automatically for each other. It was rushed and frantic, desperate to show the other they were still there. Jack let Ethan take charge, needing to be the one not in control this time. It felt so good, with Ethan between his legs, dick driving into him so deep and hard it was almost as if he was whole again.

Jack dropped back into a heavy sleep moments after they'd come and when he woke the next time, was alone in the bed.

Soft voices from beyond the closed bedroom door assured him quickly he hadn't been abandoned again. But it also made him wary and curious. This place was Ethan's sanctuary, his secret lair away from the prying eyes of the world and his own paranoid instincts. Had he really invited company over?

Yes. Yes, he had.

In a pair of hastily donned track pants and a T-shirt, Jack surveyed the scene that greeted him in the open plan living, dining and kitchen area. Mati and Lewis sat on stools at the kitchen counter, comparing things on their phones and snickering like a pair of teenagers. Meera sat on the couch, turned so she could rest one bent leg on the seat, arm on the backrest, head cradled in her hand as she listened to Ethan, who sat in the corner of the sectional piece.

It was homey and domestic. And totally not what Jack could deal with right then.

"Morning, sunshine," Lewis chimed as Jack stalked past on his way to the bathroom.

Jack showered quickly, then grumbled his way back to the bedroom for proper clothes. In jeans and a slightly nicer T-shirt, he emerged again.

"The coffee is out if you need it," Ethan supplied from the couch. He had a mug in hand already, but Jack could smell the tea from across the room.

"He is such a grouchy bear before his first cup of concentrated caffeine in the morning," Lewis said to Mati.

Jack gave him the finger and Mati laughed at the blond man. Her tune changed to a startled gasp and largely ignored, "Mum, Jack flicked my ear!" a moment later, which made Lewis laugh in return.

The couple of minutes it took the machine to burble away and spit out his coffee was the longest of Jack's life, not unlike those seconds before they got the command to go in hot on an SAS mission. He craved a cigarette, feeling like he was about go into active combat. His sister and niece, whom he barely knew, in the same room as Ethan without the distraction of immediate and shocking grief. His best friend who worked for the same secret government agency as he did was getting to know them all as well. Was this what having a family meant? It had been so long Jack had forgotten just how terrifying it could be.

And how comforting.

Coffee in hand, he turned and looked at this strange vista. Lewis and Mati were back to duelling phones and Meera had a part tentative, part curious smile as Ethan described, from what Jack could surmise through his hand gestures, driving something, probably very, very fast. It looked . . . natural. It looked right. Seeing Mati scowl, then laugh at something Lewis did, warmed his heart. Even watching his fiery, distant sister scoot a little closer to Ethan made him smile. Maybe there was hope for all of them.

This was what Jack fought for, both with the army and with the Office. This was what he needed to protect with his own life if necessary. The promise of this very image was what had drawn him back from so many edges and kept him centred. He almost wanted to snap a photo of this moment and give it to McIntosh and say, "This is why you never have to doubt me ever again."

"Weddings and funerals, man."

Jack shook himself and looked at Lewis. Mati had dashed off to the toilet and Lewis leaned on the counter across from Jack, sad smile on his face.

"Huh?"

"Drink your coffee. Your brain hasn't kick started yet." Lewis gestured around the beautiful space. "Weddings and funerals are the only reliable ways to bring a family together."

Taking a gulp he barely tasted, Jack nodded. "Speaking of which, where's Lydia today? Still working?"

Lewis dropped his gaze to his phone. "I don't know. Right now, I don't really care either."

His best friends had been Jack's relationship meter for a long time. They lived and worked together so seamlessly even their occasional arguments had seemed perfect to Jack. He knew they'd worked at it though, witnessed them compromising for and supporting each other. He had even mediated a few of the bigger issues between them. But he'd never thought he'd ever hear Lewis say he didn't care where Lydia was, however.

"Is something wrong with you two?"

"Don't worry about it." Lewis let out a long breath. "You don't need to deal with this shit right now."

Jack glanced at Ethan and Meera again, still marvelling at how well they appeared to be getting on. Mati came back from the bathroom and, showing that innate sense of awareness she'd hinted at before, quietly bypassed the kitchen and threw herself onto the couch between mother and uncle's boyfriend like she'd been doing it for years, not just a single morning.

"Yeah, actually, I think I do." Jack leaned on the counter close to Lewis. "You're family, Lew. What's going on? Is it because you haven't been working together?"

Lewis standing in for McIntosh and Lydia running an operation without him had been the furthest apart they'd been professionally in years.

"Are you still a temp director now McIntosh is back?" he asked curiously.

Eyebrow cocked, Lewis shook his head. "McIntosh isn't back at work. I'm still captaining the good ship ITA, and Tan still has his hand up my arse like the puppet master he thinks he is."

At least Lewis wasn't so far gone he'd slipped into decency.

"But she came to India to update us on the Cabal situation. She was there when she got the call about . . . about Dad."

"No one told me she was back on the job." Lewis's fingers flashed over his phone screen, typing out a message to Lydia. "And if McIntosh is up to date on Cabal shit, then Lyds has to know about it. And if she knows about it and didn't tell me . . ." He trailed off ominously.

Jack waited until the message was sent, then asked, "That's not the only problem between you, though, is it?"

"No," Lewis admitted grudgingly. "She's changed since she got control of the Cabal job."

"Power's gone to her head?" Though Jack seriously doubted it. Lydia had been the real leader of Lewis's unit for a long time. Lewis was the human computer and Lydia was the person at the keyboard. If that sort of influence hadn't affected her already, then leading a super-unit of team leaders on a globe-spanning hunt for the top tier of a very secret organisation wouldn't.

"Made her more withdrawn," Lewis muttered. "She doesn't talk to me anymore. She spends more time at work than I do and I'm doing nearly eighty hours a week. You know how she was always keen on watching political manoeuvres? Well, she's obsessed now. Ob*sessed*. But I only know that from what I hear from others. She doesn't talk to me about any of this. Not like she used to."

His phoned beeped and he looked at it, then turned it around to show Jack the message.

TTYL.

That was it. Nothing else.

"But she won't. I'll be lucky if I see her this week at all."

Everything Lewis was describing was very unlike Lydia. She was dedicated to her job, yes, they all were, but she'd never let it consume her like this before. Still, she was Jack's friend and he tried to see reason.

"It's a big job. Big and complex, and yes, consuming. I got lost in it too."

"For really important personal reasons." Lew gestured vaguely towards Ethan. "And I'm working all the jobs right now, Jack. That's what McIntosh does. She overseas every single fucking move any ITA asset makes, and some made by Intel and ETA as well. I'm doing all that and yet I still found the time to be there for my friend when his dad died." The bitter diatribe ended with an apologetic wince and a swipe at his damp eyes. "Sorry."

"Don't be," Jack assured him. He squeezed Lew's biceps comfortingly. "I understand."

"Good. Explain it to me, then." He sighed and slumped over the countertop.

"Everything all right?" Ethan came around the counter and brushed his hand across Jack's back as he went to fridge.

"Relationship issues," Jack murmured.

"Oh. I'm sorry, Lewis."

Lewis waved at him from his face-plant on the counter.

Ethan closed the fridge. "We don't have anything to feed our guests, Jack."

Very carefully not saying he didn't invite them around, Jack offered, "Want me to head out and get something for breakfast?"

Lips pursed, Ethan shook his head. "I'll take Meera and Mati out in Victoria. You and Lewis finish talking."

"Thanks," Lewis muttered. "'Preciate it."

The promise of another ride in the Aston Martin had Mati bouncing. Meera wasn't quite so excited, but she gave Lewis a knowing look, then followed Ethan and Mati out.

Once alone, Lewis sat up and rubbed his hands over his face. "I get it, Jack. I really do. This job is nothing like anything we've ever gone after before. Not even ETA has undertaken anything on this scale. I get that she's completely focused on it. What I don't get is why she won't let me help her with it."

That was surprising. Lewis had an uncanny ability to see patterns in what appeared as chaos to anyone else. He could sift through mountains of data and instinctively pull together all the fragments to make a cohesive whole. This was exactly what they'd needed while chasing Ethan as he searched for the Cabal leaders. And Jack had thought they had it.

"You mean you weren't working the job at all while we were running around after Ethan?"

Lewis shook his head. "Nope. Tan took control of it right from the start. Lydia didn't even put up a smidge of an objection."

"Jesus. You would have been exactly what we needed."

"Not to blow my own whistle, but yeah. And yet . . ." Lew spread his hands in a universal but-here-we-stand-screwed gesture. Then he frowned. "I'm starting to wonder if it's intentional."

Jack had been as well, but he knew to let Lewis talk through his process. "Why?"

"Let's timeline this shit. First of all we get the green light on the biggest investigation the Office has ever undertaken. Spearheaded by humble moi. Then suddenly, McIntosh, who has never, ever, shied away from the big deals, needs some personal time off. Next thing I know, I'm wearing her pumps. The ones with the mega high heel and pointy toes. Uncomfortable doesn't even start to get there. And because I'm such a newb, Tan's all over me like a really bad case of shingles. I get swamped in everything but the big, fun job all my friends get to play with. Now we have McIntosh showing up in India when she's supposed to be on leave. Significant because *leave*, and *India*."

"Shit." Jack thumped the counter with the side of his fist. "That's what I was missing. I knew McIntosh showing up in the field was weird, but I was forgetting that Australian citizens trying to get into India right now is difficult."

"Which means the Office got her in on the super down-low, and if that's the case, why not just send a field asset, or redirect one of the ETA assets already there?" Lewis got up and began to pace, just a few strides either way. "I think, Jack, I think she was already in India. Before it all blew up politically."

Jack's stomach clenched. "Before the leaders of the Cabal arrived even. She told me we'd pegged the wrong person as a Cabal leader. It wasn't Sakamoto. It was Balakrishnan all along. Oh fuck. She knew before Ethan and I got to his house."

"But how?" Lewis muttered.

"I don't think our director is as straightforward as she seems sometimes," Jack answered just as softly.

Lewis met his grim expression. "She can't be working with them. Surely."

Their silent contemplation was interrupted by the buzz of the intercom. Jack checked the security system, finding Lydia at the private lift in the foyer. She looked nervous and he hoped she was. The way she'd been treating Lewis lately and her no-show at the funeral weren't making her his favourite person right then. But if she was here, maybe she was willing to talk.

"Come on up," he said into the intercom and put in the code for the lift to open for her. "It's Lydia," he told Lewis and opened the door for her arrival.

Lewis slid off his stool and ran his hands through his hair. "How do I look?"

"Shit has been known to look better."

His mate scowled at him but disappeared into the bathroom moments before Lydia stepped out of the lift. She crossed the foyer with a hopeful smile.

"How are you, Jack?"

"Getting there," he said flatly and waved her in.

Her smile died as she passed him. "I deserve that. You're alone?"

Wondering if she would be more likely to talk if she thought no one else was around, Jack said, "Yeah. The others have gone to get food. What's up?"

When Lydia faced him, she had a gun in hand. "We have a lot to talk about, Jack."

THIRTY-NINE

Mati graciously allowed her mother to sit in the front of Victoria, claiming she had already experienced the Aston Martin from that seat. The young woman clambered into the back, commenting how no one had fixed the car up from when "Jack smashed it into the Alfa over and over."

Ethan claimed they had been too busy since then to deal with Victoria but that he planned to get right onto it. He didn't want to admit that seeing her still beaten up was an almost physical pain. As was seeing anyone other than Jack in her, but this was Jack's family and Ethan vowed he would do anything for them, especially in light of their recent loss.

With that thought in mind, he took them to GiGi's, Jack's favourite patisserie. While the women picked out a variety of pastries for breakfast, Ethan carefully chose several pieces of fudge. Some to share with everyone, some just for him and Jack. He paid for his selection and turned around to look for Meera and Mati. He found Jack's sister first, chatting with a tall blond woman by the pastry counter.

Donna McIntosh.

And beside them was Mati. She was looking warily at the man looming behind her.

Ten.

Director McIntosh glanced over at him and nodded once. Saying something to Meera, she gestured for them all to go outside. It would be easier to fight out there, so Ethan waited until everyone had left, then followed them.

"No sudden moves, Mr. Blade," McIntosh said calmly once he'd joined them. "We're not here to cause trouble."

Ethan looked pointedly at Ten. "Then why is he here?"

"Merely to ensure your cooperation."

"What's going on?" Meera demanded, holding Mati behind her.

"Nothing that involves you." Ethan held out the car keys to Meera. "Take the car, go back to Jack." He cocked an eyebrow at the director. "Is it all right for them to go back to Jack?"

"It should be. I've got someone talking to him as well. It will only get dangerous if he makes it so."

Everything fell into place. Why McIntosh had shown up in India so soon after their confrontation with Balakrishnan. Her confidence that he was a Cabal leader. Her "leave" from work. Why Ten was standing passively by her side.

She was with the Cabal.

"Meera, go to Jack. Tell him I'm sorry."

"Ethan—"

"Ms. Reardon," McIntosh said firmly. "Take your daughter and go."

Meera wasn't silly. She took the keys and went. Mati didn't argue, memories of the frantic car chase still fresh in her wide, panicked eyes.

"If anything happens to them, I will kill you," Ethan said to McIntosh.

"I wouldn't expect any less. Shall we go?"

THE TOWER

·   Ethan had followed McIntosh, with Ten on his six, to a dark coloured 4WD where, once inside, he'd been cuffed and blindfolded. They'd travelled to what Ethan believed was a small airfield outside of Sydney, where they boarded a midsized jet. While Ten piloted it, McIntosh gave Ethan the tiny, ceramic-shielded beacon to hide under the skin of the open wound on his hip—so it wouldn't be detected by scans or body searches—then sedated him for the remainder of the trip back to the Cabal.

After getting above ground, cracking the ceramic casing and letting the beacon send its signal, then glimpsing McIntosh in the lift,

Ethan was herded back into his cell. He was strapped to the cot and his leg broken, as per the Doctor's command.

He barely felt it while it was happening. It was shocking how easily he'd fallen back into the unfeeling place he'd learned to retreat to as a child. The defence mechanism he'd had to perfect in order to survive. Then he'd watched Eleven die by his own hand and it had felt as if the knife had cut him instead of his brother. A sharp, stinging slice followed by a dull but persistent ache he could no longer ignore.

He'd tried to hide it, desperately did *not* want to be the weak one again, the "bad luck," but hadn't succeeded. Two had seen the change in One-three after Eleven's death. As had Seven. Even Two had doubled down on him, One-three hadn't been able to go back to how he'd been before. He'd resisted and fought and felt himself slowly being worn down. Seven had been his rescue in those days. She hadn't consoled or defended, but rather given him a quiet place to simply be himself. When he cried, she hadn't insulted. When he slept, she hadn't attacked. When he wanted a kind touch, she at least hadn't punched, even if there wasn't much warmth in the cool hand she'd put on his back or cheek or head.

After fracturing his left fibula, they set it and wrapped it in a stabilising bandage and brace, and allowed him to remain on the cot, rather than string him back up. They clearly didn't mean to cripple him permanently, just ensure he didn't make another attempt on the lives of every guard on the island. And perhaps it meant the Doctor didn't want him dead at all.

Was that the goal of the sessions? To assess if Ethan could be brought back into the Cabal and used as he once had been? They'd lost all of their assassins bar Ten, so was this them trying to salvage what they could of the program?

No. This most definitely wasn't how the plan was supposed to go.

If Ethan had known the Doctor would be here he wouldn't have come as quietly as he had. The Cabal had forced him to be something he didn't want to be, warped him until he had no choice but to be their pet monster. He'd resisted as much as he could, causing himself pain and heartache, but in the end it had been worth it. He'd found Jack, found a life outside of the one the Cabal had made for him, and had found value in being himself. But the Doctor . . . what he had done to Ethan, to all of them, was something Ethan didn't think he'd ever recover from. The whipping and broken leg were negligent compared to the sessions with the Doctor.

Still the pain from his leg, back, and throat were constant and made him restless, which only aggravated them further. Wanting some relief, Ethan ran through a meditative technique he'd learned when they grafted the neural implant to his brain. It took a few repetitions, but eventually, the pain faded and he drifted into a light sleep.

Which was a pattern for the coming days. He slept and was only visited by wary guards delivering food and water. No more tea with the Doctor—no more Doctor, thankfully—just pain, simple fare and no communication. On the third day, someone came and replaced the brace and splint on his leg. No one gave him any pain relief. Day five saw a touch of despair creep in. He'd been here a week and his options were incredibly few and far between. It was hard to keep his hopes up when all he could do was wait.

Then on day six, he got a new visitor.

Tumbling locks woke him from meditation. It was his latest attempt at distraction and worked slightly better than simply sleeping. He felt marginally more optimistic as he hauled himself up into a sitting position, though waves of pain from his leg sapped that minor relief fast. His throat and back had mostly recovered, only worrying him if he ate too much or moved too fast respectively.

The door opened and Zero rolled in. "You've been busy, One-three." He eyed the brace on Ethan's leg.

Dropping his gaze, Ethan murmured, "I learned my lesson."

"Didn't I warn you about making trouble?"

"You did. I'm sorry I couldn't listen to it."

Zero studied him, shrewd but tired eyes narrowed, fingers drumming on the wheel of his chair. "Couldn't? Always with the plan." He slipped a hand into his chest pocket and retrieved three small, white pills. "For the pain."

Ethan had resisted the first time Zero had offered him relief. Taking anything "freely" given by the Cabal was always fraught with hidden agendas and costs. This time, however, the ache in his leg, combined with the doldrums of the past several days, and the fact that the Doctor was close by and could want a "session" at any time, made him yearn for even that small escape. Yet he managed to shake his head.

Zero rolled a little closer and his voice dropped into a quiet, insistent tone. "Take them. I think you'll need it."

One of the things Ethan had learned to trust was that Zero wouldn't lie to them. He might not tell them everything, might hedge a few details, but what he did say was always true. He'd been right about Dejana's death, and that Ethan could deal with his brothers while also ensuring Jack's family weren't harmed.

That he was undoubtedly being truthful about Ethan's need for the pain relief meant something was about to happen. Something big and potentially painful.

Ethan held out his hand. Zero wheeled over to him, gave him the pills and then produced a bottle of water from a pocket on his chair. Ethan washed the pills down with the entire contents of the bottle.

"Right." Zero rolled backwards to the door. "They want you up top." At his knock, a guard opened the door and Zero said, "Bring the crutches."

A moment later, two guards entered, one carrying a pair of metal forearm crutches, the other covering his fellow with a bullpup rifle. The crutches were tossed onto the cot from a safe distance and then the guards backed out.

Pain relief and potential weapons. Zero was definitely pushing the boundaries of his position. It had to be something major.

Swinging along on the crutches, Ethan followed Zero out. The guards fell in around them, four front and six behind. They definitely hadn't been taking any chances of him breaking out again, broken leg or no.

"Up top" meant the observation deck Ethan had been shown after his breakout. The sky was overcast, the water dark and choppy. Black clouds loomed to the north while the setting sun blazed red and golden to the west. Furniture had appeared, three comfortably plush armchairs and small, round side tables. They faced the inner wall, where a blank screen had been hung. People fussed about, placing drinks and trays of hors d'oeuvres on the tables, ice buckets with champagne beside the chairs. A couple of steel-topped tables were set up with more food and drinks. There were also a lot of armoured and armed guards.

The pain relief had set in. Ethan's leg had settled into a barely-there ache, but only the very periphery of his senses had gone fuzzy. The benefits of being a Sugar Baby.

Zero positioned Ethan and himself to one side of the activity. The escort from the cell remained with them. The other security staff eyed them cautiously as they patrolled. Fifteen minutes after their arrival, the lift doors opened again and a familiar figure stepped out.

Mahavir Balakrishnan wore a three-piece, pinstriped suit, a gold watch chain looping across his left ribs. He had two of his personal guards with him. Balakrishnan sent Ethan a smug smile before strolling over to the centrally placed chair and taking a seat like a king on a throne.

The next of the Cabal bosses to arrive was a man of Arabian appearance. He was under average height, pleasantly round and smiling, his dishdasha white and ghutra red.

"Zahid Farooq," Zero murmured. "One of the richest bankers in the Eastern Hemisphere. Don't let the smile fool you. He's pure predator."

Farooq took a chair beside Balakrishnan and started up a lively conversation in English. Balakrishnan sipped his drink and nodded but didn't contribute much beyond a "Hmm" or "Of course."

Not more than two minutes later, the final boss arrived.

"Lord Walton Prentis Camdon-Smythe. Inherited title and money. His father looked like he was going to live forever but took ill rather suddenly three years ago. Papers said it was 'old age' that got him. I believe Two took a leaf from your book and poisoned the bugger. Walton got the title, money, and clout to get a position at the top of the Cabal." Zero's top lip lifted in a silent snarl. "He's the newest of them. At least until tonight's vote is over."

"Vote?" Ethan watched the tall, lean English lord in an Oxford suit stride directly to his chair, imperiously directing one of the waitstaff to bring him his scotch.

"There are two empty seats." Zero nodded to the two vacant chairs on either end of the row. "Potential replacements are usually mined from the next layer of members, the candidates present their cases for inclusion, then there's a vote."

"What happens to those who don't get selected?"

Zero shrugged. "Death. Or if they're particularly useful to the leaders, they have to prove their loyalty."

Ethan didn't need to ask. He knew just how the Cabal demanded someone prove their loyalty. "You said candidates are *usually* selected from the next hierarchal layer."

The handler cocked his head, as if listening for the hidden agenda in Ethan's words. "Yes, usually. Sometimes, like today, there are special circumstances that allow another candidate to step forward."

Knowing he had pushed a little too much, Ethan kept quiet while Camdon-Smythe sampled his scotch, turned his nose up and sent the server away with very detailed instructions on which bottle to pick. Ethan scanned the area, noting guards and waitstaff. There were six servers and two dozen security personnel. The Doctor was absent, but then this side of the Cabal hadn't appeared to interest him. It wasn't power or money the Doctor was after, but knowledge, and his pursuit of it had been as relentless as the Cabal bosses seeking wealth and influence.

Once everyone was settled, all but a couple of the waitstaff were dismissed and Balakrishnan commanded the first candidate be brought in.

There were four of them in total. The first three—a Turkish industrialist, a Brazilian tech developer, and a United States senator— all spoke about money, prestige, and the new territories they could help bring into the Cabal's sphere of influence. It all sounded good, but clearly didn't impress the existing leadership, and Ethan could understand why. A reason that was highlighted by the final candidate.

Donna McIntosh stepped out of the lift and paused to take in the observation deck. Ten was a silent, stone sentinel at her shoulder. It was unclear if he was guard or guardian. Ethan doubted McIntosh had managed to subvert Ten's loyalty, so it had to be the bosses making sure this new initiate into the Cabal didn't run amuck. Not that anyone noted Ten's presence behind the woman. She looked amazing in her fitted skirt suit in blood red, sky-high heels, blonde hair curling over her shoulders, but it was the attitude she carried before three of the most powerful people in the world that made her glorious. She stood there like they were the suppliants and she the one with the power of veto on their lives. Whereas for the first three, the bosses had barely looked amused, now they were rapt. She must have been a force of nature when she was a field asset.

"Hello. I'm Donna McIntosh, a director with the Meta-State Office of Counterterrorism and Intelligence." She repeated it in Hindi and Arabic, receiving respectful nods. "Thank you all for allowing me to stand before you today. I understand how great of an honour it is for you to grant my petition an audience. I heard the other presentations. I listened as they told you they could deliver you greater access to more wealth, greater opportunities for power and control. But that's all they brought to the table. Opportunities." McIntosh gave each of the bosses a long, direct look. "I don't bring you opportunities. I bring you prizes. The first, your errant asset, Experimental Boy Thirteen."

Ethan went still as every eye in the room turned to him. The security people sceptical and the bosses smug. They finally had him back. It was easy to see that this time, they wouldn't be letting him go. Just as they hadn't let Zero go.

"But One-three is not the only thing I have brought you, up front, with no guarantee of my inclusion amongst your ranks. I have another gift. As I'm sure most of you know, there was a recent leadership spill in Australia. The old prime minister was deemed unfit to lead thanks to the revelations of an . . . unfortunate incident involving Australian soldiers on Indian soil."

"Unfortunate." Though Balakrishnan didn't sound at all sad about the loss of life.

Movement in the sky over the horizon caught Ethan's attention. A black shape against the dark clouds, glinting metallically as it passed through shafts of light thrown up by the setting sun.

"The old PM was Minister for National Security at the time of the incident. It was his signature that gave the go ahead for the operation. Once that knowledge became public, it was simple for the Deputy PM to call for, and be granted, his leadership challenge. The party barely needed to vote. The old PM had to stand down, and the Deputy PM, John Nelson, is now Australia's prime minister."

"Information we are already very well aware of, Ms. McIntosh." Farooq glanced at his Patek Phillippe watch. "We don't have all night. My chopper will be here very soon."

Yes. The distant aircraft, getting closer, was a chopper. It was coming in low over the water, moving fast. Faster than a civilian chopper should move.

McIntosh nodded to Farooq. "Then I'll get to the important part. The information about the failed Jharkhand mission had been seized by the AFP during the arrest of an opposition front bencher, who had in turn, paid a known underworld subject for the data. What this means is, anyone who knows just how Mr. Nelson came by that data controls him." She paused and looked each boss in the eyes. "I know how he got that data. Sirs, I bring you Australia."

Any questions the bosses might have had were drowned out by the sudden roar of the approaching chopper. It swept up from the ocean surface, coaxial rotors thumping deafeningly. The sleek, predator shape of the Kamov Ka-52 shot past the observation deck window so close the thick ballistic glass shook under the pressure of its passing. Then it was gone, disappearing out of view overhead.

"What the hell?" someone demanded.

"Farooq? Was that yours?" Camdon-Smythe demanded.

Before the Saudi man could answer, the chopper was back. It swung into the air outside the window, hovering just far enough back that the spinning blades didn't hit the building. It looked lethal and intent.

And then it opened fire.

FORTY

Jack lifted the Kamov Ka-52 off the deck of the Australian Navy frigate in the Indian Ocean and turned it towards the coordinates the beacon planted on Ethan had given them. His location had been determined five days ago and even though the Office had kicked into high gear instantly, Lydia had made them wait for a pre-determined date—when McIntosh had assured her *all* of the Cabal bosses would be there.

Even just thinking about that conversation with Lydia the day after his father's funeral boiled Jack's blood. Once again, McIntosh had used him mercilessly for her own purposes. He was starting to think Tan might have been the smarter choice. At least he'd always been upfront about his intentions to extract every iota of usefulness from his assets.

The entire time Lydia had been telling him about how McIntosh had been working this job on her own since Ethan revealed the existence of the Cabal, Jack had wanted to scream and punch something. He barely heard as she explained how his trusted and respected director had worked on her own to uncover the truth behind a stolen data stick full of information about the top secret SAS mission in Jharkhand and how it had somehow ended up with the deputy PM. Jack couldn't care less how Nelson had used that information to discredit the current prime minister in a leadership challenge he ultimately won, and how it was all connected to the Cabal. He didn't even want to hear about McIntosh drawing Lydia into her investigation, demanding absolute secrecy of her and, ultimately, driving a spike into his best friends' relationship.

Jack didn't want know any of it, because all he really focused on was Lydia saying, "She used the information of Blade going after Jäger to get the Cabal bosses to listen to her. That's how they knew to put Ten into play in Mumbai. Now she needs Blade as a bargaining piece so they'll let her make a bid for a seat on the Cabal leadership. He was supposed to be caught in Goa, but you and he managed to escape, but he's with her now. Blade will get the beacon into whichever black site they end up at and once he sets it off, we'll be able to track it and find them. And end the Cabal. That's been her purpose all along, Jack. You have to understand it was the only way."

Which was when Lewis burst out of the bathroom, furious. "No! It wasn't the only way. You should have come to me, Lyds. Why didn't you tell me?"

Lydia had barely held back tears. "I wanted to. I did! Donna wouldn't let me. Please—"

"Wouldn't let you? She wasn't your boss then! I was!"

And on that completely wrong thing for Lewis to say at that time, Jack left his friends screaming at each other, determined to catch McIntosh before she went anywhere with Ethan.

He'd made it as far as the underground carpark of the building, where he found Meera and Mati getting out of Victoria. The moment Mati saw him she erupted into tears and threw herself at him, shaking uncontrollably. In clipped words—a sure sign of just how angry she was—Meera told him about meeting with McIntosh at the patisserie. When Jack hadn't believed that Ethan had just gone with her so easily, Mati had told him about the man with McIntosh. From her description of "cold, inhuman," he guessed it was Ten and understood.

"You'll find him," Mati had said earnestly. "You found me. You'll find him too."

It had woken him up. Kick started his brain. Sent him back upstairs to split the quarrelling lovers apart and interrogate Lydia for every bit of information she had. Two days later—with Meera and Mati willingly back under protective watch—they had a plan Jack could live with. Five days after that, he was speeding towards a Cabal black site in the Ka-52.

The *Anzac* class frigate, HMAS Mackay, remained just over the horizon from the Cabal island, situated approximately halfway between Perth in Western Australia and the Maldives. The frigate would approach at flank speed once the surprise was lost, her compliment of four Blackhawks launching then as well. The Ka-52 had the capability to cover the distance fast enough that by the time someone saw them it would already be too late.

"Majority of heat signatures are at the top of the tower," Keira reported as they roared across the surface of the water.

"Good. We'll get the bastards all at once."

"What if our people are up there?"

Jack stared at the rapidly growing island. "If Ethan's there, he'll take care of McIntosh."

The ETA field leader glanced at him, her eyes hidden behind sunglasses, but the thinness of her lips told him exactly what she was thinking.

"He'll be okay." Jack wasn't sure if he was assuring her, or himself.

And holy hell if he wasn't right, McIntosh wouldn't know what had hit her.

Jack could understand the director's secrecy, because if he had known what she'd planned, he would have vetoed anything and everything—with bullets, if necessary—right from the start. So, understand her motives, yes. Agree with them, fuck no. But he would do everything he could to make this part of the craziness work.

The island—if the tiny chunk of rock almost swamped by ocean waves could be classified as one—had been a secret ally base during the second world war. On official record it had been destroyed by a Japanese battleship. That report had been greatly exaggerated apparently. Satellite images had shown no activity on the surface and no signals had originated from the base. Probably standard operating procedure for a Cabal site.

Right in the middle of the rock was a tower about four storeys high. It was thick and appeared impenetrable to anything other than a missile, a couple of which were attached to the underside of the helicopter. Jack couldn't use them, however, not until they knew exactly where their people were. Which required a recce.

Their first pass of the tower was all about shock and awe and told them all they needed to know. The tower was it for buildings, on the surface at least. Original plans for the base were long lost, but Jack didn't doubt that there would be underground portions. Probably cells and hidden caches of weapons. It also showed them a helipad on the roof. The only sign of how to get on and off the rock. There wasn't even a dock. The Mackay would have to deploy boats to get troops on shore.

"Let's get this started." Jack hovered the bird over the helipad.

Keira's grin was pure and deadly. "Let's." With her bag of gear, she jumped out of the chopper, hit the cement roof in a controlled roll and came to her feet with a pistol out and scanning.

Jack lifted back up, swung sideways, and dropped over the side of the tower. He pointed the nose of the Ka-52 at the concentrated heat signature and opened fire.

The glass was bullet proof, but that was true only up to a certain point. Several hundred rounds impacting in under thirty seconds would shatter it no worries. Inside, people scattered to either side of the field of fire, some not fast enough to make it before the glass blew inwards in a million little ballistic fragments. Jack drifted the chopper to the left, chasing black clad figures and a few, more colourful ones as they raced away from the flying glass shards. He caught flashes of bright red, hoping that was McIntosh on the move. He didn't see anyone that made him think "Ethan."

Back where he'd first blown out the glass, Keira rappelled down from the roof and swung into the observation deck. FN P90 at the ready, she stalked into the confusion. A moment later, something on the roof exploded. Crazed glass Jack's bullets hadn't yet cracked shattered under the violent pressure. People inside dived for cover. Then a second explosion, from the base of the tower, shook the whole structure. Keira's devices should have taken out any stairs and lifts, effectively trapping everyone at the very top and delaying reinforcements from below.

Jack returned to the roof, landed, and grabbed his own bag of gear. Keira had left him a rope ready to go and with his own P90, back up pistols and knives in place, he went over the side and down into the fight.

Three dead guards sprawled across the floor just inside the broken window. Jack rolled over them, unhooked his harness and came up on one knee, scanning rapidly. A portly man in a white dishdasha lay near the wall, blood coating the back of his robe. He didn't move. Keira had set up behind a knocked over, wingback chair, returning fire that came from the right.

"There's about twenty troops, maybe a half dozen non-combatants, and the targets," she reported as Jack dove into cover with her.

"Any sign of our people?" Jack watched the other direction, rifle up and ready, but no one seemed to be coming back that way.

"Saw McIntosh go that way." Keira pointed to the left. "Haven't seen Blade."

"Okay. Give me a sec to contact the Mackay, then we'll sweep the area."

Keira nodded and sent a short burst of gunfire after the quickly appearing then disappearing figure of an enemy scout.

Jack closed his eyes and went *sideways*. He sent the prepared message to the frigate, got a confirmation, and came back to awareness just as several of the enemy made a combined effort to flush them out. Some stayed pressed to the inner curved wall, sending covering fire towards their position, while another pair slid along the outer rim to get a different angle of fire.

"Time to move." Keira sprayed bullets without aiming, leaped over the chair and backed away from the encroaching enemy.

Jack went with her, watching where they were going, trusting her to keep their backs free of immediate pursuit. Just as he caught sight of the enemy ahead and fired, a startled scream sounded behind him. Wanting nothing more than to turn around and see what the sudden eruption of thumps and smacks meant, Jack concentrated on keeping the enemy in front pinned.

"Keira, talk to me."

"We got help. Going to lend a hand."

It had to be Ethan. "Go. I'll keep this side back."

The presence at his back moved away and he backed up with it. Thanks to the curve of the space, the enemy in front advanced as he retreated. The sounds of hand-to-hand ramped up behind him as Keira joined the fight. She was as lethal with her hands and feet as she was with a gun.

Then suddenly the enemy in front surged forwards. More troops appeared, spreading out and firing on full automatic.

"Oh shit." Jack turned and ran. "Incoming," he yelled as he went.

Ahead, Keira was locked in a hold, enemy arm around her neck as she wrestled for control of a gun in the man's other hand. Closer to the gaping hole in the glass wall, Ethan was an elegant blur of sweeps and kicks, swinging a pair of forearm crutches as weapons. At Jack's shout, Ethan broke away from his opponent, planted the crutches firmly and swung both legs out, feet hitting the other man in the chest. He tumbled out of the tower with a wild yell. The moment Ethan's feet touched down, he gave his own cry of pain and staggered towards the open air as well.

Jack grabbed Ethan by the back of his shirt as he raced past, shot the man holding Keira in the back, and all but threw himself and Ethan behind a barricade of overturned tables. Rolling, he came up on a knee, rifle pointed at the strange man sitting against the inner wall, pistols in both hands.

"Jack, no." Ethan grabbed his arm and pulled his weapon down. "He's friendly."

Keira crashed over the barrier and Ethan had to stop her from shooting the man as well. He was older than Jack by at least twenty years, greying hair buzzed to the scalp, a scar down one side of his face, and his legs were the thin sticks of a long time paraplegic. The man was bleeding from his right shoulder. Next to him was a wheelchair riddled with bullet holes.

"He's Zero, our handler," Ethan said breathlessly. "He's helping us."

"Us?" Jack asked warily.

"McIntosh went that way." Zero's English was accented, though Jack couldn't tell where the accent originated.

Having worked out that the resistance was gone, the enemy closed in from their left, bullets impacting the steel tabletops and flying overhead, keeping them pinned.

"She went after the bosses." Ethan had lost one of the crutches, and the other one lay beside him, his hand resting on it, ready to snatch it up on a second's notice.

"I'm surprised you didn't go with her," Jack said as softly as he could.

After a few moments, Ethan shook his head, the action weary. "That's not what I need anymore. They're not important to me. Not like you are."

Holy fuck and damn. Jack was ready to throw Ethan over his shoulder, get back to the helicopter and fly the hell away. He'd been half worried that McIntosh would have caught Ethan up in her plan to rid the world of the Cabal from the top down. But it was still the plan and Jack knew his director wouldn't leave it half done.

"Guys." Keira had made a small gap in the tables and was firing through it. "Could use some help here."

Zero tossed Ethan a gun and then pulled himself closer to the barricade. He added single shots to Keira's sweeping automatic fire.

"Go after McIntosh," Ethan said to Jack. "We'll keep them occupied here."

Wondering why Ethan was opting to stay put, Jack finally put it together. Zero had a wheelchair, so the crutches were for Ethan. The weariness on Ethan's face wasn't about being tired. Now that he was still for a moment, Jack noticed the leg brace, the fading bruises on his neck, the stiffness of his shoulders. These weren't injuries from the current battle.

The anger came white hot and all consuming. Anger at whoever had hurt Ethan, at the Cabal bosses for orchestrating it all in the first place, and at McIntosh for putting them all back in this situation without bothering to ask first. She was his director, he respected her, knew she had a harsh job and that often personal feelings didn't work well with the decisions she had to make. But right then, that meant little to nothing. She'd thrown him into the snake pit unprepared once before, and now she'd done it again.

"Be right back," he snarled.

Hefting his rifle, Jack rolled over the barrier and raced after McIntosh.

He found her about a quarter of the way around the loop. She was pressed into the shallow recess of the stairwell door, rifle taken from a fallen enemy across her chest. Her hair had been pulled back into a messy knot and her shoes kicked off. The skirt was torn up both sides, jacket gone, and a red mark showed a hard punch had landed on her right cheek.

"Thank you for the timely arrival, Jack," she said as he joined her in the meagre cover.

"Don't thank me yet. I'm really pissed with you right now."

A smile flittered across her lips. "I figured you would be. Sorry."

A black clad figure was creeping up along the outer rim. Jack sent three bullets their way and they crumpled to the floor, unmoving. "Consider this my resignation, Donna."

McIntosh leaned out of cover, fired, and ducked back in as it was returned by an unseen enemy. "Yes, I figured that too. On three?"

"On three," he agreed grimly.

"Three."

They moved out together, covering each other as they advanced around the curve. The enemy didn't retreat quickly enough and four armed troops came into view. Behind them was a white man in an expensive suit that looked decidedly roughed up now.

"Camdon-Smythe," McIntosh said tersely. "He's a boss." She swept her fire across the ranks of troops. Two dropped to lucky hits, most of the bullets impacting armour.

The prick was pressed up tight to the inner wall, shouting at the remaining troops to "Kill them. Kill them now!" He must have been paying them a very good wage because they gave it a fair shot, keeping Jack and McIntosh pinned.

"We'll never get him at this angle," McIntosh said.

"They won't let us retreat and come at them from the outer rim."

"I'll do it."

"I've got the armour," Jack corrected. "I'll do it. On three."

Grudgingly, McIntosh said, "On three."

"Three."

McIntosh stepped out from the wall, firing rapidly. Jack sprang out further, tumbling into a controlled roll as bullets whizzed by him. One screamed by his left arm, leaving a burning wake, but he came up on one knee, aimed, fired and rolled back into cover.

Enemy fire immediately stopped and Jack and McIntosh pressed against the wall, listening. No more desperate demands for them to be killed, no more obedient fire from the troops.

"Got him," Jack muttered.

"You hit?" McIntosh asked.

"Winged only. I'm fine."

"That's goo— Jack!"

McIntosh shoved Jack hard and he staggered as she stepped out in front of him, gun raised to fire.

Bang!

FORTY-ONE

Ethan watched Jack vanish around the curve and wished he had stayed, or that Ethan could have gone with him. The pain meds had worn off quickly thanks to his Sugar Baby constitution and his leg was throbbing. Using it for support while kicking with the other was almost as bad as the other way around. The best he could do right then was make sure the troops here stayed focused on them and didn't head back around to where Jack and McIntosh were hopefully together now.

He joined Zero and the female asset in keeping the troops occupied. The pistol had a very limited number of shots, though, and he and the handler ran out fast. The asset—who introduced herself as Kiera—shrugged off her pack and told them to use it. Inside were more handguns and magazines. Furnished with new guns, they kept at it until Ethan noted movement on the horizon. A large ship was powering toward the island from the southeast. Two large choppers were racing ahead of it and a third was lifting from its deck. Reinforcements. They only had to hold out for a bit longer. Which wasn't soon enough for Keira.

"There's barely a half dozen of them left. We need to end this sooner rather than later."

"She's right," Zero said. "We'll run out of ammunition before them, then they'll pick us off."

Ethan had to agree and as he looked around, he got an idea.

While Ethan and Zero kept firing, Keira worked on Ethan's distraction and in under a minute, they were ready to go. Leaving Zero propped up against the wall, Ethan and Keira moved out from behind the cover slowly. Keira pushed the wheelchair in front of them, dead body strapped into it, empty guns tied to the arm rests.

With an extra shove, she sent the chair rolling toward the enemy fast enough they wouldn't want to take the time to make sure it wasn't a real threat. Sure enough, the enemy changed aim to the chair and the body jerked as it was pummelled with bullets. Distracted, the troops missed Ethan and Keira coming around the inner wall.

Six. Seven. Eight shots and it was done. The last six enemy troops were down. Just beyond them was Balakrishnan, who had one of the female waitstaff as a shield, his arm around her neck and gun pointed to her head. Ten stood in front of them, S&W 500 in hand.

"It's over, Balakrishnan." Keira aimed for him. "If you come with us willingly, you'll live and be treated fairly. If you resist, well that's a whole other story."

Ethan kept his sight on Ten. His leg was throbbing, the brace not made to support his weight, but he did his best to ignore it. Weakness in front of Ten was like chum in the water.

"It won't matter what you do to me, the Cabal will always exist," Balakrishnan said. "It always has and it always will. Kill them."

Ten was moving before Balakrishnan finished speaking. Ethan had started moving even before his brother. He knocked Keira out of Ten's line of fire, then dropped down, balancing on one hand and swept his good leg through Ten's. His brother jumped, predictably, but that just gave Keira the opportunity to leap back in. A flying kick took the gun out of his hand and the follow through caught him in the ribs, making him stagger back.

Ethan rolled out of the way as Keira pressed the advantage. She was highly skilled, keeping Ten on the defensive as she drove him away from Balakrishnan.

Slowly standing, Ethan raised his own gun and sighted Balakrishnan's head. Which was currently ducked down behind that of his human shield.

Leg burning, Ethan settled into his stance. "This won't work, Balakrishnan. Let her go and surrender."

Balakrishnan said nothing. Ethan scanned him for another vulnerable spot. He could get him in the leg but he might still shoot the woman. As far as collateral damage went, she wouldn't be the worst Ethan had left behind, but he really didn't want to be the sort of person who could do that and walk away anymore.

There was a hesitation in the sounds of the fight to his right. Ethan glanced that way.

Ten blocked a blow from Keira, knocking her arm out wide. His other hand jabbed in and Keira threw herself out of the way of the blade in that hand—directly into the one in his other hand, springing out from a wrist sheath. He got it in under her raised arm, through the gap in her armour. It was jammed in so hard that when she fell with a startled gasp, the blade ripped out of his hand.

Ethan didn't know Keira but Jack had spoken about her with admiration and respect when he'd told Ethan about their search for him. She was an Office asset, fighting to keep her corner of the world safe. It could have just as easily been Jack.

The gun swung and he pulled the trigger, calm and deliberate. He was in pain and he was tired. It was time to go home with Jack and get out of this life he didn't choose once and for all.

Balakrishnan screamed as his knee blew out. He didn't fire his gun, just flailed wildly and fell. The woman tumbled out of his hold and scrambled away as Ethan stalked towards the last of his targets. The man lay on the floor, clutching at his ruined knee, blood seeping out between his hands. He was crying in pain, but when he saw Ethan standing over him, he shut up quickly.

"If you could know the full pain of what you put me and my siblings through, I wouldn't hesitate to show you. But as there is no way you could ever understand just what you stole from us because you are a heartless, cold-blooded piece of fucking shit, I guess I'll just kill you, like you made me kill so many others. How does it feel?"

He didn't give the man time to answer. The bullet slammed into Balakrishnan's head between his wide-open eyes.

It didn't feel like closure. It didn't feel like an end. Ethan had told Jack the truth. Balakrishnan and the others didn't count anymore. It felt like nothing.

"It's over," he said, even though he didn't feel that way himself. "No more orders. No more control. We're free."

Ten smiled. "You are free. I was never caught." He threw his knife.

Ethan stepped into the trajectory, intercepting the spinning weapon a second sooner than he should have. The handle knocked into his chest and clattered to the floor. He was still moving when

Ten met him with a fist. Ethan took the blow on his shoulder, shrugging it off as he rammed his forearm against Ten's throat and drove him backwards into the glass wall. Ten pulled another gun and Ethan knocked that arm down, then jammed his elbow back into his brother's face twice. He grabbed Ten's arm and slammed it against the glass, trying to dislodge the weapon. It took a twist of the wrist to make him let go and it flew away.

Ten reversed the grip and wrenched Ethan's arm up and back. Spinning with the pressure, Ethan dropped to his knees and hauled Ten over his back, slamming him to the floor. Something moved in his leg and Ethan's gasp was silent, the sudden, searing agony stealing his voice.

A boot slammed into his gut, throwing him back against the glass wall. His leg twisted under him. This time he screamed. Then Ten was there, right in front of him, fist driving for his face. Ethan pushed off the slick glass and slid downwards. Ten's knuckles crashed into the wall above his head. Ethan brought his good leg up between Ten's, knee aiming for his cock and balls. Flinging himself away, Ten rolled one way and Ethan went the other.

The throbbing in his leg was intense, pressure building in the tissues. Any weight on it was impossible. That was the sort of pain he couldn't ignore, couldn't grit his teeth and work through. He tried to get away when Ten came for him again, but his able-bodied brother was faster. Two strides and he was over Ethan. Ten came down on one knee, letting his weight and gravity drive his fist into Ethan's solar plexus. Something snapped inside and fire lanced through his chest, air bursting out of him so hard it felt like it was made of razors. Ten punched him in the jaw, twice, three times, and stars flared in his greying vision. Ethan tried to knock aside the blows, but there was too much pain when he moved his right arm and Ten slammed punch after punch into his gut.

"Stop."

The fist coming for Ethan's face halted, inches away. Even Ethan froze with the ingrained obedience at that voice. Zero pulled himself closer, powerful shoulders and arms holding his torso up, useless legs dragging along behind him. His face was stony as he stared at Ten.

"I don't have to listen to you anymore," Ten said.

"You barely listened to me in the first place." He nodded to Ethan. "Why are you attacking your brother? There's no one left to give you orders."

Good question. Ethan was very interested in the answer, but he was also interested in the shard of glass just beyond the tips of the fingers of his right hand. It felt like he was breaking every rib on that side with each millimetre he moved but he . . . was . . . almost . . .

"I don't need orders. I want to do this," Ten said in the lifeless tone that sent shivers down Ethan's spine. Not even now, when he was doing this because it was something he wanted, did he show any spark of humanity.

So there was absolutely no qualm about ramming the shard of glass into his brother's side. Ethan's scream as agony tore through his ribs and lung drowned out Ten's startled yell, and the solid thwack of Zero's fist punching into Ten's jaw. He tumbled off Ethan, the improvised glass knife ripping out of his body in a spray of blood. Hand pressed to the gushing wound, Ten scrambled to his feet and backed away. He didn't need to run. Neither Ethan nor Zero could follow him. Ten's face lost any sign of pain, falling back into his neutral, emotionless mask—no, not a mask. It was his true state. The Cabal had surgically removed every morsel of empathy and sympathy Ten might have been born with. If he lived, Balakrishnan would be right. The Cabal would always exist.

Ethan dragged himself after his brother. Zero came with him, his face just as determined. Ahead, Ten stooped and picked up a gun and continued. Then he stopped, raised the pistol, and fired.

Bang!

Jack's wordless, tortured yell froze Ethan's heart. Had Ten driven the final knife into Ethan's chest?

But then he saw Jack, tall and lean and beautiful in his burning rage. He stalked towards Ten, eyes narrowed, teeth barred, fist clenched. He was lethal and intent, no doubts as he came to kill.

Ten fired again and Jack was punched backwards. He hit the floor in a graceless sprawl of limbs and didn't move.

"Jack." Ethan tried to get up but his leg simply wouldn't let him. Everything was pain and his body just couldn't do what he needed it to do.

"Don't," Zero commanded. "One-three, don't."

Ten glanced back at him, adjusting his grip on the gun, as if he was considering putting a bullet through Ethan's head as well. He lifted the weapon, then went down with a startled cry as Jack swept his legs through Ten's, taking them out from under him.

"Body armour, you fuckhead," Jack snarled as he flipped over and slammed a fist into Ten's face.

Ten blocked the next blow and rolled away, coming up on his feet. He grunted as he did so, hand automatically covering his injured side. Seeing it, Jack pursued him and targeted that spot relentlessly.

Jack's fighting style wasn't pretty. It was messy and unconventional, but it got the job done. Ten was on the defensive, backing up with every blow and kick. Ethan had been on the receiving end of those once, knew the strength and sheer determination Jack could pack into a single punch, especially when he was angry, and right now, he looked incendiary. Ethan had barely kept ahead of him, and he hadn't been bleeding from a jagged wound in his side.

"You fucking piece of goddamn rotten shit." Jack punctuated each word with a punch, the last three landing right on the open wound. "You killed her. You killed her."

Did Jack know about Keira? Or had something else happened?

Either way, Ten was beaten. He couldn't hold his hands up anymore, his head sagged, and his feet stumbled until he hit the glass wall. Blood poured freely from the hole Ethan had made and already his dusky skin looked paler. He would be dead from blood loss soon. Jack didn't appear to care. He seemed lost in his rage, as if throwing punches because it was the only thing that felt effective.

"Jack." Ethan's voice was weak, his own body feeling like it was still being pummelled. "Jack."

But somehow Jack heard him. He stopped mid punch and, one forearm against Ten's throat, he turned and looked at Ethan.

"End it. Please," Ethan whispered.

Ten was his brother, but Jack was his future and it hurt to see him like this. Jack was passionate and reckless, but he was never cruel.

Light returned to Jack's brown eyes and he turned back to Ten, who met his gaze directly and didn't resist when Jack broke his neck.

Then Jack was on the floor beside him, his hands gentle even though his knuckles were ragged with torn skin and oozing blood. "Ethan, where does it hurt? Are you bleeding?"

Something inside Ethan let go. The final bit of strength he'd been living on to get this far, to find freedom at last, gave way. It ebbed and took the pain with it. He couldn't feel his broken leg anymore, or his busted ribs. Not even the light was hurting his eyes because it was dark and getting darker.

Ethan smiled. "It doesn't hurt anymore."

"Oh fuck, don't say that. Come on, Ethan. Tell me where it hurts." Jack's hands got frantic as they ran over his body. "Oh god. Don't do this. Ethan, don't leave me. You promised you wouldn't leave me ever again." His eyes were sparkling and he leaned down to kiss him. "Please," Jack whispered against his lips.

Everything was calm. His heart had slowed from its wild clamouring while watching Jack fight. He felt good. Jack was here and he didn't hurt anymore. "I love you, Jack."

"I know. I love you so much. You're going to be fine. The navy's on the way. You'll be okay. Just hang on for me. Hang on to me."

Jack was worrying for no reason. "It's all right, Jack. It's over. They're gone and I'm free."

The encroaching darkness surrounded him and Ethan let it take him.

FORTY-TWO

THE HEARING

Silence filled the hearing room. No one could look at Jack as he finished speaking. Which was good because if anyone said anything less than one hundred percent supportive right then, he was liable to rip their head off.

Three days. It had been three days since Donna McIntosh was shot and killed right in front of him. Three days since Jack had let pure rage and grief guide his hands in beating a man past defeat and into cruel abuse. Three days since Ethan had slipped into unconsciousness in his arms. It was still raw and bleeding inside and he'd had to sit here with this gaping, open wound and talk about everything that led up to it just so they could finally put this all to rest. Simmons was lucky Jack had let it go on this long, but they'd had to do this. The final part of McIntosh's plan. Jack just had to keep it together long enough to get the "nod."

"What happened then?" Chan asked gently.

Taking a deep breath, Jack said, "The Blackhawks from the HMAS Mackay arrived. They found more Cabal troops trapped in underground tunnels by the explosions. Most of them surrendered without a fight. They also found reports from psychiatric experiments conducted on Ethan's group of Sugar Babies. A Dr. Isaac Deland was the author. Originally from the UK, his licence to practice was revoked after allegations of misconduct were proven. Working for the Cabal was the only way he could continue his research on Sugar Babies. They let him experiment on the children they turned into their assassins. He had free rein to do anything he wanted, so long as he provided, and I'm quoting from his notes, 'viable products.' The doctor wasn't on the island and we haven't been able to find him since."

It was gratifying to see everyone, including Simmons and the Quiet Man, wince at the words. Jack had read the recovered digital records that morning and it had taken Lewis to calm him down. These were the monsters who'd made Ethan and the others. The quick deaths they had gotten were too good for them.

"And Ethan?" Lund's tone was strange, almost as if he didn't dare ask.

"He was choppered down to the frigate in a Blackhawk and thankfully the medics on board could save his leg. He had compartmentalisation syndrome that had been caused by trauma from the broken fibula. There was further internal bleeding in his abdomen that they discovered when he went into cardiac arrest from blood loss. They kept him alive until he could be flown to Perth for surgery. He came through that lot of surgery okay and when he was stable, they were going to transport him here, but I haven't heard anything since yesterday afternoon."

Jack was desperate to get this over and done with so he could find out where Ethan had ended up. But Simmons wasn't finished with him yet.

The minister leaned forward and clasped his hands together, as if trying to portray intimacy or concern. "I'm very sorry to be the one to tell you, Mr. Reardon, but we got word earlier in this hearing that Ethan Blade succumbed to his injuries last night. You have our deepest condolences."

Jack pushed away from the table so fast and violently his chair skidded backwards and fell over. Hands curled into fists and pressed to his forehead he tried to absorb the information. A note saying Ethan was dead. A note Simmons had put aside saying it had no importance on the current proceedings.

Fuck.

Fuck, fuck, fuck.

"Jack?"

He pried his eyes open and found Director Chan in front of him. She held out several tissues and he took them as gently as he could. Pressing them to his damp eyes, he pulled in a deep breath, and another, and another, letting them out in shaky little bursts.

"I'm so incredibly sorry," Chan murmured. "How about we recess for a while so you can . . ." She trailed off, probably realising how futile fifteen minutes would be in order to deal with that fucking bombshell.

Jack wiped his eyes and shook his head. "It's fine. Let's keep going. Get this shit over with as soon as possible."

Her dark eyes brimmed with concern, but she nodded and returned to her seat at the table. While she murmured to the others Jack righted his chair, sat down and worked really hard at not going over and smashing Simmons in the mouth.

Ethan dead, and it wasn't important enough to interrupt the proceedings. Jesus fucking Christ, the man was lucky Jack had learned some restraint in the military. Though this felt worse than what had happened at Jharkhand. Felt bad enough he could do worse than knock loose some teeth.

He was half out of his seat when the door behind the review board opened and the blonde assistant appeared. She slipped in but remained by the door, unnoticed by everyone except Jack. When she met his gaze, she gave a small nod.

Jack sank back down. This was it. Time to end it. He probably wouldn't get to hit Simmons, but this might be just as satisfying.

Simmons began gathering his papers. "We understand you will need some time to come to terms with the death—"

"Actually, sir," Jack said, voice rough from resisting the urge to shout a lot of nasty words at the man, "I'd rather we just finish this now."

One eyebrow cocked, Simmons said, "I still have a quite a bit of information to go through, Mr. Reardon. Perhaps we should continue this tomorrow. Or the day after."

"No. I think you'll find there's only one more piece of information we need to discuss."

"Which is?"

Jack reached into his case and withdrew a generic black thumb drive. "How this made its way from AFP evidence and into the hands of the then deputy prime minister."

Lund and Chan exchanged frowns while Greene began a mildly frantic search of his records.

Simmons smiled vaguely. "I believe you said Donna McIntosh was the one who—"

"I said that she *knew* how Nelson had acquired it, not that she gave it to him."

At last, the smug air around Simmons evaporated. His mouth pinched and his hands crumpled the gathered paper. The silent assistant slid in behind him, eyes narrowed behind her tinted glasses, limbs loose and ready.

"We have evidence, *sir*," Jack continued, "confirmed by the Office, ASIS, and the AFP, that you were the one who obtained the data stick from the federal police. That you gave it to John Nelson and suggested that he use it for a leadership challenge, so you could get a man in the PM's office whom you controlled. Then you would have gone to your contact within the Cabal and used that connection to gain an audience with the bosses."

Simmons spluttered objections but Jack spoke over him.

"That's why Donna McIntosh had to move as fast as she did once she discovered what you were doing. She took your plan and used it herself to gain access to the Cabal so we could wipe them out. And so we could then expose you for being the lying, greedy, manipulative traitor that you are."

"I am not a traitor." Simmons surged to his feet. "I did it for this country. To use their resources to protect us. God knows, the fucking Office isn't doing its job. You're the ones who had the traitor in your midst. I did it so that wouldn't ever happen again."

Calmly, Jack turned to the Quiet Man. "Is that enough of a confession?"

"It's a start. We'll get the rest out of him no worries." With a nod, he motioned the assistant forward.

Simmons started to turn but the blonde woman was faster. She had him face down over the desk, arm twisted up behind his back far enough he screamed in pain before Jack could even get out from behind his own table. He walked over and crouched down so he could meet Simmons' teary gaze.

"This is Seven. She's one of the thirteen kids the Cabal tortured into becoming a killer. The group you wanted to be part of. If that's the sort of thing you can excuse in the name of defence, then we don't need your brand of protection."

For the first time since Jack had met Seven, he saw her smile.

Swiftly, Seven had Simmons cuffed and she and the Quiet Man—Jack still wasn't sure which agency he was with—took him out of the room. Greene watched them go, suddenly pale and sweaty, and a moment later, he sprinted for the door, hand pressed over his mouth.

Lund and Chan both started asking questions and Jack merely shoved his case at them, saying it was all in there, and for more information, they would have to deal with Alex Tan.

"I quit," Jack told them as he backed away. "I know the Office isn't as bad as the Cabal, but some days, it's hard to tell." And he left.

Lewis met him outside the building. "How did it go?"

"We got him," Jack said grimly. "He confessed in front of Lund and Chan, so it's pretty solid. How did your hearing go?"

"Easy peasy, mate. I just threw so many spreadsheets at them they couldn't wait to give me the all clear." Lewis's smile went from smug to worried. "Um, I think they might make me director permanently, now that McIntosh . . ."

Jack's chest tightened. God. Apart from combat talk, the last things he'd said to her were that he was pissed and that he was quitting. She'd used him, and Ethan, one too many times for her own ends. Her goals might have been good, but that didn't make it much easier to deal with. Especially when it hurt them like this.

"You should take the job," Jack said firmly as they trotted down the steps to the footpath. "You'll be really good as a director."

Lewis shrugged. "Are you going to her funeral tomorrow?"

"I don't know. I want to, but I don't know if I'll handle it well." Jack hurt when he remembered McIntosh hitting the floor of the tower, blood splattering her white blouse, blue eyes frozen in death. At the same time, he couldn't forget everything she'd done to him and Ethan. "It'll depend on . . . you know."

Nodding in understanding, Lewis changed topics. He gestured to the still banged-up black Vanquish parked right in front of the government building. "How has this not been ticketed?"

"No one dares touch this car now." Jack smiled sadly and unlocked it. "You coming?"

"You want me there?"

"Yeah. Just in case."

Lewis got into Victoria and Jack drove them out to Mosman. Not to Middle Head, but to HMAS Penguin, the naval base next to it. They were passed through the gates and directed to the Balmoral Naval Hospital. Inside, a nurse guided them down long corridors to a secure section guarded by two navy police officers. Again, Jack and Lewis were allowed in and eventually, came to a room with another officer outside.

Only Jack got past this gatekeeper. He stood for a moment by the door, looking at the still body on the bed.

Jesus. For a moment when Simmons had told him that Ethan had died, Jack had wondered if was true. Despite all the hard work by the medics on the HMAS Mackay, Ethan had been in a very critical condition when they airlifted him off the frigate and to Perth. He'd arrested a second time before they got him into surgery. So the decision had been made.

Ethan Blade would die on the operating table in Perth.

Ethan—Jack's Ethan—would be transferred when stable to this secure hospital in Sydney, where once he recovered, he would get a new name and a new life.

Right now, he didn't look like that would happen any time soon. His left leg was suspended in traction and tubes drained bloody fluid from his abdomen. Ten's blows had busted Ethan's spleen, causing the internal bleed out. Most of the skin Jack could see was either mottled with black and green bruising or even paler than usual. At least he wasn't intubated anymore and breathing on his own, just nasal prongs for oxygen.

Tears traced down Jack's cheeks. His vital, vibrant Ethan. He'd come so close to losing him forever. Might still lose him to any number of complications.

Jack finally got himself moving and sat in the chair next to the bed. There was a heartrate monitor on Ethan's finger, cannulas in his arms and bandages across his chest and belly. Jack wanted to hold him close, protect him from the world, but all he could do was brush a finger along the side of his arm, from wrist to shoulder and back again.

"It's me," he said softly. "I'm here now and I'm not leaving until you wake up. Everything's over, Ethan. The Cabal is gone and we got

Simmons. I quit, too. The Office is just going to have to do without me. Find someone else to take all their hits for them. Except maybe that'll change when Lew is properly in charge. Anyway, I'm unemployed now and think I'd like to take you up on that kept man option we discussed a while back. Thing is, Ethan, you gotta be there to keep me. You promised you wouldn't leave me again and fuck it, you're not going to, even if I have to keep dragging you back by the scruff of your neck."

"You'd try."

Air caught in Jack's throat. The words were quiet and croaky, but they'd definitely come from Ethan. Resisting the urge to lunge in and kiss him, Jack settled for, "I'd win that fight."

Eyes still closed, Ethan whispered, "I'd let you."

"Jesus." Jack pressed his face to Ethan's arm, tears falling freely. "I thought I'd lost you."

"The way I feel, I think you nearly did." His hand fluttered as if reaching for something. "Glasses?"

"Oh, shit. Yeah." Jack scrambled in his pockets and pulled out his own pair. "Here." He stood and leaned over to slip them on.

After a moment, Ethan's dry lips turned up in a smile. "Hello, Jack."

"Hello, crazy bastard."

"Half right, Jack."

CODA

THREE MONTHS LATER, JACK

Jack zipped the Ducati through evening traffic, the late winter wind biting even through the leather jacket. He hadn't gotten the usual call from Ethan for a ride home but he was heading out to the rented garage anyway. It had been a long, busy day and Jack needed to see him sooner rather than later. Thankfully the traffic wasn't too bad in the outer suburbs and Jack turned into the complex minutes later. The sound of the smooth-as-fuck motorbike warned Ethan and the door was opening as Jack rolled up to it. Inside, he parked beside a polished and now completely whole Victoria.

"You finished her," he said after taking off his helmet.

Ethan leaned against the car, braced leg bent to keep his weight off it. Several operations later and it was now as good as new and just needed the added support for a while longer. Part of his recovery process—according to Ethan if not his doctors—was fixing up the damage Jack had caused Victoria while rescuing Mati and her friend from Seven. Jack suspected it wasn't so much the physicality of the work as the soothing presence of the car and actions Ethan knew and loved that had helped revitalise him.

"This morning. I spent the rest of the day getting her immaculate for the barbeque tomorrow."

Jack swung off the bike and stepped up to him. "It's just the family, no one important."

Snorting, Ethan slung his arms around Jack's neck. "Hmm. No one important indeed."

Unable to hide a smile, Jack buried it in Ethan's neck. The return of Meera and Mati to his life had been a welcome if weird change. He suspected if he'd watched Mati grow into the young woman she was now, he wouldn't be so flabbergasted when she shifted from serious discussions about politics to giggling prankster almost as fast as Ethan changed gears while racing. Meera, he was learning, was the same annoying big sister he remembered, even though her pestering seemed more about improving his life than criticising his choices now.

He took a deep breath of Ethan while he was there, letting the scents of sweat, oil—car oil, not gun oil these days—and soap roll through him. Ethan slid his hands down Jack's spine, and then back up, under the leather jacket and the suit one beneath it. Palms running up and down, Ethan pressed against him, sighing in contentment.

"How did the interview go?"

It took Jack a moment to register the words, and then a few more to remember what they referred to. Honestly, he was quite happy to simply stay right where he was for the rest of his life. The rest of the world could catch on fire and he wouldn't care. It wasn't his job to care anymore.

"Jack? The interview?"

"Uh. Okay. It went okay." Leaning back, he rolled his eyes. "I got the job. Don't worry, you won't have to support me forever."

It had been a surprise to get a call from his old "on paper" boss at the International Security Office, where he'd been a Specialist Security Advisor as a cover for working at the Office. He knew how to do the job and do it well but his relationship with John Axworthy, the officer in charge with the ISO, had been strained thanks to Jack not actually being his employee to use as he needed. Once his resignation from the Office had been finalised, so had his position at the ISO. Until Axworthy had offered it back to him.

Ethan grinned. "Congratulations. I knew you would get it. And for the record, I don't mind *keeping* you, but retirement doesn't suit you, Jack. You were driving me crazy with your bored moaning and pestering."

"Crazier," Jack corrected and got the laugh he needed to hear. "I made a few provisos though."

"Such as?" Ethan's hands kept drifting lower and lower until they were right on Jack's arse.

"Such as I get to work from home. I'll have to go to Canberra a couple of times a month for a day or so but that's all. And I get to pick which overseas assignments I take, with a minimum of three a year."

"Sounds ideal."

Jack flexed his butt in Ethan's hands. "You can do without me for that long, huh?"

Ethan squeezed. "Perhaps. I suppose we'll just have to see." His voice had lowered and gotten huskier, and as much as Jack wanted to follow that path to its happy ending right then, he had his own question to ask before he chickened out.

"Did you talk to Tan today?"

Ethan went still. Jack waited him out, believing this had nothing to do with confusion, but with fear. They'd talked a lot while Ethan was laid up in bed, and he had told Jack about his worry that he didn't know if he could be satisfied without the challenges his work had provided. He'd admitted to not following the Office requirements of keeping clear of illegal activities while Jack had been working with the police the year before. Part of it had been blackmail, but Ethan confessed he could have gotten out of it if he'd truly wanted. So he was concerned.

Also, Ethan had signed a contract with the Office to work with ETA. Director Tan had been understanding in the wake of Ethan's injuries, but now that he was all but completely recovered, he wouldn't wait much longer.

"Yes," Ethan said cautiously. "I'll go in to talk to him on Monday. Jack, I know this isn't what you want anymore, but . . ."

"It's okay. I mean it. You've got to do what makes you happy or content or whatever." Jack shrugged. "Keep the option open and if you find you need to do more or less, you can decide then."

"I suppose. If I did decide to work for Tan in the field, would you mind?"

"I'd worry. A lot." Not only was Jack not keen on Ethan going back into dangerous situations, he still wasn't Tan's biggest fan. His "ends justify the means" attitude was a little too close to the Cabal mentality for Jack's complete peace of mind. "But it's your choice."

Ethan nodded, then kissed him. Soft and swift, but Jack followed his mouth when he pulled back, wanting another taste, another connection. Huffing, Ethan let him, kissing back when Jack pressed his tongue to his lips, seeking more. Ethan opened to him and Jack delved in, groaning as his man met him with teasing touches.

God. This. So long as Jack got to do this forever, he didn't care what either of them did the rest of the time. The way Ethan pushed into him, tilted his head to get better access, clutched at Jack's arms, back, hair, all fed into him. It set off his chest grenade so that even while his heart wobbled, heat suffused him from head down to fingers and toes.

Jack gripped Ethan's arse and lifted. Legs wrapped around him and Ethan moaned as Jack sat him down on the boot of the car. Half expecting to be chided for the move, Jack was surprised when Ethan braced himself with one hand behind him and ground his hips into Jack's, his hardening dick thickening even more in this position. Jack rutted back, kissing, nipping and licking his way along Ethan's jaw to the sensitive spot behind his ear.

"Jack!" Ethan's legs hitched higher, pressing their groins even tighter together and Jack nearly came then and there.

The recovery of their sexual relationship had been gradual, growing alongside Ethan's physical recovery. Of necessity they'd been gentle and caring with each other. Which Jack had loved because he'd been feeling extra tender and attentive to Ethan since nearly losing him. Lately, though, Ethan had been hinting at more than slow, seductive blowjobs, or hand jobs in the shower, or rutting and rubbing on the couch. Jack didn't care how they got off so long as they did it together. Ethan, on the other hand, seemed to have very specific ideas today. He wriggled and moaned, leaning back further and further, taking Jack with him. His hips rolled with increasing frequency, pushing at Jack until Jack's dick was where he wanted it, pressed against Ethan's arse.

"Jack," he almost whined. "I don't want to wait anymore. I can't wait anymore."

"Oh, fuck." Jack ground on him, his dick almost ready to rip through underwear and pants.

Ethan huffed, head dropping back. "Only if you get your act together and—" He broke off with a moan as Jack rubbed against him extra hard, then laughed when the motion sent him sliding across the super glossy surface of the car.

"All right, fine." Jack pulled back, hauling Ethan off Victoria as he went. "You'll get fucked if you want, but it will be in bed at home, where I won't have to wonder if it's me or the car you're hard for."

Ethan's chuckle was beautifully wicked. "Even then, you'll never know."

Grumbling, Jack chased him into the car, then got on the Ducati, which he'd accepted as a coming-home present the day Ethan was released from hospital. He could admit he loved it now, mostly because Ethan had told him how he'd fixed it up with Jack in mind, but also because it was an amazing ride. His old Ninja still got a run every now and then, and Ethan had mentioned using it when he was given the final all-clear, which made Jack tingly at the mere thought. He'd loved, too, the simple act of having Ethan on the back of whichever bike while Victoria was being fixed up. Jack would drop Ethan off at the garage in the morning and either stay with him—being pesky, apparently—or go do a few other things, then collect his man in the afternoon. Normal and simple and heartachingly cherished. Now that Victoria was finished, that would stop, but Jack was sure whatever mundane thing Ethan found to do would fascinate him just as much.

Jack beat Ethan back to Bathurst Street, but waited for him in the garage. In the lift, they picked up almost exactly where they'd left off.

"You know," Jack muttered as he navigated his way from lift, to door, to bedroom with Ethan wound around him, kissing his neck, face, mouth, "you citing a sore leg isn't going to fly as a reason for me to carry you around for much longer." He released his hold under Ethan's arse, prepared to let him drop onto the bed, but Ethan clung on, legs tightening, hands fisting up acres of leather.

"I do recall you saying once that carrying me like this was hot." He nipped Jack's jaw.

"I was younger then. And you weren't carting around extra weight."

Ethan gasped and let go, falling back on the bed, arms flung over his head so his shirt—another one of Jack's that seemed to just be Ethan's now—rode up and exposed a quarter moon's expanse of pale skin, dark trails of hair, and well defined abdominal muscles. "You're the one who keeps feeding me pastries."

Shucking his jackets, Jack gently nudged Ethan's brace. "I meant this." Off came the tie and he started unbuttoning his shirt. "And for the record, you can eat as many pastries, fudge, and chocolate as you want and it won't change a thing about how I feel about you. However, many more of these?" Another soft prod at the brace. "That might make me a bit grumpy."

The sunglasses came off—Jack had adjusted to living in Ethan's twilight world happily as it meant he got to see all of him—and Ethan slid off the bed to stand in front of him. Wordlessly, without otherwise touching, he kissed Jack, a lingering, firm press of his lips. When he pulled back, he whispered, "Likewise."

Heart surging into his throat, Jack cleared it with several rough swallows, then in a husky rumble said, "It's agreed."

Jack pulled the T-shirt off Ethan, helped him kick off his sneakers, then removed his shorts—a necessity with the brace, even in winter—and the undies. Watching that hard dick bounce free of confinement had Jack dropping to his knees. He tugged on Ethan's hips so he sat on the edge of the bed, then hooked his knees over his shoulders and licked a long, wet strip from taint, over balls and up the thick shaft to flick the tip of his tongue over his frenulum.

Ethan thumped back into the mattress and he let out a long moan. Jack massaged the back of his thighs as he kissed up and down his dick, stopping to suck at the tight skin every now and then, moving on to pull Ethan's balls into his mouth. Ethan went non-verbal almost immediately. The priming at the garage had left him on a hair trigger and he was writhing and fidgeting as Jack teased. He wasn't the only one eager for more. Jack all but ripped open his own clothes to finish stripping. He had to back off for a moment to get his shoes and pants off. Ethan watched him with narrowed eyes and stifled a groan when Jack took himself in a tight grip and pumped.

Christ. It never failed to do his head in, seeing Ethan want him, knowing it was only Jack who did this for him. It wasn't an egotistical thing, but an oh-shit-don't-let-me-screw-this-up-for-him thing. It was an amazing turn on and a scary honour, one Jack would do anything to uphold.

Back on his knees, Jack took Ethan in his mouth, savouring the flavour and the shape and the weight. He sucked and licked until Ethan was gasping and his thighs were jumping, then Jack pulled off.

"So, I was thinking I should probably drive to the barbeque tomorrow."

Ethan's head popped up and he stared at Jack with his assassin expression in place. "Why would you think that?"

Jack dipped his head and lapped playfully along Ethan's shaft. "Well, you drove home today and apparently your leg was so sore from that I had to carry you from the lift to the bed. Seems to me a longer drive would only make—hey! That's my head." He tumbled backwards onto his arse, laughing as Ethan returned his good foot to the floor.

"Might I remind you that I have only just finished fixing Victoria from the last time you drove her?" Ethan sat up, arms crossed, eyes narrowed. His still thick dick belied the accusation in his tone.

"That wasn't the last time I drove her," Jack reminded him, slinking back into the gap between Ethan's legs. He nuzzled his face into Ethan's belly. "I managed to not prang her up further while you were in hospital." Slowly worked his way back down to Ethan's dick and ran his cheek over the head, loving Ethan's sharp intake of breath as he felt the five o'clock shadow.

"I suppose that is a point in your favour," Ethan conceded a little breathlessly. "I'm not convinced however."

"Okay, how about this?" Jack lifted Ethan's legs up, tipping him onto his back, and peppered kisses across his thighs, dick and balls between words. "If I make you come twice tonight, I get to drive."

Snorting, Ethan said, "Challenge yourself, Jack. You make me come twice most of the time."

"Fine. Three times."

Ethan's foot nudged at Jack's head again.

"Four? You really think you've got it in you?"

"I rather think, Jack, that it's *you* who needs to believe I have it in me."

Jack grinned. "You're on."

Minutes later, after swallowing, he said triumphantly, "That's one."

Still purring, Ethan hauled himself up the bed so he was lying on it completely and rolled to his belly. "Pace yourself, Jack. This is a marathon, not a sprint."

Jack crawled over him and fetched the lube from the bedside table drawer. "Shouldn't you be more concerned about your own stamina than mine?"

"Enough talking. More shagging."

Laughing, Jack obeyed. Kneeling between Ethan's legs, he lubed up his fingers and worked the first one into his impatient man. He all but hypnotised himself by dragging his other hand over all that smooth, pale flesh on display for him, lining his fingers up with the faded scars that never failed to tug at his heart painfully. After the medics had stabilised him on board the navy frigate, they'd reported on all the injuries Ethan had suffered while being held by the Cabal. Learning that they'd whipped him again, Jack had almost swum back to the island to make sure every last one of them was thoroughly dead. Thankfully, those lashes hadn't been deep enough to scar, but Jack could still see their angry red lines overlaying the older marks. Ethan was home now, though, mostly healed, and happy. That was what Jack chose to concentrate on.

"Turn over." Breath caught in his throat as he spoke, sharp with the ache of how close he'd come to losing the man he loved.

Ethan did, expression concerned. "Jack, are you all right?"

"Yeah." He leaned over, seeking his mouth. "Just need more of you."

Which Ethan gave, wrapping him in arms and legs and pulling him close. Jack grabbed their dicks and stroked them together, swallowing Ethan's moans, cherishing every single one. Jack could have come like that but Ethan was insistent.

"Jack." He pushed up against him. "Inside me."

Letting their dicks go, Jack pressed his palm to Ethan's belly. "Are you sure?"

With a frustrated growl, Ethan bit his jaw. "Yes, I'm sure. If you don't do something now, I'm going to have to take charge."

Flames licked through Jack's entire body at the thought of Ethan taking charge. There were few things hotter than Ethan indulging his every naughty impulse at Jack's very willing expense. But that would derail Jack's overall goal for the night, and tomorrow.

"Fine." Jack worked a couple of fingers back into him, slowly thrusting and stretching again. "I just need one tiny, little, itty bitty thing first."

Eyes rolled back in bliss, Ethan barely managed a, "Which is?"

Jack put his mouth right next to his ear and whispered, "Say it."

Gasping, Ethan's whole body jerked. He grabbed a handful of Jack's hair and pulled until they were looking directly at each other, then slowly, deliberately, Ethan said, "Fuck me, Jack."

ETHAN

Ethan woke with a start. For a moment, he couldn't recall where he was, why he was sitting up, or that he'd even fallen asleep in the first place. The moment the hum of the smooth engine registered and the landscape of green hills came into focus, he remembered.

With a little sigh, he adjusted his arse in the bucket seat. It still held a pleasant ache from the night before. Jack had definitely delivered on Ethan's demands, keeping him up most of the night in his effort to win their little bet. Ethan couldn't even be sorry he'd lost. Letting Jack drive wasn't as big a deal as he'd pretended, and he had gotten exactly what he wanted for the night, twice, and two other orgasms that had been just as glorious and fun.

"Hey, you're awake." Jack reached over to pat his thigh. "I was worried you might never wake up."

Snorting, Ethan really looked at the passing landscape. This didn't look very familiar. He and Jack had made a couple of trips down to Helensburgh to visit Meera and Mati since he'd been released from hospital, and the ladies were supposed to be hosting today's barbeque.

"I'm starting to suspect, Jack, that my falling asleep, after being sexually exhausted on purpose last night, was all part of a grand scheme you concocted to not only get behind the wheel of my car, but to then kidnap her and me both. Where are we?"

Jack's chuckle sounded forced and his tone when he answered was almost hesitant. "There's been a slight change of plans. It's a surprise for you."

The strange wariness made Ethan wonder what the surprise could be. When organising today's get-together, Jack had asked him a couple of times if he would like to invite Seven and Zero. While

Ethan had been pleased to find an ally within the Cabal in Zero, and he was happy Seven had escaped the destruction, he wasn't quite ready to bring them back into his life. Not now that he had a life he wanted. Not while he was still negotiating the intricacies of who he himself was in this new life. He didn't think Jack would go behind his back and invite them, but he couldn't imagine any other surprise Jack might have for him.

Cautiously, he asked again, "Where are we?"

"About ten Ks out of Cessnock, but our destination is about five Ks out of Pokolbin, so about half an hour before we get there." Jack still didn't sound overly confident.

"The Hunter Valley. Are we going wine tasting?"

Jack shrugged. "We can, if you want, but the barbeque's still happening, just . . . relocated."

"Why? Didn't Meera want to host it?"

"Meera's the one who suggested it. Who commanded it, actually."

Watching the siblings work at this new stage of their relationship had been intriguing. They were actively trying to change attitudes, yet they still didn't always find a mutual point of agreement. Which, Ethan suspected, was simply a part of being a family. They didn't always agree, but now rather than start a protracted fight and split apart over it, they could move on to something they could see eye to eye about. And usually that thing was Mati.

"So Meera and Mati will be there?"

"Yup. Lewis too. He's picking up Mr. Cesare and Shorty on his way. And just as a warning, I also invited Lydia."

Ethan winced. "Is she coming?"

"She said she might pop by. I told Lew and he's okay with it." A few kilometres went by, then Jack said, "She betrayed him but he knows why now. He said he's okay with her at work, but he moved out of their place the other week."

"I know he was spending some nights at your Leichhardt apartment. Did he move in there?"

"No. He found his own place, said he needed somewhere completely new. Start afresh and stuff."

Something was off about Jack's answer. It wasn't a lie but it wasn't the entire truth, either. Did it have something to do with the surprise?

"Have you chosen a name yet?" Jack asked before Ethan could interrogate him.

Thoughts successfully diverted, Ethan turned back to watching the scenery. "Not yet."

"You really need to pick something soon. Tan's not going to wait much longer and if he ends up picking, you'll be John Brown for the rest of your life."

Ethan snorted. "There are worse names."

"Fuck yeah, but there are better ones, too." Jack squeezed his thigh and gently said, "You could be Paul St. Clair, you know."

His head shake was instinctive. "I couldn't. He's gone. I'm not the man that Paul St. Clair would have become."

They reached Cessnock, the small town creeping up around them until they were driving down a main street and through the central business area. Jack made a turn and a sign announced Pokolbin eleven Ks away.

"What about Sinclair, then?" Jack persisted as they left Cessnock behind. "You've used it before."

"It's a possibility. I've also used Saint."

"Speaking as a lapsed Christian, I like it."

Surprisingly, discussing surnames was a pleasant distraction, especially when Jack started proposing ones that sounded dirty. It was such a good distraction that Ethan missed Pokolbin.

Jack laughed. "There's nothing to miss. It's pretty much all vineyards." Then he got serious again as he made another turn onto a narrow road that headed towards the hills just beyond the neat blocks of grape vines, looking more like coils of brown wire in the winter than plants. "We're almost there."

Curious and wary, Ethan studied the landscape. It looked dry but, like the vines, everything was winter brown. There was green on the hills and that was where they appeared to be going, turning off the road onto a gated driveway. Jack pulled up beside a security post, wound the window down and punched a number into the keypad. The tall, wrought iron gate rolled aside and they went through.

"This is private property?" Ethan asked.

"Yeah. We have the owner's permission." He threw Ethan a slightly worried smile.

Ethan frowned. "Jack? What is going on?"

The drive curved around a large dam, a small flock of wild ducks paddling on the water, while large domestic white, brown and grey ducks wandered around the edge. Trees rimmed the water and the driveway, and the grass was green as it spread away to either side. There were paddocks fenced in white logs though no animals were in sight. Through the trees, there was a house slowly appearing.

"It was a hobby farm. They had horses, goats, couple of cows, chickens." Jack gestured. "Ducks, which the old owners left behind because they're 'part of the landscape.'"

Suspicions growing, Ethan said, "And the new owners?"

"Don't mind the ducks. I mean, they're kinda cute, right?"

The drive circled around a neatly trimmed garden-bed of roses and lavender before the house, as well as continuing on around it to disappear behind the large, single storey structure. Most of its size, Ethan guessed, was the wide wrap-around patio festooned with hanging baskets of flowers and potted plants. The house was off-white render with green trim on the windows and a dark red roof. Chimneys graced either end of it, the north one sporting an old-fashioned weathervane. Solar panels interrupted the rustic air.

"Looks okay, doesn't it?"

Jack sounded so worried Ethan's suspicions were pretty much confirmed. "I like it." And he did. Mostly for the fact that he couldn't see another house, but also because it was beautiful, nestled into this gorgeous part of the world. "It'll be a chore to get it secure, but I'd love to live here with you." He leaned over and kissed Jack's surprise-parted lips. "You sold your Leichhardt apartment, thus Lewis couldn't live there anymore, and you bought this place for us. Jack, I love the surprise. I love you, so much." He kissed him again and this time Jack had the wits to respond.

A long while later, Jack said, "You haven't even seen the best bit yet."

"There's more?"

"Just you wait." Putting Victoria back in gear, Jack slowly drove around the house and the rest of the property opened up for Ethan.

More paddocks, a small vineyard—it was the Hunter region, after all—a large undercover entertainment area, a pool with natural rock landscaping, and a long, six-bay garage. Jack parked Victoria in the bay closest to the house and turned her off.

"I thought you could bring your other cars out here," he said. "Or you could start another harem if you wanted. But the moment I saw this, I knew I had to buy this place. I think they had tractors in the last two bays because they're larger. Maybe you could turn that into a work space so you had room too—"

Ethan crawled into Jack's lap to kiss him again. Jack laughed, the sound muffled, and wound his arms around Ethan.

"You like it, then?"

"It's perfect," Ethan enthused between kisses. "You're perfect. I don't deserve you. I want to fellate you, right here."

Jack kissed him like he was seriously thinking about it, but he pulled back with a small moan and pressed his forehead to Ethan's. "You deserve me. You deserve this. You deserve everything and anything you ever want."

"You." There was no hesitation, no doubt, no worry. "You, Jack. I don't care where we are, or how many cars I have, so long as I have you."

"Good. Because you got me."

As much as Ethan also wanted to stay right where he was, his healing leg was mashed between Jack and the car door and was starting to ache. They untangled themselves, got out, and Jack took his hand, leading him.

"There's one more surprise." There was a wicked gleam in his eyes this time, all nervousness gone.

"Another one?" Ethan was already breathless with warm shock and love. He couldn't imagine what else there could be, especially one that had Jack smirking like that.

"I didn't think we'd be able to pull this one together in time, but God smiled on me, thankfully. Well, that and a whole heap of sugar cubes helped, too."

Mute with wonder at Jack's overwhelming joy, Ethan let himself be led around the garage. Stables backed onto it, surrounded by small yards. One of which was occupied.

Sheila was sunning herself on the far side of the enclosed space but before Ethan could say her name, she seemed to sense him. Her head whipped around and, grunting happily, she flung herself into motion. Big feet slapping on the grass, she barrelled into the fence to greet him.

Ethan threw his arms around her long neck as she snuffled excitedly at any part of him she could reach. He couldn't believe it. The six-bay garage attached to a lovely house, surrounded by beautiful scenery and isolation was one thing, but this? If he hadn't already believed Jack loved him, this single act would have convinced him. Ethan buried his face in shaggy hair, not even caring that her camelid scent would stick to him all day.

It was ridiculous to have such an attachment to a half-feral camel he'd found while preparing for the Valadian job. She'd wormed her way into his heart over those few weeks with a needy persistence that had won him over. Jack hadn't been so easily enamoured, even now keeping a little distance as he patted her shoulder, but he'd known what it would mean to Ethan to see her again, to know she was fine and happy.

"When did you find her?"

"Couple of weeks back. I found this place, saw the stables and sort of got nostalgic."

Ethan chuckled. He let Sheila go and turned to Jack, leaning against the fence. Sheila plopped her chin over his shoulder and blinked long, languorous lashes at his beautiful man.

"It made me think of this dumb lump." Jack gestured at the camel. "So, I said I was going to Canberra for that week, remember?"

"Hmm. The one where Mati had to babysit me."

"It wasn't babysitting, it was just coincidental that she was coming to the city that week to check out universities."

Ethan merely cocked an eyebrow and Jack smirked.

"Either way, I went to WA and spent two days looking for her. She finally showed up, bit me, and ran away before I could get her into the trailer."

Sheila snorted and Ethan laughed.

"I managed to coax her in with sugar cubes and then Lewis had a couple of junior assets from the Perth branch drive the trailer over here. She apparently bit them a couple of times, too."

"Poor baby." Ethan soothed the camel with a pat.

"Poor assets. Imagine being called on for a super-secret mission, only to find out it's to haul that stinky critter across the Nullarbor, who then bit them for their troubles."

"She was scared and confused."

"She's pretty much pure evil and you know it. Come on, the others will be getting here soon."

Sheila grumbled about being left alone again, but Ethan promised he'd be back with more sugar, and followed Jack to the house.

The entertainment area had already been decorated with twinkling lights, long table and chairs in the middle, with wicker lounges, footstools and glass topped coffee table to one side. A large barbeque sat at one end and a bar at the other. Jack took him into the house, gave him a quick tour of the four bedrooms, two baths, office, living room, separate dining room, family room, and well stocked modern kitchen, all on polished hard wood floors, with soaring, exposed beam ceilings. Ethan was dazed by the time they grabbed beers from the fridge and went back outside to wait for the others.

"Do you like it?" Jack asked as he leaned back on the banana lounge.

Ethan settled in between his legs, back to Jack's chest. "It's an awful lot to take in so quickly. But yes, I like it. I love it."

Jack's arm tightened around his middle. "Thank fucking Christ for that. Do you know how many times I second-guessed all this? I thought you'd hate it or hate that I'd done it without talking to you. And it's not like I'm saying we live here full time. I don't want to abandon the penthouse because I know it's where you feel the safest. I just thought we could have this, too. Somewhere to be completely alone with each other, or on our own if we need some time apart. If you don't—"

"Jack?"

He stumbled to a stop mid nervous ramble. "What?"

"Trust me, I love it. You had me hooked the moment I saw the garage."

Jack took a few sips of beer, then said, "I knew it. You do love your cars, and that camel, more than me."

"So long as you know your place in the pecking order."

"Fuck you, Blade, and the camel you rode in on."

Ethan laughed.

"So, any more thoughts on a name?" Jack asked when he'd calmed down.

Sighing, Ethan relaxed into Jack's body. "Some. I think it has to be Ethan."

Jack's hand, which had been idly rubbing his belly, stopped. "Are you sure? Seven told me how Ethan Blade came about."

"I'm sure. I'm not Ethan Blade, but I *am* Ethan. I have been since you first called me that in the desert, after Valadian died and we were in the stable. I may have only realised it six months ago, but that was when it happened. You said it without anger or derision. When you looked at me and didn't see an assassin or an enemy. You saw *me* and said 'Ethan.'"

"Jesus," Jack whispered, face pressing into his neck. "I'm so sorry I was a dick for so long. I should have realised then how much you meant to me, how good you were for me. I'm sorry."

"You don't have to be sorry, Jack. I didn't know either."

It took Jack a while to gather himself, and when he did, his voice was rough with emotion. "So, Ethan is a good start. What about a middle name?"

"Do I need a middle name?"

"You do. I need to shout at least three names when you piss me off."

"Hmm. All right. How about Paul?"

"Ethan Paul. That's not bad. Now surname. Ethan Paul Sinclair." He repeated it louder and angrier. "I can work with that."

"Ethan Paul Sinclair." Ethan tested it out several times. "I think that's it."

Jack clinked their bottles together. "Cheers, Ethan Paul Sinclair."

"Cheers." Ethan took a sip and, wiggling out of Jack's hold, stood. "It is a good name. For now."

Jack gaped at him. "For now? What the fuck does 'for now' mean?"

Ethan smiled, leaned over, kissed him, and said, "Just that perhaps one day, maybe soon, you might want it to be Ethan Paul Reardon."

He left Jack in stunned silence and went to start his new life.

ACKNOWLEDGEMENTS

I wanted to keep this one very short and very sweet (along the lines of "I love yous all!") but thought I better name names . . .

May Peterson . . . I owe you this entire book. No. This whole series! Without your tireless work on book one, book three and all the ones in between wouldn't exist. You were a massive part of making WDMTD the book so many readers loved and you saved me again with this one.

L.C. Chase . . . Your eye-catching and stunning covers and layout speak for themselves. And you did it all while dealing with me. Thank you so much for being so accommodating and understanding.

Erin, Anna, Layla and Allison . . . You all supported me for so long during this journey and I am so very grateful for all you did.

Riina Y.T. . . . You're a great friend, and awesome rock and sounding board, particularly with this book. You helped me get back up when I fell down. This book wouldn't be here without you.

The Rotorheads, Chris Ostler, Mike Toms and Andrew Vintner . . . Thank you all for answering my weird questions about helicopters and how to crash them. I learned an awful lot and any helicopter faux pas that made it into the book are totally my mistake.

Lastly, to all the readers who took a chance on the new-to-them author with the weird back-and-forth timeline book, to all of you who stuck with Jack and Ethan (and me) all the way to the end, I love yous all! None of this is possible without any of you. All the thanks and cheers in the world to you!

ALSO BY L.J. HAYWARD

M/M Romantic Suspense

Death and the Devil Series
Where Death Meets the Devil, #1
Where Death Meets the Devil: Coda, #1.2
Bargaining with the Devil, #1.4
When the Devil Drives, #1.6
Devil in the Details, #1.8
Why the Devil Stalks Death, #2
Dealing in Death, #2.5

Urban Fantasy

Night Call Series
Blood Work, #1
Demon Dei, #2
Here Be Dragons, #2.5
Rock Paper Sorcery, #3

ABOUT THE AUTHOR

L.J. Hayward has been telling stories for most of her life, a good deal of them of the tall variety. She loves reading but doesn't seem to have enough time between wanting to be a more disciplined writer, being the actual erratic writer she is, and working for dollars in a dungeon laboratory. She also lives on the Gold Coast in Queensland, but rarely sees a beach and can't surf, though she thinks living on a houseboat might be fun. At least then she'd have an excuse to get a cat.

Visit L.J. at her website, ljhayward.com; on Twitter, @ljhayward; or on Goodreads, goodreads.com/L.J.Hayward.